Vengeance

by

Brenda Huber

Chronicles of the Fallen, Book 4

Vengeance

Cover Art by *Rae Monet, Inc. Design*

The Wild Rose Press, Inc.
PO Box 708
Adams Basin, NY 14410-0708
Visit us at www.thewildrosepress.com

Publishing History:
Previously published by Samhain Publishing, 2016
First Black Rose Edition, 2021
Trade Paperback ISBN 978-1-5092-3427-1
Digital ISBN 978-1-5092-3428-8

Chronicles of the Fallen, Book 4
Published in the United States of America

Why did she get the feeling she was in over her head? Way, way over her head.

"Thank you," she said, gritting her teeth in determination. Perspiration beaded her upper lip as she managed to get into an upright position. She clutched the sheet to her chest with one hand and reached for the pile of clothing with the other. "I appreciate all you've done for me, Sebastian. You've been...beyond kind."

He stopped halfway across the room and slowly turned. The smile he sent her nearly stopped her heart.

"Sweetheart, there are three very important things you need to know about me...know and remember above and beyond anything else. First, I don't have an altruistic bone in my body."

Phoebe blinked.

"Second, when I want something, I won't ever stop until I get it. *Not. Ever.*" He paused, stared at her for a long moment, stared hard, as if to make certain she not only heard but completely understood every last word. A heavy sense of foreboding settled in the pit of her stomach and she frowned.

"And third... *I. Want. You.*"

The smile he gave her left her with no doubt in her mind over what he'd meant by that last remark. And then he vanished. A long moment later, she sucked in a shuddering lungful of air. That old adage about frying pans and fires came back to her once more.

"What did I just get myself into?"

Dedication

I'd like to dedicate this book to the librarians. Here's to all the women and men who strive to broaden our horizons, enrich our lives, and promote our creativity through fact and through fiction. Here's to the people who encourage young minds through reading programs and helpful literary suggestions, who teach us not only to explore but also to fall in love with the worlds and the characters who live within the pages.

This book is also dedicated in fond memory of Irene Simonsmeier, the first librarian to kindle within a younger version of me a burning love of books and a driven desire to write them through the simple use of small, gold-colored, plastic trophies and summer reading programs. And especially to Angie at the Swea City Public Library, Mary at the Bancroft Public Library, and Darcy, Judy, and all the women at the Algona Public Library for helping me to get my children excited about reading. You should all have superhero capes!

"Avenge not yourselves, but rather give place unto wrath, for it is written, Vengeance is mine; I will repay, saith the Lord."

~Romans 12:19

"Not if I get there first."

~Sebastian, Demon of Vengeance

Prologue

"Please, *please*, do not tell me I just missed her!"

The balding little man behind the counter jumped at Sebastian's tone. Sweat beaded the clerk's brow as he fidgeted with a stack of travel brochures. "Well, I'm sorry, but you have." He hitched a thumb over his shoulder toward the window behind him. "In fact, there she goes now."

The edge of the countertop cracked beneath Sebastian's fingertips as he watched the twin engine Cessna taxi down the runway. He'd chased that double damned woman all over this Godforsaken town. Port August, Michigan had become his own personal version of limbo from which it seemed he could not escape. A never-ending loop of always being one step behind the cursed woman and never lucky enough to quite catch up. The storm brewing inside him boiled closer to the surface as the front wheels of the plane left the tarmac.

Breathe, Sebastian reminded himself.

And there she went, slipping through his fingers. *Again.* A red haze winked over his vision for a moment. The little gnome took a cautious step back, sweat streaming down the sides of his smooth forehead now, his eyes wide as saucers behind thick rimmed spectacles.

Just breathe.

Sebastian let out a really, really, long breath. His

palms sizzled. The little man behind the counter took another step back. The colorful pamphlets in his shaking hands spilled across the counter and fluttered to the floor.

Going demonic and decimating the small airport wouldn't bring the wayward professor back. Nor would it make him feel any better, at least it wouldn't once he'd retaken his human form and his conscience caught up to him.

In demonic form, he'd definitely enjoy himself.

Probably a little *too* much.

Seething, Sebastian turned, stalked from the building, and climbed inside the car he'd "borrowed". Keeping his temper in check took far more control than he was comfortable admitting. Halfway across the parking lot, his phone began ringing. His temper clicked up another notch. He was in no mood to deal with anyone else's problems today. And that would be the only reason any of the others would call him. Either the proverbial shit had hit the fan, or it was about to. He jerked the device from his pocket and checked the display.

Xander? He closed his eyes, tipped his head back and groaned aloud. *Damn it. If the Slayer is calling, it's gotta be bad. Really freakin' bad.*

Sebastian gritted his teeth, teetering on the edge of saying fuck it and smashing his phone rather than taking the call. Somehow, his default role in their merry little band of misfits had become mediator, voice of reason, and general all-around shitstorm-cleaner-upper. As a rule, it didn't bother him. At least, not usually. After all, he had far more patience than anyone else in their crew. Legendary patience he'd used once upon a time to dole out his particular brand of justice. He was, or had been, the demonic version of karma. Didn't matter how long it took, who you were, or how well you hid, sooner or later, Vengeance always, *always* caught up with you.

Now whenever something went wrong, his brothers-in-arms called him without giving it a second thought. Why? Because they knew he had a long, long, *long* fuse.

Only they had a tendency to forget about the epic bang at the end. Forget about it until it was too late. By then things had already begun to explode and burn and then the only thing to do was get the hell out of his way until the storm blew over.

Well, the end of that long fuse was getting closer and closer. Every minute, every second that ticked by and he didn't have his hands on that damned professor—the Guardian of the missing Sword of Kathnesh—poured fuel on the flames.

His conscience—or whatever meager shreds of decency he had left—got the better of him. Something end-of-the-world-bad had to have happened if Mr. I'd-Rather-Be-Tortured-Than-Talk-On-A-Damned-Phone was heating up the airwaves. Sebastian so didn't have the time *or* the patience to deal with anymore shit today.

He hesitated just long enough that the phone went silent. But he didn't bother breathing a sigh of relief. He knew what was coming.

And three, two, one…

The phone screeched to life once again.

Yeah, thing about Xander? He didn't do voicemail. He'd just keep hitting redial until he drove you insane.

"Yo," Sebastian barked into the phone. "Listen, man. Right now isn't a good time to—"

"Stolas has Mikhail."

Sebastian's entire body went stiff. He scowled at the steering wheel, unseeing, as all the air in his lungs deserted him. His hand fell to his lap, leaving the keys dangling from the ignition as he tried to wrap his mind around this unexpected news.

No. No way *I heard that right.*

"Come again?"

"He wants to trade Mikhail for Maggie."

"Maggie? Wait, the Halfling Maggie that Gideon was supposed to retrieve?" Sebastian shoved his splayed fingers through his hair. "How the hell did Stolas get his hands on *Mikhail*?"

The Demon of War was the strongest, meanest, most lethal bastard Sebastian knew. Mikhail carried the chip on his shoulder—and its corresponding temper—around like it was his due, and he had the skills and the experience to back it up. If Stolas or one of his minions—or, considering this was Mikhail they were talking about, probably an entire legion of Hell's finest—could perform a bag and tag on Mikhail, then the Fallen were collectively screwed. And not in a way that might encourage one to bask in a pleasant, post-coital afterglow.

"I haven't been off grid that damned long. What did I miss here?"

"Nutshell. Best guess, they took Mikhail via portal. The Halfling mated Gideon. She's pregnant, probably with The Chosen One. Ashïek is involved," summed up Mr. Twenty-Five-Words-Or-Less. "Clear?"

Ashïek? Son of a bitch! Just like that, Sebastian's

blood turned to molten lava. The steering wheel crumbled like aluminum foil in his unforgiving grip.

Even as angels, Ashïek and Sebastian had maintained a not-so-healthy rivalry. And that rivalry had only grown more conflicted after the Great Fall, more often than not turning downright bloody…with a *lot* of collateral damage. One of Lucifer's most favored forms of entertainment had been pitting the two against each other at every opportunity. He'd fueled the flames of hatred by rewarding the one who fought the dirtiest, regardless of who the victor had been.

While Sebastian's rank had risen quite high in Lucifer's army, Ashïek was every bit as formidable. The things Ashïek could and would do—the abilities he possessed, abilities like opening the aforementioned portals—gave Sebastian a case of the cold sweats. It had taken every last ounce of ruthless, brutal determination on Sebastian's part to best Ashïek. But best him he had. Many, many times.

To hear Ashïek was involved…well, it didn't exactly make Sebastian feel all warm and fuzzy inside.

"Are you sure this isn't some kind of trick?"

The words had no more than left his mouth when his phone vibrated with an incoming text.

"You tell me," Xander suggested. "We believe the vortex Ashïek opened up to take Mikhail was something like what he opened for Mortikaï to capture Kyanna and Maggie."

While Sebastian had yet to meet Maggie, he'd grown quite fond of Xander's mate Kyanna. The way that leggy blonde Guardian had managed to get under the Slayer's skin made her worth her weight in gold.

A river of ice sluiced through Sebastian's veins,

chasing the hot glow of hatred. Mortikaï was a slimy bastard. Dear God, what had he done to Kyanna and the Halfling once he'd gotten his deformed hands on them? Nausea roiled through Sebastian at the mere thought.

Damn. Sebastian knew he'd fallen out of the loop for a bit while on his wild goose chase, but *WTF*?

Just as quickly as his dread for Kyanna's safety surfaced, it receded. No way would Xander be chatting it up on the phone if his mate was still in the hands of the enemy. Nor would the demon who'd abducted her still be alive. Xander would have already torn Heaven, Hell, and all of Earth asunder to get his woman back. And had she been seriously harmed—or, God forbid, killed—Earth would already be burning.

So, if Sebastian were a betting demon, he'd wager that Mortikaï's entrails were already decorating Xander's cabin in the mountains.

All the same, he found himself asking, "You handle Mortikaï?"

"Gideon did. One piece at a time."

That gave him a brief moment of surprise. Not that Gideon wasn't more than capable. Sebastian had just assumed Xander, in his fury, would have beaten anyone else to the kill. From the sound of things, Gideon was just as possessive, just as protective of Maggie as Xander was of Kyanna. Guess this mating business was touchier than Sebastian had assumed.

With a shake of his head, Sebastian opened the text, and let out a foul curse at the gruesome image filling the screen.

Oh, yeah. Stolas had Mikhail all right.

And the Demon of War was in a bad, bad way.

Any plans of chasing after the wayward professor

just got shoved to the back burner. "Where do you want to meet? The farm or your cabin?"

"Keep to your mission."

"But—"

"Secure the new Guardian. She's the only chance we have of recovering that sword. The rest of us will rescue Mikhail. Just watch your back. So far, there's no way to predict when or where these damned portals can open. And if Stolas can get to Mikhail, he can get to any of us." As close to mother-henning as Xander was ever likely to get. "It's personal now."

There was just one point Xander didn't understand, not fully. Ashïek had always made it personal where Sebastian was concerned.

In his short, not-so-sweet, Slayer-typical way, Xander disconnected the call before Sebastian could say or ask anything else. Sebastian wondered what his brothers-in-arms were planning, knowing only that there was no way on God's green Earth Gideon would ever agree to give up his mate.

His *pregnant* mate.

Dude's gonna be a daddy. Sebastian still couldn't wrap his head around that revelation.

In the Great Fall, along with his wings, Gideon had been stripped of his ability to ever again know the touch of a human. Almost two hundred years ago, Lucifer had...*modified* Gideon's Heavenly curse when he'd punished the Demon of Temptation for disobedience.

Hypocritical asshole, thy name is Lucifer.

Lucifer had taken Gideon's curse and run with it, tweaked it a bit, making it so that Gideon *could* touch again. But only while in demonic form. In human form, though he still couldn't touch anyone, Gideon was temptation incarnate, able to discern a person's darkest cravings and offer them up on a silver platter. And the moment that person took the bait, it triggered his demonic form. Gideon became death, bloody and brutal. He became the monster.

Problem with that little scenario was Gideon had no control in demonic form. Once Gideon went demonic, once he *became* the Demon of Temptation, he couldn't differentiate friend from foe. He'd be more prone to kill you than to stop and ask questions.

Sebastian and the others had searched high and low—though they'd been vigilant to never let Gideon know of their quest—for something, *anything* to lift the curse. By unspoken agreement, they'd decided each successive failure would eventually crush Gideon. And fail they had. Again and again. But they'd concealed their search in vain. Gideon had spiraled into a self-destructive depression anyway, a downward plunge from which Sebastian and the others had feared Gideon might never recover.

Which begged the question, *how?* How had he managed to touch the female? Had the cuffs Sebastian finally secured from Asher worked better than anticipated? Heaven knew the cost had been even higher—and more unusual—than Sebastian had anticipated. A sworn blood contract of one favor, unspecified in description, collectible at any given moment.

But if those cuffs had been the cure to the curse, then why hadn't Asher offered them sooner?

Or had it been the Halfling herself?

However it had come about, Sebastian was just grateful. Gideon's curse had been broken. So no. No way, no how would Gideon give up his mate. Not even for one of his brothers. And they wouldn't expect him to.

Mikhail sure as hell wouldn't expect it of him.

Sebastian understood. He, of all demons, couldn't blame Gideon for wanting to keep his woman. Not after watching Xander with his fierce little Guardian wife, or Niklas with his feisty, yet all-too-fragile human mate.

Jealousy's jagged, poisonous claws twisted in his gut.

It was extremely rare for a demon to commit himself to one mate, preferring instead to…well, cavort with as many or as few partners as he desired whenever the whim struck, so to speak. And it was more than a little unnerving to realize just how much Sebastian had come to envy his brothers and the relationships they'd chosen. Those two women—three now if you included the Halfling—represented something Sebastian had long ago given up on. Hope for a happy ending. Something to strive for, to look forward to.

A future that wasn't filled with death, blood, destruction, and more death.

If he'd ever been lucky enough to have claimed a mate of his own, Sebastian would have done whatever it took to keep her safe. He'd have protected her from all harm and cherished her as none other ever would. Nothing and no one would have kept them apart.

Probably not even the female herself.

Grim, filled with renewed purpose and knowing time was running out for the Demon of War, Sebastian decided to hell with shocking any nosy neighbors with the blunt reality of their world. He'd been to the professor's house once before, and he remembered the lay of the land well enough. At least if he shimmered now, he wouldn't risk materializing with a tree limb sticking through his gut, and he wouldn't land in the middle of the damned lake gulping water with the fishes.

Sebastian centered his focus, picturing in his mind the professor's tidy little Cape Cod home on the shores of Lake Superior. He geared himself up for a little B&E and shimmered to the beach behind her house.

He'd resisted breaking into her abode before, hoping he'd be able to do this the honorable way. Intercept the woman and learn what he needed to know directly from her. Well, that plan had just flown right out the window. He'd have to play the hand he'd been dealt, like it or not. Ethical or not. He'd need to know everything he could about the woman and her ill-timed trip as quickly as possible if he hoped to recover the Sword of Kathnesh—the one sword capable of taking Lucifer's head. And he was damned tired of being one step behind.

No more playing fair.

Once he'd solidified on the beach and her back door was within sight, Sebastian shimmered one last time, dropping himself onto her deck. Closing his eyes, he let his senses expand all around him.

Something niggled at him, something was...*off*.

But he couldn't quite—

Of course! Why hadn't he noticed it the first time he'd come here? There were no wards, no enchantments. No mystical protections designed to fend off or repel his kind. Frowning, he opened his senses and did one more search, just to be certain.

Nada. Not so much as a chip of a ward stone. Not a

wisp of lingering enchantment.

W. T. F?

No wonder these people had lost the sword. Damned careless, if you asked him. With a growl, he knelt to pick the lock. But the moment his hand brushed the doorknob, the door popped open.

Not even locked.

Of all the inexcusable, incompetent, lazy...

He straightened, opening his senses up once more as warning bells went off in his head. Suspicion stirred.

Too easy.

Still, he could sense no other demonic presence, nothing human or angelic. Was this some kind of trap? Sebastian paused for a moment, just to make sure there wasn't an electronic alarm system either.

There wasn't. He snorted and shook his head, disgusted all over again.

How stupid. A woman living alone, and a Guardian no less. Of all people, she *should know better.*

Sebastian eased into what appeared to be the living room and closed the door. He glanced around, looking for a good place to start.

The term *organized chaos* came to mind.

Stacks of corded newspapers rested near the door. As if someone had bound them with the intention of carrying them out for recycling, but then gotten sidetracked. Indeed, the majority of the house was in much the same state. Baskets of clothing sat near the foot of the staircase, clean and neatly folded, but someone had neglected to take them the rest of the way upstairs and put them away.

A vacuum cleaner waited near the end of the couch

with its cord wrapped up in perfect order. The floor was spotless, but the vacuum had yet to be put away. A green, reusable grocery bag rested on the counter dividing living room from kitchen, half unpacked and pretty much forgotten. Everywhere he looked tasks were partially completed.

His attention landed on the coffee table. A notebook rested atop a tidy stack of papers. A file box sat on the floor nearby, lid open. After scanning through the papers on the table, he found what he realized was her itinerary.

Could she make this any easier?

Again, the uneasy feeling of walking into a trap rippled over his skin. He perused the detailed schedule. The script was feminine and flowing. He smiled when he located not only her destination, but also the name of her guide.

Piece. Of. Cake.

He should have just done this earlier, rather than chase her all over town. Then he'd be the one a step ahead. But he'd thought he'd be able to catch up to her and just snatch her off the street. That she'd eluded him time after time, without even *knowing* she was eluding him, jerked his chain all over again.

A bloodcurdling screech rent the air, catching him off guard. An enormous ball of pissed off orange fur came hurling at him from out of nowhere. Searing pain exploded down the side of his face as he fought to tear the yowling monster away. Instead of dislodging the little beast, he only succeeded in fueling its fury. It sank spiky claws into his shoulder and chest, ripping streaks of fire across his flesh. Sebastian bellowed in shock and pain.

His mind raced as he sought to fend off the attack. But the damned thing clung like a bur. Animagi? But what kind? It didn't smell like Animagi, though. And he'd never encountered one so small before. Was this a hybrid? Each wound the creature inflicted throbbed and pulsed as if injected with venom of some kind. But weak venom, as it didn't induce immediate hallucinations or paralysis, but damn did it burn all the same.

And just like that, the fiend was gone. Only then, as the devil crouched, hissing and spitting in the corner, back arched and luminous irises glowing, did Sebastian get his first real look at his assailant.

A damned cat.

Sweet saints, he hated cats. And they hated him.

Witness exhibit A.

His chest, scratched to hell and back, stung something fierce. Wetness dripped onto his now shredded T-shirt. Scowling, Sebastian probed his burning cheek. His fingers came away smeared with crimson. He snarled. The double damned cat let out another screech and scurried for cover.

One thing was for certain. Professor Phoebe Mackenzie better enjoy her brief reprieve. Because once he caught up with the woman, he damned well might strangle her with his bare hands.

Chapter One

Phoebe hefted her carry on and stifled a huge yawn. She readjusted the shoulder strap as she strode down the terminal in Alberto Acuña Ongay International Airport. She'd made it to Campeche, Mexico without incident.

When's the other shoe going to drop?

Nope, don't do it, she scolded herself the moment that traitorous self-sabotaging thought slipped out. *Don't jinx yourself.*

Phoebe skimmed the crowd at the gate, looking for her guide. She didn't see him, but she was familiar enough with both Ricardo as well as her general location that she wasn't the slightest bit anxious. Mexico—particularly the jungles and all its small hole-in-the-wall villages—were a second home to her and she spoke the regional dialects like a native.

She should. She'd pretty much grown up here.

Even before her quest to recover the stolen sword had begun, Phoebe had already been well-versed in many of the archeological ruins of Mexico. She'd spent more of her formative years exploring them at her father's side than learning in a traditional classroom. The mythology. The art and architecture. Creation stories. The very ruins themselves. It was all in her blood, as it had been in her father's. He'd taught her everything he knew.

Perhaps one of the most important things she'd learned from his tutelage was to hire a dependable guide, one she could trust with her very life. After all, no one knew the lay of the land as well as a local.

That guide was Ricardo Esteban Reynosa Alcalá. Her father had relied on Ricardo without reservation. Phoebe did as well, and he'd never let her down. In fact, on their last trip together, Ricardo had saved her life, at great risk to his own. If Ricardo said he would meet her, then meet her he would.

But then, that wasn't strictly true, she corrected herself. Not the meeting part, the worry part. She was plenty worried. Not that Ricardo would stand her up. What troubled her was that she would be exposing Ricardo, and any other innocent villagers they hired, to the increasing dangers she faced. She was terrified over the prospect, but she had no choice. The fate of something far greater hung in the balance.

That understanding still didn't mitigate the guilt. Ricardo had already been put at risk, had almost *died* because of her. If anything else happened to that sweet man, she just didn't know what she'd do.

She caught herself tracing her fingertips along the jagged, puckered scar tissue running from the edge of her jaw, just below her ear, down to the center of her throat. She made a conscious effort to drop her hand to her side. Drawing a deep breath and stiffening her spine, Phoebe gripped the strap on her bag with renewed purpose.

The sword prophesied to be the tool that brought about the end of the world had been stolen. Her father, the sword's Guardian, had been slain by Hell's minion. A demon.

A demon just like the one that had—

She forced a swallow and shook that frightening thought away, squaring her shoulders. That left her—and her alone—to locate the ancient artifact and secret it away once more. Hide it and protect it with her life if need be.

Talk about the weight of the world resting on the wrong shoulders.

Grim, Phoebe scanned the crowd again, looking for her ride. And, even as she did so, she found her thoughts wandering over the details of her fruitless search, picking it apart. Time was ticking away. She could feel it like a giant, razor-sharp guillotine poised over her head. Urgency pushed her to hurry, though she didn't know why. Knew only that something—something *momentous*—was happening. Somewhere. And it involved that sword. She had nothing more than a gut feeling—and the theft of the sword, of course—as proof, but she couldn't shake the certainty.

She'd begun her quest to reclaim the sword by retracing her father's last excavation…the location of her father's murder. For the thousandth time, she wished she'd gone with him on that trip. Wished she hadn't let other obligations stand in the way. Maybe if she'd gone along things would have been different…

And, even as she was filled with regret and guilt, she knew the truth. If she'd gone along, if she'd been there with him, she would most likely be dead now too. And there would be no one left to shoulder the burden.

So was it her sense of duty and the lifelong lessons she'd been drilled to accept as a child of a Guardian that drove her to recover that sword?

Or was it survivor's guilt?

Not like she could sit down on a shrink's couch and have her emotions, her beliefs and her drives, professionally analyzed. First, if she didn't end up locked away in a psych ward, at the very least her good name and all her research would be tainted. Second, and maybe more importantly, her father had insisted, through his journals, that secrecy was of the utmost importance.

No, she wouldn't be discussing her family legacy. Not with anyone.

Well, no one but Ricardo...but he was family, so that didn't count. Not really.

Whatever it was that drove her, she wouldn't give up. She felt the weight of responsibility pressing down on her like a mountain on her chest. And she still struggled with the crushing grief. A grief that had been her constant companion ever since the moment she'd received her father's final letter. A letter that had begun with those cursed, cliché words.

My dearest Gum Drop, If you're reading this letter, then I didn't make it out of the jungle alive. I'm so sorry, angel, but I leave to you a terrible burden...

His revelation had turned her world upside down. On her first expedition after her father's death, she'd scoured the ruins of Los Guachimontones or—more accurately—a small area less than two miles south of the ruins. As close as she could guestimate to where her father's maps and encoded journals had indicated something of importance was hidden. As close as she could guestimate to where her father had been slain. Though even in the coded language that only the two of them knew, he was ever-careful never to refer to it by name, surely, he had to be pointing her toward the sword.

She hadn't found her father or his grave. Nor had she found the sword. But she had found another journal, as it turned out.

That had also been the sight of the first in a long series of brutal attacks. That particular incident had resulted in the death of an innocent worker. And yes, she was keeping score, her conscience would allow for nothing less. The running tally was currently three. She could only pray to God there wouldn't be any more destined for the books. But she couldn't stop now, couldn't risk the fate of the world over the risk to a single human life, even if it was her own.

Her search had already taken her back into the jungles of Mexico. La Venta Olmec and Toniná, otherwise known as the House of Rocks. She'd located another journal, and a series of encoded maps. She'd extended her search to those of Chacalán, referred to by the locals as The Valley of the Throat Cutters.

But there she'd come up empty handed, the sword eluding her yet again.

Well, maybe not empty handed. She'd walked away with a pile of clues, another of her father's many journals…and a nasty scar to remind her that someone out there would do whatever it took to keep the pilfered sword.

She caught herself fingering her scar once more and gritted her teeth. It had become a nervous habit. Forcing her hand to return to the carry-on strap, she scanned the crowd. Her search for the sword had become a big scavenger hunt.

The stakes were astronomical, and failure was not an option.

Though she still struggled to reconcile why he'd waited until his death to tell her about the sword, she understood why her father had encoded everything in his journals. Concealing the clues, leading her on an exhausting chase. He didn't want to make it easy for the other team. And he'd known she was up for the challenge, had prepared her for this himself, in his own way. Teaching her their special codes, drilling them into her. Telling her the mythological stories over and over. Training her to decipher the secrets of the past. He believed in her.

Had believed, she corrected, blinking away the sudden sting of tears. Even now, faced with the most complicated challenge of her life—maybe especially now—it was difficult to grasp that he was gone.

So yes, she understood it was necessary. But it was also damned frustrating.

This time, armed with the latest coded journal, and the last of her hopes, Phoebe was headed to Balamkú in Campeche.

Balamkú, known as Jaguar's Temple, was one of the Mayan Ruins located in the Rio Bec Region of the Yucatan Peninsula. Calakmul and two other ruins were located nearby, so close together they could be visited in one day if necessary. Which made this expedition convenient if she'd misinterpreted the clues and the first location turned out to be a bust.

She'd taken a hiatus from lecturing—provided she returned to her job at all—which allowed her two months for the trip. God willing, she wouldn't need even a quarter of that time. After all, should she succeed in finding the sword, reinventing herself and finding a new place to live—a new place to hide—took time.

Time she wasn't sure she had.

In all their travels, she and her father had not visited these particular ruins. According to her research, Balamkú was small, a series of detailed reliefs covered by a stone temple. So she wouldn't spend a lot of time there, would instead devote her energy to searching the grounds around the temple before moving on to Calakmul.

Access to the interior of the temple at Balamkú was limited to a single door. And that door was kept locked at all times. But you could enter with the aid of a worker on the site. While the pyramid wasn't supposed to be very spectacular from the outside, the interior was documented to hold beautiful designs consisting of the three large images of a rabbit, an alligator, and a jaguar. The major reliefs were flanked by many small animal carvings.

In all honesty, search for the sword aside, Phoebe couldn't wait to see the ruins. All of them. Mayan culture, thanks to her father, had become an addiction for her. A link to him, if she were being truthful.

A short, squat woman bumped into Phoebe in her rush to join a group of people nearby. Men and women milled all around the airport terminal. Some holding name placards. Others laughing and hugging. Businessmen talking on phones and tourists with their maps and their huge rolling suitcases strode this way and that.

Her attention snagged for a moment on a tall man at the far end of the crowd. He stuck out like a sore thumb amidst so many swarthy *Mexicanos*. His mussed hair was bleached blond, his skin lightly kissed by the sun, and wow was he tall—at least six foot five if he was an inch. Golden stubble covered a lean jaw that looked as if it could take punch. Although he was dressed like he'd just stepped down off some billboard for designer jeans, he looked as if he'd be more at home at the helm of a Viking longship with battle hammer in one hand and a bolt of lightning in the other.

She snorted over that bit of fanciful imagination. A Viking god? Exhaustion must have taken a greater toll than she'd realized. More likely, he was nothing more than a surfboarder who was a god only in his own mind.

His stop-your-heart-handsome face was screwed up in a frown as he stared hard at something in his hand. A piece of paper...or a picture maybe? She craned her neck for a better look, her curiosity piqued. She just couldn't seem to help herself.

But then someone called her name nearby. The surfboarder's head snapped up, and for just a split second their gazes connected. Electric blue eyes seared her, pinning her in place. An odd awareness, foreign and hot, sizzled through her.

"Professor Mackenzie?" A heavily accented voice called once more from her right.

Phoebe sucked in a shuddering breath and blinked, breaking the connection with Surfer Boy. She pushed her glasses up the bridge of her nose with her index finger as she turned to the burly man calling her name. He wasn't much taller than she, but what he lacked in height he made up for in girth. His dark hair, what was left of it, had been slicked back. His goatee was well trimmed. His olive complexion was sun weathered and pockmarked. He wore a short-sleeved button down with a palm leaf design, khakis, and loafers. He held a placard with her name on it.

"Here," she called, waving. He reached her side and thrust out a beefy paw.

"*Me llamo Juan, Señorita*," he introduced himself. He released her hand and reached for her carry on. "*¿Habla español? ¿Cómo estuvo tú viaje?*"

"*Sí, hablas español*," she assured him, and then continued on in fluent Spanish, "My trip was just fine, *gracias*."

He nodded, smiling a huge gap-toothed grin as he accepted her bag. The fact that she spoke Spanish like a native must have just made his job infinitely easier.

"Did Ricardo send you?" she queried, once again thankful she picked up foreign languages as easily as some people picked up the common cold. The driver wasn't a huge surprise. Ricardo had sent them before.

"*Sí*. He has been detained. I am to take you to meet him at *el Cantina*. The car is this way," he replied, rambling cheerfully in his native language as he maneuvered her toward the exit. "You have more bags, no? If you would like to wait in the car, I will return for your things."

"*Gracias*." Phoebe rubbed at the knots in her neck. She'd been so lost in thought, focused on her search, that her other bag had slipped her mind. *Ugh!* Some days she'd forget her head if it weren't attached.

Another yawn snuck up on her. As they exited the building, a wall of steamy heat slammed into her. The driver never took his hand from her elbow as he more or less tugged her along. Probably afraid she'd pass out from the temperature or something. The heat didn't wilt her, not as is did some people. She'd grown up with it. It was like a second skin to her. But, as tired as she was, it didn't exactly energize her either.

She should be used to flying by now, but she just never seemed to be able to relax on a plane, always feeling a strange, itchy sensation just under her skin the moment the wheels left the ground. And the flight after the last layover had been particularly turbulent. All she wanted to do right now was take a long, cool shower and crawl onto a feather soft bed where she could sleep for the next two days straight.

What she wanted and what she was going to get were, however, two very different things. Not only was she avoiding any sort of layover in a major city on purpose, she was headed into the heart of the Rio Bec Region. A true jungle.

She'd chosen to do it this way for a reason. The more people she interacted with, the greater the risk. At best, she knew she could look forward to rainwater camp showers and a sleeping bag on the hard floor of a cramped tent.

If she was lucky.

At worst? Well, she'd once spent two nights in a row with her back pressed to Ricardo's atop crumbling ruins, both of them wide awake, clutching guns to their chests as they scoured the dancing shadows of the jungle, flinching at every shush of leaves and snap of a branch. And did she mention? Her throat had been flayed open and bandaged with scraps from a filthy shirt at the time. Trips like that had given her a whole new meaning for the term "roughing it".

She glanced at the heavy, silver watch on her wrist as they all but jogged along the sidewalk. The scuffed, much-loved timepiece was the only thing she had left that had belonged to her father, aside from his journals.

He'd had Ricardo mail the package to her along with his final letter should he not return from his final trip by a certain date. A trip he'd completely out of character refused to allow Ricardo to accompany him on. The package had been a proof of life kind of thing. Or rather proof of death, as it were.

Grimacing at the memory, yet still grieving too much to part with the reminder, she made a mental note to reset the watch for the current time zone.

"Will it take very long to get to *el Cantina*?" Maybe, if Ricardo didn't already have all their equipment ready to go, she could sneak in a short nap.

"*Ah, Señorita, no problemas.* I'll get you there *muy rapido*," he said with another of his big grins.

A raucous broke out somewhere on the street behind her, but Juan was already steering her toward a plain brown sedan. With one firm hand gripping her elbow, he opened the car door, and then all but shoved her inside. She'd no more than righted herself in the seat, gasping in shock, when he tossed her carry-on at her.

Juan slammed the door in her face. And then, he disappeared.

Phoebe froze for a split second, stunned. Then she bolted forward and jerked at the door handle. A dark chuckle came from the front seat, startling her. Sucking in a sharp breath, she shot a glance over her shoulder. Juan looked back at her through the mesh wire partition. He'd gotten there much too fast for a normal human. Like a slap to the face, she understood her mistake.

This was no driver, at least not one sent by Ricardo.

"Who are you?" she demanded, pressing against the back of her seat in horror.

How could they have found me already?

"I am Sïnsobar," he said, his Spanish accent replaced with one very closely resembling a British intonation, one completely incongruous with his appearance. "You can call me Sin," he drawled, offering her a lewd smile.

That wicked grin made her very, very uneasy. As if the present circumstances hadn't already put her on edge.

She looped her carry-on over her head and across her body, and then scrambled for the door handle with renewed purpose. The knob on the lock had been removed, preventing her from opening the door. Truly frightened now, she glanced at the opposite door. It, too, had had the lever removed.

"Let me out," she ordered, cursing herself for the way her voice shook.

"I don't think so, Guardian," Sin replied.

Her blood turned to ice with that single, damning word.

Her captor's focus swerved to the rear window. His eyes turned black. Not just the pupils. Not just the irises. But the whites too.

Complete, bottomless black.

Demon black.

She'd seen eyes like that before. Three times before, to be exact. The first two times, she'd been very, very young. The last, not all that long ago. But those memories had been seared in her mind. Because in those moments, her life had forever changed.

Oh no. No, no, no! How could I have been so

stupid? So careless?

He scowled at something behind her, whipped around to face the front, and stomped on the gas. Phoebe was thrown back in the seat. She scrambled to regain her balance, twisting around to peer out the rear window.

Surfer Boy had followed them out onto the road and ran behind them now.

Had he seen her abduction? Was he trying to help her?

Praying as she'd never prayed before, she managed to get up on her knees despite the madly swerving car. Her pulse pounded in her ears.

"Help!" Phoebe shouted. She slapped her palms against the back window again and again. "Please, help me!"

But Surfer Boy was falling farther and farther behind until she couldn't see him anymore. Frantic, Phoebe spun in her seat. Her palms stung from slapping them against the window. She searched for another way out as pavement gave way to dirt roads and they sped along over dips and ruts. Desperate, bouncing up and down on the dusty, hard seat, she kicked at the door to no avail. She kicked at the window. Kicked at the mesh divider. Nothing.

She sat up and opened her mouth to plead with her captor once more. But her words morphed into screams. They were headed straight for a squat stucco house with a piece of corrugated tin propped over what looked to be a porch. The demon behind the wheel wasn't making any effort to turn, or even slow down.

Without warning, the demon—Sin, he'd called himself—reached back and slashed fiendish black claws across the mesh wires separating them. His massive fist shot through the jagged opening. Then that claw-tipped hand wrapped around her forearm. The world around her blurred, and she had an intense sensation of falling. Her stomach pitched into her throat as bright color swirled around her. Images and sensations assaulted her, here and gone too fast for her to register.

****

Sebastian raced after the sedan. He'd recognize that face anywhere. Her image had haunted him since the moment he'd first laid eyes on the picture he'd pilfered from her home, the picture still tucked inside his right hip pocket.

Phoebe Mackenzie had beaten on the rear window as the sedan pulled farther and farther away. Her lips had been moving. He hadn't needed to hear her words. The look on her face said it all.

She was in trouble, and she knew it.

The car was moving too fast, swerving too erratically for him to lock onto it and shimmer inside. He was more likely to solidify in the trunk, or in the engine block, than on the seat beside her. All he could do was follow behind and hope he could catch up before the Carpathï—a species of demon with the ability to change forms, otherwise known as skin-shifters—who'd taken her could shimmer away with her.

He just wished he knew the identity of the demon driving. That might give him some clue as to where they were headed. Maybe. Though he had a sneaking suspicion. He just prayed he was wrong.

As fast as he was running—yeah, he was probably

garnering all kinds of attention that he shouldn't be—despite the traffic slowing the sedan, Sebastian was losing them.

Damn it all to hell.

They soon came upon an intersection…one it didn't appear the professor's abductor had any intention of slowing for. Sebastian spied a motorbike, its driver waiting for the light to change. Keeping all his attention on the speeding sedan, he pounced. Without breaking stride, Sebastian displaced the stunned motorcyclist and was burning rubber on the pavement.

Concrete soon gave way to pitted dirt as the sedan turned off the main highway leading out of the city. After a few harrowingly close calls with oncoming traffic, they tore into a small village. Carts and people, squawking chickens and excited dogs soon cluttered the irregular cobblestone road. The sedan barreled around corners, unmindful of pedestrians, traffic, or who had the right of way, and Sebastian kept pace.

Impoverished buildings whizzed by right and left now. Sebastian paid them little heed, his single-minded focus locked on that sedan. But then an ancient, rusted out truck with poultry-filled wire cages stacked in the back lumbered onto the road in front of him. The bike teetered beneath him for a moment. Sebastian kicked at the ground for balance as the rear wheel fishtailed. Dust and feathers billowed up all around him.

He craned his neck as he revved the motorcycle and launched around the rear of the truck. He watched, helpless, as up ahead, the car careened into the front of a stucco shack. Clumps of dirt, clouds of dust and stucco flew through the air as the sedan came to an abrupt stop.

Sebastian tore onto the scraggly yard and vaulted from the still sliding motorcycle. He rushed to the car and tore the back door open, ripping it from its hinges. But even as he did so, he knew he was too late.

The car was empty.

He didn't waste time swearing or cursing his piss poor luck yet again. Sebastian closed his eyes, centered his focus, pulled in his abilities, and opened his senses.

He didn't yet know the name of the demon that had taken her. Or where they were going. Hell, he could be headed straight into a trap for all he knew. He didn't give a flying rat's ass. All that mattered was that he wasn't going to sit back and let the professor be snatched right out from under his nose. Not when he'd been searching for her for this long. Not when she'd been so close.

Not again.

The moment her emerald green eyes had connected with his across the airport terminal had sealed her fate, sword aside. He couldn't shake that electrical zing that had arced between them.

She wasn't getting away from him.

Scowling, Sebastian searched for that fragile, already fading luminescent trail all demons left behind when they shimmered.

And he smiled with grim purpose.

Chapter Two

When the world stopped spinning, Phoebe was able to draw a breath at last. A sharp gust of air hit her hard, slightly cooler than before, but so foul and dank she doubled over and gagged. She squinted through watery eyes, scouring the gloom for some clue as to where she was. Dim light filtered in from a small opening a short distance away. All around her, dark, water splotched, rough stone walls absorbed the rest of the light.

A cave?

And they weren't alone.

Hideous creatures writhed in the shadows, shifting in and out of the twilight making odd hissing and clacking sounds. They bowed to the demon still in possession of her arm. Glancing over, she swallowed in dismay and tried to pull away as his form began to mutate.

And then she gaped in shock. One moment the swarthy, slick-backed, portly Hispanic man stood beside her. And in the next minute, a tall, lean *humanlike* creature took his place. Humanlike…but *not*. His skin was blood red. His shoulder length hair was jet black. As black as his eyes. He smiled at her, flashing a set of fangs a la Dracula.

She couldn't believe what she was seeing. It was like history repeating itself. The resemblance, the sense of familiarity was uncanny. He looked so much like the one who'd—

"This female belongs to Dimiezlo," the creature—
Sïnsobar, she corrected herself again—said, his voice
layered and deep. His pronouncement was met with
livid snarls and disappointed growls from the surging
mass of creatures moving around the cave. He snarled
right back. The angry noises died away and, although
the mass still shifted and hissed, Phoebe sensed a
sudden wariness filling the room.

"She is a gift for Stolas." Hisses erupted once
more. Fear, unmistakable and ripe, filled the air.

She tugged at Sin's grasp to no avail, terrified of
the demon, and yet afraid to move any closer to those
seething, slathering shadows.

"But, Master," a whiny, thin voice begged from
somewhere too close for her comfort. "We've been so
long without a female. And she smells so...*delicious*."
The last word was said on a shivery, lustful shudder.

Phoebe cringed at the implied intent.

And then she froze, breath arrested, as realization
dawned. These demons weren't speaking English, or
Spanish. Nor were they speaking French, Italian, or
Russian. She would know, as she spoke each of those
languages—along with several dialects of native
cultures—fluently. And yet she'd understood every
guttural word they'd spoken.

Every. Single. Word.

How? What is *this language?*

"Stolas will be displeased if she is in poor
condition when he receives her."

Again, the crowd of monsters recoiled at the mere
mention of the name.

Whoever this Stolas was, he seemed to be her best

chance of walking out of this cave alive and in one piece.

"But, Master, she is not a Halfling."

Phoebe cringed. Why wouldn't that…that *thing* give up?

"It doesn't matter. She is a Guardian. He wants her kind too. And you know he likes them with enough spirit to last at least a few hours in his little dungeon of horrors."

Okay. So maybe this Stolas guy wasn't looking like such a stellar option after all. Especially not the way this horde of ghoulish nightmares cowered every time Sïnsobar said his name.

"Please, Master," whiny voice wheedled. "We'll be exsssstra careful with her."

Sïnsobar studied the mass, seemed to be gauging the temperament of the room.

Oh, God, he's wavering!

"No!" she cried, fighting his hold. "You can't do this."

But her demands only seemed to seal her fate.

"Fine," Sïnsobar relented. "But don't drain her. And for Hell's sake don't kill her. Stolas wants her alive and able to… Well, talking, I imagine, won't matter so much."

With that, Sïnsobar thrust her into the surging darkness. The shadows swarmed her. Phoebe screamed, and screamed again as rough, calloused, clawed appendages began pawing at her, tugging her hair and ripping at her clothing. Careless grasping drew blood and left welts. Fingers—at least, she hoped they were fingers—pinched and squeezed. Something sharp punctured her wrist, and her whole body seized as fiery acid flooded her veins.

A dark roar reverberated through the cave, and the crowd of horrors around her froze. Phoebe searched for the source of that roar, struggling against the tentacle-like arms that squeezed and pulled at her. Had this Dimiezlo come for her? Would she be spared this indignity? This violation?

Or was she in for far worse?

A nightmare come to life appeared in the middle of the cavern. He was huge. Ginormous. And, judging by his next roar and the expression on his fierce face, pissed off to the extreme.

His muscles bulged with supernatural strength. His skin was the color of ash and soot. His eyes were similar to Sïnsobar's, a deep bottomless black, only somehow more frightening. And his fangs made Sïnsobar's look like fake Halloween adornments—scrawny ones at that. The big, curved horns on the top of his head skimmed across the roof of the cave like steel on flint, leaving a shower of sparks in his wake. But it was the black wings snapping open behind him that snared her attention. Hers and everyone—every*thing*—else's in the chamber. His wings were massive and coated with shiny black feathers. Feathers that looked like some kind of high-tech metal plates.

"*Vengeance*," something whispered. The note of horrified terror filling its voice was sharp.

Phoebe swallowed. Ally or foe? Frying pan or fire?

Sïnsobar swore and roared, "Attack!"

Still the shadows hesitated, apparently cowed by the newcomer more than they were by their master. Sïnsobar swiped at the shadow closest to him, and blood sprayed in a wide arc as the shadow burst into ash at his feet.

"Damn it, I said attack!"

Finally, caught between a monster and a nightmare, the mass of shadows surged forward, surrounding the newcomer. Sïnsobar himself had disappeared somewhere along the way. Phoebe—clearly the spoils of this impending battle—was shoved, less-than-gently, toward the back of the cave. She looked on in horror as the nightmare erupted into action.

Claws and fangs mauled and tore, shredding their way through Sïnsobar's army. But it was those massive, shiny black wings, unfurling and swiping and slashing, that truly decimated the beings swarming him. No shadow monster stood a chance. None could withstand the strength, the lethal brutality of those wings. None could dodge them. None could evade them and get close to him…unless he wanted them close. And if ever he let one get close…

Well, the wings would have been the more humane way to go.

Something heavy and slimy hit her from the side, toppling her to the ground. Sharp fangs ripped into her shoulder. Though she fought with everything she had, she couldn't dislodge the creature. It began slurping at the jagged wound it had inflicted, all the while grinding itself against her hip and grunting in the most lewd, disgusting way.

Phoebe cried out, squirming and twisting in an effort to get away. But it was no use. The creature clung to her like an octopus.

The winged nightmare gave a mighty roar, and then the creature pinning her to the sandy floor was wrenched away, its fangs leaving behind mauled flesh.

Phoebe screamed as she pressed her palm to her bleeding shoulder. The pain was excruciating, beyond anything she'd ever experienced. Black dots began to swirl around her vision.

The winged demon turned toward her, her struggling assailant dangling several feet off the ground from one of his gigantic fists. Without looking away from her, the ash-colored demon clamped his huge hand on the top of his victim's skull, severing head from body in one brutal twist. He dropped the remains, already forgotten, to the ground.

The nightmare's massive chest was heaving, his muscles rippling. The tops of his black wings arched above his shoulders, the bottom tips brushed over the ground behind him as he approached her. Phoebe shrank back, pressing against the damp, uneven rock wall. Blood poured from her wound, seeped between her fingers, and ran down her forearm to drip from her elbow. Despite her best efforts, a whimper escaped her.

"Do not fear me." The beast spoke in that same layered voice and guttural language Sïnsobar and his creatures had used. He held his big hand out, palm up to her, though he didn't come any closer.

"I'm here to help you," he said, in English this time. "Do not fear me. We must go before Sin returns with reinforcements."

Phoebe blinked at that blood covered hand and forced down the bile rising in her throat. The cave had begun to come in and out of focus.

She straightened her glasses, but it didn't help. A wave of icy air swept over her, and she shuddered. Her head had begun to pound, her body to ache. She felt awful. Like she had the flu, only worse.

Way worse.

"Who are you?" she managed to get out. Her throat was raw. She glanced down at that big, bloody hand again, cringing.

A frown pinched the demon's brow, and he drew his hand back. And then, the beast's form shifted, all the blood and gore disappeared.

Phoebe's mouth fell open. She couldn't believe it. She had to be hallucinating.

"You!" she shouted. Or, at least, she tried to. Her voice emerged little more than a hollow whisper.

Surfer Boy? How was this even possible?

****

The Guardian looked so bedraggled and shell-shocked, leaning against the wall of the cave as if it were the only thing keeping her upright. Her hair was a mess. Her clothing was torn and bloodied, hanging from her in shreds. And the scent of her fear was sharp, stirring his anger.

But she blinked up at him, the will to survive written all over her beautiful face. Something jumpstarted inside his chest, as if a livewire had been hooked up directly to his soul...or the withered empty husk of what was left of his soul anyway. For a moment, he lost his purpose. Lost his train of thought. Lost his very reason for tracking her here. All he could see, all he could hear, or smell, or sense was this female. He didn't know why, only that those stunning eyes of hers had captivated him somehow.

She flinched and readjusted her grip on her bloody shoulder.

If he could have, Sebastian would have brought every one of Sïnsobar's minions back so he could rip them apart all over again. But his rage wouldn't help her. And so, he battled for calm. Battled to hear the voice of reason inside his own head.

Sebastian thrust his now clean hand out once more. "Come on, we have to hurry."

Her emerald green stare turned to the mouth of the cave over a hundred yards away. He watched, awed and more than a little irritated, as she pushed to her feet and began wobbling her way toward the exit. She cut a wide arc around him, refusing his assistance. Between each unsteady step, she braced a shaking hand on the rough cave wall, leaving smears of blood in her wake. Her pace was slow and labored, but she hadn't uttered a sound.

After what she'd just seen, after what she'd just been through, he couldn't fathom how she was still even conscious.

She was stubborn.

She was strong.

She was…

"*Magnificent*," he whispered.

He wanted to let her keep whatever shreds of pride she still clung to with such fierce determination, yet he knew they didn't have time. He hadn't exaggerated. Sin could return at any moment.

She took a misstep and nearly went to her knees, catching herself at the last moment. Sebastian's heart lurched. With his chest aching in an odd, uncomfortable way, Sebastian strode forward.

"I'm sorry, professor, but we're gonna have to do this my way."

He scooped her up in his arms. That first contact zapped a shot of lust straight through him like a bolt of lightning. So much so that he almost dropped her. She let out a muffled shriek and clutched at him for balance.

Cursing beneath his breath, Sebastian lifted her higher against his chest and tightened his hold on her. "It'd probably be best if you close your eyes now. We have to make a few jumps to displace the shimmer trail before we stop, and I've been told women don't like this part very much."

He couldn't help himself. He peered down at her and before he realized what he was doing, he pressed his nose to her hair and dragged her scent in soul-deep. His instincts were firing all over the place, going haywire. He felt like he was coming out of his skin. His knees were weak, and his whole body was inexplicably shaky.

Yet he'd never felt more powerful or more alive in his entire existence.

What. The. Hell?

Chapter Three

About the seventh or eighth hop, Sebastian figured they were safe. The professor hung limp in his arms, conscious but barely holding on. For a moment, he thought she might have passed out. But then she moaned and buried her face closer to the side of his neck. And once more, he felt as if he'd been hooked up to a mega-watt power station, his pulse jumping erratically.

Time to go home. He focused on his farmhouse, on the kitchen. She was a mess. How much blood had she lost? He needed to get her cleaned up, patched up. Then he'd have to sit her down and get her talking. He needed as much info out of her in the shortest amount of time possible. He needed to find some way to steal the sword back from Stolas. And he needed to go after Mikhail.

Even now the others might be embarking on a suicide mission to free the Demon of War. His brothers needed him.

Sebastian glanced around in confusion as soon as they solidified. Fury settled in shortly thereafter. He stood at one end of the kitchen near the table, the professor cradled in his arms, and he turned in a slow circle. Had his place been hit by a tornado? Cupboard doors and cabinet drawers hung open, though the walls and ceiling were still intact. Chairs were overturned.

Pots and pans, cooking utensils, and canned goods were...*everywhere*.

Small appliances, broken and mangled, littered the countertops, tabletop, and floor. Shards of broken dishes, shattered glass, and busted stoneware crunched beneath his feet among swathes of spilled flour, sugar, and coffee beans. His disbelieving stare skimmed over and then shot back to a butcher knife embedded in a cupboard door.

What. The. Hell!

And then he remembered the call he'd gotten from Gideon a while back—something about the Halfling remodeling his kitchen—and he cursed. Oh, yeah, his place had been hit by a tornado all right. At least an EF-3 by the looks of it. And that storm had a name. Maggie.

That rotten bastard had let his mate decimate Sebastian's kitchen. The least Gideon could have done was clean up the damned mess.

I'll have his head for a Christmas tree topper.

Clenching his teeth, Sebastian carried the professor from the kitchen into the living room. Only then did he let out the pent-up breath. The destruction had been limited to the kitchen.

Lucky bastard.

Handling her like she were made of glass, Sebastian lowered the professor's feet to the floor. It took everything in him to let her go and step back. Tearing off his own skin would have been more comfortable.

His breath left him in a stunned whoosh. He was acting like—

He staggered back a step, feeling like someone had

just belted him in the gut…with a railroad tie.

He was acting like Xander acted around Kyanna.

Like Niklas behaved with Carly.

What the hell is wrong with me?

"Oh, God," she gasped. "I think I'm going to be sick."

Faster than she could draw her next breath, Sebastian conjured a trash can and thrust it into her hands. And then he stood there, watching helplessly, as the professor sagged to her knees on his living room rug and proceeded to toss her cookies.

Confused by his reactions to her, he waited till she looked like she was done. He then conjured a wet washcloth, a bottle of mouthwash, and a glass of soda, handing each to her in turn. He vanished everything as soon as she set it all aside and leaned back on her heels.

The moment the items in question disappeared, she squeaked, losing what little color she'd regained. He cringed. Yeah, should have probably warned her about that. Well, there was no help for it now. He lifted her onto the sofa.

"Better?" he asked, taking the seat beside her. He couldn't stop staring.

And the fact that he couldn't stop staring made him feel like a fool.

"Not so much." She peered at him as if she expected him to sprout a second head. "Who are you?"

"I'm Sebastian."

His mind had somehow kicked from neutral into high gear.

Why was she affecting him this way?

The question whirled around in his mind, though he was careful not to voice his quandary aloud. He studied her in the bright shaft of sunlight pouring through the window. Her pictures hadn't done her justice. She was…his mouth went dry. She was so beautiful it took his breath away. Another surge of desire swam through his blood, and his body reacted as though he'd been given a shot of undiluted adrenaline…adrenaline and a concentrated dose of aphrodisiac. He shifted in his seat uncomfortably.

Tall as she was, the top of her head had barely reached Sebastian's chin. And she was slim, almost boyishly so. Exactly as she'd been described to him by the oh-so-helpful residents of Port August, otherwise known as Hell on Earth.

But her skin was porcelain with a faint dusting of freckles. Like cream and cinnamon. Nobody had mentioned that.

He caught himself wondering how all that cinnamon and cream skin might taste.

Her features were sharp, her chin pointed, her cheekbones pronounced. The angle of that chin bespoke a stubbornness he'd already witnessed. But there was a softness about her too. She was…dainty. Delicate. And she was so pale right now he feared she might pass out after all. Dark shadows smudged her remarkable eyes, and her lips were almost blue.

The curve of those lips made him want to sample them.

"I'm Phoebe," she introduced herself, holding out a hand that still trembled. "I guess I should be thanking you?"

He took her hand in his. And he held on long after she tried to release him, marveling at how fragile her bones seemed and the softness of her skin, which wasn't like him at all. Nor was he the type to sit and stare in mute, starry-eyed fascination. And yet, that was precisely what he was doing. His mind raced, and yet he was tongue tied.

Googly-eyed and all but drooling.

She frowned, squinching her eyes closed as she pressed the heel of her free hand to her temple.

"Are you going to be sick again?"

Maybe all the shimmering had been too much for her. Was she in shock from her earlier trauma at the hands of Sin and his minions? Had she been injured when the car had collided with the house? Did she, even now, have internal injuries, putting her at risk?

Realizing he was on the verge of hyperventilating, he forced himself to breathe. God, he'd never tease Niklas and Xander again. Or Gideon. Gideon had a mate now too, didn't he?

Scowling, Sebastian drew back, all of a sudden, though he didn't release her hand just yet. Why was he even thinking about mates? He blinked at the professor. Sure, she was attractive...hell, she was downright alluring in an exotic sort of way, if he were honest. But it wasn't as if he was desperate with burgeoning, unspent lust. He hadn't exactly been celibate all these years, not like the others, and that had been his cross to bear. So why was he acting like a crack addict, and she the fix he'd been craving?

"I don't think so, just a little dizzy," she said.

He waited while she struggled to gain her bearings, still gripping her hand in his. Just the thought of releasing her was abhorrent. Why?

Why did he feel like he was having some screwed up kind of clouds-part-sun-comes-out-heavenly-angels-singing-ah-ha moment?

Even as the thought crossed his mind, one cold certainty settled inside him. He'd never experienced this before. This fierce need to possess. To protect and to provide for. Or this sense of bone-deep attraction.

The certainty of that knowledge floored him.

Her free hand reached up to press against the blood-soaked tatters of her shirt over her shoulder.

Damn, that's a lot of blood. Maybe I should—

"You're a demon? Like them?"

That took him aback, her calm analysis. But then it shouldn't. She was a Guardian, after all. As such, she should know all about them. Not all of it might be correct, but she'd have the basic grasp of things, he was sure.

"Demon, yes. Like them, no."

She seemed to weigh his words. A tiny frown knitted her brow. She looked as if she wanted to argue, but then thought better of it. "Where am I?"

"I brought you home. Ahh…to my farm. You're safe now."

"I'm sorry," she said, shaking her head. "This has all just happened so fast. I've been on one airplane after another for hours and hours, and then I thought Ricardo had sent…" Her voice trailed away for a moment. She frowned, and then her lovely emerald eyes shot wide. "Ricardo! Oh, he must be so worried."

"Let's just take this one step at a time, yeah?"

She licked her lips and nodded. "That…that demon, he said his name was Sin or something. He was waiting at the airport for me. Like he knew just where to find me. I don't know how he—"

"He—or one of his minions—probably slipped into

your place and checked out your itinerary." Sebastian shrugged. "It's how I found you."

"So that's where I left it," she muttered. She shook her head again, her lips compressed, and she sighed.

But then her attention flew back to his face. "Wait...*you* broke into my house?" She scooted back on the sofa, still clutching at her shoulder as she inched away from him. He still held her free hand, so she didn't get far.

"It wasn't like the door was locked." Great, now he sounded defensive.

"It wasn't?"

"No."

She frowned, her focus turning inward. Heaving a sigh, she pushed her glasses up the bridge of her nose with the tip of her index finger. "I probably forgot to lock it."

Hearing that did not make him happy. Rather than scold her as he wanted to do, though, he changed the subject. Time was, after all, of the essence. And it wouldn't matter anymore anyway. From now on, she'd be under his care, his to protect...at least until he got his hands on that sword. And once he got the sword...

Sebastian frowned. Then what? Would this odd connection he felt to her be gone by then?

"I've been looking for you for a long time."

Her expression became downright alarmed, and she tugged at her hand with renewed force. "Why?"

"I need you to listen to me, to everything I have to say, before you freak out, yeah?"

She didn't look like she was going to believe anything he had to say. In fact, the freak out portion of this evening's entertainment looked like it was already well underway.

"Look, I saved you back there in that cave. You owe me. The least you can do is hear me out," he said. Her reticence struck a nerve he hadn't known he even had. Where was his vaunted patience now?

Her brow puckered, but Phoebe nodded after a very, very long moment. Still, she tried once more to pull her hand from his. And that irritated him too. So he held on, and ignored her bid for freedom.

"I know about the sword," he began.

At that, panic flooded her expression, and she began jerking at her hand, half rising from the couch. She glanced around the room, searching for an exit.

"Be still, and listen," he ordered as he yanked her back down beside him, closer this time. He didn't want to hurt her, but he wasn't ready to sever contact just yet either.

She quieted, but her hand, her whole body, was rigid now. A fine sheen of perspiration dotted her forehead and upper lip. Sebastian readjusted his grip on her. Her skin was so warm.

He frowned.

Her skin was *too* warm.

He peered hard at her. Her eyes were glassy. Her breathing was shallow and rapid.

"Are you okay?" Damn it, he was starting to sound like a broken record.

Phoebe shook her head, then moaned. "I can't...I can't breathe."

She pushed her hair back and fanned her face. The tattered shreds of her shirt parted. It was then that he got his first good look at her shoulder. He'd known she'd been injured, but then she'd gotten sick, and he'd realized he wanted her for his own, and—

Damn it, that wound is bad.

Sebastian blinked, his body vibrating with the need to destroy something. He should have noticed sooner, paid better attention.

He conjured bandages, thick pads of gauze. Beside him, she jolted, let out a soft cry, and tried to scoot away again.

Her shoulders rose and fell on shaky breaths. The vicious scar that ran down the side of her throat did nothing to calm him. Someone had done their damnedest to take her head off. It didn't matter that she'd survived. That wound could have easily ended her.

Ended her before he'd ever found her.

How had he missed the scar or the wounds before? Granted the cave had been dark, and her long hair had been down, torn from the bun she'd worn earlier, tangling around her neck and shoulders in wild disarray. But he could see it now. And the sight of it was doing some freaky stuff to his insides.

"It's so hot in here," she slurred.

Sebastian's attention shot to her face. Alarm flooded him. Hot? It couldn't be more than sixty-five degrees in the house. He always kept his place cool. Maybe cooler than most. Kyanna and Carly were always complaining, accusing him of deliberately trying to freeze them out. But having spent a good deal of time roasting in the fires of Hell, AC was a luxury he refused to skimp on. No, the room wasn't hot. Not by any means.

Phoebe swiped the back of her free hand across her damp forehead. Sebastian frowned and grabbed her arm. He turned it over with great care and examined the small red puncture wounds surrounded by angry purple bruises on her wrist.

Shit!

She'd been bitten. Not that the huge gashes in her shoulder couldn't already be contaminated with venom, but the puncture wounds on her wrist and the angry coloration confirmed it. What kind of venom was the question? There'd been more than one species of demon in that cave. Best case scenario, it'd been a Charocté Demon. Worst case scenario, a Carpathï.

Not such a huge issue either way…if she were a demon. An angel stood a fighting chance. Slim, but a chance all the same. Even a Halfling with diluted blood might survive. Maybe.

But a human?

Not a snowball's chance in hell.

His blood ran cold.

Now that he knew to look for it, he was beginning to scent the sticky sweet smell of venom taking hold in the blood seeping from her wounds. And he panicked. Not Carpathï venom, but something nearly as bad. Diffenidus venom. Beyond a doubt. He could tell by the distinctive scent, very similar to that of roses.

Why hadn't he detected it before? Had the poisoning been too new, the venom not circulated enough through her system yet? Or had he been too wrapped up in his attraction to her?

Once, a very long time ago, Mikhail had tried to heal a couple of humans they'd rescued from a Diffenidus nest. But the humans hadn't responded to his treatment. Instead, they'd suffered torturous misery so bad that, to this day, Sebastian wondered if it wouldn't have been kinder to put them down rather than let the poison run its course. In the end, the humans hadn't survived anyway.

No human had *ever* survived.

All the same, Mikhail was her best bet. But with Mikhail out of the picture, Sebastian had no idea how to heal her. What was he going to do? He couldn't let her die.

He'd only just found her. And he hadn't even had a chance to question her about the sword.

And, even as he tried to deny it, he couldn't pretend that the sword was his only interest in her now.

"I think I caught a bug or something," she murmured, and then her eyelids fluttered closed, and her body went limp.

Sebastian caught her before she hit the floor. Sweeping her up into his arms yet again, he cursed. She was burning up, what was left of her abused clothing damp with sweat.

His mind raced. He'd watched *ER*, and *Grey's Anatomy*, and countless other medical dramas thanks to Gideon's addiction to primetime television programming. But Sebastian wasn't a damned doctor. Besides, not even a real human doctor could fix what was wrong with her.

That odd ache in his chest intensified until he had trouble breathing.

He wasn't giving up. It wasn't in his nature. He'd do whatever he had to do to give her a fighting chance.

First things first, he had to get her temperature down. He shimmered them both into the shower in the master bath. With a deft mental flick, he turned the water on, ice cold, and vanished what was left of her clothing. She came to with a gasp. He wasn't sure if consciousness was a blessing or a curse for her right now. She moaned and struggled in his arms, a feeble protest at best, but he held her beneath the spray, as gentle as he might hold a newborn babe. She shivered, mindlessly trying to burrow close to his warmth.

Holding her at arm's length when it was obvious she was so miserable was one of the hardest things he'd ever done. What he wanted was to cuddle her close and sooth her. Comfort her. Urges completely foreign to him. Yet he'd never felt this overwhelming tenderness, this gripping protectiveness for a female before. It humbled him.

He directed his attention, and his soapy hands, to the wealth of fresh bruises, welts, and cuts covering her lean body, and did his best to otherwise ignore the fact that she was naked in his arms. With as much care as possible, he cleaned her injuries. He focused on the puncture wounds on her wrist, cleaning them twice, but since the poison was so far into her system there was no point in trying to draw it back out through those wounds. It would only cause her further harm.

Her shoulder had been mauled, and he hated to touch it, knowing he would only cause her more pain. However, on the off chance there might be more Diffenidus saliva in the wound working its way into her system, he knew he needed to get it cleaned out. The ragged flesh still seeped blood, though much more sluggishly now. He touched the wound, and she cried out, pulling away.

The sound of her pain pierced his heart. Sebastian bit down on his lip, wrapped an arm around her to hold her to him, pinning her arms at her sides, and he forced himself to continue his ministrations. He was hurting her, though it was for her own good, and it was killing him.

That she hadn't passed out already was a wonder. The pain he must be causing her. And yet, it was the only thing he could think of to do. He would see her better. He would not lose her now.

Sebastian held her beneath the spray of chilly water until his own teeth started to chatter. Only when her skin was cool to the touch did he turn off the water. He conjured a towel and wrapped it around her. His instinct was to bundle her chilled flesh in layers of soft, fluffy blankets and kindle a huge blaze in the fireplace. But he knew that was wrong, would only cause her temperature to rise once more and all the misery he'd just put her through would have been for nothing.

So he conjured himself clean and dry and clothed in jeans and a T-shirt, and then carried her to his bed. There he laid her down and eased her wet hair from her face. He conjured bandages for her shoulder and, not knowing what else to do, sat by her side and held her hand. And he prayed.

Her eyes soon fluttered open, but she seemed dazed. He managed to coax her into taking a couple Tylenol and drinking most of a glass of water.

Unfortunately, neither stayed down long. The violent spasms wracking her body as she got sick scored him with guilt all over again.

There had to be help for her somewhere. Desperate, he called Kyanna, but neither she nor Xander had heard of a cure for a human infected with Diffenidus venom. Kyanna suggested some herbal concoctions to alleviate the symptoms, and crystals to reinforce his ward stones in case the demon that had bitten her had forged a link. But he was pretty certain he'd already killed that bastard. More the pity. He'd happily decimate Sïnsobar's nest all over again to seek vengeance over what they'd done to her.

He glanced at Phoebe. He couldn't think of her as the Professor any longer, not after having tended to her in the shower. Desperate, he picked up the phone one last time. He didn't know what else to do.

"Talk." Asher's deep, sleepy voice came over the line.

"Is there a cure for Diffenidus venom?"

"Hmm…not a cheap one."

Asher was a legendary and lethal demon mercenary the Fallen had come to regard as—if not one of their own—then an ally, of sorts. He wouldn't straight out agree to join their ranks, yet he hadn't sold them out to the highest bidder either. That was saying something, considering the highest bidder was Lucifer himself, and the bounty on their collective heads was so high no demon in his right mind would turn it down.

There was very little Asher didn't know or couldn't find out. He never reneged on a contract. And he never failed when he was hired, be it for something as simple as locating an item or as damning as carrying out a cold-blooded assassination. Of course, Asher's assistance always came with strings.

And a very steep price tag.

"At least, not cheap for a demon or angel," Asher clarified, sounding a little more awake now. "Now if you got a human on your hands, you might as well call the priest and buy a shovel."

"There's nothing I can do? Nothing at all?"

Sebastian asked, his voice catching despite his struggle to remain calm.

A long moment of silence stretched on. A deep sigh. "So, we *are* talking human."

"Yeah."

Another long pause. "Bring her to me."

The fine hairs on the back of Sebastian's neck stood up. "I didn't say anything about this being a female."

"Am I wrong?"

"Where are you?" he asked, ignoring the smirk he heard in the other demon's voice.

"Home," Asher said, and then hung up.

Without a second's hesitation, Sebastian conjured a T-shirt—one of his own—to cover her and scooped her up in his arms.

When Asher said home, he meant the castle. A castle of which, to the best of Sebastian's knowledge, no-one but a very select few even knew about. Possibly no one else but him. Centuries ago, Asher had called in a steep debt Sebastian had owed. As repayment of that debt, Sebastian had helped Asher lay siege to an honest-to-God castle in the highlands of Scotland and claim it for his own. And he'd been sworn to secrecy on the castle's location. Asher's home boasted turrets, tower rooms, and dungeons…the last of which, rumor had it, Asher made ample use.

Sebastian shimmered them to the courtyard and waited for Asher to come to them. The mercenary had his own protections over his lair. Protections Sebastian wasn't stupid enough to mess with. Not even in the current circumstances. He wouldn't be any use to Phoebe if he was missing his head or he'd been turned inside out. Literally.

A moment later, Asher appeared beside him. "Give her to me," he instructed, holding out his arms.

"She doesn't go anywhere without me." Sebastian made no effort to pass her over, or to hide the surge of possessiveness sweeping through him.

"It's like that, is it?" Asher asked, arching a brow. Sebastian narrowed his eyes. He didn't like the way the edge of the mercenary's mouth curled up, or the hint of interest that now gleamed in his chocolate brown eyes.

"Droppin' like flies," Asher murmured, shaking his head. He turned and, as they stepped up to the thick wood set in even thicker stone, he waved a hand over the front door.

A low rumbling mixture of syllables and sounds passed Asher's lips. Something far older and far more sinister than Sebastian had ever heard. Sebastian's skin crawled at the surge of energy emanating from the demon beside him, an energy he shouldn't, by rights, even be able to detect. That was Gideon's thing. But sense it he did. He felt the protective layers over the castle waver and change. Not gone completely, yet Sebastian was able to follow Asher inside without incurring physical injury.

As soon as they cleared the doorway, Asher waved over the massive double doors, raising the protective barrier once more. Sebastian's skin crawled.

Dark magic. Very dark magic indeed.

Extra enchantments that hadn't been here the last time Sebastian had had cause to visit.

As if reading his thoughts, Asher called over his shoulder, "New wards thanks to Xander."

Xander? Now Sebastian was truly puzzled. While

Xander took precautions like the rest of them, he'd never been big into wards and enchantments. At least, not until Kyanna had come along. His Guardian mate gave a whole new meaning to the phrase *packin' heat.*

But these were definitely not angelic enchantments. Sebastian frowned. Did this have something to do with the day Xander had nearly died? The Fallen been engaged in an epic battle with angels as well as demons in a meadow near Xander's cabin. Sebastian recalled that day clearly. It was the first and only time he'd ever suffered a broken wing. Excruciating. It had ranked right up there with a horn removal, and that didn't bear remembering.

Xander had disappeared with Kyanna, and some time later Asher had deposited a hysterical Kyanna on Sebastian's doorstep. She'd been beside herself, going on and on about Xander dying and flaming swords and angels of death, so much so that Sebastian had been forced to ask Asher to use dark magic to bespell her into unconsciousness for fear she might hurt herself. Everything had turned out all right in the end. But that day in general had been a freak-show mess from the get go.

"Follow me," Asher instructed as he strode down one barren, drafty, stone hallway after another.

Phoebe shivered in Sebastian's arms. Her skin was clammy now. Her lips were blue again. She moaned and curled closer to his chest. Frowning, he glanced down. He didn't want her fever to return, yet it didn't feel right to let her freeze either. So he conjured a pair of those thick fleece lounge pants he'd seen Carly wearing once when she'd been under the weather, replaced the thin T-shirt with a long-sleeved thermal shirt, and put warm woolen socks on Phoebe's feet.

At the end of the last hallway, Asher stopped and opened a heavy oak door. He arched a dark eyebrow at Phoebe's new apparel, but withheld comment.

Wise demon.

"Put her on the bed," he instructed as Sebastian followed him inside.

Sebastian glanced around. The room looked as if they'd stepped back in time. Straight into a fairytale. All they were missing was the sleeping princess.

A luxurious, massive four poster bed dominated the room. Expensive, forest green bed curtains hung from the canopy, open to the room on three sides. Feminine, antique furniture dotted the room, hand carved and delicate. A dresser here, a wardrobe there, a vanity complete with mirror, backless seat, and a silver brush set over there in the corner. Plush green carpet padded every step. The room had been painted a powder blue, and the ceiling looked like puffy clouds. Open. Airy. Spotless and dust free. Sebastian hesitated.

This couldn't be Asher's bedchamber, could it? Surely the very masculine demon wouldn't claim a room so obviously designed for a woman's use. But everything here was so...*fresh.*

The idea of placing her in the mercenary's bed didn't sit well.

"It's the guest room," Asher commented with a wry twist of his lips.

A guest room? Why would this anti-social demon need a guest room? And a frilly one, at that?

To the best of Sebastian's knowledge, Asher didn't have a mate.

"I don't," Asher gritted out, patience clearly

dwindling.

Sebastian looked over at him, wary. He'd heard stories of Asher's abilities. Were they true?

"It wouldn't take a mind reader to translate the look on your face just now, Vengeance," Asher informed him. It didn't go unnoticed that he hadn't answered the unspoken question, though.

"Put her down," Asher barked.

Sebastian placed Phoebe on the bed and stepped back.

Asher sat down on the side of the bed, hip to hip with Phoebe. He peered over his shoulder, his expression dark.

"You're hovering."

"Sorry."

Sebastian backed up several steps. But he didn't take his attention off Asher, watching every move like a hawk.

Turning back to Phoebe, Asher laid one hand on her forehead, one hand on her chest directly over her heart, and closed his eyes.

After what seemed like forever, Asher opened those unfathomable dark eyes and pierced Sebastian with a look that would have worried any other demon. In all honesty, it even unsettled Sebastian, just a little bit.

"I thought you said she was human," he hissed.

Sebastian's mouth fell open and his brows snapped together. "What do you mean? What is she?"

"Not human," Asher snapped as he turned back to his patient. Sebastian watched every move Asher made even more closely now. He tensed as Asher conjured a small vial of gelatinous, luminous green liquid. At the same moment, a parchment appeared before Sebastian. The figure on the contract was, as usual, astronomical.

"You sure you don't just want my first born?" Sebastian growled as he pricked his thumb and pressed his bloody print to seal the bargain. The parchment disappeared.

"Not yet," Asher murmured, all his intense focus on Phoebe's face.

Sebastian's brows snapped together. What the hell was *that* supposed to mean?

That was the other problem with Asher. Everything was a damned riddle. One that, more often than not, came back to bite you in the ass when you least expected it. Before Sebastian could question him further, Asher lifted Phoebe's head with far more care than Sebastian would have thought the demon capable and eased the slimy green concoction past her lips.

Sebastian held his breath as Phoebe resisted at first, her precious face screwed up in disgust. But after a moment or two she acquiesced, accepting every last drop of the vile looking elixir. He expected her to get sick again, the way she had when he'd given her the Tylenol. But, though her eyes remained closed, her brow relaxed.

Without warning, a punch of power rippled through the room, and Sebastian tensed.

What the hell was that?

The power wobbled, and then settled down to a faint simmer, damned near unnoticeable. And it was coming from Phoebe.

Asher vanished the now empty vial and waved a hand over her mauled shoulder, conjuring a fresh bandage. He stood.

"Take her home. Change that bandage every few hours until the wound is healed." He produced a small lidded container and handed it to Sebastian. "Put that salve on the wound. Keep her comfortable. And under no circumstances are you to give her any more human medicines."

"She's going to recover, right?" Sebastian asked as he accepted the container, unable to look away from the woman on the bed. That odd energy was still wisping through the room, causing the fine hairs on his forearms to stand on end.

"She will. Or she won't." Asher shrugged. "That's up to her. There's nothing more I can do for her."

Sebastian didn't like the sound of that. But he knew he wouldn't be getting any more reassurance.

"Thanks," he said as he gathered Phoebe in his arms.

"I'm assuming you have ward stones around your place?"

That gave Sebastian pause. Discussing the protections around his home with anyone other than his brothers-in-arms or Kyanna didn't sit well. Suspicious, he held Phoebe just a little tighter as he turned to face Asher. Was the mercenary planning something? Did *he* intend to try to take Phoebe from Sebastian?

Sebastian's grip on Phoebe grew even tighter. Just let the bastard try. He'd slice and dice the mercenary. He'd start with the demon's horns and work his way down. He'd—

"Oh please," Asher scoffed. "You think I'm that stupid. You Fallen and your mates. Only an idiot—a *suicidal* idiot—would try to break that shit up."

Sebastian shot Asher a dark scowl before dropping

his attention to the woman in his arms. What the hell was the mercenary talking about? Mates? Why would he even suggest something so crazy? So utterly ridiculous?

So far out there that it wasn't even…

No…

No way.

But he stilled as he searched her face.

Was it possible? He didn't even know her, not really.

And yet…

And yet he wanted her. Badly.

The question was, did he want her *permanently*? Did he want her enough to lay *that* kind of a claim on her?

"Get rid of 'em."

"What?" He blinked up at Asher, lost.

"The ward stones," Asher clarified, eyeing Sebastian like he couldn't decide whether to be annoyed or amused. "Get rid of 'em."

"Why the hell would I—"

"You don't get rid of them, she'll be dead inside a week. Your call."

Sebastian scowled at Phoebe once more. *What the hell?*

Asher waved his hand over the window. Sebastian, sensing the protective barrier weakening, knew it was time to go. He'd figure this all out later. He shifted Phoebe higher in his arms and she snuggled close, tucking her head against his neck with a contented sigh. The soft sound stroked at the ache in his chest.

It didn't matter what she was. Mate or no mate, she would live. He would not allow anything else.

Asher stared on, his expression inscrutable.

Disconcerted, Sebastian shimmered them back to the farm. He returned Phoebe to his bed and, careful not to jostle her, he climbed in beside her. He braced his back against the headboard, stretched his long legs out on the bed, crossed his ankles, and settled in. But within a matter of minutes, she began to worsen. Sweat beaded her brow once more. Her face scrunched up in misery. Her legs began to shift restlessly.

Brow drawn tight, Sebastian rolled Asher's warning around in his head. He hated to leave her, but it didn't look like he'd have much choice. It took longer than he thought it would, but he shimmered all around his property, gathering up ward stones. By the saints, he'd forgotten some of these were even out here. He even called down the protective spell Kyanna had given him. Once he was certain he had them all, he shimmered to the foyer of Gideon's plantation.

A spare moment later, Gideon appeared at the top of the grand staircase, barefoot, dressed in nothing more than a faded pair of jeans. He hadn't even bothered to button them, and the wood he was sporting was barely concealed. His hair stood nearly straight on end in wild disarray. His lips were swollen, and a healthy flush colored his skin. Even from this distance, the scent of woman and sex wafted down the stairs to Sebastian.

"What are you—"

"No time to talk," Sebastian blurted, dumping the ward stones in a pile by the door.

"Are those—"

"Ward stones, yeah. Keep 'em. I gotta go."

"But don't you need—"

"No."

Sebastian, worried Phoebe might have gotten worse while he was away, shimmered back to her side. He touched her brow. Cooler, good. She looked to be resting more comfortably as well. Maybe the ward stones had been exacerbating her condition? Well, whatever was going on, he wasn't taking any chances.

Off and on, he monitored her temperature and her pulse. She seemed to be holding steady, but she had yet to awaken. And that worried him. As Asher said, either she would recover. Or she wouldn't. It was all up to her now.

He cursed himself for not being able to do more.

And he puzzled over Asher's comment. *"Not human."*

What the hell does that mean?

Damn it, Asher.

It would have been nice to know what he was dealing with here. He knew she wasn't an angel, or a Halfling. He would feel it, sense it as he could sense other angels. And she wasn't a demon. He could tell that too, just by the lack of that noxious taint of brimstone all demons gave off in some small amount. To him she simply smelled like…Heaven. Yet he couldn't sense her lineage, couldn't sense anything past the overwhelming effect she was having on his system.

But if she isn't human, then what is she?

One word leapt out at him, catching him completely off guard.

Mine.

His mind went blank for a few moments, and then began skipping around like a broken record.

He hadn't received some Divine sign. No mystical, predestined mate awaited him. Only this gut-wrenching animal attraction. This instinctive, protective reaction. And the dead to rights certainty that she should—that she would—belong to him.

He didn't even know her.

But he wanted her.

And every minute, every second he spent with her that wanting only grew stronger.

He'd witnessed her courage in the cave. Surely that was a start. As was her will to live. She'd survived this long against the venom, hadn't she? So she was a fighter. That would be necessary for the kind of life that he led. The rest would come, in time.

He eased onto his side, propped himself up on one elbow, and he studied her with an intensity that probably would have frightened her had she been awake. Primitive instinct insisted that he'd already fought for her, already won her…it was only right that he claim her for his own.

But that was crazy. Insane.

He wasn't some Neanderthal, some wild animal.

And yet she drew him as nothing else ever had.

I could make her mine.

The tempting thought swirled up from the bottom of his soul, where his deepest darkest desires were buried, and held him enthralled.

So the real question was, what was he going to do about it?

Without warning, Phoebe began convulsing. Her skin flushed bright red and sweat broke out on her skin. The fever had returned, pushing all other thoughts from his mind. And so back into the shower they went.

Chapter Four

Phoebe groaned. Had someone used her as a punching bag? There wasn't a single square inch of her entire body that didn't ache. She tried to swallow. Her mouth was so dry she couldn't even form spit. Her head throbbed like a bass drum in a really bad rock band.

A gentle hand lifted her head from the pillow, and something hard and cold pressed against her mouth. Water, cool and welcome, trickled past her lips. Greedy, she gulped. The glass was withdrawn.

"Slowly," murmured a deep voice. The glass returned and, fearful of it being taken away again, she heeded the warning, taking only small sips.

Weak beyond belief, she let the hand beneath her head settle her upon the plumped pillow once more. She heard a whisper of movement, and what she thought might be the creak of a chair. With another small groan, she peeled her eyelids open. The room was dim, the shades drawn against the harsh sunlight, and yet she squinted and blinked. A blurry motion in the corner caught her attention.

"My glasses," she managed to croak.

The blurry shape moved once more, clarifying as it came closer.

Her Surfer Boy. He held something in his hand and offered it to her. Her glasses. Grateful, she took them from him, and then slid them up the bridge of her nose.

Her hand was shaking. She made a weak fist and pressed it to her chest.

He returned to a chair near the bed, watching her with acute, unsettling awareness. No. No, that wasn't right. He wasn't a surfer. At least, not that she knew anyway.

And he certainly wasn't hers.

Slowly, details came back to her foggy mind. His name was Sebastian, he'd said. And he looked like hell, like death warmed over. His mussed hair stuck up at odd angles. His clothing was wrinkled, as if he hadn't changed in days. Dark shadows smudged his turbulent blue eyes, and the beginnings of a full, golden beard shadowed his jaw.

"Would you care to explain to me," he asked, quiet and deliberate, "how you survived a Diffenidus bite?"

"I don't know what that is."

He gave her a level look, his expression not giving a clue to what was going on behind those brilliant blue eyes. "A demon. A very, *very* poisonous demon."

Phoebe tried to push herself up in the big bed. But she was just too weak, and she slipped back down. "Good immune system?"

She watched as his broad chest rose on a particularly deep breath. He popped his jaw. "Try again."

Did he already know? Was he trying to trip her up? She licked her dry lips. Was it possible that, in the throes of her illness, she might have—

With the graceful ease of a natural born predator, he rose from the chair, startling her into losing her train of thought. A tube of Chapstick appeared from out of nowhere, and he settled on the side of the bed, hip to hip. His hand was steady as he smoothed the ointment over her lips. The lip balm vanished from his hands, and he then brushed the hair from her brow, tucking it behind her ear. After plumping her pillow beneath her head with the utmost care, he settled the blankets more securely around her.

He seemed very comfortable performing those basic tasks for her. And that made her uneasy.

How long was I out?

Sebastian rose and began prowling the room. He was a closed book; he gave nothing away.

"I'm waiting." His voice boomed in the room, and she jumped.

Phoebe fidgeted beneath the weight of those blue, blue eyes. "Sheer dumb luck?"

He let out an audible, irritated sigh.

"I don't think so," he said at last. Too calm. Too quiet. For some reason, his calm set her teeth on edge far worse than had he screamed threats and waved a gun at her. Or turned back into that smoke-colored nightmare again.

Well, maybe not quite *that* nervous.

Her mouth went dry again.

"Let's try one more time, shall we?" he offered as he settled in the chair once more. He braced his elbows on the arm rests and pressed his fingertips together. "And before you attempt to hand me some other creative line of bullshit, let me enlighten you. Diffenidus saliva is, on average, toxic to angels. In fact, very few survive." He shook his head. "But you're no angel. Nor are you a Halfling. Diffenidus saliva is also lethal to humans."

He held a finger up to cut her off before she could

interrupt.

"*All* humans, *no* exceptions," he clarified. "But then you're not human either, are you? At least, not *completely* human." He tilted his head and considered her with that same unsettling intensity. She wanted to squirm like a bug under a microscope. "Diffenidus venom, however, isn't lethal to other demons. Not usually. Instead, it causes severe reactions. Hallucinations, raging fever, delirium, vomiting…and I'm betting right now you feel like you've been hit by a truck, yeah?"

Phoebe glanced away. She knew his name. Knew he'd rescued her from Sin's cave of horrors. But, other than those two basic facts, she knew absolutely nothing about this guy…this *demon*. And he was a demon. She knew that as well, had seen him transform. Had seen the mind-blowing monster he'd become. It didn't make her feel any better. And it sure as hell didn't induce her to spill all her deepest darkest secrets.

"Where am I?" she asked, changing the subject.

He regarded her in silence. After a long, uncomfortable moment, he informed her, "We're at my farm in southern Minnesota."

She looked to the window, though she couldn't see past the heavy drapes. "Minnesota!" She gaped. "You took me from Mexico?"

"Technically, Sïnsobar took you out of Mexico. I took you away from him."

"Well, I have to go back," she insisted, her panic and fury at last giving her the energy she needed to push herself up on the soft bed.

The sensual line of his lips compressed. A muscle clenched in his jaw. His expression tightened, and his hands fisted on the armrests of his chair. His nostrils flared. "You aren't going anywhere." He sounded hoarse all of a sudden. Strained. He looked down, then back to her face, then down once more. His eyes flickered, going completely black, then blue, then black again, once, twice.

"You can't keep me here." Panic seeped through her, cold and insidious.

But she couldn't give in to the threatening hysteria. She had to figure out what her next step was in getting back to her search for the sword. She struggled to the side of the bed. It was only when her bare feet touched the chilled floor that she realized she was naked, the corner of the sheet pooling on her lap.

Mortified, she jerked the sheet up and around her. "Where are my clothes?"

Sebastian stared at her, hard. His face a study in raw, carnal hunger. The way he looked at her set off a strange trembling deep in her core.

"Gone," he replied at last, his tone level, strictly controlled, despite the fire shimmering in his eyes. "I didn't figure you'd mind as they were pretty much trashed anyway."

His sultry stare skimmed down over her, over the thin sheet she clutched to her like a shield. His attention dipped to her bare legs, caressed their way down to her glittery, Scarlet Kiss painted toenails, and the heat in his expression intensified until she feared it would consume him. Consume them both. Nervous flutters winged through her stomach. Careful to keep the sheet in place to shield her modesty, she scooted back in the bed and reached for the blanket as well, covering herself from toe to neck.

"And as to the other"—his stare met hers—"you're wrong."

"Wrong? Wrong about what?" She was having trouble keeping up with the conversation. Those mesmerizing electric blue eyes had woven some spell on her senses, certainly on her body. She was having all sorts of strange visceral reactions to him.

He leaned forward, dropped his elbows to his knees and assessed her once more, his attitude…his body language…now reeked of sheer male power. Power and possession the likes of which she couldn't even begin to fathom.

"I *can* keep you." The edges of his mouth curled up, making her heart stutter. "In fact, I have every intention of doing exactly that."

She blinked at him, as her lips slowly parted in shock.

****

Those words, combined with the recent visual reminder of that supple body—the very same body he'd spent the last four days intimately tending—took on a whole new appeal. Sebastian clamped down hard on the lust swelling in his groin, but he wasn't able to suppress it. Not completely. Hell, not by a long shot.

Answers, he reminded himself. He needed to get answers first. Before anything else. The others were counting on him.

And Mikhail…

Christ in Heaven, the tortures Mikhail was enduring even now. Stolas had periodically been sending them sadistic photos of Mikhail's brutal treatment. Apparently the bastard demon prince got his rocks off not only on vicious and inventive torture, but on immortalizing his efforts with candid shots of his handiwork. The pictures, Sebastian rationally knew, were designed not only to degrade the Demon of War, but to break him and to destroy his fearsome reputation. They were also designed to taunt the Fallen. To demoralize them. To weaken them from the inside out. To shake their resolve.

Instead, all Stolas had done was fuel their rage. Fuel it and reinforce their determination. Sebastian wanted to destroy the bastard with his bare hands. The only thing keeping him grounded right now was his focus on Phoebe. Xander, Niklas, and Gideon had been preparing to leave on a rescue mission the last time he'd spoken to Niklas. That had been nearly two full days ago. Since then, nothing. Not a peep. Not an SOS. Not a blip on the radar.

He'd even called Kyanna and Carly as he'd waited for Phoebe to recover. They hadn't heard anything either. Not for days. Nor had Maggie, they'd informed him. And they were all beside themselves with worry and fear.

Not good.

The last shreds of his control were stretched to the breaking point from his need to take action—*any* kind of action. And the tiny little spikes of energy that came from Phoebe whenever she became worked up about something drilled into him, making him want to push for answers.

Patience, he reminded himself. Phoebe wasn't a rogue demon to be interrogated. She was a fragile mostly human being. As such, he needed to use kid gloves here, not brass knuckles dipped in Ralsha venom.

Still, he was mindful of every second that ticked by.

"Why do you have to go back to Mexico? In case you didn't notice, somebody's trying to kill you."

He watched as she lifted her hand to finger the scar on her throat. He didn't think she was even aware she was doing it. Her throat moved as she forced a swallow, and then her hand fell limply to her side.

"I'm a Professor of Archeology, currently on hiatus. I lecture at Redmond College in Port August, Michigan," she informed him. "I am a leading expert on the Mayan culture, particularly Mayan mythology. I've spent the last year obtaining academic funding and trudging my way through enough political red tape to make your head spin in order to get the permits necessary to coordinate a dig near Campeche. I have to get back *now*. My window of time is closing."

She'd just given him, he was sure, the same song and dance she'd no doubt used to obtain all those necessary permits she'd spoken of. But the answer sounded too convenient, a little too rehearsed.

And he wasn't buying a syllable.

He leaned back in his chair, crossing his arms. "You know what I think?"

She lifted her chin and arched a regal brow.

"I think you're looking for the sword."

A huge spike of energy slammed through the room, powerful but unstable all the same. He was surprised the windows hadn't blown out.

He had to give her credit though. She barely blinked. But he could see the cogs spinning, trying to gain traction, as she scrambled for something to say. If he hadn't been watching her so closely, or felt the surge in her energy, he might have missed the minute physical giveaways.

"A sword?" she asked, her voice perfectly regulated. "I don't have any idea what you're talking about."

Sebastian braced his hands on the arms of the chair as he glanced around the floor in mock concern. Then he lifted his feet in the air.

She frowned. "What are you doing?"

"If the bullshit gets any deeper in here we're going to be floating, and these boots are brand new."

Her mouth snapped closed, and she glared at him. Clearly, she didn't find his comment the least bit amusing. That was fine. He didn't have the time to waste on verbal sparring anymore either. He had a feeling Xander and the others were in over their heads on this rescue mission. He should be with them. Should be helping to set Mikhail free. Should be skewering Stolas to the wall of his polished, onyx great hall for starting this whole damned war to begin with. A primal need to punish leaped up inside him, thirsting for blood. He pushed it back down, ruthless and determined.

Dropping his boots to the floor with a loud thud, Sebastian leaned forward once more and clasped his hands between his knees. "Let's cut to the chase. I'm running out of time and so are you. So, let me tell you what *I know*." He put special emphasis on the last two words so that she understood he was serious, and that there would be no more evasions, no more half truths.

"I know you are descended from a line of Holy Guardians charged with protecting the Sword of Kathnesh. Given your profession, your love of antiquities, and your dedication to learning the fine details of the places and people you study…" He paused, offering her a ruthless smile. "Yes, I know what Google is, Professor—you have an impressive reputation, by the way—I'm assuming you also know the history, The Prophesy, pertaining to that sword. How the Sword of Kathnesh, the one weapon prophesied to be capable of taking Lucifer's head, along with the Arc Stone, the Scrolls of Prévnar, under the control of the Chosen One will be powerful enough to overthrow Lucifer.

"I'm also guessing that you know if that happens, the world as you know it will be overrun with demons bent on the destruction of Earth and the enslavement and, ultimately, the complete annihilation of mankind. I also know you're now looking for a way to recover the sword because the last Guardian lost it."

As he'd recited the Prophesy to her, she'd lost what little color she'd regained. But, at his last accusation about the former Guardian, anger glittered in her emerald eyes and color rushed back to her cheeks. "It wasn't like he had a moment of forgetfulness and misplaced the damned thing."

The instant the words passed her lips, her expression registered her shock. She clamped her mouth shut, but it was too late.

Sebastian cocked his head and let one corner of his mouth lift. *Gotcha.* "Out with it. You've already given yourself away."

"Who are you?" she asked, subdued.

"I already told you, I'm Sebastian."

"No. I mean *who* are you."

He rolled the dice. She might as well know exactly what she was dealing with. "I am the Demon of

Vengeance."

He watched the blood drain from her face once more and her eyes widen. Shit. Was she going to get sick again?

"Vengeance," she whispered. She drew a deep, shuddering breath, and pressed, "As in 'Death comes on the wings of Vengeance'?"

Another tiny spike of energy.

What the hell is she?

Judging by her expression, his reputation had preceded him. He hadn't heard that phrase in centuries. He'd starred as the boogeyman in many a native culture. Still, that she knew the phrase surprised him a bit.

That was all right though. It would save time.

"You saw me. You saw the wings. You know what I can do. Kind of stupid to deny what I am now," he added.

Would she finally come clean about what *she* was?

He watched as she looked to the door, then to the window.

A stronger shot of power pulsed from her for a moment before withering away.

Hoping for a way out, princess?

Finally, her attention returned to him. Her lips set in a mulish line.

Apparently no easy admissions would be had here today.

Yet again, she displayed a complete lack of trust. His instincts roared inside him. Over the course of the last several days, as he'd tended her and nursed her back to health, Sebastian had reached the conclusion that she was the one for him, the woman he was set to claim as his mate. The connection he felt to her was just too strong to ignore, too powerful to deny. Did she not feel the connection? She sure as hell wasn't acting like it. And it was driving him crazy.

Still, he sought to reassure her. "You, of all people, have no reason to fear me."

"Sure I don't," she hissed. "You only managed to singlehandedly decimate a cave full of those…those other *creatures*. And you've just told me you intend to keep me prisoner. But I shouldn't fear you? Ha!"

Okay, maybe she should fear him. Fear the fact that he wanted, more than just about anything else on Earth right now, to turn her over his knee and—

His vaunted patience snapped like a brittle twig. "I killed those demons to save *your* life. Demons, if you hadn't noticed, that were doing a damned fine job of making a meal of *you*. And then I saved your life *again* from venom poisoning…at great expense to me, I might add. You've been damned near comatose—and at my *complete mercy*—for four entire days. If I was going to kill you, I would have done so already."

"Why would you do all that? Why save me?"

He leaned back in his chair and crossed his arms. How much to tell her? How much before she ran screaming for the hills? Roll the dice again and tell her the truth—that he'd decided to make her his mate?

No. He didn't think she'd handle that too well. Not yet anyway.

Better stick with the party line. He was a patient demon. She'd come around to his way of thinking. He just needed time to convince her.

"Because I am of the Fallen. No longer a warrior of Hell. I, along with my brothers Xander, Niklas, Gideon, and Mikhail have thrown off Lucifer's rule and strive for redemption. We work to reclaim our places in Heaven. We want only forgiveness."

She watched him for a long moment, her eyes narrowed shrewdly. "Yet you seek the very weapons that will kill Lucifer."

Of course, she would lock on that point. He clenched his fists in his lap and inhaled deeply, striving for self control.

"Only to prevent them from falling into the wrong hands. To keep the barriers between Hell and Earth from toppling. The balance between good and evil must be maintained. We, myself and the other Fallen, will keep the Sacred Relics safe. While we no longer follow Lucifer, we will keep those weapons from the hands of those that seek to end his reign and enslave all of humankind. That's why it's so important to get the sword back from the demon prince who now has it."

"What demon? Who's trying to overthrow him?" she asked. He noted the way her fingertips had crept up to trace the scar on her throat. Again, he didn't think she was even aware of it.

So she didn't know who was behind her attack? His mind immediately began turning that puzzle over and over, looking for ways to use it to his advantage. It was all about information right now. Information he had that she wanted. Information she had that he needed.

So he took a gamble. "I can tell you about him, the one behind the attacks on you."

Her attention flew to his face, and he knew the hook was set. He just had to reel her in.

"I can tell you about him." He waited a long beat,

just to set the hook a little deeper. "But I require a sharing of information."

She bit down on her lower lip, her brow scrunched. She was waffling. He waited, wouldn't speak until she finally gave a faint nod.

"His name is Stolas, the one who's making the power play. He's Lucifer's own grandson." She was hanging on his every word now, sucking the information up like a dry sponge. And he knew he'd chosen the right tactic. "Stolas is the one who took the sword and killed the last Guardian... Or rather his minions did, as Stolas is trapped in Hell. But he's actively working on changing that. My compatriots have already prevented his summoning once. If he gets his hands on the rest of those relics, your world is going to burn. I'm here to stop that from happening. But I need your help."

She eyed him, suspicious, as she sat up a little straighter, tucking the blanket beneath her armpits, baring those delicious shoulders to his hungry eyes, or one of them anyway as the other was still covered beneath a thick pad of gauze. "You're keeping me here against my will. How can that be deemed as an act of someone wanting forgiveness?"

"Say the words, honey. Tell me what I want to know, and I'll take you back to Mexico. Hell, I'll even *help* you summon the damned sword back to Earth." Yeah, he'd take her back in a heartbeat. But he wouldn't be leaving her. He'd never let her go.

"So you can steal it for yourself, you mean?"

He stared at her, hard, and he pledged from the bottom of his black soul, "I give you my solemn vow I will never take the sword from you. It shall remain in your possession, always. And I vow my protection to you until the day I die."

She weighed his offer in silence, a deep frown etching her features. With a small shake of her head, she asked, "Why would you make that promise?"

Because you are mine.

Mine to keep. Mine to protect.

She wasn't ready to hear that truth of what he wanted from her though, not yet. That was plain as day. So, he guided her in another direction. "I'm guessing this latest incident with Sïnsobar isn't the only bit of trouble you've experienced. And I'm guessing you got that scar from one of Stolas's minions. You should know, things are only going to heat up from here on out."

Her brow puckered. She was cornered and, he could see, she didn't like it. Not one bit. She clenched her hands in her lap. "Why are the attacks getting worse? Why now?"

Not exactly falling at his feet in gratitude and unconditional acceptance. But her body language had relaxed a bit, and her frown wasn't nearly as suspicious as before, only more curious. Ah, sweet progress.

"My brothers and I have already found the Arc Stone and the Chosen One." No way was he going to tell her *how* they'd managed to obtain the Chosen One, at least not just yet anyway. Or that Stolas had captured their most dangerous warrior. No need to freak her out if he didn't have to. "I'm sure Stolas must be feeling pretty desperate. Logic dictates those attacks are just going to get worse. Only I can keep you safe. You need me."

He fell silent, letting the implications sink in. She

closed her eyes and rubbed her hands over her face, her fingertips sliding beneath her glasses to massage her eyes. Saints above, she was adorable when she did that.

But she was tiring faster than he'd anticipated. Asher's antidote might have cured her, but the venom had still taken its toll. She pushed her glasses up the bridge of her nose with her index finger and settled back on the bed with an exhausted sigh.

Concern for his mate battled with the pressing worry for his brothers, his need to save Mikhail and recover the relics.

"Admit it," he coaxed, feeling like a rank bastard for pressing his advantage. "I could be a very useful ally. I'll be the brawn to your brain. I can protect you while you search. And just think, no more need for airplane tickets, no more bumpy rides."

At least, not on a plane. He fought to restrain the wicked grin pushing at his lips.

Staring up at the ceiling, Phoebe huffed out a mirthless laugh. "I think," she said with a great deal of wary resignation, "there's far more brain in that head of yours than you'd have me believe."

His cheek twitched. She had his number. She knew it. And she was going to make damned sure that he knew that she knew too. Praise God, she was perfect for him.

She lay there so long he feared she might be slipping back into unconsciousness again. But then she let out a disgusted groan.

A patented sound of aggrieved acceptance if ever he'd heard one.

"I don't have any choice here, do I?"

"Nope," he said, doing his best to keep his tone as

far from gloating as possible.

At last, she gave in. She turned her head on the pillow to look at him. "What do you want to know?"

"Everything."

Chapter Five

Sebastian sat back and crossed his arms like judge and jury.

Easier said than done. Her father's journals had cautioned her to the extreme, insisting that she must never confide in *anyone* about the sword. For any reason. Not until she was ready to pass the mantle on to her own child.

Besides, she felt like death warmed over. Her limbs were as useless as rubber, heavy as if weights had been strapped to her wrists and ankles. Her shoulder throbbed where that...that *thing* had sunk its fangs into her. She probed at the thick pad of gauze covering the wound, grimacing. Her body hurt everywhere, but at least the racking, fiery pain had subsided. She wanted to sleep for another week. Or two. But her mind whirled. According to him, she'd already been out for four days. She didn't have any more time to lose.

If all he'd said was true...then she owed him. Owed him huge. He *could* be a useful ally.

If she could trust him.

That was a big *if*...

She wasn't sure she could. He was a demon. And, up to date, her experience with demons had been less than pleasant.

All she could do was go with her gut. Go with her gut and ignore this stupid physical attraction that had her all tied up in knots. Rely on what she'd seen with her own eyes, what she'd witnessed in that cave. She remembered bits and pieces of her illness, fragments of moments, really. His face close to hers as she'd slipped in and out of consciousness, his brow creased with worry. His gentle hands as he'd forced her to drink. Over and over. His steadfast strength when he'd held her as she'd gotten sick. His soothing voice murmuring encouragement, telling her over and over that he would not allow her to die. How he forbade it.

So she'd trust her gut. But she'd also use her head. Just because they were on the same side didn't mean she had to play *all* her cards up front.

Another memory surfaced, and she felt her face grow warm. Cold water. Icy cold. Cascading down her naked body. And…

And someone had been in that shower with her, holding her up, bracing her. Unbelievably strong arms wrapped around her with such tender care, supporting her, cradling her against an equally naked, very hot chest as that bone chilling water beat down upon her. And, quite honestly, that *hot* could be taken in more ways than one.

Oh, dear God, please let that have been a hallucination.

Rubbing her lips together, she pushed that thought aside. She'd never be able to work with him, never be able to look him in the eyes again if she thought for one minute that—

The very idea left her mortified.

And all her girly parts shockingly aroused.

Business, she reminded herself sternly. She needed to look at this as a business arrangement. Work with him until it no longer worked in her favor.

Or maybe she was just exhausted and delusional.

Either way, she really only had one option.

So to hell with it.

Still, there was a niggling iota of self preservation swimming around somewhere inside her that hadn't completely drown in exhaustion. Self preservation and a horrible sense of *un*reality. She could do this on her own. Without him. She *should* do this on her own, she told herself.

Just because you can*, doesn't mean you* should*.* Her father's all too frequent warnings to her came back to haunt her. She ground her teeth.

"So…if I tell you what I know, you promise you'll help me find the sword? Help me find it, but you won't try to take it away from me?" Sweet Mary, she couldn't believe she was doing this. "You'll swear on whatever it is you hold sacred that you won't betray me?"

She watched, wary, as Sebastian rose from the chair. He crossed the distance between them in three determined steps and sat down beside her, hip to hip. He took her hand and clasped it between his like a medieval knight pledging troth to his lady as he stared deep into her eyes. His hands were slightly rough in texture, strong, and oh-so-warm. His expression was so serious it created an uncomfortable ache in the pit of her stomach.

"I swear to you, on everything I hold sacred, I will never betray you." He placed her palm flat on his chest, directly over his heart, trapped it there with one of his hands. The heat of his flesh burned her though the thin cotton. His muscles felt like granite beneath her touch. His free hand, he laid gently over her own heart.

"I vow to you, I will protect you with my own life, now and always," he said in a deep, oddly layered voice, using a language she shouldn't understand. Shouldn't but did. Words that left her completely baffled, and shockingly compelled to repeat them back to him.

Something odd shifted inside her, seemed to click into place. Unsettled, she pressed her lips together, fearful of what she might let slip out, and listened as he went on, "I will safeguard your happiness and put you before all things. I bind myself to you. *Qui et illisium speccaté.*" *Now and forevermore.* "I will do everything within my power to help you find that sword, and I will not take it from you, ever," he finished in English.

Had he not realized she could understand everything that he'd said? All of it?

Umm, all righty then.

She hadn't been expecting anything quite so excessive. A simple *yes* would have sufficed. Phoebe didn't know how to respond to his pronouncement. At least, not rationally. But her gut was telling her he'd meant every word. And she always trusted her gut.

But the things he'd said…

And the *way* he'd said them…

He'd sounded as if he'd meant something far more serious—far more permanent—than just searching for the sword.

No, she scoffed. That was just crazy. She'd misunderstood somehow. It was her illness, her exhaustion making her misinterpret things.

Uncomfortable with his grave demeanor, she twisted her hand until she could shake his in a curt, businesslike manner. "We have an arrangement then."

He tilted his head, the strangest look crossed his face as he leaned back. "An arrangement?"

"Yeah." She frowned. "You know, a deal. Business."

"Business." A lethally seductive smile crept over his face. Her heart stuttered in her chest.

Business. Business, she repeated. *This is just business.*

He turned her hand over in his once more. Slowly—oh Lord, so slowly—his steady stare locked on her, he lifted her hand to his sculpted lips and pressed a lingering, very *un*businesslike kiss to the center of her palm. Those blue, blue eyes held her captive.

She couldn't move. Couldn't look away. Couldn't jerk her hand back, though that was what she *should* be doing.

At last, after what felt like an eternity of oxygen deprivation, he drew his lips from her skin. Taking far longer than *he* should. "We have an…*arrangement*."

Oh, why does that sound as if he means something entirely different than what I intended?

Troubled, hoping that strange, intimate vow and his stomach-fluttering kiss had just been an odd demon way of sealing a deal—some cultural thing she wasn't aware of—she drew her hand away. The weight of his prolonged stare made her fidget. Just when she didn't think she could take it a second longer, he stood and returned to his chair in the corner. She cleared her throat.

"My father's people have been Guardians of the sword back to the beginning," she said, eager to break through the sudden tension clogging the room. She went on to tell him what she knew of the Prophesy, strikingly similar to the version he'd told her earlier.

"I was ten years old the first and only time I saw the actual sword. It was the night of the fire. The apartment building where we were living at the time burned to the ground. It was dark, and the smoke was thick. I was very young, but I remember it like it was yesterday. I still dream of it once in a while. It happened pretty quickly, just a glance really, but it made an impression. Especially since the circumstances were so intense, and I'd never seen my father carrying a weapon before, *any* kind of weapon."

She looked to Sebastian, expecting him to begin questioning her then, but he just nodded, waiting in silence for her to continue.

"The sword seemed so out of place given Dad's area of expertise, you know? Anyway, Dad's journals documented it pretty thoroughly so I would recognize it again, if ever I saw it. The sword was actually a medieval broadsword. Forty-five inches in length. Three inches across the forte. Just over four and a half pounds. The fuller—that shallow center indentation that runs the length of a straight double-edged blade—was etched with symbols, glyphs of some kind. Dad was never able to interpret them, nor were any of our ancestors." She rubbed at her temple as she recited what she knew, the facts that her father had documented in his coded journals.

"The cross guard was inlaid with silver," she said. "When Dad first came to be Guardian, he had a very trusted and ethically unshakable mentor working for a respected antiquities museum. Dr. Brewster was also a leading expert on several ancient languages. Dad, being the archeologist that he was, asked his mentor for a favor, asked him to analyze the sword. But Dad was cautious, swearing Dr. Brewster to secrecy, making him promise not to show the sword to or talk about it with anyone else. His mentor, of course, agreed.

"According to the documentation in Dad's journals, Brewster ran extensive tests. Unfortunately, even after studying the sword in great detail, he was unable to decipher the glyphs on the blade. However, he did date the sword back to the early sixth century. He gave Dad all the results of his findings, everything pertaining to the sword. The strongest indicator that there was something...*unique* about it came in the materials used to make the sword. His findings showed that the grip was made of—"

She broke off, glancing away, uneasy.

Sebastian leaned forward, drawing her focus back to him. "Made of what?"

She licked her lips. "It's not unheard of for the grip on these types of swords to be fashioned from horn. But Dr. Brewster believed this grip was actually crafted from bone." Phoebe drew a deep, fortifying breath. "The one and only test Dad had allowed was a tiny sample to be taken for DNA testing to determine what kind of bone it was. But the tests were...inconclusive. Bone of unknown origin, they read. It didn't fit anything in the database, mammalian, reptilian, or other. He never did figure out exactly what kind of bone it was, or what it might have belonged to. And Dad, for obvious reasons, refused to allow the sword to be sent in for further testing.

"But Dr. Brewster had also found one other even more disturbing clue. Grips on these kinds of swords were often wrapped in leather. This bone grip was covered with *skin*. Dr. Brewster had also taken samples of that too, but he didn't tell my father, not until the results came back. According to the tests results, the skin was something close to, but not quite, human. Of unknown origin. And, although there were no known dyes present, the skin itself was distinctly red in pigmentation. Red with some kind of distorted black markings. Only the black segments showed dyes. Dr. Brewster believed the black segments were actually tattoos of some kind."

"So the bone would have been demonic in origin," Sebastian surmised, rubbing his jaw, his expression thoughtful. "Or even angelic, I guess. But the skins would most definitely be demonic. No angel that I know of would have red skin. The problem is, there are a lot of demons with that skin pigmentation. Maybe Animagi? Or Carpathï?"

"My father later wrote in one of his journals that he feared Dr. Brewster had let something about the sword slip to someone. Or that he'd retained samples from the grip for further examination. Maybe took pictures, or something."

"Why would he think that?" Sebastian asked sharply.

"Less than twenty-four hours after he'd returned the sword to my father along with the documentation, Dr. Brewster was found in his lab in the basement of the museum, murdered. His lab had been ransacked."

"Could his murder have been related to something else he might have been studying?"

"Museum officials insisted everything on his inventory lists was accounted for. Dr. Brewster hadn't gone on an excavation in decades. The man practically lived in the basement of the museum. According to my father, Brewster had taken on researching the sword as his final project before retirement. He wasn't researching anything else, nothing at all."

Sebastian seemed to be rolling those facts around in his head. His brow was puckered, his focus now distant. "Anything else?"

Anything else? The damned thing was made of bone and skin! An innocent man had been murdered because of it. Isn't that enough?

She stared hard at him for a moment. She *felt* like she could trust him. Like she *should* trust him. Still, sharing this much information, willingly, about the sword…it was taboo. As if she was crossing some invisible line.

"A single, rough cut, blood red stone was set in the pommel. Fist sized," she admitted with a great deal of reluctance.

"Ruby?"

She shook her head. "Red Jasper. It's among the oldest known gemstones. In fact, Red Jasper is even mentioned in the Bible. The high priest, Aaron, was said to have one in his breastplate. It was called *Odem* then. Red Jasper was held in high esteem with the inhabitants of ancient Babylon and Egypt, and was made into protective amulets. Red Jasper was often referred to as the stone of perseverance."

"I remember," Sebastian muttered.

She'd already opened her mouth to finish her story, but his words registered, and she stopped cold. "You remember? What do you mean, you remember?"

Sebastian gave her a hooded look, one she couldn't

interpret to save her soul. "I wasn't Hellborn."

"Um, what does that mean?"

A deep frown settled upon his brow. For a moment, she thought he might refuse to answer.

"It means," he finally said, "that I was created *before* the Great Fall, not after. It means that my wings weren't always black."

Her mouth fell open and her lungs froze. She blinked at him, unable to form words.

"Do you remember anything else about the night of the fire?" Sebastian asked, all his attention locked on the here and now. Locked on her.

She couldn't respond, just kept sitting there staring like a dolt with her mouth hanging open.

Now he looked peeved. He snapped his fingers in front of her face. "Phoebe. Focus. The night of the fire? Did anything else stand out as odd?"

She blinked and shook her head. Oh, they'd be coming back to that topic, to be sure. He couldn't just drop a bombshell like that—*oh, by the way, I'm one of the original angels that fell from Heaven*—and expect her not to ask questions.

She struggled to drag her focus back. "My father was frantic. I remember that night, fire aside, because his behavior was so unusual. Normally, Dad was efficient and calm. Always patient. Always so…so steady."

"He woke me up in the middle of the night. He was yelling, beside himself. Flames licked at the walls. The heat was so intense. The smoke was black, billowing, and so thick it was hard to breathe. My eyes burned and it was difficult to see. He snatched me up, right out of bed. He had this old burlap satchel slung over his back, the one he always took with him on all his digs, and this big glittering sword strapped to his side. Those were the only things he grabbed—the bag, the sword and me. I don't remember anything else about that night.

"We spent the next several weeks in one hotel after another…it was all a blur. He tried hard to make it seem like a grand adventure. But, looking back, I can see now that he was nervous, always looking over his shoulder. Always packed and ready to go at a moment's notice. Eventually, we went back to Mexico, back to the jungle to begin a new excavation. Only then did he start to relax. After a while, everything went back to normal. Or what was normal for us, anyway. I never saw the sword after that night."

"Do you remember where that dig was? The first one you went to after the fire?"

"I'm sorry, I don't." She frowned, looked down at her hands as one name circled her memory, unspoken. One she knew all too well. One she'd only recently connected the dots to. One that, for some reason, she held back from speaking aloud now. Trust wasn't instantaneous in her book. It wasn't something you gave away randomly. It was something you earned. And he hadn't quite earned hers. Not just yet.

"At that age, one ruin had looked much like another. I was only interested in exploring the jungle and the physical ruins at the time, I'm afraid I didn't pay much attention to names."

Her eyes flew wide, and she caught her breath.

"Dad's bag!" she blurted. "When that demon kidnapped me, I had a leather satchel—oh, my God! I have to find that satchel. Dad's last journal was in there. And—"

"There was no satchel, no bag in the cave with you."

She looked at him, but she wasn't seeing him. Her mind was in a whirl, scrambling to figure out what had happened to that bag.

"He must have taken it with him when you came. He has to have it, the demon who took me."

"Sïnsobar," Sebastian hissed.

She nodded, pushing up on trembling arms. The sheet started to slip, and she made a hasty grab for it. "I have to get it back."

The lightness on her left wrist finally registered. *Dad's watch! No, not that too.* Filled with anguish, she gripped her bare wrist, far more frantic over the loss of the watch than she had been over the satchel.

"What's wrong?" Sebastian's brow puckered in alarm as he came forward in his seat.

"Dad's watch," she whispered around the lump welling in her throat. "It's gone."

He reached for something on a small table beside the bed.

A flash of silver landed in her lap with a heavy thud. She snatched it up and held it to the meager light. Tears slipped down her cheeks, unchecked.

"That's it, isn't it?" he asked.

Phoebe nodded as she slipped the battered time piece onto her wrist and clutched it to her chest, too grateful for words. Frowning, Sebastian settled back in the chair, scrutinizing her in an odd way. Clearing her throat, Phoebe gathered the shreds of her dignity.

"I'm afraid there's no hope for the satchel," Sebastian warned her.

She closed her eyes and took a deep, leveling

breath. Okay, all right. It wasn't the end. Inconvenient? More like a royal pain in the ass. But not the end.

"I've read and reread that journal so many times, translating Dad's code and double checking to make sure I haven't missed anything, I've pretty much memorized it. It would have been nice to have as a point of reference, but it's not going to break us. The maps might be a little trickier. I'm pretty sure I can replicate them. Probably."

"Wait, he had maps?"

"Yes, that's where the real danger lies. Dad used the code to label the maps, denote landmarks. But if someone recognized those landmarks, they might be able to fit the puzzle pieces together."

She'd feel much better about the situation when she was back in Mexico and actively searching for the sword herself.

"Sïnsobar mentioned another demon that was supposed to be coming for me. Somebody called..." *Oh, damn, what was that name?* "Dim something. Dimy?"

"Dimiezlo. One of Stolas's minions," Sebastian confirmed, nodding. "He's a nasty piece of work."

"Well, they probably have Dad's last journal now." She mustered the strength to roll over on her side to face him. She tugged the blankets up, tucking them firmly in place. "It shouldn't be a major issue, not unless they're familiar with the region. My father encrypted all his journals. It was a code he only ever taught to me. It started out as a game when I was young, but then, after the fire, it became serious. Eventually it was the only way we communicated about anything, at least in writing. They won't be able to read the journal themselves, I'm sure of that much at least."

"Then we still have a slight advantage."

"Not with me in this bed," Phoebe pointed out, filled with determination. Once more, ignoring the trembling of her limbs and the shaking in her hands, she made to sit up.

But Sebastian was on his feet before she could blink. His large hand pressed against her good shoulder, careful but insistent, urging her back against the pillows. "Oh, no, you don't. Not yet. You're not strong enough. Tell me where to go, what to look for."

"That's just it. *I* don't know." She gave up struggling and sagged into the mattress, exhausted. No way was she going to let him hunt for it while she languished in bed. He'd find the damned thing and she'd never see him or it again.

Not that it mattered if she saw *him* again. She bit her lip, unhappy with the taste of the lie souring her mouth.

What should it matter?

Answer? It shouldn't.

But it did.

And she didn't know quite what to think about that.

"Every journal I found was filled with clues. Clues and more clues. A hodgepodge network of riddles I had to work through. Riddles only *I* could work through. The clues form a map of sorts leading to yet another journal. It's a complicated process, one I'd hoped I was reaching the end of." She studied his face, bit her lip. And decided to test the waters. Would he keep to his word, or was he no better than the other demons she'd encountered? No better, just sneakier? "Dad said he would leave a trail of breadcrumbs, should the sword ever disappear."

"So there *is* a way to recover it, even though it's in Stolas's hands?" He leaned forward, his expression avid.

His excitement set off faint warning bells. Was it just ingrained caution? Or something more sinister? She hesitated. She needed him to trust her, regardless of whether or not she trusted him. If he trusted her, he might relax his guard. If his guard was down, she might be able to escape if need be.

Besides, he already knew most of the crucial information. She wasn't confirming anything new. Not yet, at least.

"Yes."

"Yes, for sure. Or yes, you hope?"

She licked her lips as she considered her answer. Automatically, he reached out and smoothed Chapstick over her lips again, catching her completely off guard. She blinked at him, nonplussed.

Stirring herself, she replied, "Yes. Definitely, yes. He would have ensured there was some way to find it, no matter what. I firmly believe that. But we can't wait. Too much is riding on that sword."

Sebastian sat there, his hip pressed to hers as he leaned across her, his expression inscrutable. His palm was braced on the mattress beside her hip, pinning her in place. He regarded her with such intensity she fought the urge to squirm.

"What are you?" His question came out of left field.

She sucked in a sharp breath. How could he know? How had he figured out that she wasn't—

"I know you don't trust me, not yet. But in order

for me to do my job, in order for me to protect you to the best of my ability, you have to tell me what you are."

He waited. She swallowed. He cocked an eyebrow. She blinked. He was clearly growing impatient by her continued silence. Still, she couldn't do it, couldn't tell him what had happened to her, what she'd seen in the mirror the day she'd learned of her father's death.

Eventually, Sebastian heaved a sigh. "Mark my words. I will find out, Phoebe. I don't know what you're so afraid of, why you fear telling me. But I'll find out." He stood and bent over her. And then he flattened his hands on either side of her shoulders, pinning her as he got in her space. "I *will* find out. And I'll still stand beside you. I'll protect you anyway. Even if I have to protect you from yourself."

He dropped a soft kiss on her forehead, shocking her speechless, before he straightened and moved toward the door.

"If you can get up, can get dressed on your own, and meet me downstairs in twenty minutes, I'll take you back to Mexico tonight. Otherwise, the trip will have to wait until you're stronger."

"I don't have any clothes," she pointed out, cursing when her arms shook violently, threatening to give way as she pushed up on the bed once more. Phoebe squawked in surprise when a stack of neatly folded clothing appeared beside her without any warning.

Why did she get the feeling she was in over her head? Way, way over her head.

"Thank you," she said, gritting her teeth in determination. Perspiration beaded her upper lip as she managed to get into an upright position. She clutched the sheet to her chest with one hand and reached for the pile of clothing with the other. "I appreciate all you've done for me, Sebastian. You've been...beyond kind."

He stopped halfway across the room and slowly turned. The smile he sent her nearly stopped her heart.

"Sweetheart, there are three very important things you need to know about me...know and remember above and beyond anything else. First, I don't have an altruistic bone in my body."

Phoebe blinked.

"Second, when I want something, I won't ever stop until I get it. *Not. Ever.*" He paused, stared at her for a long moment, stared hard, as if to make certain she not only heard but completely understood every last word. A heavy sense of foreboding settled in the pit of her stomach and she frowned.

"And third... *I. Want. You.*"

The smile he gave her left her with no doubt in her mind over what he'd meant by that last remark. And then he vanished. A long moment later, she sucked in a shuddering lungful of air. That old adage about frying pans and fires came back to her once more.

"What did I just get myself into?"

Chapter Six

Ashïek strode inside Stolas's great hall, flicking a cool glance at the Charocté near the door. He noted the one crouching at the end of the dais waiting to rush forward to serve Stolas's every whim, as well as the one hovering beside a smaller door at the rear of the room. Disgust simmered through him. He'd never understood Stolas's need to surround himself with servants.

No, perhaps *slaves* would be a better term. Slaves, the finest in crystal and tableware, excessive furnishings, and objects brought back from Earth. All on display for everyone who entered Stolas's domain. As far as Ashïek was concerned, it was just overkill. Every last piece of it. Just like this mausoleum. Ostentatious.

Ridiculous.

The bastard was clearly overcompensating.

But Ashïek kept his thoughts to himself and his face carefully blank. Stolas might be an egotistical little prick, but he was also Lucifer's grandson. As such, he had a hell of a lot more wiggle room than most, and Lucifer's ear.

You'd think that would be enough for a demon, wouldn't you? As Ashïek approached the long polished black table, he rested his hand on the pommel of his sword and tipped his head in acknowledgement. "Your highness."

Thanks to his rank in Lucifer's army, he didn't have to offer a more elaborate greeting. Not like the Carpathï currently dusting Stolas's onyx floors with his knees. Ashïek would rather have his head removed than be forced to kneel before this entitled asshole.

He took the seat Stolas irritably motioned him toward and hid his smirk over Stolas's position at the head of the table, and the throne-like chair the prince occupied. Ashïek's attention flickered over Sïnsobar, the only other notable demon present. The Carpathï, a skin-shifter of great repute, met his stare for a split second before returning his attention to Stolas's feet. The skin-shifter's arms were crossed over his chest, his fists pressed to his shoulders.

Distaste for this submissive, groveling position left an unpleasant taste in Ashïek's mouth. Yet one more example of Stolas's insecurities, his need to maintain such rigid formalities. Truthfully, the demon prince was powerful. But his strength and his standing had come by his bloodline—he'd not earned it.

Not the way Ashïek had.

"I am not pleased with your report," Stolas snarled. With a wave of his hand, he motioned to the Charocté near the rear door. The slave bowed low and opened the door admitting another demon. The Animagi hobbled inside and across the room.

Ashïek arched a brow at the minion's condition. For reasons unknown to most, Dimiezlo had curried special standing in Stolas's legions.

Oh, how far the mighty had fallen.

The fur coating the creature's goat-like legs was matted with dried blood. His face was a pulpy mess.

The skin covering his chest was a sheet of solid pink, fresh skin newly grown from where the old had been peeled away. When Dimiezlo reached the dais near Sïnsobar, he prostrated himself on the ground without a sound, not an easy position given the anatomy of his lower body. His back was flayed open with dozens upon dozens of fresh slashes. The skin on his wrists was ringed with blisters and burns. Ashïek knew of only one metal that would leave that kind of damage on a demon's skin. Quini. Double the torture, double the fun.

But the most heinous of his injuries came not from the wounds to the minion's flesh. His horns had been removed…torn from his head, very slowly, judging by the bloody uneven stumps. One of the most severe and vicious punishments that could be meted out to a demon.

Oh, they'd grow back. Eventually. And that was yet another form of torture. Regeneration of a body part was, oftentimes, more excruciating that its removal. But regeneration of horns?

Ten times worse still.

Dimiezlo must have seriously pissed Stolas off.

"I will not accept failure again, Sïnsobar. Am I clear?" Stolas berated the kneeling demon, spittle flying from his black lips.

The skin-shifter glanced sideways at Dimiezlo, his focus on those bloody stumps. He turned a bit green around the gills and forced a visible swallow. "Yes, your highness."

"Leave," Stolas commanded, his fury making the veins in his forehead and neck bulge and his face turn a darker shade of red. "Both of you."

Ashïek looked on, unimpressed, as the two minions shimmered away in a heartbeat. He understood all too well Stolas's purpose in summoning him here at this moment, and in staging this little show. Dimiezlo's torture had been designed to teach Dimiezlo a lesson. Dimiezlo's appearance had been a warning to Sïnsobar. And the entire performance had been orchestrated to intimidate Ashïek.

Apparently Stolas had missed the memo. It took a hell of a lot more than that to put a Hunter like Ashïek in his place.

"Would you care for some wine? Perhaps something more substantial?" Stolas asked, suddenly the epitome of a gracious host.

That was the other thing about Stolas. The only thing predictable about Stolas was his unpredictability.

Ashïek declined with an abbreviated shake of his head.

Stolas's expression soured, most likely because Ashïek had thwarted the opportunity for yet another pompous display of gluttony. With an irritated sigh, Stolas settled back upon his throne. He braced his elbows on the armrests and tapped his fingers together.

"How are your plans coming along?" he finally cut to the chase, a condescending, narcissistic king passing judgment on his lowly, incompetent troops.

Bloody arrogant little prick.

"You know I don't discuss my activities…with anyone."

Stolas's eyes flickered red and the muscles in his jaw clenched. He took another deep breath, and his eyes changed back to their customary black.

"I trust you do not anticipate any…complications?"

"I always anticipate complications. That's why I always win."

Hatred seethed in Stolas's expression. His nostrils flared and he dragged in another breath, let it out slowly. Ashïek toyed with the idea of asking him if the breathing technique actually worked or if it was all for show.

"I have had word the Guardian has disappeared," Stolas said.

"She will resurface."

"Sïnsobar reported she was on her way to the ruins."

Ashïek held his tongue, waiting. He hadn't been able to figure out why Stolas was so concerned with this particular human. He already had possession of the Sword of Kathnesh. What difference did it make what this woman did, or where she went?

"I want to know why. What does she hope to find?"

Again, Ashïek remained silent. His lack of response was getting under Stolas's skin. Ashïek didn't think he would have cared one way or another but, quite frankly, he was beginning to enjoy himself. Just a bit.

"I don't have to tell you what will happen if she somehow finds a way to take the sword from me, do I? Especially not now that Temptation's Halfling bitch is pregnant," Stolas spat those words out like they were poison upon his tongue.

Ah, so his little fertilization experiments aren't going so well.

And just the fact that Ashïek knew about those experiments was yet another reason why Ashïek never discussed his plans with anyone, nor would he willingly surround himself with prying eyes and ears. As long as even one other being knew what you were up to, nothing was a secret. Ever.

"I don't want the Guardian or the Fallen anywhere near that temple."

Ashïek tilted his head. What was Stolas so worried she'd find? Perhaps this temple warranted a closer look.

Stolas shifted in his seat, drained the goblet on the table before him, and then set the crystal stemware aside. "Sïnsobar said the female is cloaked with a dampening spell. An extremely powerful one. So powerful, in fact, that at first he mistook her for human."

Now that finally stirred his interest. So the new Guardian wasn't human? At least, not fully. *Interesting.*

But the old Guardian *had* been.

And he'd died like one. Bleeding and screaming. A lot.

But she wasn't a Halfling either, judging by Stolas's lack of rush to acquire her. That meant her mother would have been a demoness. But who? And where would the mother have found a cloaking spell? Whose grimoire had she taken a peek into? Not to mention, a cloaking spell with the kind of power to last at least two, nearly three, decades? He could only guess at one such spell book. And only an idiot would attempt such a feat.

An idiot...or one damned determined female looking to protect her offspring.

"One other thing. I have a special...project for you." Stolas let a self-satisfied smirk roll across his thin lips. "I have someone I would like you to spend a little time with. Someone I want you to exercise your considerable talents on."

"And who would merit my time?"

Stolas drew the moment out, as if savoring it for all it was worth. "The Demon of War."

Ashïek slowly straightened in his chair. "I don't have time for games, Prince Stolas."

"This is no game." Stolas leaned back in his seat, steepling his fingers before him. "When your portals went awry and the Fallen's mates escaped—"

"My portals did not go awry. Your scheme failed because you trusted the wrong gutter trash when you allowed Mortikaï in on your plot."

Stolas growled low, snapping his teeth. Ashïek wasn't intimidated, or amused. Stolas's carelessness could send them all on a one-way, torture-filled trip straight to Oblivion should Lucifer ever find out.

"I commissioned another, shall we say, more…motivated minion to portal the Demon of War straight to my dungeons," Stolas finished as if Ashïek had never spoken aloud.

Ashïek gritted his teeth. Great. Another loose end. He was done dealing with loose ends. "And the demon you commissioned?"

Stolas waved a careless hand toward the far wall. Ashïek turned in his seat to look at a severed head atop a polished golden spike in the corner.

Finally, the prince had done *something* right.

"I'll take War with me."

"You will torture him here."

"No. You want War to suffer? It will be done my way, on my terms, in my domain."

Stolas looked like he was about to burst a vein.

Frankly, Ashïek didn't give two shits. Nothing in this mausoleum was safe. Even the conversation they were currently engaged in left him uneasy. Too many ears equaled trouble.

Finally, when Ashïek refused to relent, Stolas conceded petulantly, "Fine. Have it your way. But I will require proof he is being dealt with…appropriately."

"Proof you shall have." Proof, but nothing that could be traced back to Ashïek.

"It is done then. And, General, when you bring me the Guardian," Stolas went on, his condescending tone grating on Ashïek's last nerve, "you can keep Vengeance's head for your trophy wall."

"I don't want his head," Ashïek sneered, slowly rising from his chair. He stared down the length of the table at Stolas through cold eyes, determination to defeat his nemesis deadening him to all else. "I want his wings."

****

Phoebe opened her eyes and blinked around her living room. Sebastian released her hand, and she stepped forward feeling like a drunken sailor regaining her sea legs. The falling sensation that accompanied shimmering wasn't unpleasant, not as Sebastian had warned. It just took some getting used to. Now that she wasn't sick from venom poisoning, the experience was actually enjoyable. In fact, it was almost…fun.

"Make it quick," Sebastian warned as he moved farther into the room.

"I will." She'd glanced over at him as she'd spoken. But she stopped to watch him, confused. He held himself rigid, a vicious looking dagger palmed and ready, as if imminent attack was anticipated.

Clearly, he'd lost his mind.

Who would attack them here? Shaking her head, she retrieved a spare backpack from the closet, then crouched to dig through the baskets of folded clothing near the foot of the stairs. She really should take these upstairs and put them away before they left. After removing several changes of clothing and undergarments and stuffing them into the huge bag, she turned to the coffee table.

As she sat on the couch to shuffle through the papers stacked there, she caught movement from her peripheral vision. Completely baffled, she watched as Sebastian eased from one shadowed corner to the other, dagger still at the ready. Her lips parted and her brow puckered when he suddenly jerked the long drapes near the French doors away from the wall and peered behind them. The only thing missing was the dramatic "ah, ha!" at the unveiling.

His shoulders relaxed, ever so slightly, only to tense once more as he began stalking on hunter's feet toward the shadows in the kitchen. He paused for a moment, then flipped the kitchen light on and leaped into the room in an obvious battle stance. His stare darted this way and that as he searched for…something. When he didn't find whatever it was he was looking for, he slowly relaxed, a look of consternation darkening his brow.

Fascinated, entertained despite her promise to hurry, Phoebe leaned back against the couch, the papers in her hands forgotten as she observed his odd actions. She watched as his eyes narrowed once more, and he slipped from the kitchen, intent on the stairs.

She couldn't take it anymore. And she couldn't

hide the humor from her tone. "Sweet Kinich Ahau, *what* are you doing?"

Sebastian paused long enough to shoot a curious glance her way. "Sweet what?"

Phoebe absently waved his question away, "Mayan sun god. Now tell me what you're doing?"

"Shh." He padded past her, constantly, warily searching.

"What are you doing?" she whispered back, stifling a giggle.

"I'm looking for that damned little monster," he hissed.

Phoebe twisted around and went up on her knees to keep track of him. She braced her forearms on the back of the couch. "What monster?"

Sebastian paused at the foot of the stairs and peered up into the darkened recesses. He placed one big boot on the bottom step and eased up like a master burglar. Or an assassin on a mission.

"Sebastian," she insisted, louder now. "*What* monster?"

"Your cat," he snapped, his voice filled with disgust.

She straightened, and then pushed to her feet. "I don't have a cat."

His head whipped around, and he peered at her with a truly alarmed expression. Like he might fly to her side and shimmer her out of there in the next instant. "Damn it. Maybe it *was* a shifter. Or a *comptestra*. I knew I should have fried it when I had the chance."

"Fried it?" He was making no sense at all. She crossed the room to stand at the bottom of the stairs and stare up at him. *Wait a second—*

She tugged on his wrist. "What's a *comptestra*?"

"Certain species of demons take animals as familiars...to be their eyes and ears, sort of like planting an innocent looking spy in the enemy camp."

"You think there's a possessed cat in my house?"

"No, not a possessed cat. A familiar. You know, like they claimed witches had black cats as familiars."

She took this in for a moment as he eased up another step. The tread squealed beneath his weight and he cringed as if someone had fired a gun.

"I'm telling you when I was here before, there was a big, hairy, orange ball of devil's piss. The demented little sucker shredded my favorite shirt and my face, damn it."

"I'm telling you there isn't any—" Phoebe sucked in a sharp breath. "Oh!"

Goodness! She'd forgotten all about it.

He peered down at her from three steps up. "What?"

"Jezzibel!"

He scowled down at her. "I've been called a lot of things, sweetheart, but never that."

A puff of laughter escaped her over the absurdity of the situation. "Jezzibel is my neighbor's cat. I was cat-sitting for Mrs. Sullivan for a couple weeks. She was scheduled to come back from her daughter's the day after I left for Mexico to pick the cat up." She shook her head and laughed. "The threat is gone, GI Joe. You can come down now." She returned to the couch and took up her papers once more.

Heavy footsteps followed her across the room. "So, you're not a cat person?"

He sounded so hopeful, it was comical. And confusing. Why should he care?

"Oh, I'm a cat person. And a dog person. Probably a hamster person too. I like all animals. And they usually like me." Except for that one bad tempered snake in Toniná. But she wouldn't count that one. It had only bitten her once, and it really had been her fault. She hadn't been paying proper attention to her surroundings. Besides, the snake hadn't been very poisonous despite Ricardo's dire reaction. She'd ended up with nothing more than a mild headache and a touch of an upset stomach.

Phoebe heaved a regretful sigh. "I just can't devote the proper time to a pet right now, so I don't have one."

"Hmm." The couch sagged when he sat beside her, and she had to brace herself before she rolled into him. His masculine scent went straight to her head.

Phoebe stared blindly at the pages in her hand. Not a single damned word made sense. She cleared her throat, pushed her glasses back up the bridge of her nose, and tried to center her concentration.

She couldn't do it. He'd taken up every last bit of her attention.

She was hyperaware of him as he leaned back and braced his arm along the sofa behind her. She twitched her wrist, blinking to bring the paper back into focus. But as he propped his ankle on his knee and bounced that big boot up and down, the typed words went blurry again. His body heat toasted her entire right side.

Why couldn't he have picked any other seat in the living room? Why had he chosen to sit in the middle of the damned couch, not three inches from her? *Great!* And now she couldn't even remember what she was supposed to be searching for.

Taking a deep breath—which turned out to be a big mistake because now his scent was branded into her nostrils—she offered him a tightlipped smile. "Can't you find something to do? Go...I don't know, watch TV or something?"

"I have something to do," he replied solemnly. Oh, she didn't like the way he was studying her. Not one bit. Okay, okay. Maybe she did like it. A whole lot, truth be told. Too much, in fact. And that was a bad thing, she reminded herself.

Bad.

Very, very bad.

"I'm watching you." He smiled that dangerous smile of his. The same one he'd given her after shocking her silent with his announcement—or warning, however she chose to take it—that he wanted her. "And you, sweetheart, fascinate me."

Yep. So bad! Crap.

Chapter Seven

Pressing her lips together, praying he couldn't see how strongly his words affected her, she turned to glare at the papers in her hand. And she still couldn't read them. She readjusted her glasses and peered closer.

An itinerary? Oh yes, that's what I was looking for. Wasn't I?

Without warning Sebastian tugged at her bun. Her hair unfurled down her back. She jerked her head around to admonish Sebastian, only to find him focused on a handful of her hair with startling intensity, a strange look on his face.

He rubbed the strands between his thumb and forefinger, over and over. He held it up to the light, and studied each strand, carefully separating them by running his thumb along his finger, fanning them out.

Sebastian released the strands slowly, letting them sift through his fingers. Then he slid his hand into her hair once more, tunneling deep this time, until he was cupping the back of her head. Phoebe was trapped, unable to look away. Unable to draw breath.

But he wasn't done tormenting her. He eased his hand through her hair again and again, before finally capturing yet another handful of long tresses. He lifted them to his face, and, holding her captive with nothing more than his smoldering stare, he slowly smoothed her hair along his cheek. The sight did strange things to her body. Turned her muscles to jelly, her bones to mush, and sent the beat of her heart racing hard enough to crack her ribs.

She swept her tongue along her lower lip in an effort to moisten it. But her mouth, too, had gone dry. And she watched as his attention dipped to study her mouth. His eyes—

She sucked in a sharp breath.

His eyes had flickered black. Just for a moment. Bottomless, demon black. And then they were that stunning, magnetic, metallic blue once more. The sight should have terrified her, should have sent her running, screaming for help.

Instead, it set fire to her blood and released languid, liquid heat rushing through her core.

She lost herself in his gaze. The blue seemed electrified now, shimmery and intense, drawing her in. Heat pulsed off him in waves. Then again, maybe it was just her?

He hadn't released her hair. She only now realized that. He was still holding it captive. Her lips parted, but she couldn't form words—couldn't even *think* of words—as she watched him, slowly and deliberately, wind that hank of hair around and around his fist.

And then he used that fisted hair to slowly, inexorably draw her closer, not stopping until she was leaning into him, off balance, bracing her hand flat on his chest. Her lips were so close to his now that she could feel the moist heat of every one of his exhalations feather across her sensitized skin.

She wasn't sure who closed the distance, but the brush of his lips across hers caused stars to explode behind her eyelids. His lips were firm, masterful as they stroked along hers. And then the tip of his tongue swept across the seam of her mouth, begging entrance, demanding it. She was helpless to resist.

She opened for him, and that skillful tongue plunged inside. The warm, rough skin of his free hand cradled the side of her face for a moment before easing into her hair and cupping the back of her head.

She was too busy playing with his wicked tongue to pay much attention when he unraveled his fist from her hair. Not until the heat of that hand settled on her lower back and urged her up and over. And then he tugged her down until she straddled him. Her knees rested on either side of his hips, but that wasn't close enough for her. Nor for him either, it seemed, as he grabbed hold of her bottom with both hands and, gripping it tight, pressed her closer still.

He rolled his hips beneath her and groaned into her mouth as the steely ridge of his arousal rode the apex of her thighs. Her insides quivered in response. She feared she'd fly apart at any moment, come right out of her skin, so she moved her hands up, up that heavily muscled chest, over those broad shoulders, and around his neck to hold on tight.

The moment that hard wall of muscle met her breasts, Phoebe moaned. As if the sound had triggered a reaction in him, his arms came around her then, and he crushed her tight, breast to chest, rock hard erection to sensitized female heat. Sebastian slanted his mouth over hers, dragging her deeper into the heat of his raging desire. She was utterly consumed.

Just like that, she lost control. She became a mindless creature focused on need and sensation and pleasure. Phoebe widened her thighs, and arched herself into him, rocked against him. His hips rolled again, and he ground his shaft along her core, a harder, longer stroke. She melted against him, melted into him, malleable clay in his arms to hold and mold as he would. He ravished her mouth and began exploring her body with inquisitive hands. He gripped her hips, spanned her waist, splayed his fingers over her ribcage. Cupped her breasts. Flicked and tugged at her nipples.

Her own fingers were anything but idle. She smoothed them through his hair and then gripped the back of his neck. More. She needed more. Phoebe clutched at his broad shoulders, dug her fingertips into thick muscle, urging him closer.

Not enough, not nearly enough.

Panting, near delirious with need, she made to pull back, but he resisted, growling a firm warning against her lips. His arms came around her again, like steel bands, holding her captive.

"No," she mumbled against his lips, "wait."

She wedged an elbow between them and pressed her hands against his chest. He growled again, deep in his chest, a dark sound rife with displeasure, but he allowed the space, his grip on her loosening with obvious reluctance. The sound sent shivers through her, cranking her desire up another notch. But she had her own goals here, and she wouldn't be denied. Her fingers grasped the hem of his shirt and tugged up, up, up revealing smooth slabs of taut muscle. Her mouth watered.

His body went absolutely still at her actions. His grip on her hips tightened as he searched her face. His expression, the sheer intensity of his desire, made her breath hitch. Understanding dawned in her lust fogged brain. He wanted her, wanted her to *see* him wanting her. Wanted her to *know* he had every intention of taking what he wanted.

She shivered at the raw intent and utter resolve in his unwavering stare. His fingers dug into her hips, relaying his reluctance to let her go, even to meet so basic, so necessary a need as removing the layers of clothing separating them. His cheeks were flushed. His lips, a little swollen, glistened from their kiss. And his eyes burned bright with need.

But he paused for a heartbeat. To make sure she was onboard and in agreement with where this was headed? Or to make sure that she understood he was in control of this ride and had no intention of stopping until they'd reached the final destination?

She couldn't think right now, didn't want to think. Didn't want to worry or care. Only wanted skin on skin. Heat to heat. Searing away everything but this inferno that had roared to life between them. She gave his shirt another tug, this one more insistent. His eyes narrowed, just the slightest, as if warning her of the danger she recklessly courted. Sebastian arched his back off the couch and whipped the shirt over his head.

Before she could react, he was reaching for hers. Her shirt was gone in the next moment. Only then did a wave of hesitation, of self-consciousness, finally hit her. But it was too late for second thoughts now. Too late to slow him down.

He let out a worshipful groan and ripped her bra right down the middle. Sebastian shoved the wispy material out of his way and cupped both of her small breasts, staring at them as if he'd found the Holy Grail.

"Perfect," he whispered. And then, louder and with

such fierce possession it stole her breath, he announced, "Mine."

And then his mouth was on her, swirling and suckling, devouring her, and she lost her mind. Her head dropped back on her shoulders, and her eyelids sagged closed. Her lips parted and she gasped as he drew her nipple deep in his mouth. The pressure, the wet suction sent spears of pleasure shooting straight to her womanhood. A wanton moan tumbled from her lips.

She sank her fingers into his hair and made a couple fists of her own. But she was helpless, a slave to her body's needs. And her body was captive to his whims.

A strange falling sensation caught her by surprise. She gasped, her eyes flying open. Phoebe found herself flat on her back, pinned into the couch cushions by two hundred and fifty pounds of lust driven male. Sebastian had worked one arm beneath her, his hand splayed in the middle of her back. He'd wedged his narrow hips tight between her thighs, rocking against her as he kissed his way up the side of her neck.

Lost to sensation, Phoebe gripped his shoulders, pulling him closer. He scraped his teeth along the ridge of her jaw, creating delicious friction that sent shivers skating through her. And when he claimed her mouth once more, she wrapped her legs around his waist and whimpered. Need, fierce and all consuming, burned her inhibitions to ashes.

Sebastian moved over her, rubbing against her. He plucked and strummed her nipple with callused fingertips, sending a fresh wave of sharp pleasure shooting through her. He mastered the kiss, tangled his tongue with hers and took control. He drifted his hand down her side until it rode her hip, then he slipped it below her and gripped her bottom, lifting her into him.

More. She needed more. Now. She reached down, pushing her hand between them, not stopping until she cupped his rock-hard erection through the denim. Phoebe pushed her palm along the length of him, dragging a tormented groan from deep in his chest. But still it wasn't enough. She wanted it in her hand, wanted to wrap her fingers around him. Wanted to draw his thick shaft to where she ached for him and urge him to fill her. Frustrated, she reached for the button on his jeans.

The ringing of a cell phone jolted her. It took a second to regain her senses, and a moment longer still to break the kiss. Sebastian didn't seem to notice. Instead, he turned his wicked tongue to the pulse point beneath her earlobe. She trembled and almost caved then and there.

But the phone kept ringing, and reality was calling. What was she doing? This had gone beyond a mere bad idea and straight into the realm of complete insanity. Somewhere there was a padded cell and a straightjacket with her name spelled out nice and neat in bright pink sequins all over it.

"Sebastian," she whispered, cleared her throat and tried again. "Sebastian."

He murmured something unintelligible against her skin, and then he turned his lips to the slice of scar tissue running across her throat. He nipped and nibbled and suckled his way from one end of her scar to the other and she knew, in an instant, that from that second on, whenever she touched it or saw it again, she would always remember this moment, would always remember his mouth upon it, and the memory of how she'd gotten it would no longer haunt her the way it had before.

But then he turned hot, openmouthed kisses to the curve where neck met shoulder, and all rational thought slipped through her fingers. The phone had gone silent…or had she just gone deaf? Either way, she was back in the fire and ready to burn.

He found her lips once more and plunged them both into ravenous need. She felt a tug at her waist as the button on her jeans popped free. The rasp of his callused fingers as they dipped just beneath her waistband made her shiver, and a small sound rippled up the back of her throat. Encouraging him. Urging him to hurry.

The peal of a phone tore through the room. Reality crashed over her like a shower of ice.

Phoebe dug her fingers into his shoulders as she tried to get his attention. It took a lot longer than it should have for him to hear the ringing. Or maybe it was just that he didn't care. He lifted his head and stared down at her, searching her face for the slightest indication that he should ignore the phone and keep going.

Sebastian shifted his position and pressed his arousal even harder against her, sparking a cascade of sensation that rushed through her core. She nearly begged, nearly whimpered. But inside her mouth, something shocking happened. Her incisors shot long. Really long, and really sharp.

She had fangs in her mouth.

Oh, dear God no! This can't be happening. Not

now.

But, as if to argue, her fangs sliced into her tongue drawing blood. Horror hit her like a tidal wave. She pressed her lips together, her brows pinched tight as she struggled to conceal what was happening inside her mouth.

His focus, still simmering with desire, skated down to her tightly closed lips, as if viewing it as a challenge. When it looked as if he might just take the decision out of her hands, might ignore the phone and resume laying siege, laying claim to her body, Phoebe panicked. She shook her head, frantic, and shoved at his shoulders with fresh determination. She couldn't give in, couldn't give either of them what they wanted.

She needed to figure out what had just happened. Why her body had just betrayed her. Why she suddenly had a set of chompers like that monster who'd kidnapped her and taken her to that cave of horrors.

He must have finally recognized the denial in her expression. Sebastian dropped his forehead to her shoulder and heaved a miserable sigh. Something melted inside her. Not with passion or pure lust. But something…sweeter. It was all she could do not to wrap herself back around him and pet him in an offer of comfort.

"This better be damned important," he muttered beneath his breath as he pushed himself to his feet.

The sudden loss of his weight and heat left her bereft. The moment he was on his feet, fishing the phone from the pocket of his now straining jeans, she sat up and scooted back, scrambling for her shirt. She peeked up at him, unable to stop herself. He was watching her as she draped the shirt over her chest, and the look of ragged disappointment on his face sent a fresh wave of longing through her.

He took a half step toward her, but then stopped and closed his eyes for a second, the still ringing phone clutched in his hand, the muscles in his forearm straining. He was a man waging a violent inner battle, his war was plain to decipher. Answer the phone, or crush it in his fist?

A smart woman wouldn't wager on that fight.

At last, he heaved an angry sigh and turned away, jamming the phone to his ear. "What?" he snarled.

Phoebe jumped at the fury in his voice, thankful it wasn't directed at her. She scrambled from the couch and returned to the basket of laundry. It took a moment to focus, but she eventually found a new bra and tugged it on, cursing the way her hands shook as she tried to hook the tiny clasps. She jerked a shirt over her head, and mentally kicked herself.

Dear God, what was I thinking?

How could I have let things get so far out of hand? Thank heaven for that phone, or we would have—

Right now we'd be—

She shook her head and shoved her fingertips beneath her glasses to massage her eyes. Lord, she'd been so wrapped up in him she hadn't even taken her glasses off. Resettling her glasses, she puffed out a breath and looked around her, tried to think. The foreign-feeling fangs in her mouth were still there. She ran her tongue down the length of one, testing it, and nicked herself again. Damn it. Panic began to rise again.

What had triggered this to happen? She'd been intimate before, she'd had sex. *Before.* But she'd never reacted so strongly to anyone else, never lost control, not like this.

She hadn't been able to stop herself, hadn't been able to hold back. Not with Sebastian. Just the reminder caused her gums to ache, her fangs to throb.

She turned away from him, worried that he might somehow notice, though her lips were still pressed firmly together.

Oh, why won't they go away?

It had to be him. Something about *him*. Sweet Mary, she and Sebastian couldn't do what they'd just done, not again. Not ever again. The dark urges that had come over her left her shaken. There at the end, she'd wanted to...to bite him, for God's sake. She'd wanted to mark him. To put a stamp of possession upon him. *Her* possession.

It was insane. What if the rest of her changed the next time? What if she couldn't stop it, couldn't shut it off?

Drawn by the sound of his voice, she turned to watch him, unable to resist, and wrapped her arms around herself.

What if I'd hurt him?

"Slow down, Gideon," Sebastian instructed the caller. He raked a hand through his hair and began pacing the living room. "Did you find him?"

A furious spat of illegible sound spilled through the phone. Sebastian stopped in his tracks and swore.

"Are you sure it belonged to him? Mikhail's got a tattoo on the back of his right hand of a—"

Another explosion of agitated speech erupted from the other end of the call, then Sebastian said, "Yeah, just between the thumb and index finger." Another spat of words from the caller, then Sebastian hissed, "Fuck."

Sebastian resumed pacing, and Phoebe took up post near the couch, indecisive. Her fangs would start to recede, and then she'd look at Sebastian, and they'd push longer once more, throbbing uncomfortably. Okay, watching him pace a whole through her living room floor was a bad idea.

And yet that was what she found herself doing. Unable to look away for more than a few minutes. Irritated with her lack of self control, she snatched up a stack of papers and one of her father's journals and shoved them into the backpack with her clothing before dropping onto the couch.

And she was back to staring.

Apparently, she was bent on being the poster child for bad decision-making skills.

"I'll come back," Sebastian barked, and Phoebe sat up, her attention now on the call rather than the delicious muscles on display, tensing and flexing every time he moved.

"Yeah, I did," Sebastian went on. "But—" More garble from the other end. "No, she's here with me now. We can—"

A long stretch of conversation came from the other end, cutting Sebastian off every time he tried to insert his opinion. Phoebe studied his face, watched as frustration and anger mounted, darkening his expression. The changes in her own body had finally faded, thank heaven. The fangs were gone at last, the burning sensation in her chest receded.

"Fuck Xander," Sebastian suddenly exploded. "I don't give a damn what he thinks. You're going to need me."

More talking, but this time the tone was quieter, and distinctly female. Phoebe's claws curled into the couch cushions as something dark and ugly coiled inside her wanting to spring free. What woman dared talk to Sebastian in such soothing tones? Her eyes began to burn, her fangs shot long once more, slicing into her lower lip this time. The salty tang of blood blossomed in her mouth.

At that moment, Sebastian turned in his pacing. He glanced up, looked away, and then his attention shot back to her face. His eyes went wide, and he frozen in his tracks, his mouth hanging open. All his attention was on her now, the phone in his hand all but forgotten.

Phoebe snapped her eyes closed and ducked her head. *Breathe. Breathe. Just breathe through it.*

"What?" Sebastian asked, his tone distracted now. "Yeah. Yeah, okay. Just…the next time they go after him, I go too. Got me?"

She heard a faint beep and the rustle of fabric. A long silence stretched on. And then heavy footfalls crossed the room. The couch dipped beside her. She shot to her feet and darted across the room.

"Phoebe?" Sebastian asked slowly, cautiously.

"No," she blurted, throwing her hands up, motioning him to stay where he was. She dragged in a deep breath, willing her body back under her control. Still, she held her hand over the lower half of her face, just in case. No way could she explain fangs. "Don't. Just…don't. That should never have happened. What we did. The kissing and… It will never happen again."

"Like hell it won't," he barked, coming to his feet.

She finally risked looking at him. At least her eyes weren't burning anymore. A quick swipe of her tongue to check her teeth confirmed those damned fangs had gone away. Finally. But the salty tang of blood remained, and she worried that the damage had already been done. She licked her lips and lowered her hand.

He was going to argue. She could see it all over his face. Something in her expression must have changed his mind. He drew a deep breath and fisted his hands at his sides.

"Sweetheart," he said in a placating tone, "do you realize that just a few seconds ago your lip was bleeding, and your eyes were—"

"Who was that on the phone?" *Please. Please, don't press the issue. Please.*

He stared at her, long and hard.

Please.

A deep sigh slipped from him. "That was Gideon. I've been waiting to hear from him for a couple days now."

Phoebe smiled then, positive that gratitude was written all over her face, but she couldn't do anything about it.

"I didn't mean to listen in on your conversation, but it was hard not to."

"It's okay. You're part of this now. You should be kept in the loop. Especially because the next time they call, I'm probably going to have to leave—"

"Leave!" Where had this crushing disappointment come from?

His hands flew up, and he motioned in a conciliatory way. "Only for a short while. And I won't leave you alone, I swear."

That didn't help. He'd promised that *he* would be the one to protect her. Not someone else. And where this irrational, illogical fear had come from, she couldn't say. Nor could she say she cared much for it. She was a grown, independent woman. So she squared her shoulders and strove to at least sound calm and rational. "Where will you go?"

He glanced around, his unease palpable. "I'm not trying to blow your questions off, sweetheart. But we really need to go. Are you packed? We've been here too long as it is. It's probably a safe bet Stolas's minions know about this place. I'd rather not be the welcoming committee if they show up, yeah?"

"I'm ready." She indicated the bag on the floor near his left boot.

He picked the bag up and held his hand out to her. With a great deal of trepidation, and more than a few second thoughts, she placed her hand in his and closed her eyes. His hand closed over hers, firm and strong, gave it a gentle squeeze. The falling sensation was barely noticeable this time. Phoebe opened her eyes. She and Sebastian were standing in his bedroom.

"Why are we here?"

"I need to grab a few things too. It's nice to have backup if I'm too weak or injured and conjuring isn't an option."

"Conjuring? Oh, you mean that thing you do where you make things appear and disappear?"

"Yeah, that," he said over his shoulder as he headed to the closet, a dimple flickering in his cheek.

She walked over and sat on the edge of the bed, watching as he pulled what seemed like random items from his closet and dresser. He'd tossed them haphazardly into the duffle beside her and then go off to find something else.

"Are there limitations to conjuring?"

He paused for a moment, turning his attention fully on her. "Yeah, I guess so. Conjuring affects us each differently. Like right after we've morphed—changed from one form to the other—we're usually too drained to extend that much energy. The morphing also creates a lot of stress on our bodies, so it's hard to concentrate, can even be painful in certain circumstances. Morphing doesn't bother me all that much, but it gives Niklas raging migraines and leaves Gideon drastically weakened.

"Anyway, conjuring. How big the item is that we're conjuring determines how much energy we need to use. For instance, a shirt or a bottle of water won't take much energy at all. But a car or a house would drain us to a critical level and leave us in a vulnerable state. So, as I'm sure you can imagine, we generally avoid those kinds of things if at all possible. And we can only conjure inanimate objects. Never anything living."

She absorbed this in silence for a moment as he turned back to his scavenger hunt. At length, his muffled voice came from the depths of his closet, "It's not all that difficult. Just concentrate, picture what you want in your mind. The weight of it. The textures. The taste or scent. The shape of it. Then call it to you. Will it into being." The movement stilled for a moment, and his voice became coaxing. "Try it. Think of something. Something small at first. And call it to you."

Conjure something? Her?

Now that *was* crazy. So crazy she wouldn't even dignify it with a response.

She asked, "I'm still waiting for you tell me what

that call was all about. Where are you going when you leave?"

He stepped from the closet then, and stared at her, long and hard for a moment. She pressed her lips together and lifted her chin, arching a defiant eyebrow at him. Shaking his head, he crossed the room, a pair of jeans in his hands. He tossed them in the duffle, and then sat beside her.

"I don't know where I'll be going, not yet anyway. We don't have that intel, at least nothing reliable yet."

"Who is *we*?"

"Xander, Niklas, Gideon and myself."

"And who are you looking for?"

"Mikhail. The Demon of War."

Were her eyes bugging from her head? They sure felt like it. She blinked. "You mean...not *The* Demon of War, right? Like the four horsemen of the Apocalypse War?"

Grim, Sebastian nodded.

"*He's* one of your brothers?"

Again with the grim nod.

"Shit," she whispered, then immediately blushed. She might slip in her head once in a while, but she generally made it a rule not to cuss out loud. But...

Shit!

"Stolas, the demon prince behind the plot to overthrow Lucifer? He managed to get his hands on Mikhail. We think maybe with a portal or something. I'm not too clear on that just yet, it happened while I was searching for you. Anyway, he has Mikhail, and the others and myself are going to go after him. As soon as we get credible info on where Stolas might have him stashed, we'll move in. So far, the only place we've been tipped off about didn't pan out. They'd already moved him by the time Gideon and the others got there."

"How do you know he was even there?"

Now Sebastian rose, fidgety all of a sudden. Phoebe frowned, wary. "He just was." Sebastian moved away and crouched down to retrieve a big pair of black boots.

"Sebastian." She waited until he looked up at her. "How do they know?"

Anger radiated from Sebastian. Anger and pain and…guilt. "Because they found his hand."

Her mouth fell open. "His hand?"

Sebastian gave a terse nod. "Nailed to the wall."

Her mind whirled. "I don't mean to sound insensitive, but…how do you know it was *his*?"

"After the Great Fall, we all lost our wings and the gifts that were unique to us. In return, Lucifer granted us—those of us who'd proven useful to his cause—special *gifts*. Mikhail received the ability to heal with a touch of his hands. When he received this gift, his palms were branded. The hand nailed to the wall bore the mark. He also has a tattoo on the back of that hand."

"Wait, why would Lucifer give Mikhail a gift to heal? Doesn't that defeat the purpose?"

Now Sebastian looked uncomfortable. Finally, he admitted, "In certain circumstances, taking a human right up to the point of death, only to revive him, only to give him hope, then take him back to death's door, over and over, is far crueler than simply taking his life and being done with it. The more torment in life, the more despair a soul feels in death. Lucifer likes to toy with souls like that."

Phoebe cleared her throat. "So, this Stolas took Mikhail's gift from him, then, when he took his hand?"

Now Sebastian looked like he wanted to be sick. He shook his head. "No."

"But you just said—"

"That he took his hand. Possibly both of them. Bastard probably kept the other one for a souvenir." Sebastian swiped his hand over his mouth. "They'll grow back."

"What?"

"That's one of the perks of our species, sweetheart. We regenerate. But it's damned painful. After all, what better punishment is there than to have to continually regenerate the same appendage over and over and over?"

Oh God.

And then another thought occurred. "So if Stolas took his hands, and that's where his ability was, then how do you know he won't lose his gift anyway?"

Sebastian's face turned to stone. "Because Mikhail lost a hand once before, long ago. When it regenerated, the gift came back with it." He stood, hefted the duffle bag over his shoulder, and held his hand out to her. "We need to go."

Phoebe didn't know what to say. Could barely wrap her mind around the gruesome images now filling her mind. Poor Mikhail.

Poor all of them if Stolas could get his hands on a demon like Mikhail, a freakin' horseman of the Apocalypse. If Stolas could torture and maim like that, without regret, without conscience…how could they keep anyone safe? Knowing someone like that wanted the sword, wanted to overthrow Lucifer and conquer a world full of innocent humanity? She shuddered.

She had to find where the sword was hidden. As soon as possible. Find it and hide it away once more and protect it at all cost.

She reached for his hand, then paused. "What were your gifts? The one you lost? And the one you gained?"

He smiled at her then, but it didn't reach his eyes and it left her feeling cold, wishing she'd never asked.

"Once upon a time, I could hear a person's deepest desires. Just by standing near them, I could read their soul and know exactly what they wanted more than anything else. In some cases, if the wish was pure, the soul true, and it pleased the Almighty, I was able to grant those prayers. Heal someone, bless a union, bring a child to the barren, that sort of thing." The look on his face was difficult to describe, lost somewhere between needful yearning and wondrous awe.

She couldn't bring herself to ask what he'd gotten in return for defecting with Lucifer. She didn't need to.

He turned haunted eyes her way. "After the fall, I lost my ability. And I just traded one pair of wings for another."

Her brow puckered as she remembered the sight of him in that cave in all his demonic glory. And those massive, lethal, midnight black wings.

"Time to go," he said again. Translation: subject closed. She had more questions. But how could she push him on this when she had secrets she would rather leave buried?

Chapter Eight

Sebastian watched her cross the dusty cantina and pull out a chair next to a squat man with a thin mustache. She'd taken all the information he'd given her earlier surprisingly well. He couldn't help but admire her strength. Most in her shoes probably would have buckled beneath the strain long ago.

She spent the next several minutes deep in conversation with the man, her hands constantly moving, her face animated, while Sebastian leaned against the bar and waited. She was in her element.

Though he was ever-vigilant of their surroundings and mindful of the other patrons, his thoughts wandered back to only a few hours ago. Just the memory of how she'd felt in his arms, the taste of her, the silk of her skin, had him shifting uncomfortably and fighting to control his own body's reactions. She was a champagne bottle shaken and ready to erupt, the passion building and building inside her until, sooner or later, it had to detonate. He intended to be the one to release the cork.

She took his breath away. But, more and more, the longer he was in her company, he was coming to realize it wasn't just her body that drew him. She called to him on every level. Her dogged commitment to upholding her familial legacy. Her loyalty to her father's memory. Her resilient nature.

He wanted her more than he'd ever wanted

another.

And he knew, sure as he was standing there, they would have made love right there on her couch. He would have claimed her, taken her as his mate. His body vibrated with the knowledge and the need. If it hadn't been for Gideon's call…

My mate.

Those two little words sent a flood of heat through his body. She held a single-minded determination that could be daunting at times. The way she focused on that sword, for example, could give a lesser demon a complex. But then there was the way she got sidetracked in the middle of simple tasks. She was a puzzle.

Though she hadn't turned it on him just yet—and he was dead certain the time would come sooner or later when she did—the woman had a temper. He wasn't fooled. He'd caught a glimpse of it now and again. And, sweet Lord in Heaven, she was stubborn. Hell bent on doing things her way. Polite, but always firm. It was all he could do step to back and let her take the lead. Just like the argument they'd had when they'd arrived here at the cantina a short while ago. She'd insisted she be the one to talk to the patrons, the one to search out information. Claimed he'd intimidate the men here.

He'd finally conceded her point. He hadn't liked it. Especially when his instincts were screaming at him to do just the opposite. But he'd relented.

Yeah, she had her quirks, but they just made her all the more adorable.

She reached up and jammed a wisp of loose hair back into that tight bun. Yet one more thing about her that drove him crazy. Seeing all that long, sable glory constantly tucked up in a staid bun made his fingers itch. He wanted to take it down again, feel it against his skin once more. The memory of how all those silky strands had felt wrapped around his fist as he'd kissed her—

He groaned aloud.

Phoebe and her companion both stood and shook hands. The man immediately left the cantina, and Phoebe returned to Sebastian's side. The urge to wrap her in his arms and shimmer them someplace private so they could take up where they'd left off was, perhaps, one of the greatest temptations he'd ever resisted. But she wouldn't appreciate his interference right now. And that was how she would probably view it. He could see it on her face. She was a woman on a mission.

He fought to bring his hunger for her back to a controllable simmer and straightened away from the bar.

"That was Pedro, Ricardo's cousin. He's going to find Ricardo and send him to meet us later at the hotel. I'm sure he'll still have our supplies stored, but it's too late to set out tonight. So we'll get a couple rooms and head out first thing in the morning."

He frowned. "Ricardo is staying at the hotel tonight?"

"No, we are." She arched a puzzled brow and shook her head, as if she'd already moved on to the next page in their playbook and was annoyed to have to go back to cover old ground. Never mind that she had failed to give him a copy of the plan. "He'll stop by later to iron out any details we need to go over. Why?"

He could already see where this was heading.

Bracing himself for the argument that was sure to come, he said, "We'll only need one room."

Yep. There was that familiar stubborn streak glinting in those beautiful eyes.

"No," she said slowly, as if speaking to an imbecile. "We'll need *two*."

"Only one, love."

She scowled, punched her fists to her hips and dipped her chin. After a quick glance around to make certain no one else was listening, she hissed, "Just because we almost—" She growled low in her throat, honest to God growled. Sweet saints, he wanted to kiss her. "Damn it, I'm *not* sleeping with you."

He really shouldn't. But he couldn't resist. Sebastian let a wicked smile curl his lips, and he lifted a suggestive brow, deliberately misunderstanding. "Well, I guess sleeping could be optional. I'd just assumed you'd want to be well-rested for tomorrow. But I'm always flexible if you'd rather—"

"That is *not* what I meant, and you know it!" Rosy color rode high on her cheeks. Using her index finger, she pushed her glasses back up. Man, he'd never realized something like that could be such a turn on. But every time she did it, it made him want to drag her to the ground and go at her like a starved sex demon.

"You and I are *not* sharing a room," she whispered furiously, glancing to both sides to make sure no one was eavesdropping.

"You know, you're really cute when you get all prim and proper like this."

Her lashes fused together as she sputtered. For a split second, those beautiful emerald green eyes flashed black. Pure, unadulterated lust exploded through his system. He still couldn't figure out exactly what she was—those flickering eyes proclaimed demoness despite the fact that she didn't fire off those instincts inside him—but her scent said otherwise. The only brimstone he could detect on her was in her temper. The rest of her was all…human?

Heaven have mercy on him, she had him so tied up in knots he couldn't tell. Her obstinate resistance to discussing the subject frustrated him to no end.

Whatever she was, he wanted her. Bad.

Sebastian leaned closer to her, enjoying the way her green-again eyes instantly darted to his lips. He savored the way she smelled, exotic flowers and all woman. For one moment, he thought about tugging her hair down just to see how she'd react. But one visual sweep around the cantina convinced him he didn't want to share even a glimpse of those decadent tresses with anyone else. So instead, he eased his mouth just a bit closer to the delicate shell of her ear.

"And, sweetheart, make sure you get a room with a really big bed. I like to move around a lot when I"—he turned his head a little, deliberately feathering a suggestive breath along the sensitive skin below her ear—"sleep."

A tremor slid through her, so powerful, he could *see* it. Delicious. Filled with a very male sense of satisfaction, he eased around her, careful to make certain he brushed against her, just a bit, before he walked toward the door, leaving her to follow. Or not.

He didn't even bother trying to hide the grin.

At the cantina exit, he paused and turned to hold the door open for her. Oh, she'd followed all right. And it looked as if he were about to get that firsthand knowledge of her temper sooner rather than later. He vanished the keys from her hand and conjured them into his. He'd noticed earlier the way her focus on the road tended to waver when she became distracted.

And right now, she was as distracted as a girl could get. Well, as distracted as a girl could get outside of a bedroom, that is.

They barely made it to the rental car before she exploded.

"You're being unreasonable," she hissed at him over the roof of the sedan. "Unreasonable and unrealistic."

"Unreasonable, no. Practical and very realistic, yes."

Phoebe rolled her eyes and growled at him. Again. It was all he could do not to burst out laughing. God in Heaven, she was adorable. Adorable and sexy as hell. She shook her head, jerked the car door open, and threw herself inside, slamming the door behind her for good measure. Sebastian let the grin he'd been fighting burst across his face for a split second before schooling his features into, what he hoped, was something more sober. Clearing his throat, deciding to be the voice of patient reason, he opened his door and climbed inside the car in a much more controlled fashion.

"How, for one moment, do you even imagine our sharing a room is in any way, shape, or form practical or realistic?" Phoebe asked, clearly not ready to listen to reason as she twisted in the seat to face him.

"I can't very well protect you if I'm in another room, now can I?" There, that was patient and very reasonable. Logical even.

She peered at him through narrowed eyes. "You

mean, you can't try to seduce me from another room. And this entire argument is moot. I will not give up my privacy just because you use some lame excuse in order to…to…to try to catch me in the shower or some other vulnerable position. I'm more than capable of taking care of myself, thank you very much."

"First of all, what do you mean, '*try*'?" He tilted his head and let his heated gaze skim down, down, up, up. Taking note of the way her eyes flickered green to black and back again with desire, the way her breathing hitched, the way her pulse fluttered at the base of her throat, the way her nipples pebbled against the thin layers of cotton. He licked his lips, imagining how that decadent flesh would taste as he swept his tongue over each one in turn. Nipping. Suckling. Dragging in a deep, shuddering breath, he forged on. "And second, if you recall, you were at my tender mercy for four days. Four. Days. Had it been my intention, I could have taken advantage of your weakened state at any point in that time span. And yet I chose to take the honorable road."

"You say '*try*' as If I'm a foregone conclusion. A sure thing! Of all the arrogant, conceited—" she sputtered. Becoming color bloomed in her cheeks.

"You said '*try*' first, not me. Even if you refuse to admit it, I know what happens when we touch," he cut her off, warming to the subject. Or rather his temper was. How dare she accuse him of…well, maybe he had pushed his limits a time or two. But still. Where she was concerned, he'd been a veritable saint. Considering the fact he'd been walking around in a veritable state of unceasing arousal around her, he should be applauded for his self-restraint, not taken to task! The more he thought about it, the more it got under his skin. Nothing would stand between him and his mate. He didn't care if he was behaving overly possessive. She was his mate. She might not know it yet. But, damn it, he did. He leaned toward her, letting his voice drop with intent. "Bottom line, sweetheart, you can rent as many rooms as you want. It won't make a damned bit of difference. Where you go, I go. Where you sleep, I sleep. From now on, I'm your shadow. End of discussion."

"The hell it is," she fumed, getting right up in his face. She didn't fear him one bit. Lord, she was magnificent. "You're not sleeping in my bed...room! You're not sleeping in my room!" Phoebe amended quickly.

"What's the matter, love?" Sebastian gave her a half-lidded stare, quirking one corner of his mouth up as he searched her eyes. "Ah, I see. Maybe it's not *me* you don't trust to keep their hands to themselves?"

Her jaw dropped for a moment, and outrage filled her expression. "You egotistical asshole," she snarled. Then, just as quickly as the words left her mouth, her horrified eyes went wide, her face flooded with bright color, and she slapped a hand over her mouth.

"Now, sweetheart, that wasn't very nice," he drawled, his brows drawing together in feigned affront.

Her hand dropped to her lap and fisted as she glared at him. "You—"

He cut off whatever she'd been about to say by sinking one hand into her hair, dislodging her bun completely, cupping the back of her head, and dragging her into his embrace. His lips sealed over hers, and he swallowed her startled yelp.

For all of half a minute she resisted, her small fists

coming up to push ineffectively at his chest. But as he slid his tongue along the seam of her lips, those small hands stopped pushing. Soon her open palms started doing a little sliding of their own. Sliding slowly, exploratively up his chest and eventually her arms slid around his neck.

With a stifled groan, he slipped his arm around her back and dragged her across the seat, until her chest pressed firmly against his. He fisted his hand in her hair and tugged her head back a bit, deepening the kiss. Sinking in. Drowning happily. Before long her fingers were tugging frantically at his shirt, and his chest was heaving as if he'd just been in the fight of his life. She wiggled closer. She was practically in his lap now, and the only thing he wanted to do was strip her of every last offending scrap of clothing and take her right there in the car on this public road and not give a damn if anyone saw.

Public. No, that was not how it was going to be between him and his mate. When he took her, every inch of her bare flesh would be for his eyes only.

With a stifled oath, he tore his lips from hers and gently but firmly put her back in her seat. As he leaned across her to click her seatbelt in place, he made the mistake of glancing into her eyes. Her completely black eyes. It was nearly his undoing. He sucked in a shuddering breath, dragged a shaking hand through his hair, and grasped the steering wheel in a death grip. And as he started the car, he prayed he had enough self-control to make it back to the hotel before he changed his mind.

Phoebe rode the rest of the way to the hotel in seething silence. The memory of their argument still made him smile, despite his anger at her resistance. Who knew winning an argument with her was as simple as kissing her senseless? That was one weapon he'd be more than happy to keep in his arsenal.

Sebastian palmed the key and followed her inside the hotel room, *their* room. It was your average, basic, no frills hotel room. One queen sized bed. One nightstand. A single dresser with an old TV, a small table in the corner, and an adjoining bathroom the size of a postage stamp.

He was smart enough to hide the smirk tugging at his lips. Luck had been on their side, or at least it had been on *his* side, saving him further argument. Apparently there was a senior tour group occupying eighteen of the twenty rooms in the small hotel. And a honeymooning couple had just rented room number nineteen not an hour before they'd arrived.

He didn't bother rubbing in the fact that if she hadn't argued with him, they would have arrived sooner, and she might have had a shot at renting both rooms. First, he could see she'd already done the math in her head and didn't like the sum she'd come up with. And second, it wouldn't have mattered anyway. Like he'd said, where she slept, so would he. He stood with his back braced against the closed door and watched as she tossed her bag on the bed and scowled at him.

And he'd thought her stubbornness cute? Must have been his dick talking, because it damned sure wasn't his sanity.

"This is ridiculous," she grumbled beneath her breath as she ripped the zipper on her backpack open.

He clenched his teeth to keep from retorting. He might be willing to bend on a lot of things for her, but not this. Her safety was more important to him than anything else. She'd just have to get used to having him around.

Why did his mate have to be the stubborn one? He'd never seen Kyanna complain about having Xander constantly underfoot. And that bastard was as overprotective as they came. Likewise, he'd be willing to bet Carly never gave Niklas grief like this. And no way in hell, he was absolutely positive, would the Halfling put up a fuss over Gideon hovering. Temptation probably had the woman wrapped around his little finger already, eating out of the palm of his hand.

Sebastian snorted at his luck as he watched her dig through her bag. Her grumbling intensified, and the scowl on her face, if possible, grew even darker.

"What's wrong?"

She huffed out an aggrieved breath. "I was paying more attention to you playing Sebastian the Great Cat Hunter, and then we were—" She choked off the words, but he knew what she'd been about to say. *Kissing. Making out.*

Nearly having sex.

Oh damn, he had to stop before he gave himself another erection…oops, too late. Looked like he had a few things to get used to as well. Like walking around in a perpetual state of arousal whenever she was near. Or when the subject of kissing came up. Or whenever he thought about her. Which was pretty much all the freakin' time now.

And there it was again, that spike in energy radiating from her whenever she was angry or upset…or aroused. To be truthful, he'd grown rather used to the constant, low grade hum of power that he hardly noticed it anymore, though it still left him puzzled as to exactly what she was. But these sharp little jolts sure caught his attention.

And that worried him. Because if he could feel them, then surely other demons would as well. Then what? How many males would he have to fight in order to keep her?

The answer surprised him.

As many as it takes.

He gave himself a mental shake and struggled to focus on her words. She was holding up a tube of toothpaste in one hand, and a stick of deodorant in the other. "…and I forgot to pack a toothbrush."

Was that all? Sebastian conjured an assortment of packaged toothbrushes across the bedspread. Phoebe blinked, and her mouth fell open. She snapped her mouth closed, shot him a dirty look, swiped up a random toothbrush and stormed to the bathroom.

"You're welcome," he called after her.

She slammed the door behind her.

The warning about the portal that had snatched Gideon's and Xander's mates right from beneath Gideon's nose came back to him. He was across the room in a flash and shoved the door open without bothering to knock.

She whirled around, clutching her toothbrush like a weapon. "What part of 'closed door' do you not understand?" she demanded.

"What part of 'you don't leave my sight' did *you* not understand?"

"Get. Out!"

"You. Don't. Leave. My. Sight."

She threw the still packaged toothbrush at him. It clipped his shoulder. "Kiss my ass!"

If it weren't for the scandalized look on her face, or the way she quickly covered her mouth, he probably would have been a lot more upset with her. As it was…

He was in her face in an instant, their noses practically brushing. "If I ever hear those words leave your luscious little mouth again," he said, very softly, very forcefully, "I will take them as an invitation. And I won't stop with that tight little ass of yours either."

Her eyes went wide at first, but then they narrowed, and she took a step back.

"Be reasonable," she insisted in a placating tone. He was pleased to note that her tone had changed, becoming much more conciliatory, though he didn't like that she was still arguing. "I'm not going to be directly in your line of sight every single minute."

"Yes. You are."

"No!" She threw the toothpaste next, her attempts at calm reasoning blown sky high. "I'm not. I'm not showering with you standing there watching. And absolutely under no circumstances will I—" She looked to the toilet in the corner. "Oh, hell no."

He ground his teeth.

"Fine," he grudgingly compromised. "But the door stays open."

"No."

"It stays open or I'm in the room. Take your pick, sweetheart."

If looks could kill, he'd be kissing Oblivion right now.

"Just a crack," she finally allowed.

"All the way," he countered.

Her eyes narrowed. How long before they flickered black again? Heaven help him, as worked up as he was right now he didn't think he'd be able to keep his hands off her if they did. Wouldn't be able to resist taking her. Claiming her. That bed was too close.

A wicked little voice in the back of his mind teased him. *The wall's closer.*

"Halfway," she allowed, disappointing him when her eyes stayed green. "And not an inch more."

He drew a deep breath. If he wanted to encourage her to be reasonable, to work with him, then he had to be willing to do the same.

Instincts. Screaming.

"All right," he conceded.

"Fine."

"Fine," he snapped, holding on to his temper by the tips of his claws.

"Okay then."

She was going to push him right over the edge.

C.R.A.Z.Y.

They stood glowering at each. And then something changed. Her focus dipped to his mouth, just for a split second. But that was all it took. The temperature in the tiny room rocketed with a new tension.

It took a moment for Sebastian to register the knocking at the door. Swearing beneath his breath, Sebastian scooped up the toothbrush and toothpaste and tossed them back to her. Not waiting to see if she caught them, he pivoted on the balls of his feet and stormed from the bathroom.

Scowling, Sebastian jerked the door open. An older man of medium height and build stood in the hallway. His skin looked like old, creased shoe leather, his mustache was bushy, and Sebastian wouldn't have been surprised to learn that the beat up, old hat on his head had rolled in with some tumbleweeds. His faded jeans and button-down plaid shirt were well-worn, as were the dusty boots on his feet.

The man frowned and took a step back, his eyes turning to the number on the door.

"*Lo siento mucho*," he said, dipping his head. "*Disculpe por favor*." He turned on his heel, but he didn't make it more than a single step before Phoebe cried out.

Sebastian spun around, his palm up, ready to form a plasma ball to kill whatever had startled her. But she was alone. Before he could question her, Phoebe sprinted across the room and nearly knocked him over in her rush to get through the doorway.

"What—"

But she wasn't paying any attention to him. She threw herself at their visitor, wrapping her arms around his neck as he swung her around in a bone crushing hug. To Sebastian's utter chagrin, he experienced a shot of jealousy so swift and so strong he had to make a fist to extinguish the plasma ball that he couldn't even remember forming.

A barrage of Spanish passed between Phoebe and the man as he set her back on her feet and patted at her cheeks, moisture glinting in his crinkled brown eyes. Sebastian knew enough of the language to understand what was being said, and he forced his jealousy back.

So this was Ricardo. Phoebe was, even now, apologizing for not meeting the guide as previously planned. Making all sorts of excuses. Then she caught Ricardo's hand and dragged him back to the room.

"Come inside," she insisted, glaring Sebastian out of the way.

Sebastian stepped back to allow them entrance. He closed the door and followed them into the room, stopping only when he'd reached Phoebe's side. Ricardo peered at him with unmistakable curiosity.

"Sebastian, this is my old friend Ricardo Esteban Reynosa Alcalá. Ricardo, this is Sebastian—"

"Phoebe's fiancé," Sebastian blurted, slipping his arm around her waist and drawing her into his side.

She went stiff as a board and started to pull away. Sebastian quickly and unobtrusively subdued her, pinning her in place beneath his arm. He gave her a warning squeeze, all the while offering Ricardo a wide smile.

Sebastian thrust out his free hand. "It's a pleasure to meet you."

Ricardo shook Sebastian's hand, looking warily between the two of them. It was obvious the man wasn't buying it, though he was apparently willing to play along. For now. "Congratulations. I did not know Phoebe was to be wed."

Phoebe started to open her mouth, but Sebastian quickly cut her off. "It was very recent."

A troubled frown darkened Ricardo's brow, but he said nothing.

Phoebe frowned up at Sebastian. She made to move away again, but he held firm. And then it was his turn to tense. Razor sharp nails dug into his back, giving a little warning of their own. Gritting his teeth behind his smile, he glanced down at her. She offered him a tight-lipped smile right back.

Okay, point(s) taken.

He released her.

"I'd like to leave first thing in the morning," Phoebe said as she moved out of his arms and walked to the small table in the corner. "Are the supplies still ready?"

"*Si*," Ricardo said, following her. She motioned the old guide to take the seat across from her. Left with nowhere else, Sebastian dropped onto the bed. He listened intently as they discussed the finer details of their expedition into the jungle.

It soon became obvious the two had done this before. Many times. They seemed to fall into an old rhythm, one of long-time partners. One of...if not friends, then certainly another dynamic. Something even closer.

Something like father and daughter.

At length, as they wrapped up their discussion, Ricardo said, "I will see if I can locate an additional tent for your intended."

"That won't be necessary," Sebastian piped up. "Phoebe and I will share. Isn't that right, sweetheart?"

Ricardo turned to Phoebe, his face revealing nothing. And yet, Sebastian sensed a deeper communication was, even now, passing between them.

Phoebe reached out and patted Ricardo's hand. But the smile she sent Sebastian's way promised retribution. "Yes, *precious*. That's right."

"Very well," Ricardo said as he got to his feet. "I will see you both in the morning."

Phoebe walked the older man to the door, where she hugged him goodbye. Seeing Phoebe in another man's arms—even someone like Ricardo, whom she clearly viewed as a fatherly-type figure—caused jealousy to rear its ugly head. Sebastian had to tamp down the urge to attack. His hearing was exceptional. As such, he couldn't miss the whispered conversation that commenced as soon as the two embraced.

Ricardo breathed urgently into her ear, "Do you need help?"

"Have no worries, my friend," Phoebe assured him with a pat on the back. "He is just overprotective. He fears something might happen to me if I leave his sight for five minutes."

Ricardo leaned back and looked to the scar on her throat. His questioning stare returned to her face. Sebastian scowled once more at the reminder that he'd almost lost her before he'd even found her.

Phoebe lifted a hand to her throat. A weak smile flitted over her lips. "Yes, he knows. Now go, my friend. Tomorrow will come soon enough."

****

Phoebe closed the door and turned back to the room. She hadn't realized how much she'd missed Ricardo. He was thinner than the last time she'd seen him. But he was still the same, still the stoic, practical, protective friend she'd always relied on. She felt calmer just having been in his presence, insulated and safe. Loved.

She'd only ever felt that way with one other person. Her father.

Sadness settled upon her, leaving her with an aching void in her chest that threatened to swallow her whole.

But then she caught sight of Sebastian. That ache subsided and unease settled in. Unease and a disturbing sensation of anticipation.

He stood in the center of the room, staring at the bed.

"Oh no. Get those ideas out of your head, right this minute," she demanded. But was she talking to him…or to herself?

Didn't matter, she decided in the next instant. She'd already made up her mind about this. And once she'd made up her mind, she never changed it. She was *not* sleeping with him. Or doing anything else in that bed with him either.

"Bad idea," she muttered beneath her breath as she marched back to the miniscule closet and dragged down a pile of extra blankets and a pillow from the top shelf. She spun around and came very close to colliding with the object of her torment.

He leaned in close, his hands closing over hers where she held the blankets, one on the top, and one on the bottom. His lips hovered dangerously near her cheek.

"Just because it's a bad idea," he whispered, "doesn't mean it wouldn't be a good time."

The heat in his eyes and the seductive tenor of his voice sent lust skating through her. She jerked her hands out from under his and backed away, leaving him holding the bedding.

"And just because you can, doesn't mean you should," she snapped right back. "I'm going to go take a shower. Alone." She cleared her throat and pointed to the floor across the room. "You might as well make up your bed while you're waiting for your turn. And no, I don't want to hear any remarks about conserving water and showering with a friend."

His lips twitched, but he held his tongue. Phoebe

turned and swept up a change of clothes before heading toward the bathroom.

She'd just started to relax when he called out, "Sweetheart?"

She stiffened all over again. Hearing him constantly calling her these endearments did funny things to her insides. But she was also waiting for the other shoe to drop. She did her best to keep her features calm when she turned back to face him. She wouldn't let him see how much he was getting to her. She just wouldn't.

"Make sure to leave the door open." His simmering stare devoured her, languid and sexy as all get out, from the top of her bun right down to the tips of her shoes and then back up, lingering in the most sensitive places. "I want to be able to hear you, you know, if you need me."

Yep. Thud. There it went. The other shoe.

She should have known better than to expect to walk away unscathed.

Before she could reply, he turned and, right before her eyes, the room transformed. The dresser, table and chairs disappeared and a very inviting bed—complete with a snow white, fluffy comforter—appeared on the wall opposite her plain, uncomfortable looking bed.

"If yours isn't to your liking, you're always welcome in my bed." He smirked over his shoulder at her. "I'm willing to share. Anytime."

"I bet," she grumbled. Then louder, "Weren't you the one who said you don't have an altruistic bone in your body?"

He grinned, melting her bones as he turned to fully face her. And then, his stare holding hers captive, he began slowly undressing. One boot, and then the other. His shirt. So. Very. Seductive. All those luscious, rippling muscles on display. His golden skin gleaming. His small brown nipples puckered. Mouthwatering.

As his nimble fingers flicked the button on his jeans open and slowly started to ease his zipper down, Phoebe realized she was staring. And nearly drooling. She whipped around, nearly crashing into the wall, and hurried to the bathroom. His dark chuckle echoed from the next room, taunting her.

And she couldn't even close the damned door to block out the sound.

Chapter Nine

Phoebe woke early the next morning before her alarm clock even went off. She yawned and stretched, rested as she hadn't been in too long to count. But then, as she became aware of her surroundings, she frowned.

The bed beneath her wasn't the same bed she'd gone to sleep in. Gone was the rock-hard mattress. Gone were the stiff, scratchy sheets and the too thin blankets. Her body was supported in the most luxurious, softest bed she'd ever slept on. The sheets were the finest silk, and the comforter felt like clouds against her skin.

Everything felt different. Even her clothing. Her frown intensified. The ratty T-shirt and boxer shorts she'd hastily dressed in after her shower were gone, replaced by—

She lifted the comforter, looked down at herself and gasped.

A dove gray, silk nightie.

That high-handed, sneaky bastard!

She swung her wide-eyed, accusatory glare toward the corner where Sebastian had set up his own bed. But it wasn't there. And neither was he. Everything in the room had been returned to normal. Everything but the bed she'd slept in.

She sat up, letting the decadent bedding fall to her lap as she looked around. Her mind raced. Last night, after Sebastian had stepped inside the bathroom for his turn in the shower she'd beat a hasty retreat, crawled into bed…and what? What had happened?

She'd fallen asleep before he'd gotten out of the shower and slept like the dead all night long. That was what had happened.

Uneasy, she glanced to her side, to the plump pillow untouched by a sleeping head. The bedding was smooth. A sigh escaped her. At least he hadn't climbed in bed with her after she'd passed out.

Or had he? And then just made that side of the bed back up?

Lord, she was being silly. He wouldn't do something like that.

Or would he?

She shook her head. Impossible. Ever since she'd begun this quest to reclaim the sword, ever since she'd received that last life-altering letter from her father, she'd slept with one eye open, ready to flee at the drop of a hat. She'd had to keep herself on the razor's edge, always alert, always prepared, never allowing herself to completely let go. Even if she had, it wouldn't have mattered anyway. The nightmares that often plagued her sleep were deterrent enough.

But last night, she'd slept like the dead.

Had it been the bed?

She caught herself fingering the scar on her throat, remembering the feel of his lips there.

Or had it been *him*? Subconsciously knowing *he* was close, watching over her?

The water pipes clanked, and the shower shut off. Phoebe caught herself stretching her neck to check out the mirror in the bathroom as the curtain on the narrow tub swished.

Sebastian pulled the cheap plastic curtain back and stepped from the small tub. Phoebe bit back a groan. His golden hair was plastered to his head, like dark honey. Water sluiced down his neck and over his broad chest. The liquid glistened, and her mouth went dry, greedy for a sip. She licked her lips and watched as the streams of moisture ran down the ropes of muscles lining his abdomen, moaned as they trickled into a dark goodie trail below his navel. And her hungry stare followed that goodie trail as it dipped low. So low. She craned her neck to see better, only to slouch with a huff as her view ended abruptly, disappointingly where the mirror cut off.

She let her hungry stare wander slowly back up his reflection, savoring every sinful, tempting inch. And then she met glittering, electric blue eyes and a wicked smirk in the mirror.

Busted.

She forced a swallow and jerked her stare away. But not before she'd caught the knowing, smoldering look on his face.

"Good morning, love," he greeted as he stepped farther into the room, his voice deep and husky.

"Good morning," she replied primly. Phoebe sank her nails into the comforter on her lap, willing herself not to look, not to check him out. Had he covered that gorgeous body yet?

Damn it, she looked.

And she couldn't make herself stop this time.

There he stood, in all his naked glory, watching her watch him. All those beautiful muscles she'd been peering at through the looking glass now proudly displayed. Her lips parted as her focus inched down, down. She visually devoured what the mirror had denied her. He stood with his feet braced slightly apart, powerful thighs flexing.

His erection stood at attention, thick and long and proud. Begging for attention. Phoebe's body quivered. Lava seeped into her veins. Her nipples beaded painfully against the delicate silk. Fire erupted deep in her core.

His entire body flexed, went rigid.

Somewhere far off, the distant echo of sanity whispered, reminding her that she couldn't do this. They couldn't do this.

"Get dressed," she croaked.

And then she cringed, heat swamping up her neck and flooding her face. Had that hoarse whisper—a beg, really—come out of *her* mouth?

Those scrumptious lips of his parted on a tempting smile. Scrumptious, because she already knew how they'd taste. *Exactly* how they'd taste.

Just like heaven.

"You first," he drawled, dipping his chin as he canted his head. The fire in his blue, blue eyes challenging her.

Daring her.

She trembled. All it would take was a tiny nod. A lick of her lips. A crook of her finger. Hell, even a blink. And he'd be all over her. She could see it in his eyes. She could see it in the way he clenched his jaw and the way he held his body, tense and prepared to pounce.

And so she froze. Not daring to so much as breathe. Like a deer in the headlights.

And he kept right on watching her, waiting.

Before she gave herself time to reconsider, in one fluid motion, Phoebe tossed the covers back and bolted from the bed, lightning fast. She barely gave herself time to register his surprise. She snatched up the strap of her backpack on the fly and darted into the bathroom, shoving the door behind her, catching it only at the last second and pushing it back to a forty-five-degree angle. Precisely. She wouldn't give him any excuse. None whatsoever. She didn't trust herself to deny them both a second time.

She let the bag fall to the floor at her feet as she clutched the edge of the sink and dropped her head.

Breathe, she reminded herself. *In. Out. Good.*

Phoebe lifted her face and peered into the mirror. And she could have cried. Her eyes were bottomless black. She hung her head and clutched the edges of the sink, unable to face the truth.

****

Sebastian raked splayed fingers through his hair. He bounced along in the back seat of the Jeep, cursing every pothole in the long, narrow road and the straining erection in his pants that just wouldn't go the hell away. He couldn't get the sight of her out of his head. Her sitting there in that bed this morning, desire pouring from her in tangible waves. He'd been half-way to the bathroom door, hand reaching to shove it open, when he realized what he'd been about to do.

Force the issue. Push her until she admitted that she wanted him too.

She was his. His mate. He would wait for her to come to terms with the reality. But there was also no escaping it. Not for him. And not for her. He was working on a full court press, but he didn't feel like he was gaining ground fast enough for his control to hold out.

He just prayed the wait wouldn't last much longer.

The Jeep's front passenger tire dropped into a particularly deep hole, and Sebastian's head smacked the window frame. The driver didn't even blink. Ricardo shot a glance over his shoulder, then looked back to the road. Phoebe sat beside Sebastian, staring out the opposite window, lost in her thoughts. She hadn't seemed to notice.

Well, he had. All this rocking and rolling, with the vegetation whipping by right and left, was starting to make him carsick. Demons weren't meant to travel like this. But he'd not been to the ruins where they were heading, didn't know the lay of the land, so it wasn't exactly safe to shimmer there.

Not yet anyway. He'd offered to make a blind test run. After all, if things didn't go…smoothly, he'd heal. He'd hated the thought of leaving Phoebe behind, unprotected, even for a few minutes. But taking her with him had been out of the question. He might heal, but she was still too much of a question mark. No way would he risk Phoebe that way.

Besides, Phoebe had been correct when she'd reminded him that while it might be faster for them right now, it would cause all kinds of complications down the road. After all, how would they explain to Ricardo and the rest of their crew if they just disappeared here, only to reappear there? And so, they were forced to rely on more conventional methods of transportation.

After what seemed like endless hours, they stopped

at a small shack with an armed guard standing sentry. Sebastian waited, tense and suspicious, prepared to grab Phoebe and shimmer away at the first sign of trouble, while the driver conversed in Spanish with the checkpoint guard. Ricardo passed a handful of folded currency to the driver, who in turn handed it over to the uniformed official at the station, and then they were on their way once more.

Still, Sebastian couldn't relax. The feeling that they were being watched—or that something was about to happen—hung over his head.

Beside him, Phoebe caught her breath. Sebastian turned quickly to see what had drawn the sharp reaction from her. She was peering out the window, her expression one of awe. He used the excuse to slide closer. His chest brushed her side, and he dipped his head to see what she was looking at, which put his face nice and close to hers.

Phoebe didn't speak, nor did she move away. Her attention was too firmly fixed on the massive ruins coming into view in the distance, her face a study in awe. Sebastian didn't know whether to be irritated by her single-minded focus or amused.

"It beautiful," she whispered.

Amused, he decided, leaning back against the seat. Sebastian casually propped his arm along the seat and began toying with the tendrils of hair that had worked their way loose from her bun. She didn't seem to notice that either.

But Ricardo sure did. Suspicious brown eyes drilled Sebastian from the rearview mirror. Sebastian just smiled.

"We're in the Petén Basin," Phoebe said, drawing

his attention. She continued to watch the ruins, visible just over the canopy of the jungle, as she spoke. "Archaeologists call this Campeche Petén. It's a poorly drained plateau really, bordered by seasonal swamplands. We're about thirty miles or so from Calakmul, by the way."

He gave a small murmur of interest, hoping she'd keep talking. Hoping she'd keep absently toying with the seam of his jeans along the inside of his knee.

"Balamkú was first occupied from around 300 BCE to between 800 and 900 CE. The ruins were discovered by Florentino García Cruz, a Mexican Archaeologist, in 1990. He came with a group of INAH custodians to investigate a report of archaeological looting. They found a looters' trench that had partially uncovered a painted stucco frieze. The site was excavated in 1994 and '95."

Feeling a little bolder—most likely pressing his luck—Sebastian slipped his hand to cup her shoulder and, by slow degrees, eased her closer to his side, brushing his thumb slowly back and forth. He was taking blatant advantage of her distraction. But she leaned so willingly into him it was hard to feel guilty. Phoebe tensed when the ruins were temporarily blocked from view by vegetation, but then relaxed against him when the site came back into view, as if soothed by the ancient stones.

"Balamkú has one of the largest surviving stucco friezes in the Mayan world," she added, and he found it hard not to get caught up in her enthusiasm. "An almost intact fifty-five-foot-long painted stucco frieze dating from 550-650 CE. I can't wait to get up there and start poking around."

"Will we go there first?" he murmured, pressing a light kiss against her hair, encouraged when she didn't get upset with him.

"No, we'll go to our base camp, get set up first before we start…ah, exploring."

The ruins disappeared, lost in the jungle. Testing, Sebastian ran the back of his fingers up and down her arm in languid, seductive strokes. She must have realized where she was, what he was doing. And how cozy they must appear to the occupants of the front seat.

She went stiff as a board, shot a swift look to the front, and then glowered at him. "Stop it," she whispered furiously, trying to squirm a little room between them.

Sebastian smiled down at her, unrepentant, holding her right where he wanted her. Well, *almost* where he wanted her. But the way Ricardo had been drilling holes with his eyes through Sebastian all morning, the older man might become more vocal in his displeasure if Sebastian hauled her across his lap.

Phoebe jabbed a very pointed elbow in his side and hissed, "Move over."

He toyed with the idea of deliberately misunderstanding, moving closer to her, but then figured he'd pushed his luck enough.

For now.

With a chuckle, he scooted back to his seat, his mood greatly improved.

Chapter Ten

It didn't take long to reach the small fishing village of Mahahual. There, they would gather the last of their supplies. Because their base camp was located well off the beaten track, deep in the dense heart of the jungle, they would have to leave their vehicles behind and finish the final lap of their journey on foot.

Phoebe had explained to Ricardo that secrecy was of the upmost importance. She'd instructed him to hire only a fraction of the crew they usually employed, and only those he knew to be the most dependable workers, ones he'd already had prior experience with.

As they stood beside one of the small shacks where they'd purchased supplies, Phoebe took a moment to follow up with Ricardo. Earlier that morning, he'd sent most of those workers ahead with the bulk of the expedition's supplies and gear and very specific instructions. Satisfied everything was going according to plan, Phoebe approached Sebastian, where he leaned against the back of their vehicle.

"We hike the rest of the way," she said, offering him a chilly smile. She was still a little peeved with him for snuggling up to her in the Jeep. He shouldn't have done that. It gave off the wrong impression. To everyone.

And it had been entirely too *nice* for her own peace of mind. She couldn't afford to let herself get used to that kind of behavior. He was a demon. She was a Guardian, despite the fact that she was also—

No. A line has to be drawn somewhere.

Shaking off that thought, she mentally ran down her checklist. She had everything she needed so they could—

She caught sight of her bandana on the back seat. She reached through the window and snagged the red cotton, rolled it up and tied it at the back of her neck. There. Now she had everything. It was time to get a move on. The ruins were calling to her. Hefting the bulky pack onto her back, she hitched it up and balanced herself against the weight.

Sebastian straightened away from the Jeep and crossed his arms. His frown deepened as he watched her cinch the strap around her waist. "What do you think you're doing with that?"

She shielded her eyes with the blade of her hand and peered up at him. The cool of the morning had already started to wear off, and a fine line of sweat trickled its way down her spine. "Um, carrying it?"

He shook his head and moved forward with his arm outstretched. "No, you're not. That thing has to weigh at least forty pounds. Give it here. You can't—"

"Actually, it's probably closer to fifty." She took a step back. "And yes, I can. I carry one just like this every time I come out here."

"That was before." He tried to get behind her, but she turned to face him, denying him the opportunity to take the decision, and the pack, out of her hands. Or off her shoulders, as it were. "It's different now."

She planted her fists on her hips. "Different how?"

"It just is." The muscle in his cheek bunched, and

his nostrils flared. Once more he tried to get around her, and once more she countered his move.

"Not good enough. So, again, how is this any different?"

He looked away from her for a moment, watched the others move around the clearing as they each prepared for the trek.

"Sebastian," she snapped, all out of patience when it looked as if he might try to dart behind her yet again. "I don't have time to waste dancing with you right now. So just answer me. How?"

His hands went to his hips, and blue fire shot from his eyes. "I wasn't around before. But I am here now. And I'm not going to let you—"

"Whoa." She slapped a hand to his chest when he made to reach for the pack again. "Back that train right up. You're not going to *let* me?" She was surprised steam wasn't rolling from her ears, that fire wasn't spewing from her nostrils. "Just who the hell do you think you are? This isn't my first camping trip, buddy. I've been carrying packs like this since I was twelve years old. I'm not some simpering southern miss, and *I* will not *let you* behave otherwise."

He'd like nothing more than to turn her over his knee. It was written all over his face.

Let. Him. Try.

A shrill whistle broke the tense standoff. She glanced over her shoulder and found Ricardo standing beside the other two men.

"Are you two done with your pissing contest yet?" Ricardo called.

Phoebe hissed out a long breath. Damn it, he was right. She was burning daylight arguing with Sebastian like this, and they had a lot of ground to cover today.

"You're pack's over there." She tossed a thumb over her shoulder and she moved to join the others, ignoring Sebastian as he sputtered in her wake. "Better get a move on, or you'll get left behind."

"Absolutely out of my freakin' mind," she heard him mutter.

Whatever.

Damned irritating…demon. She nodded to Ricardo and they set off leaving Sebastian scrambling to catch up. They walked for the better part of two hours, stopping only for short breaks now and again to rehydrate. Despite the close, muggy heat, one of the many—and possibly one of the most deceptive—dangers of the jungle was dehydration.

After one such stop, Phoebe decided to cut Sebastian some slack. Though he refused to walk anywhere but directly behind her, she hadn't heard him complain once. He couldn't possibly be used to the humidity or the constant physical exertion. And yet he continued to plod along after her.

He'd even been gentleman enough to catch her by the elbow when she'd tripped over an exposed root. She'd been too focused on the vegetation at eye level, listening to the many voices of the jungle. The symphony of sounds was a balm to her soul. One she'd missed a great deal. She should have been paying more attention to where she was putting her feet. She knew better.

She had to give him points. He didn't scold or point out her clumsiness. Just held her waist till she got her balance and then fell in behind her in silence once more.

Maybe she had been a little hard on him back at the village. As they began moving again, she pushed a big leaf out of her way and decided an olive branch might not be out of order. Phoebe began telling him about the different flora and fauna of the region, detailing various plants as she held a few examples up for his inspection.

He seemed interested, asking questions and making observations, so she continued talking as they walked, really getting into her subject. She even related an old anecdote about a pack of Guatemalan black howler monkeys that had decided to lay siege to their camp one time when she was younger, and the extreme measures Ricardo and her father had taken to finally drive them off.

"The howlers are more active at dawn and dusk, so of course, whenever we were trying to either get our day under way, or trying to shut it down for the night, they would come out and make a raucous." She smiled when he reached around her to hold up a wide fan of leaves. "Hands down, one of the most exhausting trips I've ever been on."

"Ever have any problems with predators?"

"Not so far. Though the jaguar population in the region is one the largest anywhere in the world, estimated at roughly around four hundred," she said. "They're primarily located in the Calakmul Biosphere Reserve."

She kept moving down the freshly beaten path, the last of the workers some thirty feet or so ahead of her. Phoebe reached up to snag a big flat leaf. Suddenly, she was plucked from the ground before she could take her next step, snatched from behind and jerked back against Sebastian's chest. He held her there, her feet dangling nearly a foot above the ground.

"What the hell?" she squawked.

Though he kept one arm around her waist, kept her anchored to him, he pointed at the ground directly in front of them. A snake had slithered into their path and she'd been so busy talking that she hadn't noticed. Again.

She patted his forearm, a gentle admonishment to let her go. He did so...reluctantly. Which caused her heart to thump a little harder. Determined to get them back on an even keel, she took a closer look at the snake. When she went down on one knee and reached for it, Sebastian hissed and made to grab for her once more.

"Don't," she cautioned in an even, smooth tone. "Unless you want me to get bitten for sure. You'll startle it."

Behind her, he froze.

Phoebe slowly eased her hand down and, palm up, patiently waited for the snake to come to her. The small red head lifted from the ground and, tongue flicking this way and that, the serpent moved fearlessly into her loose grasp. Sebastian drew in an audible breath, let out a nasty—if soft—curse. But he didn't move.

Carefully, supporting the snake in both hands, Phoebe stood and turned to Sebastian.

"There," she murmured, soft and easy. "Nothing to worry about."

"Nothing to—" He sounded like he was choking. Phoebe glanced up from the snake she'd been smoothing her thumb over. Sebastian's expression was alarmed, his body tense, and his eyes were glued to the creature in her hands.

"Phoebe, sweetheart, that's a snake," he said very slowly.

"Very observant." She bit the inside of her cheek.

"Put it down," he ordered with forced calm. Lord, he acted like she was handling a bomb here.

She managed, just barely, not to smile. "Are you afraid of snakes?"

As expected, his back stiffened. "Of course not. We have an understanding. They don't mess with me, so I don't mess with them. No one gets bitten that way."

She held the snake up, inches from her nose to look into those little black eyes. So uncomplicated. Such basic desires. Hunt. Eat. Rest. Mate. Basic survival 101. Would that all life were that simple?

"Then we're in luck that you're in such a good mood, aren't we?" she cooed.

"Please, baby." Sebastian swallowed audibly, his tone gone hoarse. "Just put it down."

The poor guy. She decided to take pity on him. "Red on black."

"Is that supposed to mean something?"

"See the bands of color on him?"

She risked one more glance at Sebastian. The vein in the side of his forehead bulged. The muscle along his jaw bunched. He eyed the snake, nodded, though he remained tense.

"It's like the saying goes…red on black, friend to Jack. Red on yellow, kill a fellow. Now this little guy here is red on black. A tropical milksnake. Another indicator is the color of a snake's head. See how his is red? The poisonous coral snake will have a black head."

Taking her time, she lowered the snake to the

ground, then opened her hands and let it slither away. She brushed her hands together as she stood to face him. "He's harmless. You can relax now, Indiana Jones."

She made to turn back to the trail, but he grabbed her elbow. "Don't *ever* do anything like that again."

"Like what?" she asked, jerking her arm free.

"You scared ten years off my life."

"You're immortal. I think you'll survive." She struggled to control her own temper now. Why was he getting all bent out of shape like this over a little, harmless snake?"

The look he gave her spoke volumes about what he thought of her comment.

But he didn't say anything, and his strained expression didn't relent, so she took a deep breath and a mental step back. Okay, she could see how, to someone unfamiliar with—or someone who actively went out of his way to avoid—snakes, the situation might have seemed a bit risky.

Patience.

"It's pretty rare to find a coral snake, though they are present in this region." She smiled encouragingly up at him, pleased to note his shoulders were gradually loosening and he wasn't holding himself quite so rigid anymore. "Besides, he was feeling far too mellow to bite me."

Sebastian's eyes narrowed and a groove dug in between his brows. "How do you know what kind of mood he was in?"

Phoebe went still, blinked, licked her lips. Then she shrugged and laughed if a bit nervously. "Male moods tend to improve on a full belly. And his was pretty fat.

I'd say he had a mouse in there or something." She spun away and, letting out a silent breath, Phoebe set out at a determined pace. "Besides, I'd be more worried about the creepy crawlies if I were you."

The heavy thuds of his boots had begun following her. The swish of vegetation denoted his proximity. Close. Too close.

"Creepy crawlies?"

"Hmm? Oh, yes," she said, feeling a little spiteful despite her determination to remain patient and understanding. A little devil rode her shoulder. "Wolf spiders, tarantulas, scorpions. That sort of thing. You'll want to make sure you shake out your boots in the mornings before you put them on. Probably shake out your sleeping bag too at night before you climb in. 'Course, that's not to say they won't decide to join you anyway round about the midnight hour."

All movement behind her halted. She kept right on walking. When he resumed crashing along through the foliage, he was cussing a blue streak beneath his breath.

Phoebe smiled.

****

The afternoon seemed to stretch on forever, wearing on his last nerves. He couldn't shake the sight of Phoebe picking up that snake earlier. The damned thing could have been poisonous, her cute little rhyme notwithstanding. Black on yellow, red on black, freakin' blue on green, he didn't give a shit. Just the memory of her holding the creature so close to her face still made his heart stutter. He'd seen her at death's door, fighting off poisoning once already. He had no desire to ever do so again. Where she was concerned, he wasn't taking any chances.

As if Phoebe's stunt with the snake wasn't enough to try the patience of a saint, even the jungle seemed out to drive him insane. The edges of some of the leaves would catch him unawares, slicing his arms to ribbons with a thousand thin paper cuts. Sweat would trickle into the cuts and burn like a mother. Then the insects would come out in droves—drawn by the scent of blood, no doubt, the vicious little suckers—driving him insane with their buzzing and their stinging nips. No wonder Phoebe had chosen to wear khaki cargo pants and a long sleeve shirt.

Just when he thought he couldn't take another second of it, the bugs would finally go away. Leaving him with nothing to focus on but the sweltering, stagnant waves of heat. And Phoebe's sexy ass in those pants…and him not able to do a damned thing about it but play host to one erotic daydream after another. Which cranked his internal temperature sky high. It was a vicious cycle. By the saints, he was in Hell all over again.

Up ahead, Ricardo came to a stop. Phoebe turned to Sebastian and offered him a canteen. Her hair clung to her scalp. Loose strands were plastered to her forehead and neck. Her skin was slicked with sweat. Dark patches had begun to show on her shirt, under her armpits, down the front of her chest. He'd lay odds her back was soaked beneath her pack. His sure as hell was.

And her eyes…sparkled.

Dearest God in Heaven, but she was…*enchanting*.

He gave his head a rueful shake, but admiration still curved his lips upward. Here he was, wishing for a nice cool stream to roll in—hell a freakin' snowbank to dive headfirst into—and there she stood…excited, unfazed by the physical discomforts of what was turning out to be quite a strenuous trek.

She's having the time of her life.

He accepted the canteen, tipped it to his lips and drained it.

"We should be reaching camp soon," she offered with a tired but happy smile.

Sebastian grunted in response. If she could do this, walk mile after mile after mile in this heat without complaint, then he damned well could too.

Phoebe turned to speak to Ricardo, an animated discussion in Spanish with lots of arm movement and waving hands. Sebastian listened with half an ear. He conjured the canteen full of ice-cold water and then upended the thing over his head, savoring the delicious chill. He quickly conjured it full once more and held it out when Phoebe turned to face him again.

Smiling, she accepted the canteen and put it to her mouth. The sight of her lips pressed where his had been only a moment before brought to mind the last time he'd had his lips on her.

Instant. Painful. Erection.

Stifling a groan, he waited as she tipped her head back and closed her eyes before unobtrusively readjusting his fly. From the corner of his eye, he caught the way she jolted at the first contact of that ice-cold water. Brilliant green eyes flew wide open, and Phoebe turned a radiant smile on him.

That smile made every second of their grueling hike worth it. His chest swelled as she brought the canteen back to her mouth and took another series of long, greedy gulps.

"Thank you," she said when she finished, capping

the canteen. "That was a rare treat out here."

"Anytime," he said, falling into step close behind her, closer than he'd been for the last mile or so. "Really," he reminded her, softly so the others wouldn't hear. "All you have to do is tell me what you need, anything you want, and I'll conjure it for you."

"I already have everything I need," she responded, just as quietly, and picked up her pace.

Sebastian hitched his backpack up and fell in line. But the silence had stretched on too long between them. The sound of her voice and the stories she told took his mind off the heat, so he moved closer again and asked, "Talk?"

"About what?"

"I don't know. Tell me about the region some more. Tell me a story."

She went quiet for a moment as she climbed over a fallen tree. Sebastian reached up and took her elbow, balancing her until she was safely over. She smiled back at him, watched as he hopped over the tree, and then resumed walking.

"The Toltec culture, lead by Quetzalcóatl, rose up in this region around, um, 987 CE, I believe."

"The name sounds familiar."

She nodded. "Toltec became the dominate culture before the arrival of the Spanish conquistadores."

She fell silent for a moment. "There is one interesting story that comes to mind."

"Tell me," he encouraged.

"The first Spaniards to visit the region were actually survivors of a shipwreck. Only two survived. Jerónimo de Aguilar and Gonzalo Guerrero. In time they were considered members of one of the tribes.

Guerrero later married the daughter of a Chetumal tribal chief. De Aguilar was eventually rescued during the Spanish explorer Hernán Cortés's expedition."

"Did they have children?"

"I believe so, yes. A son."

"So he was sort of like the father of the Mexican nationality?"

"Well, I don't know about that. And, the proper name for a child of mixed race, particularly of Mexican and Native American descent, is Mestizo." She reached up and scrapped sticky hair from her cheek, hooked it behind her ear. "Actually, you could offend some by referring to them as Mexican in general, rather than Mayan for the Indigenous population or Campechanos for the Hispanic population."

Was there no end to what she knew? Even her brain fascinated him. And the way she came alive in the telling, there was just a way about her.

Geez, he was turning into a dope.

"I'm probably boring you," she said at length.

"I like listening to you lecture."

"I'm not lecturing," she argued, stopping to shoot him a frown.

"Okay, you're telling stories then." He couldn't resist. "I bet all your classes were packed, weren't they?"

Her frown deepened. "Usually. But why would you say so?"

He smiled. "Just a feeling."

She eyed him for a moment longer. Then, with a shrug, she turned to the trail. "You know, you're welcome to walk at the front of the line with Ricardo," she offered. "He could probably tell you a few more interesting, less academic stories about the region."

"Nope. I'm fine right where I am."

She shot an exasperated glance over her shoulder. "Dare I bother asking why?"

He grinned, unabashed, and let his focus wander south. He cocked his head to make it very obvious where he was looking. "The view from where I'm standing is killer. If I haven't mentioned it, I really like your ass in those pants, just in case you were wondering."

Her mouth fell open. She blinked. And then she sputtered.

He chuckled and gave her his best, wicked smile. "Suppose they'd notice if we slipped off the beaten path for a while?"

Phoebe gave a little harrumph, color brightening her cheeks. She spun away and nearly smacked into a tree trunk. Righting herself, she hastened her steps to catch up to the others. Sebastian's mood soared. He even took up whistling.

Could he help it if the only song that came readily to mind involved pouring sugar on him in the name of love?

They broke into a clearing a short while later. Once there, Sebastian stood back, out of the way as directed, and watched as Phoebe hustled around the camp, inspecting, nodding approval, pointing and redirecting. She darted into one of the tents, then came back out a few moments later, sans her backpack. He made a mental note which tent, just in case, then observed as she launched back into motion. It was almost exhausting to watch. One would never be able to tell she'd just spent the better part of her day tromping through the jungle.

The ease with which she interacted with Ricardo, relied on him, was testament to their relationship. The way the six workers responded, respectfully and efficiently, attested to Ricardo's judgment. And, confident woman in her element that she was, Phoebe took their behavior as her due. Just watching her boss people around—not that she actually bossed, it was more like politely and firmly instructing—was a turn on. As she had informed him in the heat of their battle, this wasn't her first camping trip. If he had any doubts before, they were history now.

Eventually, she directed Sebastian to the second in a hodgepodge cluster of tents. The same one she'd ducked into before. Sebastian breathed a sigh of relief. He really hadn't wanted to have that argument all over again. Especially not out here with an audience.

He lifted the flap and stepped inside. "Home sweet…" His voice trailed away as he looked around in dismay. He dropped his bag on the canvas floor and, resisting the urge to spit the now sour taste out of his mouth, he finished, "Home."

He stepped farther inside the tent. This wasn't going to work, not at all. First, he couldn't even stand up straight. Even hunched over as he was, the back of his head still pressed against the top of the tent. And Phoebe wasn't exactly short. It couldn't be much better for her. Second, the place smelled like…well, like a tent. An old one. Third, by the time Phoebe had finished stacking her crates in the middle of the back wall, spread the two single sleeping bags on the narrow cots against the opposite sides, and hung the lantern at the tent's highest peak, there wasn't enough room to turn around, let alone live for the foreseeable future.

Which brought his attention back to the cots. The itsy-bitsy, teenie-weenie cots. And the ratty, musty looking sleeping bags.

That shit sooo ain't happenin'.

Her backpack had been tossed onto one of those cots. He moved farther into the tent, letting the flap slap closed behind him. Sebastian eased onto the free cot, very cautiously. It creaked beneath his weight, but he didn't end up on his ass on the floor, so he figured that was something at least.

He looked around, already missing his overstuffed couch, his big screen TV, and his refrigerator all the more.

Oh no. Or, in Phoebe's choice words…oh *hell* no.

The figurative light bulb went off over his head, and he smiled. He could do much better than this.

Much, much better.

Chapter Eleven

Supper was a relaxing affair, eaten around the campfire. The fare itself was good, tasty and filling, if a little spicy. Ricardo had found an exceptional camp cook. Phoebe could have lingered longer, listening to the workers, six in all, as they spoke in hushed tones. But she was tired. It had been a long day, and an even longer, grueling trek, and she wanted nothing more than to take a quick shower and to turn in for the night. As she well knew, the first rays of dawn would come all too soon.

Standing, stifling a yawn, she dug her fist into the small of her back. She'd just dart inside her tent—ugh, the tent she was now sharing with Sebastian, heaven help her—and snag a change of clothing before taking a go at the camp shower, such as it was. But she caught sight of the smug smile on Sebastian's face, and she paused. He'd been grinning like that off and on for the last hour or so. Her eyes narrowed.

What's he up to?

Pressing her lips together, she made her way to her—*their* tent. Phoebe ducked as she pulled back the flap and stepped inside.

She straightened, and her eyes widened in disbelief.

"Sebastian," she hissed.

No. She had to be imagining things. The heat had

gotten to her. Or exhaustion. Something. What she was seeing just couldn't be possible. Shaking her head, she backed from the tent, letting the flap fall back in place. Ignoring the strange looks she garnered from her crew, and the smug look on Sebastian's face, she surveyed the outside of the tent once more.

Plain, dark, water-stained canvas, patched here and there. It was as familiar to her as a comfortable pair of old shoes. This tent, as well as the one Ricardo was using, were the same tents they used whenever they went on an excavation together. There was no way what she'd just seen could have possibly fit in a tent of these dimensions.

Perturbed, she stepped back inside. It was exactly as she'd witnessed it a moment before. Gone were the sleeping bags and cots. Gone the rough crates, the lantern, the bare tarp floor.

The inside of the tent now had to measure twenty-five by twenty-five. At least. The walls were still material, only now they appeared to be made of luxurious ivory silk. The floors were covered with some kind of glossy dark wood. An expensive looking, tall wardrobe, the top lined with lit candles, stood in one corner and in another corner sat a beautiful writing desk complete with antique lamp and comfortable looking chair. In the third corner rested a big, overstuffed couch with a coffee table in front of it and a mini fridge doubling as an end table. A tasteful arrangement of candles of various thicknesses and lengths nestled in the middle of the table. The candles bathed the entire room in soft white light.

But the focal point of the room was the massive, four poster bed draped in crimson silks. Overhead, a paddle-bladed ceiling fan whirled gently, stirring the air. Air delicately scented with exotic flowers and tropical fruits.

Air that was at least a full twenty degrees cooler than the air outside the tent.

It was a room of fantasy and luxury. Something you'd expect to find in a lavish bungalow on some alluring beach with the shush of the tide rolling in nearby.

It was a room designed for a romantic seduction, right down to the gleaming claw foot tub in the remaining corner. An elegant end table and a silver towel stand draped with two thick white towels stood beside the tub. The top of the table was littered with an assortment of glass jars filled with colorful bath salts, body scrubs, and gels.

The heavy weight of large hands settling on her shoulders made Phoebe jump.

She whirled around, ready to blast him, both for startling her and for…well, the room. But he quickly laid a cautionary finger against her lips.

"Shh," he warned. "We wouldn't want Ricardo or one of your crew to come charging to the rescue, now would we? After all, how would you explain all this?"

Fuming, she shook off his finger, and hissed, "How do *you* explain it all?"

"I conjured it for you." He walked over and dropped onto the sofa with a grateful sigh.

She rounded on him, planting her fists on her hips. "I didn't *ask* for this."

"I know you didn't." He shrugged. "I'm just looking after you."

"I don't need looking after. I'm perfectly capable

of taking care of myself. Now change it back."

He looked around the room, and then back at her. "No."

She couldn't believe he'd just tossed that word out there so casually. As if she'd asked him if he wanted coffee after supper.

She narrowed her eyes. "This isn't going to work, you know."

The look he turned on her was entirely too innocent. "What won't work, sweetheart?"

She ground her teeth. "You know exactly what I'm talking about. This"—she swept her arm around the room—"is not *normal* on a trip like this."

"Why rough it when you don't have to?"

"Because this is a jungle. This stuff doesn't belong here."

"I say it does, and I can provide it, so..." He shrugged again. *Damn him.*

She drew a long breath, counted to ten, then counted to twenty, before letting it all out slowly. Somehow, she managed to find a patient, reasonable tone. "I don't need all this luxury. I've made due with what was here before just fine, many times."

"Just because you can, doesn't mean you should," he quipped, throwing her own words back at her.

Phoebe gasped, outraged. She snapped her teeth together, clenched her fists at her sides, and growled, "Change. It. Back."

He only smiled. That irritating, obstinate, infernal smile. *Damn it. Damn it. Damn it.* She wanted to stomp her foot.

"You might as well get used to it, sweetheart. I can give you all this and more."

"I don't *want* all this," she snarled. *I don't want you.* But she couldn't speak the lie aloud. That he would do this? That he would think to provide this oasis, this tiny slice of paradise in what could potentially be a very physically demanding search drove her crazy. It maddened her.

It also touched her, deeply.

Not the luxury. But the thought—the intent—behind it. The idea that he wanted to make her comfortable, take care of her. Even if a portion—however small or large—was driven by lust.

And it was more than she felt she could deal with.

"Please, change it back."

Finally, a flicker of irritation flashed in his eyes. But it was gone just as fast as it had appeared, and all that easy charm was back in place. And so was that wicked smile. Seduction on steroids. "Are you sure?"

His stare never left her, didn't waver for a second, as he slowly stood. The spell wasn't broken until his face disappeared for a split second while he pulled his shirt off over his head.

"Why don't you give it a night? Sleep on it, love," he said, drawing her unwilling attention to the decadent bed. She snapped her focus back to him, only to curse herself because she knew she was weakening. His muscles rippled in the soft candlelight luring her closer. "Think it over. If you're not completely...*satisfied* in the morning, then I can always change it back."

Realizing how close she'd been to drooling—literally drooling—Phoebe swallowed and forced herself to blink. But she got all caught up again when his long fingers began slowly working the button at his waistband loose. Suddenly, she couldn't breathe. She waited on pins and needles until that tiny round piece of metal finally popped free.

"Would you like me to fill the tub for you?" His softly spoken question barely registered.

She stood trapped, frozen in place, lusting, craving, as he eased his zipper down, down, down, seemingly one tooth at a time.

"Fill the—" What was he talking about. *Why* was he talking? "Fill what?"

She couldn't track the conversation. Honestly, couldn't even remember the words that had just come out of her own mouth. And then his thumbs slipped into the sagging waistband of his pants and, bit by bit, began working them down, one stingy inch at a time. Right. Left. Right. Revealing a patch of short curling hair. Her eyes widened. She moistened her lips. And giddy flutters spun through her womb when the thick root of his manhood was revealed at last. How much further would he go?

"The tub. With water," he clarified, and chuckled.

Water? What the hell did water have to do with anything? She finally managed to drag her gaze up, up over the luscious muscles roping his stomach, the heavy slabs of raw strength that formed his chest, and over those broad, powerful shoulders.

He tilted his head down, just a little, and he peered at her with startling intensity, with *knowing* that shook her to her core. His sculpted lips tipped up at the corners.

Phoebe sucked in air like a drowning woman and spun around. The room tilted. *Oh, God!* She was going to pass out.

"What are you doing?" she squawked, unmindful,

uncaring if anyone heard and came to investigate.

"I thought that was obvious," he said. The dark desire in his voice made her tremble.

"Well, stop it."

"But I prefer to bathe *without* clothing," he said, the damned tease.

The slosh of water pricked her ears. Knowing it was a bad idea, knowing she had no business doing it but drawn against her will, she peeked over her shoulder. Soon her whole body followed suit, turning to fully face him. She was blatantly staring, and she couldn't seem to help herself. He'd already gotten in the tub. Water lapped at his small, puckered nipples. His strong arms rested along the rim as he leaned back, an iniquitous grin on his sinful lips.

If she went up on tiptoe, could she see through the water?

No! She bit the tip of her tongue. *Bad, Phoebe! Bad!*

"I should probably warn you," he drawled, dipping a finger into the water, sending tiny ripples over the surface, "I sleep naked as well."

Her vision blurred. Her knees nearly buckled. *Oh sweet Mary, I'm going to have a stroke.*

"You're welcome to join me," he coaxed, drawing slow figure eights in the water with the tip of one finger. She couldn't look away. "The water's perfect, nice and cool. Though I can make it hotter if you like."

She just bet he could.

Oh God. Oh God. Oh God.

"Oh God," she whispered aloud, nearly hyperventilating. Phoebe cleared her throat, and still, all she could get out was a hoarse, "Get out of there!"

His grin widened. "Okay."

So amenable.

Bracing his hands on the sides of the tub, he made to rise. Phoebe threw her hands up. "*No!*"

He sank back, and water sloshed over the sides. "Change your mind about joining me, love?"

"I need a shower," she muttered, shaking her head, still unable to close her eyes or look away. "A really, *really* cold shower."

Sebastian's lips twitched. The writing desk in the corner disappeared, and in its place stood a roomy glass shower stall. The water was already running. Where it came from, where it went to once it disappeared down the drain, she couldn't say.

She stared, unmoving.

"Not to rain on my own parade here, but you might want to take advantage of that shower sooner rather than later. Conjuring a constant stream of water takes considerably more energy than a simple tub full."

"I'm not—"

A privacy screen appeared between the tub and the shower. A sigh escaped her.

"I'm not going to win this one, am I?"

"The way I see it, you have four options. You can use that shower and go to bed feeling clean and refreshed. You can use the camp shower, in which case I will have to leave this comfortable tub to follow you, and then stand guard outside the shower until you're done. Not nearly as comfortable for either of us. Or I can conjure you clean. Not as relaxing, but just as effective. You decide."

"What's the fourth option?" The words were out of her mouth before she gave it a second thought.

His smile grew. "You can join me."

She'd just had to ask.

It took only a second longer for her to decide. In the end, the idea of standing beneath a piddly trickle of water in the camp shower while scrubbing herself clean at breakneck speed in the near dark swayed her.

"Fine," she ground out, moving behind the privacy screen.

"Fine," he said, sounding entirely too pleased with himself.

"No peeking." She tugged her shirt off, wrestled her pants down her sticky legs.

"No promises," he called, laughing when she froze, pants around her ankles.

Shaking her head, smiling despite herself, Phoebe finished undressing and stepped under the spray. Cool water streamed over her hot flesh. She barely managed to bite back the groan of pleasure.

"Too cold?" Sebastian asked.

"No. It's perfect."

She stood a moment longer, savoring the experience. But then, remembering what he'd said about using up energy, she made short work of washing and rinsing. Oh, the sly demon. She picked up a bottle of conditioner and rolled her eyes. A luxury in the wilds. One she made sure to make ample use of.

Once she'd stepped from the tub and wrapped a thick towel around herself, she called out, "I'm finished."

The shower immediately disappeared, as did the screen, and the desk was back in place. She grinned at the look of disappointment on his face. He'd been hoping to catch her naked. She tilted her head and smiled. Too late.

"I'll take the screen back," she prompted. "I still need to dress."

"I'll close my eyes." His smile said otherwise.

She'd be a fool to trust that wicked demon, at least about this. "Screen please."

"You take all the fun out of it," he grumbled. And suddenly her towel was gone, replaced by a pink nightie much like the one he'd put her in the night before.

"I prefer my own clothing."

"*All* the fun," he muttered. But the nightie disappeared, and she now wore her own tank top and boxers.

She gathered a hank of wet hair in her hand, held it up. "You sure you don't want to take care of this too?"

"No," he drawled, eyeing her with that searing heat again. "I think I'd like to watch you take care of it."

Really? He'd teased and tormented her from the moment she'd stepped inside this tent, really from the first moment she'd woken up...in his bed. Now he wanted to play this game, did he? She didn't know where the thought came from, or why she wasn't being smart enough not to give in to it, but she found herself turning the chair to face the tub and sat down.

"Brush?" she asked.

One appeared beside her on the desk.

Smiling with—at least what she hoped came across as—serene nonchalance, Phoebe picked the brush up and began running it through her hair. Over and over, scalp to tip. She drew the long strands over her shoulder, down over her breast, slowly brushing. Drawing his eyes with every sweep. But tormenting him turned into a double-edged blade. Her tank top quickly became wet, and her nipples beaded in the cool air. When his knuckles turned white on the edge of the tub, and his eyes flickered black, she decided maybe she'd pushed things about as far as she dare.

Yawning, she set the brush aside and stood. As she climbed into bed, the water sloshed behind her.

"Can we lose the silk sheets?" she asked.

Red cotton sheets soft as clouds replaced the silk in a blink of the eye.

"Anything else I can do for you, love?"

His voice was too close. She glanced over, deliberately keeping her gaze on his face. He'd dried off. But he hadn't dressed. She would not look. She would not look.

"Just stay on your side of the bed," she said sweetly, and then promptly rolled over on her side, giving him her back.

The candles whispered out, plunging the room into darkness. The moment the bed dipped with his weight, she stiffened. Phoebe held herself still, barely breathing, as he settled. Even after he'd stopped moving, she couldn't seem to relax.

A deep sigh ghosted through the tent. "Relax, Phoebe."

"I am."

"Uh-huh." He shifted.

The bed dipped, but he didn't move closer, didn't touch her.

Why was she so disappointed? Wasn't this what she wanted? Wasn't this what she'd just told him she wanted?

"You trust me to keep my word?" His voice slid through the darkness, a caress. A temptation.

She hesitated.

"Phoebe," he growled, his tone sharp.

"Yes," she grudgingly admitted.

"Good. I promise you, I won't touch you."

She caught her breath as that stab of disappointment sharpened, catching her off guard.

"Not yet," he added. Her breath caught. "But be warned, love. You are mine. I can wait till you're ready to admit it, ready to accept me. So, I won't take you. Not until you ask me to. But it will happen. Soon."

A rush of need scored her. She couldn't answer right away, still hung up on the images his words had caused to flood into her mind.

Still, he didn't touch her, didn't reach for her. And yet the intensity of his words were as bold and possessive as if he'd run his hands all over her.

At her continued silence, he said sharply, "I thought you said you trust me."

"I do."

Uncomfortable. Silence.

"What?" she asked when she couldn't take another second of waiting.

"If it's not me that you're worried about, then I can only assume you mean…" He drew a deep breath. "Oh."

"What?" she demanded now, unsettled.

"Do you really want me to say it out loud?" His voice had gone soft, warm and wanting. Oh God, so sexy.

The reality of the situation, the knowledge that he'd uncovered the truth of her feelings before she had, made her clamp her teeth together.

"Oh, just shut up and go to sleep," she snapped.

She could hear the smile in his voice. "Sweet dreams, Phoebe."

Chapter Twelve

"Niña," Ricardo's voice called from the other side of the tent flap. "The sun is soon to rise."

"I'm up, I'm up," Phoebe mumbled. She shoved the hair from her eyes, blinked blearily. "I'm up."

It took a moment to get her bearings. She'd slept so soundly again. No nightmares, no jolting awake at tiny, imagined sounds. *How?*

And then physical awareness began to take hold. Her front was cool, almost cold. But her backside, and a large area on her stomach, was toasty warm, tempting her to snuggle back and burrow in. She frowned when she tried to roll over and met with resistance, and then she stiffened, realizing that the warm spot on her belly was actually a hand.

A glance over her shoulder told her he was still asleep. And that he'd curled himself around her in the night, wrapping her up tight. His chest was glued to her back, and their legs were tangled. Phoebe managed to wiggle around, carefully worked her legs free. On her back now, she surveyed the situation.

Lord, she couldn't even get mad at him, couldn't claim he'd gone back on his word or took advantage of the situation.

She was on *his* side of the bed.

Way on his side.

Stifling a groan, she scooched and scooted, edging

toward freedom. Sebastian murmured in his sleep, threw his leg over her thighs and, tucking his hand around her waist, dragged her back. He cuddled her close, nestling his cheek against her hair. And a very thick, very hard erection pressed against her hip.

Well, this is just great. Now what do I do?

Phoebe debated her best course of action, one that would allow her to slip from the bed without waking him. One that got her out of this situation without him realizing she'd snuck over to the dark side.

Well, she'd been sleeping, damn it. She couldn't be held accountable, right? Besides, if there were no witnesses, she could pretend it never happened.

Right?

She glanced up.

Golden stubble covered the lower half of his face. He looked so...peaceful. She hesitated a moment too long, studying his face, watching him while he slept. Melting inside. And she let herself become ensnared. Knew it was happening, was completely cognizant. And she did nothing to stop it.

She'd had no nightmares again last night. Only sound, restful sleep. She eyed him, not liking where this train of thought was headed. Didn't like it. But she didn't stop it either.

The heavy, rigid length along her hip twitched. She glanced down. The sheet had slipped dangerously low. And, she remembered all too well, he wasn't wearing anything under that sheet.

Did she dare? She licked her lips. She'd seen him before, when he'd stepped from the bathroom that first night, fresh from his shower, dripping wet, and very, very naked. Surely, her memory had to be faulty. She'd made a mountain out of a molehill, so to speak.

What could one little peek hurt?

She caught her lower lip between her teeth and, holding her breath, peered at his face to make sure he was still asleep. She pinched the sheet and slipped it down, one precious millimeter at a time. His breathing remained slow and even. Feeling bolder, she pulled the sheet down a little more, just a touch farther. Just a quick glance, she told herself. And then she'd cover him back up and get out of bed.

Only a peek.

The sheet slid down, and she caught sight of just the tip of him. A little more, and then she'd stop. His arousal slid fully into view, and she caught her breath. Nope. Her memory hadn't been faulty. *Whoa mama.* Just as she nipped the sheet and eased it a touch farther, something made her stop and look up.

Sleepy blue eyes were watching her.

Busted. Again.

She didn't know what to say. Oh God, he'd just caught her checking out his goods. Heat flooded her face.

But he didn't leave her floundering in embarrassment for long. His focus dipped to her mouth, and his eyelids slid to half mast. His mouth was already so close. But he didn't swoop, as she'd expected. As she'd hoped. Then she could have blamed the kiss on him.

No, he eased closer, his mouth hovering just fractions of an inch from the corner of hers. She would have to be the one to turn her head to initiate the kiss. And he waited, not moving, not grabbing, not pulling her closer, not taking the power from her.

He just waited.

The decision was hers.

And his words last night came back to her. He was going to make her ask.

She wanted to blame lack of alertness on a poor night's sleep. Blame her impulsive reactions this morning on the curse of her own blood. Blame proximity. A moment of weakness. Or blame him for just being too damned sexy.

But there was no blame to place. Well, except for maybe the part about him being too sexy. They both wanted each other. She knew she wanted him. He'd told her, point blank, that he wanted her. There was no one else to worry about. No one would be hurt if they came together like this. As long as she could keep her reactions under control.

He brushed the tip of his nose against her cheek.

It would have taken a stronger woman than she to deny him. She was the one to close the distance, to turn her head, to pull him closer. And she knew it.

Yes, she cared. Yes, she worried.

But she wasn't about to stop.

She could control her reaction, could manage the changes in her body, now that she knew to expect them. She could be with him and not give in to the urge to bite him. She could.

She was sure of it.

Well, almost sure of it.

But the wanting was so bad, the need for him so intense, she couldn't deny it any longer.

His lips were warm silk against hers. Firm, demanding. Rubbing and sliding, slow and easy. Her heart stumbled. Fell. She tangled her fingers up in his hair. With a small sound, she turned her body into his.

Sebastian slid his hand around her waist, splayed it on her lower back. He rose over her, slipped his forearm beneath her head. And still he kept the kiss right there, floating at the edge of sensual, drifting just a sliver shy of devouring.

Again, she was the one who took it deeper. Phoebe, driven by a steadily building sense of urgency, angled her head and touched her tongue to his lips. The groan that rumbled in his chest sent heat and satisfaction soaring through her system. Emboldened, she pushed her way inside his mouth, swept her tongue along his, sampling, testing, gliding.

She could feel him holding back, waiting, questioning. She was having none of it. She angled her head a little more, slid her foot up the back of his calf. Hooking her knee over his hip, Phoebe arched her hips up to him and pressed herself against his straining arousal.

"Please," she murmured against his lips. "Please, Sebastian."

The moment his fingers dug into her bottom, flexed, squeezed, she knew she had him. He stole control of the kiss away, seizing what he wanted most. Her. And now he was the one devouring, ravenous. He pushed up over her, his mouth mastering hers. He wedged his hips between her thighs. His erection rubbed at her core, impeded by her shorts. Still, it was one of the most erotic things she'd experienced. The feel of him pushing his hand down the outside of her thigh, gripping her other knee and shoving it up, guiding it around his hip, worked a shudder through her system.

His mouth left hers, and he nipped his way along her jaw, scraping his teeth over her skin.

"Tell me, Phoebe. Tell me you want me to make love to you," he urged, his cheek pressed to hers, his breath caressing her ear, his voice strained. "I need you so much, love. Please say yes."

"Yes." She moaned and dug her fingers into his shoulders. She was still in control of her body, no fangs, no aching gums or burning eyes. Oh, she wanted him. But she was prepared this time. She could handle it.

He reared back, peered down at her, his expression almost a comical mix of disbelief and hope. "Yeah?"

She looked up at him, and nodded, too overcome with need to offer a smile of reassurance. "Yes."

His expression turned fierce, hinting at the floodgate of desire breaking within him. Phoebe reveled in it.

Now he swooped. Now he took. Now he demanded.

Her clothing was suddenly gone, vanished in the blink of an eye. Nothing separated them now, and the smooth heat of him pressing all along her body sent the last of her thoughts winging away.

This. *This* was need. *This* was desire. This was *life*.

Passion rode her, swept her up, sent her soaring. His mouth seized hers, laid claim to her soul, as he urged her legs to tighten around him. He rocked his hips against her, sliding the thick head of his erection along her damp cleft, back and forth, teasing her. But she was already wet, already eager, and his gliding thrust was slick. He moaned, deep in this throat, the sound rumbling up to caress her lips.

As the broad head of his arousal poised right at her entrance, he stopped. "Phoebe."

Her eyelids fluttered open, and she stared up into brilliant blue.

"Remember what I said last night," he prompted. She swallowed, struggling to think, struggling to push beyond the primal hunger driving her now. "You are mine, yeah?"

She searched his eyes. He was resolved in this. He would go no further until he was satisfied with her answer.

"Yes," she said.

"And you want this?"

"Yes."

His eyes narrowed. His face was beginning to show the strain, but he wouldn't relent. "Ask."

She sucked in a sharp breath. But she couldn't look away. He flexed his hips, and his rigid flesh nudged at her. She quivered.

"That's not fair," she complained.

"Ask," Sebastian insisted.

She narrowed her eyes. But when he began to pull back, she tightened her arms and legs around him and growled. *Her* terms, she told herself. "Take me," she demanded.

One corner of his lips curled up. "We're gonna have to work on those manners, love."

"Sebastian," she snapped.

His jaw tightened. His eyes flickered black. The scent of blood took her by surprise. Gasping, she gently pulled her claws from his shoulders. "Oh, Sebastian! I didn't mean to—"

He captured her mouth, searing her with a

staggering kiss. For a moment, he let her surface. Just long enough to growl, "Never apologize for your passion, Phoebe. I want it all." And then he dragged her back under.

Sebastian slowly began to fill her then, inch by unhurried inch. And, once he'd seated himself as deep as he could go, he gave one last push.

"*Qui et illisium speccaté*," he vowed, solemn. *Now and forevermore.*

Phoebe's eyes all but rolled back in her head. And then he began to move. Not a pounding, slamming urgency as she'd expected. As she'd thought she'd needed. But languorous, decadent thrusts designed to build pressure, build and build and build until a conflagration erupted to brand her as his and to consume her.

He captured her left wrist, pushed it slightly above her head on the bed. His hips continued to pump, his strong back to flex in long, slow, wondrously sensual thrusts. As he moved deep inside her, relentless and demanding, he slid his hand over her palm, laced their fingers together, and held tight. His big body flexed and moved over hers, sinuous and powerful. He left off kissing her, but only for a moment, only long enough to sample her chin or nip below her ear. But then he'd be right back, drinking in her soft cries, like a greedy man happily drowning in the finest wine.

His kisses were addictive. She couldn't get enough. She rocked her hips in time with his, so close to tipping over that glorious edge. So close she thought she might lose her mind. Yet not quite there.

With his free hand, starting at her jaw, Sebastian caressed his way down her side, pausing at the drugged pulse at her throat, at the curve of her collarbone, at the smooth skin over her heart. He teased her nipple, rolled it, rasped his thumb over it, and then danced his fingertips over her ribs. He explored the sensitive spot at the front of her hip and slid his hand along the top of her leg, smoothed it over her knee, then swept up the back to grip her thigh. The heat of his palm sent tingles rushing through her. The calluses on his hands abraded her nerves and made her blood sing.

And all the while he continued to move inside her. Sure, masterful strokes. Melding them together in an undeniable bond of intimacy she was sure she would take to her grave. Fanning the flames, feeding the fire. He murmured words of encouragement and praise against her lips, her neck, her shoulder. The scent of him intoxicated her, so masculine. Spicy and seductive.

Phoebe teetered closer and closer to losing control. She tried to hang on, struggled desperately for purchase on the slippery slopes of her hunger. But it was no use. Just when she thought she could ease back, just when she thought she'd be able to steal a second to level out and think, or catch her breath, Sebastian would twist his hips just right, or push particularly deep, deep enough to drive her into the mattress and send a cascade of sparks showering through her belly. He'd thrum her nipple again, or…or dear heaven, he'd caress her in the hundred and one other ways he seemed to savor. Seemed to crave.

He demanded a response from her with every touch, wouldn't relent until he'd wrung something from her. A moan. A gasp. A sigh. A whimper. A shiver.

And all the while, he maintained the contact of their clasped hands. Like a lifeline. Like a focal point that kept her grounded, kept her hyper aware of everything else he was doing to her body.

His hot, ragged breath puffed in her ear. He nipped her earlobe into his mouth, raked his teeth over it, suckled it.

"Damn it, Phoebe," he growled, hoarse, his breathing heavy. "Don't hold back. Give me everything. I want *all* of you!"

He reached between them then and set to stroking the tiny nub of sensitive nerves, pressing it against his cock where it drove in and out of her, unrelenting in his seduction. He rubbed that pleasure point as if it had become the center of his world, gentle but ruthless, with exquisite care but with relentless determination.

"Please, love," he whispered, his cheek pressed to hers now. "You're driving me crazy. I don't know how much longer I can hold out."

As if his words were the catalyst her body had been waiting for, Phoebe exploded in his arms, convulsing as he impaled her on his rigid length. She pressed her mouth to his shoulder to stifle her cries as wave after wave of sensation washed through her. Sebastian stiffened above her, groaned like he was dying. Like he'd found Nirvana.

Deep inside, she could feel him jerking and pulsing, feel the wet heat of his orgasm rushing into her. He buried his face in her pillow and roared as he dug his fingers into her hip, tightened his hand on hers, holding her in place as he continued to pump for a few seconds more.

And then, muscle by muscle, he relaxed into her. She kept her legs around his hips, kept her free arm around his neck, and basked in the feel of his body pressing into hers, crushing her into the mattress. Only when he began to stir did she realize what she'd done.

She'd bitten him.

In fact, her fangs were still embedded in his shoulder. Her first instinct was to jerk her head away. She caught herself just in the nick of time. *Stupid. Stupid.* She could have left horrid slashes through his skin like that. Puncture wounds were bad enough. Carefully, praying to God he wouldn't notice, she slid her fangs from his flesh. His big body shuddered.

He rose, bracing his weight on his elbows. The shift in his position reminded her that he was still buried deep inside her.

And still hard.

Warily, she watched him search her face. And, as he stared into her burning eyes, an impossibly wide smile blossomed across his face. One that made her tremble.

"You bit me," he said at last.

She could only stare up at him, cornered. Trapped.

But he hadn't sounded angry. Or shocked. Or disgusted. Or any of the other things she'd feared he might experience. Instead, he sounded almost…proud. Definitely happy. She frowned. And deep inside of her, his erection jerked, pulsed. He slid slowly out of her. But then, taking her completely by surprise, he pushed back inside, flexing his hips, grinding into her.

No, not the reaction she'd been expecting. Not at all. Strange man.

No, strange demon, she corrected.

"I didn't," she denied. Knee-jerk reaction. Pure and simple. When cornered, deny, deny, deny.

He turned his head and surveyed the tiny holes in

his shoulder. Oh, yeah, that was a whole lotta pride in his grin. She couldn't pretend otherwise. And his reaction was doing strange things to her insides. When he finally turned back to her, he looked like he was about to crow.

"Oh, yes you did." With a jerk of his head toward the shoulder—and the still bleeding wounds—in question, he gloated, "Even you can't ignore the evidence."

Cursing herself, she glanced, unwilling, at the injuries she'd unwittingly inflicted. Two small punctures. Still seeping just a teensy bit of blood. Only a fool would continue to pretend they didn't exist. But to acknowledge them meant to acknowledge everything she'd been taught to conceal.

"I'm so sorry," she whispered, unable to look him in the eyes. "I didn't mean to...it'll never happen again!"

"Like hell it won't!" he all but bellowed.

Startled, she gaped at his wrathful face.

"You *will* bite me again, whenever the mood strikes. Am I clear? I want *everything* from you, Phoebe. I told you that. I want it all. I won't settle for anything less."

Phoebe peered up at him. She couldn't even process what he was saying. How could he want that? How could he look at her without revulsion? How could he—

She was saved from having to reply, saved from lending voice to the incredulous questions circling her befuddled brain, by a loudly cleared throat, just outside the tent flaps.

"Phoebe?" Ricardo called again. "Breakfast is

getting cold."

The reality of the situation came crashing down on her. Frantic, she began pushing at Sebastian's shoulders, but he refused to be dislodged.

"I'll be right there," she called out, glaring up at Sebastian.

A muffled muttering could be heard, and then Ricardo's footsteps faded away.

"Let me up," she insisted.

"Not until you tell me you understand."

"No, I don't," she snapped. But she hadn't meant about his orders for her to bite him again, though she didn't exactly understand that part either.

No, what she didn't understand was...any of it. Her reactions to him. What had driven her to bite him? What was so messed up inside her that she could actually grow fangs, let alone sink them into someone...into him? Why? Why had she given in to this overwhelming, illogical need to...to brand him this way, mark him as hers? Like she were some kind of territorial...*thing*?

What's happening to me?

"You bit me, Phoebe. And you'll do it again. I demand it," he barked, easily subduing her when she tried once more to shove him off.

Tears, unbidden and unwanted, blurred her vision. She turned her head away and squeezed her eyes closed, willing herself not to let them fall. But she could do nothing about the way her breathing hitched.

"Damn it, Phoebe, hold still." He jerked both her hands above her head, pinned them down. Consternation passed over his features. And he asked softly, too softly, "Do you know why you bit me?"

She couldn't act like she hadn't understood him, couldn't pretend his question hadn't hit her like a ton of bricks.

She blinked, forcing herself to look him in the eye. It was the least she could do after what she'd done. She shook her head, miserable.

"You bit me, love, because you are marking me. Claiming me as your mate. As you are mine."

"Mate?" Incredulous, she blinked up at him. That was the last thing she'd expected to hear. "No." She shook her head again, harder this time. "That's…that's just ridiculous. You say that as if we were a couple of—"

"Demons," he supplied, unhelpfully.

"I'm *not* a demon," she snapped. "You are, but I'm not."

He frowned down at her, cocking his head to the side. "Why can you accept that I am, but deny it in yourself?"

"I…I don't know what you're talking about." God, she was starting to sound like a broken record. A lying, broken record. But she couldn't face the ugly truth. Couldn't accept that she—

Heaven help her, she couldn't even *think* the possibility in her own head. "And I didn't mark you as my…as a mate. I didn't."

"Yeah? Well these bite marks say otherwise. You marked me as yours. You laid claim to me, loud and clear." Damn him, why wouldn't he stop grinning like an idiot when he said that?

She shook her head, opened her mouth. But nothing came out. And so she snapped her mouth closed, pressed her lips together tight lest she do something really stupid. Like agree with him.

"Don't you think it's about time, all things considered, that you tell me what you are?"

Oh, he asked that question so calmly. Like he was suggesting a stroll in the park.

A question she'd spent the better part of her life running from, hiding from. Denying.

Even now, coward that she was, she still couldn't cop to it. Not even when faced with irrefutable proof. She jerked her hands free, gritting her teeth when she realized the only reason she'd managed it so easily was because he'd allowed it. Phoebe gave his shoulders one last good slap.

"Get off me," she demanded, pleased when her voice neither trembled nor broke. "Ricardo will come back, and next time he'll come inside after me."

"This conversation isn't over," Sebastian warned.

"I can't do this right now." Her voice broke, there at the end. Shame flooded heat into her cheeks, and she looked away.

Heaving a deep sigh, Sebastian rolled to his side of the bed, sprawled flat on his back, leaving her cold and vulnerable. Exposed. She scrambled from the bed. He pushed up on his elbows and watched her through narrowed eyes as she jerked the doors to the wardrobe open. The tears were back, worse than before. Careful to keep her back to him, she brushed them away with the back of her hand and snatched blindly at the first thing her fingers brushed.

"Fine. We won't do this now. But mark my words, sweetheart, we *will* be doing this. We will be having this conversation…soon. I've respected your wishes and held off long enough."

Phoebe jerked on a bra and underwear. She tugged on a shirt, getting it all twisted up so she had to stop and untangle herself before she could get her arms in the proper holes. She held her tongue as she wrestled with pants and socks and boots. She struggled with the clasp of her father's watch, and fresh guilt swamped her. She'd betrayed the promise she'd made him. She'd given her secret away, even if unintentionally.

She could *feel* Sebastian watching her, and the weight of his stare made her fingers clumsy.

As she marched toward the tent flap, he called out, "Phoebe?"

Against her better judgment, she halted in her tracks and spun around. "What?"

"You need to wait for me."

"Why?" She crossed her arms, her chin setting mutinously.

"Well, for starters, there's that pesky little agreement we have where you don't go anywhere without me." There was that double damned wicked grin again. "And besides, you might want to give yourself an extra minute or two before going out there."

She ground her teeth. What was he playing at now? "Because?"

"Because, love, your eyes are still black."

Chapter Thirteen

Sweat trickled like a steady stream down Sebastian's chest, ran like a river between his shoulder blades. He tipped the canteen to his lips and took a long draw of luscious, ice cold water. The sun beat down on his face. Once he'd drained the canteen, he lowered it to his lap, conjured it full once more, and screwed the cap back on.

He'd been sitting here for the last three hours or so, watching as Phoebe sifted through a pile of recently unearthed...junk. He couldn't make heads or tails of most of it, though she seemed to know exactly what every little chip was. He shook his head and watched her lift a shard of pottery into the light, watched her tilt her head as she meticulously studied it from every angle. Her face shone with wonder.

Give the woman an oasis in the jungle, a tent full of modern amenities, any comfort she could imagine with just a wish, and did he get so much as a thank you? A well done? An, *"Oh, Sebastian, you irresistible, sexy stud! You shouldn't spoil me this way"*?

Nope.

Nothing but complaints. In his head, he recited her arguments in a mocking, scornful tone. *"You can't do this, Sebastian." "This doesn't belong in a jungle, Sebastian." "Change it back, Sebastian."*

Ugh! He could pull his hair out.

So much for luxuriating in a well-satisfied post-coital glow.

How did one go about pampering a mate when she refused to be pampered?

Grinding his teeth, he scowled as she lovingly set the shard aside and picked up another piece of broken clay. His eyes narrowed. He should have conjured the damned tent full of dirty, old, broken pots. Then, just maybe, she might have gifted him with a smile.

Why was his mood so damned sour? Any other guy would be sitting on cloud nine, grinning like a loon and whistling a happy tune, after a wakeup call like he'd gotten this morning. He should have been whistling right along with them. After all, it had been, hands down, the best sex he'd ever experienced. As old as he was, that was saying something. And, she'd bitten him, marking him as her mate. He couldn't be happier about that.

No, it was what had come after that had pissed him off. And the more he thought about it, the angrier he got.

Her tightlipped resistance had snapped his last nerve. The way she acted sometimes...if he didn't know better, he'd swear she had no idea herself.

Frowning, he studied her again, only this time he tried to fit the puzzle pieces together in a different order. What if she *didn't* know? What if *she* had no idea what she was?

He scowled now, his focus drifting away. Was it possible? She'd been raised by a Guardian. Surely he would have—

Sebastian shook his head. His thoughts started to circle back on themselves. Maybe he needed to look beyond Phoebe for the answer. What if the Guardian himself hadn't known, hadn't realized he'd married and mated a demoness? What if he hadn't known he'd sired one, was raising one?

By all accounts, her father had been human. Completely human. And Phoebe herself displayed normal human traits. Hell, she even smelled human. But what if Phoebe's mother had hidden the truth from her husband? What if...

It was, he supposed, possible. After all, Kyanna's entire family had been Guardians and, according to Kyanna, half the things recorded in the precious books passed down generation to generation had been wrong. Or missing vital information. Humans—Guardians—didn't exactly have an all access pass to Hell, at least, not one with round trip tickets.

And what better place for a demoness to hide than with a human already bent on hiding something?

It stood to reason there'd be a lot of room for error on her father's part. Whether he knew about his wife—and his daughter—or not.

Sebastian rubbed his hand along his jaw, scratched his chin. What if Phoebe truly didn't understand what was happening inside her own body? The reason her eyes changed? The way her ears drew to points when she got really, supremely pissed off? The sexy little fangs? Yeah, he'd gotten a good look at them that night on the couch, though he was pretty sure she didn't know he'd seen them. And he'd gotten a damned good look at them as she'd slid them out of his shoulder. He got hard just thinking about them, about the way they felt.

But how could her father not have known? How

could he have lived with Phoebe's mother for—for what? years?—and not have realized, not have had even the slightest inkling? Or raised Phoebe and not have had some sign? Some clue? Which circled to the question of how her very presence had been masked so well?

She didn't seem to have any abilities either. At least, if she did, he'd never, not once, seen her use them. Not even when her own life had been in danger. She didn't radiate energy, not that he could tell. Though he'd be anxious to know what Gideon had to say about that. That was, after all, Gideon's gift—the ability to detect energy. Was it possible—

A terrified scream pierced the air. Sebastian shot to his feet, his focus cutting to Phoebe. But she was already in motion, sprinting up the steep steps of the ancient pyramid so fast her feet were a blur. Up above, a worker dangled precariously at the edge of a huge cut stone. They'd cautioned the workers about getting too close to the edge of the stones. Apparently, someone hadn't taken the warning to heart.

The sight of her running at top speed caused Sebastian a split second of surprise, giving Phoebe a head start. One she didn't need. She was already at the top of the ruins before he could blink.

How—

No. Now was not the time to ask how. Now was the time to move. Without giving it a second thought, he shimmered to the top of the ruins just as Phoebe, laying flat on her stomach at the edge of a massive stone slab, was dragged toward the edge, pulled down by the worker's weight. She'd stretched as far as she could go, and her grip on the worker's hands was beginning to slip. Instead of scrambling for purchase as she should have done, she stretched, securing a tighter hold on the flailing man, which, of course, dragged her even farther over the edge until she hung by her hips.

Cursing, Sebastian grabbed hold of the first thing he could get his hands on—the waistband of Phoebe's pants. He hauled her back, then, arms wrapped around her waist, lifted her clear of the ledge. The worker came right along with her. Sebastian's strength was great enough that their combined weight barely caused him any strain. No, his heart raced for another reason all together.

The sight of her hanging head down over the edge of that nearly sheer rock face would have given him a coronary, had he been human.

Gritting his teeth, he dragged her to safety, inadvertently pulling the worker along with her. Once they were back on stable ground, a safe distance from the edge, he dropped her on her butt. The worker landed beside her. And Sebastian lost the fight. He sat on his ass, hard, and fisted his hands in his hair, half a second away from pulling it all out by the roots.

By the saints! If he'd been a second later in grabbing her, she could have been dragged right over the edge. She could have died.

The urge to grab her up and shake the living daylights out of her slammed into him. Fury as he'd not known before rocked him. He sat there and breathed deeply—in, out, in, out—so that he didn't do something he'd only end up regretting later.

The worker leaped up, and a furious spat of Spanish poured forth. He made the sign of the cross, over and over, spewing prayers for deliverance from evil as he backed away, the word demon upon his lips. Sebastian rolled his eyes. The worker raced for the stairs and flew down them, almost as fast as Phoebe had ascended them.

"Damn it," Phoebe snapped, pushing herself to her feet. She dusted her ass off, and then slapped her palms to her hips as she glared down at him. "Well, that's just great! I hope you're happy now."

Sebastian could only blink up at her and sputter. And then he saw red. In a flash, he was on his feet and had his hands manacled around her shoulders. Unmindful of anyone else that might be watching, he jerked his energy in, centered his focus—or tried to anyway—and shimmered them away.

The moment they solidified, he released her and stormed off. He heard her gasp and swear somewhere behind him. But he was too angry to care, too mad to stop.

"Where are we?" Phoebe demanded.

He ignored her and kept right on walking. How dare she be mad? How *dare* she take that tone with him? She'd put herself at risk. And he'd just saved her life. *Maybe.* But did he get a thank you? Hell no. In all likelihood, she would have plummeted to her death. *Possibly.* But who the hell knew? Because she wouldn't discuss jack shit with him. Oh no. He was just supposed to fall in line, take the pat on the head like a good little demon and not ask any fucking questions.

When he reached the line of trees bordering the meadow, he spun around and stormed back, just as worked up on the second pass as he'd been for the first.

Well, no more. This conversation was overdue. Long overdue. And he'd be damned if he let this go on a moment longer. They were going to have it out.

Right here.

Right now.

Just as soon as he calmed down. Just as soon as he could talk to her without feeling the need to shake her senseless and scream bloody murder. Just as soon as he could breathe again.

Just as soon as the thought of her dangling over that ledge didn't kick him in the balls.

He reached her side, took one look at her, and then spun back around and marched off once more. It took two more passes before he didn't fear for her safety. But, just as he reached her side, determined to have this out in a calm and reasonable manner, she stepped into his path.

"What the hell do you think you're doing?" She had the audacity—the sheer nerve—to glare at him. "Where are we? You know what, forget it. I don't care. Just take me back."

Blood. To. Instant. Boil.

"Hell no!" he shouted, inches from her face.

But instead of backing down, which would have been the smart thing to do, she got up in his face and yelled right back. "Yes!"

"I'm not taking you anywhere until you tell me what the hell you are."

"I don't know," she screamed. And the moment the words left her lips, her eyes flew wide, and she stumbled back a step, as if he'd just sucker punched her.

Her mouth fell open, and she staggered back another step, sucking in a sharp breath. She jerked her hand up to cover her mouth, but it was too late.

Sebastian pulled up short. His lips parted, and his temper slowly leached away. So she *didn't* know.

"Take me back," she whispered.

"No."

"I'm not going to discuss this, so you might as well take me back now."

"No."

"Damn it," she exploded. "I have to go back. Now. These people are a superstitious lot. I'll be lucky if half my crew doesn't desert before we make it back to camp."

"Is that the excuse you're going with this time?"

"Excuse? It's cold hard fact."

"Be that as it may, we aren't going anywhere until we get a few things clear."

"There's nothing to get clear. You need to take me back." She turned and stomped away, giving her attention to the meadow. "Where are we anyway? This place looks like a war zone."

"That's because it was."

She shot an inquiring glance over her shoulder as she came to stand beside a crater the size of a small car. Grass and a few wildflowers had begun to grow in the pit, but it, like numerous other areas in the meadow were still recovering from the vicious battle. A battle between the Fallen, a flock of angels, and a nest of demons. A battle that had nearly cost Sebastian his wings, and the Slayer his woman and his life.

Sebastian gritted his teeth and strove for patience. She was trying to deflect the conversation, but it wouldn't work. Not this time.

She glanced up, scanned the tree line, took in an area over to the west where a towering forest had been sheared down to stumps. Nearby, what had once been a massive boulder now lay in shattered, ragged pieces. A short distance over, stretches of scorched earth had started to come back. Tender shoots of green had already started to form a blanket, decorated with tiny blossoms. Even the sight of nature's resiliency wasn't soothing his ire.

"What?"

"We're in the Rockies, in a meadow near the Slayer's cabin. The battle happened not quite a year ago between a group of Stolas's minions, a contingent of Michael's flock, and us, the Fallen. There were no real winners, though Stolas's followers took an ass whooping. Now, I'll tell you what we *are* going to discuss."

She turned to face him, squared her shoulders, fire glinting in her stare. But he cut her off before she could blast him. "We're going to discuss you being...not human."

The wind got sucked right out of her sails. She shook her head. "I am hu—

"Enough," he roared. Immediately, Sebastian closed his eyes and drew a deep breath. Calmer, he looked at her and tried again. "Enough. You aren't fooling anyone anymore, sweetheart. I know you're a demoness."

Not exactly the appropriate term, but he figured she'd object far less to demoness than to the term demon spawn, though that was probably just as accurate, or at least closer to the truth. The term Halfling was generally used when referring to someone of human and angelic descent. What was the correct term for human and demon mix? Not full-fledged demon spawn. Demonesses were rare enough. But a female demoness of mixed race? Unheard of.

Spawnling was the best he could come up with.

As it was, she flinched. Why did she look so...so wounded?

"Phoebe," he said, and started for her, hands held out to capture hers.

But she jumped away like a scalded cat and thrust her hands behind her back. She looked to his shoulder, the one she'd left her mark on, and then she turned her face away. As if she couldn't stand the reminder of what she'd done. Of what she was. Beneath his shirt, the already healed wounds gave a slight throb, one that resonated in his balls.

"Sweetheart, you are a Spawnling."

She hung her head, her shoulders drooped.

"Is that what they call it?" she whispered. She sounded...broken.

His heart twisted.

Determined, he strode forward and wrapped her in his arms. She was limp as a noodle at first. But then, by slow degrees, she found her spine. Her arms went around his waist, and she turned her face into his neck. And then she was holding him tight. So tight. As though he were the only thing stable in her world. He couldn't even begin to describe the sensation it caused. It floored him and left him feeling invincible.

"I'm a monster," she breathed, the confession torn from her like the blackest of sins admitted to a judge and jury.

"No," Sebastian said against her hair, pulling her closer still. "No. You're still you, sweetheart. Still Phoebe. This is just a part of you."

She began to shake her head and draw away, but he captured her face in his hands, forced her to look at him.

"You *are* still you." He peered hard into her eyes. "You. Are. Phoebe. *My* Phoebe." He pressed a quick kiss to her lips to silence her when she made to object. "You are *my* mate, just as I am yours. I will not let you deny it again. And I will not let you go through this alone. I can help you. You just have to let me."

Chapter Fourteen

That evening, the moment they arrived back at the nearly deserted camp, Ricardo shot Sebastian the stink eye and pulled Phoebe aside. Sebastian waited by the campfire, watching as Phoebe engaged the old guide in a heated discussion. In the flickering golden light, she looked like a pagan goddess. She might still be unsure of herself, and of what she was—he'd barely been able to extract anything but the bare bones of information from her—but she stood her ground with the old guide, and Sebastian couldn't be prouder of her. As she pushed her glasses back up the bridge of her nose with one finger, his groin tightened painfully.

At last, Ricardo hugged Phoebe and patted her head. Just the way Sebastian imagined a father might do. With one last angry glance in Sebastian's direction, Ricardo disappeared into the shadows at the edge of camp. Phoebe returned to Sebastian's side.

"It was even worse than I feared. We haven't lost half the workers. We lost all of them. Well, all of them except for Ricardo and Marco."

Now Sebastian turned suspicious eyes to the lone man sitting beside an empty tent not far away.

"Why is he still here?" he asked Phoebe.

She glanced over. "Ricardo said Marco fears his wife—should he return empty handed—more than he fears some demon."

Sebastian continued to watch Phoebe's remaining crewman, until Phoebe elbowed him. "Knock it off, or you'll scare him away too. Tomorrow we'll go back to the dig site we worked at today. Dad's journal indicated something of importance was concealed somewhere around there. I'm headed to bed. It'll be an early start again tomorrow."

She didn't wait for him. Instead, she rose and crossed the small clearing, not bothering to look to see whether he followed or not. Phoebe disappeared inside the tent. Sebastian shot one last glance at the remaining crewman, who still idled outside his own tent before following her. Man, right about now he was wishing he could use a massive pile of ward stones to liberally pepper this campsite. He didn't like the feeling that his mate was exposed and vulnerable.

Sebastian stepped inside the tent. She hadn't lit any of the candles. It made no difference, his night vision was excellent. Judging by the pile of clothing folded neatly on the chair, she'd already changed at land speed record. He moved toward the bed, undressing as he went. And, as he climbed into bed, the small mound on the other side of the mattress shifted, moving closer to the edge. Any closer to the edge, in fact, and she ran the serious risk of falling out of bed.

Sebastian let out a long sigh.

"Phoebe?" He sank back into the thick mattress and was met with silence. But he knew she was still awake. No one could have fallen asleep that quickly. "I meant what I said earlier, in the meadow. I'll help you anyway I can. I'll even take you to meet the others, Gideon and Niklas and the rest. And their mates. We'll teach you all about what you are, help you learn the scope of your abilities, if you have any." He waited for a moment, and then rolled the dice. "We can help you learn to control them."

Silence.

Frustrated, he pushed a hand through his hair. "I know you said you don't want to learn, but you need to. Honey, don't you see? You're a demoness, a Spawnling, whether you like it or not. Whether you chose to acknowledge it or ignore it, facts are facts. Sooner or later, others are going to realize what you are too. And then you're going to end up with a target on your back. You need to be able to defend yourself. In order to do that, you need to know what you are and are not capable of."

And damn it, wasn't that another kick in the balls? He'd finally come to the realization that he was far more like Xander than he cared to admit. The instinct to protect was strong in him. All along he'd been preaching feminist equality in battle—probably just to get Xander's goat in all likelihood, when deep down his own nature demanded he shield his woman and keep her from harm at all cost.

He couldn't have it both ways. He couldn't promise to teach Phoebe what she needed to know to survive and then expect her to play the part of the good little woman who stayed out of harm's way. Besides, his mate wasn't the kind to play it safe, tending hearth and home, while he went on battling evil where he found it—hell, seeking it out—as though nothing had changed.

Instinct demanded he be the one to defend her. He should be the one stepping into the line of fire, not her. But that wasn't fair to Phoebe. And yet, was encouraging her to fight the right path for them either? Was he using this knowledge as a carrot, knowing how independent she was? Was it a lure to get her to own who she was?

Because, if she accepted who she was, accepted what she was, then she'd also have to accept that he was her mate.

How messed up was that? Maybe that was why he felt such an obsessive need to pamper her, to provide for her in every other way imaginable. Because, realistically, he knew he wouldn't be able to keep her out of the fray. And he wouldn't be able to be her shield. Not all the time, at least. Not if she was a Guardian. Not if she was a demoness. Her very nature would insist that she be front and center in whatever battles they fought, whatever war they waged. Side by side.

He was damned if he did, and damned if he didn't.

Her continued silence almost pushed him to his breaking point. "Damn it, Phoebe. Talk to me."

She was still. Too still. Was she even breathing? Why wouldn't she talk to him?

He opened his mouth—he wasn't sure what he'd been about to say—when she rolled to her back and huffed out a breath. But still she wouldn't speak. Stubborn female.

Sebastian stared at the dome of the tent, watched the shadowed paddles of the ceiling fan slowly circle, and racked his brain for something, anything to say that might get through to her. Why was she being so resistant?

Fear of the unknown could often be a powerful emotion.

Perhaps...

Perhaps, if she knew more about their world?

"Xander and Niklas were once the right and left hands of Lucifer. Xander was the great Slayer, Lucifer's personal assassin. He has the ability to tell if someone is lying. He told me once it feels as though a thousand spiders are crawling over his flesh when someone tells a lie near him. He also used to be able to form Hellfire, though he can't do that anymore thanks to a little...ah, bargain he made." He turned his head on the pillow, though Phoebe had made not a sound, moved not an inch, and he continued, "What's Hellfire, you ask? Well, since you're being so inquisitive, I'll tell you. Hellfire is basically a superheated plasma ball that will burn through anything."

Silence.

"What was that?" he asked again. "Oh, well, you see, plasma balls are a primary form of defense for a demon. Be sure to tell me if I repeat myself, or if you've already heard this before." He lifted his hand, held it palm up in the dark above them. "How a demon forms a plasma ball is... Hmm, well, I've never really thought about it before. I guess, the best way to describe it, since you asked so nicely, is you focus inward. Call forth the heat that always seems to hover, just beneath the surface. Pull it in, focus it"—he set deed to word—"send it spinning outward, toward your palm."

A second later, a seething mass of plasma spun itself into a ball. That ball, bright and hot, floated above his hand for a moment, just long enough for him to see she was watching his every move. With a snap of his wrist, a clench of his fist, he extinguished the ball.

"A few angels can do something remarkably similar, only they call it Angelfire. Instead of orange plasma, like ours, theirs are more of a pale blue. Almost, but not quite, white. Apparently, Gideon's mate Maggie—she's a Halfling, by the way—can form Angelfire. You see, sometimes, abilities are hereditary, and her father is—catch this—none other than the legendary Archangel Michael, and Angelfire is one of his little tricks."

He waited for a long moment, but she remained silent.

Where to go from here?

"So, back to Xander. He used to be a real badass," Sebastian went on, warming to his subject. "And then he met his match. He mated a Guardian."

Now he stopped, and he waited.

After a few minutes of weighted silence, Phoebe rolled to face him, though she still didn't speak. Sweet progress. He savored it.

"Kyanna is the Guardian of the Arc Stone. She's...*almost* as stubborn as you."

Was that...? Could it be? Had she just snorted?

"She's feisty and compassionate, smart, and very beautiful."

No doubt about it. She'd just snapped her teeth at him. He grinned. "And she has Xander wrapped irrevocably around her little finger. You two are going to be like two peas in a pod, I can see it already."

Still, she remained impassive.

Okay. What else?

"Niklas's mate Carly is human. She's a little spitfire. Fragile, but she has the heart of a lion, that one. You'll like her too. And Gideon's mate, as I mentioned earlier, is a Halfling."

Finally—*finally*!—she made a tiny sound. Half a murmur, really. Nearly imperceptible. But a sound, nonetheless.

He rolled to face her, at least a foot of empty bed separating them. But the intimacy of the dark made if feel like they were the only two people in the world.

"A Halfling is someone of human and angelic descent." Sebastian reached out cautiously, and brushed her hair over her shoulder, then slowly settled his hand flat on the bed between them. He didn't get bitten, so he figured he was on the right track. "I haven't met Maggie yet, but she must be very special if she managed to break Gideon's curse. Gideon was the Demon of Temptation, in case I forgot to mention it."

The shadows deepened between her eyebrows.

"Or maybe it was his curse you were wondering about." Sebastian reached for her once more, this time sliding the back of his finger along her cheek. "Gideon was cursed to never know the touch of another. Long story, but in a nutshell, it was a bad situation all around. Dangerous. That went on for nearly two hundred years. We all tried to help him find a way around the curse, but nothing worked."

Sebastian's focus drew inward for a moment as he remembered how close Gideon had been to plunging past the point of no return the last time Sebastian had seen him. "I must admit, I'm anxious to meet the Halfling."

Another sound, maybe a growl?

Sebastian licked his lips. What now? He was running out of Fallen to tell her about. "I bet you're wondering about War, right?"

Once more, the shadows between her brows deepened.

"Well, Mikhail—that'd be the Demon of War—is a difficult guy to know. Very antisocial. I'd like to say his bark is worse than his bite, but I'd be lying."

Crickets in the peanut gallery. Sheesh. Tough audience.

"Mikhail has the gift of healing. I think I already told you that, yeah?"

Another murmur. This one more definite.

"What most people don't know is that he used to be an Angel of Mercy, one of the first in fact. But humankind's selfishness and greed thinned that flocks' ranks. Now, there are but a few left. Anyway, Mikhail lost his faith. And when Mikhail fell, Lucifer was quick to pounce. He gifted Mikhail with his healing hands and—whenever Mikhail wasn't out inciting war on Earth, decimating the human population—Lucifer forced him to use those hands to revive humans unlucky enough to be dragged or coerced into Hell, over and over and over. Or he'd use those healing hands on the battlefield, reviving those that fought with the least amount of honor, the hardened killer element if you will, after which he would send them back into the world to wreak more destruction."

A small sound of distress escaped her. Sebastian reached for her before he stopped to think. The moment he slid her hand into his, he froze, cursing himself. Now she'd pull away. Now she'd sever the connection that had budded to life between them here in the dark.

But she wound her fingers through his instead and squeezed.

Breathing a little easier, Sebastian went on with his

stories. "Niklas was the first to break with Lucifer's rule. He'd had enough despotism and couldn't take it anymore. Maybe it was his ability that drove him to break with the dark prince."

Phoebe applied just the slightest bit of pressure. If he hadn't been waiting for it, he might have mistaken it for a twitch of muscle.

"Niklas is known as the Seer. He sees emotion, like a rainbow of colors, surrounding a being. Sort of like their aura. But more shifting, more fleeting. Fear, anger, lust, hope…he can see it all. Maybe that was what caused the rift. He could still see the good in people, their love, their hope—pretty much any positive emotion, even through the fear, no matter how hard that being tried to suppress it—even when that being couldn't decipher it for himself.

"Anyway, Xander and Niklas had forged a bond in Heaven, and that bond had only grown stronger in Hell as they both faced the same tyranny. Xander knew that Lucifer would send him after Niklas, and so, before the order could be issued, he found Niklas and together they approached a few others. Myself. Gideon and Mikhail.

"I guess you could say, we were all in the same boat. Or clinging to the sides of it anyway. So together, we escaped Hell. And since that day, we've worked to thwart any foothold Lucifer might be trying to gain here on Earth." He drew a deep breath. "And now we fight against Stolas, too."

He fell silent, trying to figure out where to go from here. It would be exceedingly helpful if she'd just tell him what she wanted to know. He frowned. Maybe she just didn't know what to ask.

"Every demon has some kind of ability." Was this the right path to take? He wasn't certain. He didn't want to scare her into shutting down on him again, but he also wanted her prepared. Wanted her to know that if she did have some kind of special gift, that she wasn't alone.

"But it's different in every case. There are many, many abilities. But not every demon can do all things. For instance…shimmering. For the most part, all demons can shimmer. However, not every demon can travel between Earth and Hell. And certain species, like Ralsha for example, can't conjure. But some, like the Ralsha, can spit an acidic venom. Others, like some Animagi can emit poison from their horns. And Carpathï can secrete poison from their fangs during battle."

He paused, suddenly overwhelmed by the sheer amount of information she should probably know. "It'd be a damned sight easier if there was some book I could give you to read. Too bad Encyclopedia Britannica didn't come up with that version…everything you need to know about demons, A to Z."

That earned him a puff of breath. Great, now she was laughing at him. Sort of. Well, it was something at least.

At the end of his rope, he gave her hand a gentle squeeze. "Sweetheart, if there's anything you'd like to know, all you have to do is ask."

She remained quiet for so long, he feared he'd pushed her too hard too fast. But then her soft voice broke the stillness, and he could have shouted for joy. "Are there any others…like me?"

****

Phoebe waited with bated breath, heart in her throat. She couldn't believe she was even doing this, asking questions, talking about any of this. Her father must be rolling over in his grave right now. But she couldn't seem to help herself.

She fingered the scar on her throat with her free hand. He'd been correct when he'd said she'd have a target on her back. She already did. And people were lining up to take aim, it seemed. So he was right. She wasn't stupid. And she wanted to survive. She wanted to live.

So, she needed to know.

And to know, she would have to talk. She would have to acknowledge. She bit her lip and prayed her father, wherever he was, would forgive her for breaking her word.

"There are other demonesses," Sebastian began. Phoebe tensed, waiting for him to go on. Why did he sound so reluctant all of a sudden? "But there aren't many. Female demons are very rare."

"Why?"

"Well, no one really knows for sure. Due to the lack of female demons, male demons mate humans, though not usually with the sole purpose of begetting demon spawn, you understand. But sometimes—on rare occasions—it happens anyway."

"Why only on rare occasions?"

"Human anatomy usually isn't strong enough to withstand carrying demon spawn to term. And, for whatever genetic reason that spawn is, nine hundred ninety-nine times out of a thousand, male." He shrugged, but then his expression turned pained. "Because of their rarity..." He trailed off, his tone troubled.

She squinted at him in the darkness. "Sebastian?"

"Because there are so few female demons, they're often captured and…and held against their will. Most are kept secreted away. Bloody battles have been fought over those that have been found, entire legions wiped out either trying to keep a demoness or trying to steal one away."

Phoebe sat up and stared down at him, incredulous. "Are you kidding me?"

He sat up too, though he didn't scoot any closer, which was probably a good thing right now. She wasn't sure how she might react. On top of the wardrobe, the candles flared to life, illuminating the broad expanse of his naked chest. The sheet pooled low in his lap.

"In my entire life, I've only ever seen one demoness…besides you. I only caught a brief glimpse of her, just for a few moments. But I knew if I even acknowledged her, I'd be dead before I drew my next breath. She was a prisoner." He drew a deep, bracing breath. As if he feared her reaction. "Lucifer's prisoner. She was chained by the neck, wrists, and ankles to a wall in his personal chambers. She was very beautiful, noble and unbroken despite her circumstances."

Outrage boiled through her system. "Why didn't you free her?"

Now Sebastian seemed to weigh his words carefully. "Because those cuffs weren't coming off without a key. Lucifer kept that key on his person at all times. And—" Sebastian broke off, rubbed a hand over his eyes.

"And what?"

He searched her face, seemed to silently beseech

her to hear him out. "I was a different demon then, Phoebe, a hardened soldier who knew that to try to free the female would have resulted in certain, and very painful, death for me...probably before I'd have had the first cuff free. To my way of thinking at the time, no female was worth dying over."

The way he watched her gave her goose bumps. She found herself asking, "And now?"

"Now I know better. Now...now I have a female of my own."

Phoebe wrapped her arms around her waist and chewed on her lower lip. She couldn't deal with his claim right now. There was just too much to wrap her mind around. What he said about Lucifer killing him before he could free the female was probably true. But still, it bothered her that another of her kind would be treated like that. That *she* too could potentially be treated that way if she were discovered.

"How long ago?"

"Close to five hundred years, I guess."

She drew a steadying breath and tried to take all the passing years into account.

"I heard rumors that the female eventually escaped and slipped away to Earth," Sebastian said.

"What happened to her?" Was she still alive? Was there a possibility Phoebe might find her? Talk to her? Learn from her?

"I'm sorry." Sebastian shook his head. "I don't know."

Hope deflated, Phoebe sank back on the bed. She didn't resist when Sebastian settled beside her and drew her close. She even rested her head on his shoulder, settled her hand over his heart. The circle of his strong arms shielded her, and she felt…comforted. Safe.

The candles snuffed out, and darkness plunged them into that strange intimacy again. She found herself drawing slow designs on Sebastian's chest with light fingertips. But he didn't complain, so she didn't stop. She lay there for a long time, lost in thought. He must have understood she needed time to process all that he'd told her, because he remained silent.

"What if I don't have any special gifts?" She'd voiced the fear aloud before she'd thought to filter. Fear that she did have special abilities, or fear that she didn't? She wasn't sure yet.

Warm lips pressed to her forehead, and his arms tightened around her.

"Then you'll still be you," he whispered against her skin. He was silent for a moment, and then he added, his voice only slightly teasing, "Honestly, I don't think I'd mind at all."

"Why?"

"Because…if I'm being totally honest…if you don't have any gifts, then I can keep you out of the fighting, away from danger and safe. And I can continue to provide for you. Maybe someday you'll start to depend on me. Maybe you'll even begin to think of me as something you can't live without."

Phoebe caught her lip between her teeth and frowned.

I think that's what I'm afraid of the most.

Chapter Fifteen

When Phoebe woke the next morning, Sebastian was curled around her once more. He'd tossed his leg over her thighs sometime in the night, caged her in his arms. She didn't have to tug any sheets this morning to steal a peek; he'd kicked them off in his sleep. And his entire, very naked, very masculine body was on display for her viewing appreciation.

Still, she kept her focus above his neck. She remembered all too well the consequences of peeking. Look what had happened yesterday. No, no matter how much her body might be aching to melt into him, to wake him with kisses and see where things went, she couldn't give in to those urges. She had too much to get done today.

And until she got her seesawing emotions back under control, having sex with him was just a bad idea, plain and simple.

Carefully, she shifted and scooted until she'd managed to gain a little room. Then, before he could draw her back like he had the last time, she bolted from the bed and scurried for the stack of clothing she'd set out last night.

"Whaa? Hm?" His voice was groggy. He blinked at her, squinty-eyed, as he ran a splayed hand up the side of his face and into his wildly mussed hair. "Phoebe?"

She resisted the urge to shiver as the sound of his

voice stroked through her.

"Time to get up and get moving," she chirped with false cheer. Never mind the fact that it was still pitch dark outside and the jungle all around them was still asleep. She made short work of dressing, wound her hair up into a bun and shoved her glasses into place.

"I didn't hear Ricardo," he mumbled.

Throwing his arms wide, fisting his hands, Sebastian stretched, tempting her to look—to ogle—despite her resolve. She caught herself wavering, her focus slipping and sliding down that perfect chest, over those luscious abs, straight to his long, hard—

Her eyes snapped back to his face.

"Well, we're up early." *Perky, perky, perky.* Wait, no that didn't come out right. Or did it? *Ugh!* "I'll just go help Marco with breakfast."

"Damn it, just give me a second to wake up," he growled, grinding his palms against his eyes.

"No time to wait." She jerked the tent flap open. "Lots to do." And then she fled.

She couldn't face him this morning. It was even worse than yesterday, and that was right after they'd had sex, for goodness sake. Hot, impulsive, soul-searing sex. But somehow, the connection they'd forged last night was far more...personal. She'd finally acknowledge that she wasn't human. Not completely. Well, sort of acknowledged. She still couldn't come right out and say it. Not yet.

Besides, she had yet to uncover any of these magical gifts, so she wasn't sure how *not human* she was. And as far as the way her eyes went black, well, that was just...an anomaly. She wouldn't even think about the fangs yet. Because if she thought about the fangs, then she'd be forced to think about the biting. And then—

Nope. Not going there.

Phoebe bustled around the campsite, pleased to note Marco was already up and about. He'd already rekindled the campfire, and had a pot of coffee simmering, bless his heart.

"Good morning," she greeted him, doing her best to ignore the muffled cursing coming from her tent.

"Good morning," Marco replied with a bright smile.

"Is Ricardo up yet?"

"I hear him stirring. I think he went into the trees a little while ago." Marco pointed toward a tramped down path the men used when they slipped off to relieve themselves.

The sound of canvas slapping canvas drew her attention. She turned in time to see Sebastian step out. He paused there in the opening for a moment and took in the campsite in one sweeping glance. And then he pinned her with a look. One so intense, one so loaded, she forgot to breathe.

He crossed the clearing in long, purposeful strides that had her heart tripping double time.

"Marco already has coffee ready if you'd like some," she said, nerves making her palms begin to sweat.

And still he kept right on coming, uttering not a sound.

"Are you hungry?" Something hot flickered in his expression, and she trembled, scrambling for something to say, something to diffuse the tightness in her chest and the flutter much lower. "We have plenty of supplies. We could make—"

But he reached her side in that moment. Without saying a word, he thrust both hands up and captured her head, sinking his fingers into her hair, completely dislodging her bun, and dragged her close. Her hands went to his wrists, then his chest. The heat of him burned through the cotton. His heart beat steady and strong against her palm. Sebastian tipped his head down until his face was inches from hers and stared hard into her eyes. Having lost the thread of her one-sided conversation, Phoebe forced a swallow as her mouth suddenly went bone dry.

And then he seized her mouth with his. Without uttering a sound, he demanded complete submission. Utterly ravishing her until she melted into him. The world spun for her, his lips, his hands, his body the only anchor she had. He kept her there, boneless and mindless, for a moment longer. And then he dragged his lips from her.

Still holding her in place, his eyes drilling into hers, he said, "You forgot my morning kiss, sweetheart." With his hands still holding her head, he looked down over her body, lingered on those achy places and made them throb, before meeting her stare again. "I should probably warn you. If you don't give me a kiss in there"—he jerked his head toward the tent—"then you better expect me to come looking for one. And just so you know, I don't care who's around, or how far I have to go to find you. I will get it."

He moved his mouth closer to her ear, sending shivers of pleasure coursing through her veins as his slightly bristly jaw rasped against her cheek. "You might not want to make me wait too long or"—he moved into her again, deliberately brushing an unmistakable, very large erection against her belly—"I could get a little carried away."

"You could get carried away in the tent too," she pointed out, breathless.

"I could." He grinned, wicked to the bone.

Sebastian released her abruptly, leaving her standing there on legs limp as noodles. "I think I'll take a cup of that coffee now," he told Marco.

Dazed, Phoebe accepted a mug of coffee from Marco. She watched as a smug Sebastian accepted his own mug and raised it to his lips. His eyes met hers over the rim of his mug. The look he sent her scorched her to her toes. So much heat rushed to her face she was a little surprised her head didn't simply explode. Shaking her head, she turned away, just in time to see Ricardo returning to camp.

Breakfast was silent and hurried. Phoebe didn't have much of an appetite and ended up pushing most of her food round and round her plate, staring moodily into the campfire.

"You need to eat," Sebastian said, drawing her attention.

She wanted to argue, but knew he'd only stated what she already knew. She had a long day ahead of her, best to start it on a full tank, so to speak. Yet her mind was too full to worry about how her belly might feel in a few hours.

"I'm done," she said as she stood up.

"Phoebe," Sebastian growled, then clamped his lips tight and shook his head.

After scrapping her plate into the fire, she dropped it along with her fork into the plastic tub they used for washing. Then Phoebe went to check her pack. As she dug through zippers to make sure her tools and supplies were in place, she tried to focus on the dig, on new ground she hoped to cover today, and on what she hoped to find.

But all she could do was keep replaying that kiss. Over and over and over. Damn him.

Angry at herself for letting him get to her like that and flustered that he could when no one else ever had before, she pushed to her feet and looked to the sky. The first rays of morning had begun to paint the heavens in a masterpiece of colors.

"Let's shake a leg," she snapped, not even trying to pretend to be cheerful any longer. "I want to head out in the next ten minutes."

The look Ricardo shot her said she'd be explaining herself pretty damned soon if she didn't settle down. So, taking a deep breath, Phoebe hiked the pack onto her shoulders and clicked the straps into place.

****

The trek had been long and rife with weighted silence. But once she was elbow deep in dirt and artifacts, Phoebe finally began to relax. Before long, she was humming, all thoughts of magical gifts and inescapable legacies happily pushed from her thoughts.

A hand on her shoulder startled her. She glanced up from where she was kneeling on a thick bed of large flat leaves—Sebastian's creation to pad her knees from the damp ground. He'd come up with the idea when she'd refused to let him conjure a more comfortable cushion for her.

He offered her a cantina. "Water?"

She knew what he was asking, as he'd made the

same offer several times already this morning. Iced tea. Gatorade. Lemonade. Anything she wanted. Anything at all. All she had to do was ask.

"Water's just fine," she said with a smile, accepting the canteen. "Thank you."

She tipped the tin to her lips and drank deeply of the ice cold, sweet water. And she suffered another pang of guilt when she remembered how she'd snapped and growled at him on the hike here.

He'd only asked simple questions, like why they'd made camp so far from their dig site. She hadn't needed to be so short with him when she'd explained their logic. How they'd had their camp overrun one night in the past and lost not only their supplies, but also all the artifacts they'd unearthed. And how it had been too dangerous to try to take the camp—and therefore the dig site—back. He'd fallen silent then, limiting his questions to inquiries about her physical needs. Was she thirsty? Hungry? Did she need a break? All inquiries had been met with curt negative responses until he'd finally given up all together.

And so she was trying to be extra nice now.

He arched a brow when she handed the canteen back. "Are you hungry? You hardly ate anything this morning."

"Not yet."

He didn't like that answer. She could see it in his eyes but, to his credit, he withheld any further comment as he turned away.

"Sebastian, wait."

He peered down at her, expression guarded.

She'd been out of line earlier—all morning really—and she knew it. "I'm sorry. I shouldn't have been so crabby with you today."

He considered her in silence, then nodded acceptance. "Give me some tools, show me what to do. I'm bored out of my freakin' mind."

She sat back on her heels. "I thought you were only along for security?"

"Trust me," he said, leering down at her now. "I've only ever lost focus on my surroundings once in my life…in my *entire* life. And since I don't think you intend to let me make love to you with an audience"— he shot a glance across the way toward Ricardo—"I think I can handle digging in the dirt and still manage to keep you safe."

Her cheeks flamed. Clearing her throat, she stood and brushed her knees off. After rummaging in her pack, she came up with a backup set of tools. She brought the items to Sebastian. Kneeling beside him, she began instructing him on what to do. She was more than pleased to note he was a careful, adept student.

Once satisfied he'd be okay on his own, she gathered her tools and went to another location a short distance away that she'd had her eye on. The soothing noises of the tropical forest eased her into the zone. She lost track of time, lost touch with reality as she worked to unearth the corner of what appeared to be a rough, wooden box.

Frowning, she dug deeper, brushing away dirt and debris. This wasn't an artifact. It wasn't even all that old. Excitement flooded her. Oh, she'd seen this type of box before.

She began digging faster. "Sebastian!"

He was at her side in a heartbeat. "What? What's wrong?"

She pulled the box free, held it up for his inspection as she brushed lingering dirt from the top. "Look!"

He frowned. "It's a box."

Phoebe was too caught up to be cautious, and she blurted, "My dad made this. I'd recognize his handiwork anywhere."

She immediately began prying at the top, only to let out a muffled curse as a tiny spike of wood punched through her skin. Gritting her teeth, she inspected the wound.

"Let me see." Sebastian took her hand. "It doesn't look like it went very deep, but we better clean it out. Just to be sure."

She knew better than to argue. Out here, even a tiny cut like this risked a very serious infection. Before she could tell him where the first aid kit was located in her bag, he conjured a small white tin case.

"Sebastian," she hissed, glancing over her shoulder. But Ricardo's back was still turned to them as he continued to plug away at his own little plot.

"Shh," Sebastian said, his attention on her thumb. "He's not paying any attention, and Marco is still back at camp. There's no one around to see but the monkeys, and they promised not to tell."

Chagrined, Phoebe sat back and watched as Sebastian administered to the miniscule wound as though he were performing major surgery.

"There," he said as he smoothed the last bit of white tape in place. "All better. Shall I kiss it too?"

"It wouldn't hurt anything," she said, taking them both by surprise.

His grin turned far too sensual for her comfort, and

he pressed his lips to the tape, lingering, holding her captive with his steady stare. But he didn't stop there. Slowly, deliberately, he moved to the tip of the next finger, and then the next. One after another. Brushing each tip clean, and then kissing each one in turn. And then he moved his attention to the sensitive skin of her palm, working his way to her wrist. Like he had all the time in the world and intended to spend every second of it turning her bones to jelly.

And then, somehow, his mouth was on hers. A lazy, erotic glide of tongue, a caress of lips. On and on it went. He'd just eased his hand up to cup her jaw when Ricardo cleared his throat behind them. Loudly.

Breaking apart, they both glanced up to see Ricardo standing there, a small trowel in one hand, the other fist perched on his hip. His expression was impassive.

"If you two are about done, I found something."

"What!" Her face lit up. "Where?"

Sebastian stood, offered a hand and helped Phoebe to her feet. She tucked the box beneath her arm, thanked him absently, and nearly ran to the area where Ricardo had been working, their kiss apparently forgotten already. Which chaffed, considering it had affected him so strongly he hadn't even heard the old guide approach.

Not good, dude. N. O. T. Good.

He made to follow her, but Ricardo stepped into his path. Sebastian narrowed his eyes at the man.

Ricardo didn't back down. A part of Sebastian admired the way the smaller man lifted his chin and demanded, "I want to know what your intentions are toward Phoebe."

That gave Sebastian pause. He felt like a potential date being drilled by a girl's father. All that was missing was the double barrel shotgun. Sebastian eyed Ricardo.

"I have only honorable intentions." He refused to elaborate, regardless of whatever admiration he may or may not feel. What was happening between Phoebe and him was their business.

"I know you are not engaged," the guide replied, his bushy brows drawn tight. "I know Phoebe. She would have told me before she just showed up with you."

Now they were getting into sticky territory. Sebastian debated how much to tell the old man. He knew Phoebe held Ricardo in high regard. Had seen the way the old man behaved with her. They were as close as family. As such, he didn't want to completely alienate the man either.

Ricardo solved the problem for him. "I know what you are."

What, not *who*.

Sebastian went very still. And he waited.

"You think me foolish? You think I'm some superstitious old man, like the rest? But I know the truth." Ricardo stood firm, showing no fear. "You *are* a demon. A *real* demon."

Sebastian tensed, his mind racing.

"But you are not like the others, the demons that came after her before. The ones that cut her throat," Ricardo said. That pronouncement drew Sebastian up short.

The man had looked after Phoebe, taken care of her, saved her life. Sebastian was grateful. He owed this man much. And so, he repaid that gratitude with honesty.

"I am demon. But I am penitent," he said at last. "I have broken with Lucifer and his ways. I seek redemption by sending others of my kind, those that would harm the innocent to Oblivion. I seek forgiveness."

Ricardo regarded him in solemn silence. At length, he nodded, apparently satisfied. "You are like her."

Now Sebastian frowned, all his protective instincts firing. "Like her?"

How much did Ricardo know? Could what he knew put Phoebe at risk? The thought of eliminating the old man didn't sit well. Sebastian hadn't taken an innocent life in nearly two hundred years, and Phoebe would suffer guilt and grief at his loss. But Sebastian would do it. To protect Phoebe, he'd do it.

"I knew her father." Ricardo paused, giving Sebastian a pointed look. "And I knew her mother, knew *what* her mother was. Your heart is good, like Phoebe's. Like her mother's."

Sebastian reeled at this new information. Not once had he ever considered Ricardo might have knowledge of Phoebe's mother.

Something of his surprise must have shown on his face because Ricardo went on, explaining, "My people believe in your kind. In demons and in angels. We know evil roams the Earth. Just as good does. But you…you are different. As was Danika. As is Phoebe."

"So you know what she is?" he asked cautiously.

Ricardo looked puzzled. "Yes."

"But you still treat her like a daughter?"

"Of course." Ricardo nodded. "Because she *is* like

a daughter to me."

"Did her father know what she was, what her mother was?"

"Yes." Sadness crossed those wrinkled features. "He knew. And he figured out that I knew...and he swore me to secrecy." He shrugged.

Ricardo turned to watch Phoebe. Her back was turned to them. She was on her knees industriously clearing away vegetation near the base of what appeared to be a short monument.

"I met Danika, Phoebe's mother, many years before Phoebe was born. She was already married to Raymond Mackenzie. I thought she was human. Years later, when Phoebe was a small child, there was an accident at one of the sites. Danika revealed herself to save Phoebe's life, and in doing so, she unintentionally revealed the truth of who she was. She also weakened the spell she'd used to dampen her abilities. Some kind of magic to mask her from others of her kind, she claimed. She swore me to silence and told me the spell was to hide her and Phoebe from other demons that might be looking for her. She said she would die if she were ever found that she'd be forced to go back to Hell, and so would Phoebe. That they'd be forced to go back as prisoners. As slaves."

Sebastian frowned. He'd never heard of such a spell before, but that didn't mean it wasn't possible.

Now that name on the other hand, *Danika*...

And the circumstances the woman had related. An unshakable chill skated down Sebastian's back. He felt sick to his stomach. Was it possible? He prayed not. Oh, how he prayed not.

"They left to go back to the states soon after. I

never saw Danika again after that summer. And Raymond refused to speak of her. Phoebe was so young the first time Raymond brought her back, after her mother had gone. Too young to be out here in the jungle, but there was no one left to care for her." Ricardo stopped, his expression sorrowful. He took his hat off, swiped a forearm across his brow and resettled the hat.

"Danika was a kind woman. And she loved that child something fierce. But Phoebe still blames her mother for leaving. Raymond Mackenzie is the only parent she remembers. Danika leaving like that left a hole in Phoebe's world. She's careful not to talk about it, but the girl's never recovered from it. And she worked so hard to fashion herself into what she believed Raymond would approve of."

"Phoebe loves you too," Sebastian said, dead certain.

A tender smile eased the old man's frown. "I know." But then that smile fell away. "If you are her mate, as I suspect, then you have to watch over her."

"What do you know of demon mates?" Sebastian watched the old man, suspicious now.

"I know only what Danika told me. That last summer, after I learned what she was, Danika confided in me, telling me about her world. I don't know why for sure. Perhaps it was because she knew Raymond would never pass the information on to Phoebe should something happen to Danika? Who is to say?"

The old man paused a moment, stroking his hand along the gray whiskers covering his jaw. Sensing there was more, Sebastian waited in silence.

"I believe maybe it was because she was lonely.

She loved her husband, and Raymond loved her. But, for some reason, he could never talk to her about what she was. She understood his fear, and his mistrust of her species. It hurt her, but she understood. I never did though. If a man loves his wife, he ought to love all of her. And, despite the fact that she was what she was, she was still a good woman, a loving wife and mother," Ricardo grumbled, clearly perplexed.

So Raymond had loved her, loved her but couldn't forgive her for being what she was? But he'd also been a Guardian, taught from birth to hate demons. Ricardo wouldn't have known that. Sebastian didn't even want to speculate over the fine moral line that Phoebe's father must have walked daily. To provide safe haven for the enemy. To never fully trust the woman you loved. To cherish and raise a child of that union. To raise a Spawnling to be the future Guardian.

Sebastian looked at the older man, letting him see the truth of his words. "Phoebe is my mate," he confirmed. "And I will guard her with my life."

A look of profound relief crossed the old guide's face. "Protect her from herself. She would die for those she loves. She nearly died to save me—that's how she got the scar on her neck. She would have given herself up to spare me."

"No one's ever going to hurt her again," Sebastian vowed.

Chapter Sixteen

Sïnsobar eased right up to the edge of the clearing. He peered through the foliage at the trio, the two males standing off in the distance talking, the female—his target—on her knees by the statue. So close he could snatch her away before Vengeance even knew he was there.

Phoebe carefully cleared debris from the base of the statue. He could sense the energy sizzling all around her now, and it gave him pause.

How was this possible? He'd not felt this from her when he'd taken her from the airport. Had she been under a masking spell of some kind? Had her abilities been bound?

He'd been told before that she was a Guardian right before his first attempted kidnapping. Not even when he'd touched her before had he felt anything. Not until Sïnsobar had replaced the camp cook yesterday.

Now?

Well, he'd have to be blind, deaf, and dead not to sense the power coming from her.

Stolas hadn't been happy to learn she was still out here, still digging away. Happy? Hell, he'd been furious. Sïnsobar had barely managed to talk him into one more chance.

And so Stolas had sent Sïnsobar after her one last time, to either capture her or kill her. He hadn't been specific on the why, just demanded she be taken out of the picture, one way or another. "Get her away from those damned ruins," had been his orders. And that was awfully curious, considering the demon prince usually preferred to add to his collection of female prisoners every chance he got. Yet Stolas seemed bent on this one's death. Sïnsobar's eyes narrowed, considering.

Why?

He felt the punch in the gut as a fresh wave of energy rolled from her without warning, and his focus shot back to her. What had caused this change in her? It was as if a veil had been lifted. A shield burned away. Nothing one moment, and then in-your-face power the next. If she'd been merely bound before, he should still have been able to sense *something* in her, no matter how miniscule. Bound, she just wouldn't have been able to use whatever that something was. It had to have been a masking spell. Or a powerful combination of the two.

He watched as she moved a small wooden box out of her way with a great deal of care. Then, after a moment more of study, she began tracing intricate symbols with her fingertips. Her lips were moving, as if she were reading to herself. He cocked his head, studying her a bit closer. There was just something about her…something *familiar*.

The energy buzzing from her steadily built. Pulsing and throbbing. He eased forward, drawn like a magnet, pulled by something else, something that grew by the moment deep in his gut. Something that had nothing to do with her power, but something he couldn't quite put his finger on.

Yet.

Excitement bubbled up inside him. There was nothing he liked better than a good puzzle. And Phoebe was fast proving to be a wonderful riddle. The more he was around her, the stronger the pull. Unable to help himself, he crept closer, careful to shield his own abilities. It wouldn't do to be discovered, not just yet. Too many interesting things going on around here to put everyone's guard up. Starting with the question that begged nearly as much attention as Phoebe herself. Why was Stolas so concerned about her digging around in some old rocks?

What's he so worried she might find?

Sïnsobar's brows drew together. He watched as she sat back on her heels, reached her arm straight out, and laid her palm flat upon the ancient, crumbling statue. He glanced over to see if Vengeance and the human had noticed. They were still deep in conversation, so Sïnsobar turned back to her.

She tipped her head forward and squinted at the writing on the stone monolith. And then she began to speak. Urgent words, her tone soft and low. If he hadn't been so close, he wouldn't have been able to hear her at all. As it was, he could only make out a few words here and there. And the hair on the back of his neck lifted. Chills skittered down his spine, and his skin began to itch.

Sïnsobar's eyes widened, and he sucked in a sharp breath. She was speaking Angelic. How—*where*—had she learned to read Angelic? But what truly shocked him was the fact that her short, buffed nails had just morphed into small black claws. Her fingertips had turned red...and not a flushed, human red. This was a deep crimson pigmentation—strikingly similar to his own natural color. The change had already overtaken her whole hand and was, even now, slowly working its way up her forearm. A defensive reaction common for a Carpathï.

Her eyes flew open, and for one startling moment, he thought she'd seen him. He stood there, poised on the verge of shimmering away, when he realized she wasn't actually *looking* at him. She appeared to be in some kind of trance. And her eyes were completely engulfed in black. She continued to speak and, as her lips moved, he caught a peek at tiny fangs.

Was it possible? Was she Carpathï, like him?

A Carpathï demoness.

Holy hell!

There hadn't been one of those since—

He sucked in a sharp breath and staggered back a step.

Danika.

His head swam. Before he could react, stone scraped stone, and something fell from a hidden compartment in the statue. Phoebe blinked as the item hit her lap, as if woken from a deep slumber. Frowning, she reached to scoop up the oddly shaped stone, only to drop it with a sharp cry.

Phoebe thrust her hand up before her and peered in wide-eyed shock at her appendage. She turned it over and gaped first at the back of her hand, then at her palm. At the sound, Vengeance and the human came rushing over. Sïnsobar melted back into the jungle, but he stayed close enough to keep an eye on the female. And he frowned. She'd looked…he wasn't sure. Stunned? Surprised? Maybe horrified? As if she couldn't believe her eyes.

But the moment the two males got close, Phoebe bounced to her feet and spun to face them, thrusting her morphed hand behind her. Right where he could see it, clear as day.

He swallowed, shook his head. Could it be possible? The odds were astronomical. And yet—

"What happened?" Vengeance demanded.

The male reached up and cupped her cheek, scanning her pale features. Protective instincts stabbed at Sïnsobar. He just barely managed to bite back the growl. He didn't know why, he certainly felt no physical attraction for her—which, given his own reputation was a puzzle, but he did know he didn't like seeing Vengeance touch her with such easy familiarity. Because of this startling discovery, he melted further back and gave himself a moment to regroup.

He'd just been surprised to learn she was Carpathï, that was probably all it was. She should be with her own kind. Not with one of the Fallen.

Feeling his system leveling out, Sïnsobar began slinking toward their camp. He sent wisps of energy to his bones, his muscles, his skin, his hair—not so much so fast that it might alert Phoebe or Vengeance to his presence, but enough to get the job done—morphing as he moved through the jungle. Within the space of a few more steps, he'd taken on the appearance of a human. One familiar to Phoebe. One she wouldn't think twice about getting close to. Marco, the camp cook.

And here he'd thought he'd be bored with his latest assignment. A demoness? A *Carpathï* demoness.

His grin grew.

Well how about that?

****

Sebastian stared at Phoebe, eyes narrowed. Something was wrong. She was pale, white as a sheet. And her gaze kept darting around, like a cornered rabbit. Perspiration beaded on her forehead.

"What did you find?" Ricardo asked, frowning.

"This," she blurted, thrusting a strange looking rock up in the space separating them with her left hand. "The inscription on that monolith was in Dad's code. I read it aloud, and a hidden compartment opened, and this fell out."

Sebastian scowled, thinking the heat, the lack of food, and the stress had finally gotten to her. "Sweetheart, it's just a rock."

"No," Ricardo said, taking the stone from her. "Look at the tool marks. It's been shaped."

Sebastian peered closer at the rock. He didn't see it. The damned thing was just a rock. What were they playing at? And why was she being so careful to keep her right hand tucked behind her back?

"Turn it over," Phoebe said.

Ricardo did as she asked and made a strangled sound in the back of his throat. The surface of the stone was studded with tiny bits of jewels. Chips of red and green and clear stones. They formed a pattern. And below the pattern, a strange groove was dug in deep. The whole thing was shaped like…like an arrowhead. A fist sized arrowhead.

Frowning, Sebastian held his hand out. Ricardo shot a glance at Phoebe. When she nodded, he passed the stone to Sebastian. The moment the old rock came in contact with his skin, Sebastian sucked in a sharp breath. Unpleasant jolts of power zapped him, shooting up his arm, vibrating with a shocking intensity, reminding him of how it felt when he'd tried to cross one of Kyanna's enchantments. It stood to reason that Phoebe's father, as another Guardian, would also be in possession of powerful angelic enchantments and have knowledge of protective stones, just as Xander's wife did.

"Look at the design, and the pattern. That was carved. The stones were arranged and set with some kind of adhesive. It was deliberately shaped that way."

Sebastian glanced from the rock in his hand to Phoebe. "What does it mean?"

She caught her lip. "I'm not sure."

Well, Sebastian was sure of something. She still hadn't brought that hand out from behind her back. What was she hiding?

"Here," she said, holding her left hand out. Yet another oddity, since he knew she was right-handed. "I'm going to take it back to camp. I want to examine it, compare these stones with my reference guide."

Sebastian handed back the stone, frowning. It couldn't be much past four in the afternoon. She'd never wanted to leave the excavation site so early before, regardless of what relic they'd found.

She cradled the stone against her stomach and scurried off. Sebastian looked to Ricardo. He seemed just as puzzled by Phoebe's behavior. And then Sebastian noticed the box near the foot of the statue.

For her to leave this behind? Now he *knew* something was going on.

He scooped the box up and shot another glance to Ricardo. Phoebe had already disappeared into the verdant undergrowth.

"Go after her," Ricardo instructed with a frown.

"I'll gather the rest and follow behind."

Sebastian didn't need any further encouragement. He shot down the path after her. Panic hit him like a wrecking ball. He should have found her by now. He raced on, leaves and vines whizzing by, roots tripping him.

Around a bend in the path, he almost crashed into her. She stood in the middle of the trail, shoulders hunched, head tipped down, her back to him.

"Phoebe." He panted, more winded by worry and fear than by his mad, headlong dash. "What's wrong?"

He grabbed her arm and pulled her around. She held the ancient stone in one hand and in the other…nothing. She held her hand, fingers splayed, at eye level.

Phoebe blinked up at him as if in a daze. And then she seemed to recall herself. A swift smile flashed at him. One so fake he couldn't believe she'd even think for a minute he'd fall for it.

"Wrong?" She shook her head and shrugged. Phoebe looked to her hand, and her smile slipped, just for a split second, as if she'd never seen that hand before. But then she held it up, wiggled her fingers for his perusal. "Nothing's wrong. See? I, ah, I just thought I'd chipped a nail. But nope. It's fine. My hand is just fine."

Sebastian frowned at her. He hadn't seen so much as a scratch on her. Yet he got the very real impression something had shaken her.

"Uh-huh." She was a piss poor liar. *Something* was wrong. And he would figure it out. "You left this behind," he said, holding the box up.

Her eyes flared wide, and her mouth fell open. "Oh

my goodness!" She snatched the box from him. "I can't believe I just... How could I have—"

She cut herself off, shook her head. Phoebe clutched the box to her chest and visibly forced herself to calm down.

"Thank you," she finally said. "Would you mind letting Ricardo know we're done for the day? I know the way back."

Without another word, she spun back to the trail and bolted before he could ask her any questions. Frowning, Sebastian stared after her for a moment, his eyes narrowed.

If she thought that was the end of this discussion, she was sorely mistaken. He followed her back to camp.

Once there, he reclined quietly on the couch, biding his time, watching as she poured over the journal she'd pried from the box, another book her father had encoded.

Raymond Mackenzie. The man was a puzzle. Ricardo's candid conversation sat heavy on his shoulders, shredding his conscience.

Tell her?

Don't tell her?

Sebastian conjured a bag of chips and a bottle of beer. The first crunch of a chip drew an irritated glance from her, but she made no comment.

What was the right thing to do? He worked his way through the bag as he tried to reason it out.

She deserved to know the truth. That her father had known what she was. Known and sought to cover it up, even from her. In all honesty, as her mate, didn't he owe it to her? The unvarnished truth? No matter what it was?

But, as her mate, wasn't it also his job to protect her? To see that she was happy?

And wouldn't the truth make her miserable? Knowing that her father knew what she was and yet hid it from her? But would *not* knowing the truth make her happy either? Always fighting her very nature because she didn't truly believe?

This mating business was more difficult than it should be.

Phoebe caught her lower lip between her teeth, and her brow drew together. She bent closer to the book, tracing the symbols over and over with her fingertip. She sat back and blinked, as if she thought maybe she hadn't read something correctly, or the passage didn't make sense.

He crunched another chip, and she shot him the stink eye. "Do you mind?"

Arching a brow, he vanished the chip bag and dusted his hands dramatically.

"I'm sorry," she said, letting out a long, tired breath. "I shouldn't have snapped like that. This latest journal and the rock from the monolith has me on overload."

Sebastian watched as she rubbed at her temple, stretched her neck a little to the side. He frowned as she picked up the rock, studied it for a moment, and then, still clutching the stone, leaned over the book once more.

So what if Raymond knew what his wife and daughter were? Knew, but wouldn't acknowledge it?

Does it even matter now?

Phoebe pushed the fingers of her free hand beneath

her glasses and pinched the bridge of her nose. She blinked a couple times, resettled her glasses, and went back to her reading.

Sebastian stood and went to her, dropped his hands on her shoulders and set to rubbing. She jolted at first, but then relaxed with a groan. She put the stone back down on the corner of the desk and hung her head.

"You need to take a break."

"I think I'm on to something." She shook her head and leaned forward, angling over the journal again. "I think this rock is a key of some kind. I just have to figure out where it goes."

Sebastian reached around her and closed the book.

"Hey!"

"I wasn't asking. You need a break."

He captured her wrist, drew her to her feet and turned her to face him.

"Close your eyes."

"Close my— Oh, no. We can't just shimmer off somewhere and leave Dad's journal and the key laying around where anyone could— Hey!" Her eyes rounded in alarm. "What happened to them?"

"Trust me?"

She pressed her lips together, then nodded grudgingly. "Yes."

Barely a breath of time, the thinnest bit of hesitation. But he smiled. It wasn't an unconditional, instant yes—not like it should be. But they were getting closer and closer all the time. In fact, if he had to guess, he'd say that pause had more to do with irritation than with doubt.

"The journal and the key are safe. And they will remain so. I'll conjure them back when we return, and you can pick up right where you left off, yeah?"

He took her little huff of breath as consent.

"Now," he said, drawing her into his arms. Sebastian pressed a kiss to her forehead and whispered, "Close your eyes and relax."

Chapter Seventeen

"Where are we?" Phoebe glanced around, frowning. Maple, oak, and lilac bushes didn't grow in the Rio Bec. Nor did this cheerful mix of wildflowers.

Sebastian turned her, pressing his chest to her back, and pointed up the hill. "That farmhouse up there? That's my place."

She couldn't miss the way his voice rang with pride. She'd been here before, of course. But she'd only seen the inside of his home, and not in great detail. She'd been too sick in the beginning, and then, there at the end, in too much of a rush to get back to the jungle.

Now she took a moment to let it all sink in. The house, white, two stories with clapboard siding, stood on a hill in the distance. A thin strip of a porch ran along the back of the house, no railing, but a couple of rockers sat at one end.

No fuss. No frills.

But...*comforting*.

A monster of a barn stood sentinel just to the east and back of the house. Red paint had weathered and peeled until almost more aged wood showed than paint. Shake shingles had warped and slivered, giving the distinctive gambrel style roof character. Weeds and tufts of stubborn grass shot up around the perimeter of the barn and what appeared to be the mangled remains of a rusty old tractor, spilling into the meadow behind it until they were overtaken by the wildflowers.

Behind the barn, the land sloped down to a meadow and, on the side of the meadow opposite where they stood, the thick wall of a wooded area rose up. Phoebe turned until her shoulder touched his chest. He kept her caged in the loose circle of his arms. And he watched her, absorbing her response to his home. He must have been pleased with what he saw, because a wide grin settled upon his face.

Nearby, at the bottom of the hill they stood upon, a large pond spread out before them. The grass was longer here, pushing out into the edges of the water where it mixed with arrowhead, spiked rush, water lily, and cattails. A rickety old dock stretched over the water, inviting visitors to stroll out, sit down, and dip their toes.

"I thought a swim might be just what you needed to relax. I know I could use one."

"We don't even have swimming suits." She moved out of his arms, on her guard now. She had a gut feeling that him plus her plus water minus appropriate apparel equaled trouble.

She might not have a suit, but that didn't keep her from venturing out on the dock. Oh, it was tempting. The water was smooth as glass and so clear, she could almost see the bottom.

"Why do we need suits?" Sebastian asked from behind her. His boots thudded on the weathered boards beneath their feet as he followed her to the end of the dock. "It isn't like you haven't seen everything already."

Her cheeks burned at the reminder that he'd caught her checking him out…more than once.

"And I know *I* sure wouldn't mind seeing it all again," he added.

Yep. T-r-o-u-b-l-e.

"Be that as it may, someone could come along—"

"No, they won't."

She turned to frown up at him. "How can you be sure?"

"Well, I suppose I can't be absolutely positive. But we're miles from the nearest farm, and farther still from the closest town. And if anyone does show up, I can always conjure us dressed then. Or shimmer us away."

"Then why don't you just conjure suits for us?"

"Now where would be the fun in that?" His grin grew teasing, tempting. "Have you ever been skinny dipping?"

She blinked. "No."

"I didn't think so."

Her back went up. "What's that supposed to mean?"

He just smiled. And then he began peeling off his clothing, one article at a time. When he was naked—all that sun kissed, velvet skin bare for her pleasure—he started walking toward her. Phoebe tensed, preparing for...she didn't know what. Would he push her in? Take her in his arms? Would he kiss her?

Please, God, let him kiss me.

He stopped when there was little more than an inch separating them. Sebastian lowered his head until his lips hovered close to her ear, but he was careful not to touch her.

Sweet heaven, she wanted to do a hell of a lot more than touch him. She knew what he felt like, moving inside her, pressed against her. And she'd denied them both this morning, and last night. She shivered with hunger. She didn't want to deny either of them anymore.

"Come in with me, Phoebe. You won't regret it."

And then, fast as a blink, he dove sideways, slicing cleanly into the water, barely making a splash. The glass surface of the water broke into waves and then went rolling outward in ever-widening circles. She lost track of him as the seconds ticked by.

Phoebe frowned, moved closer to the edge of the dock, and scanned the surface. *Where'd he go?*

"Come in, love," he called from the water on the other side of the dock, and she spun around. She watched as he slicked his wet hair back from his face. Crystal droplets dripped from his eyelashes and streamed down his neck. "The water's perfect."

Phoebe licked her lips. She should object, should at least try to put up some kind of resistance. Shouldn't she? The problem was, she didn't even care if it was a bad idea anymore. She couldn't think of anything she wanted more right now than to dive in and let things play out as they would.

Emboldened by his expectant expression, Phoebe began stripping. His searing stare followed every move she made. She stood for a moment longer, gilded by the fading sun, savoring the look on his face. Then she took her glasses off, dropped them onto her clothing, and leaped off the dock.

She'd curled herself into a cannonball, but the moment the cool water touched her skin, she gasped and jolted straight. She managed to close her mouth a slim second before the water slipped over her head. As she knifed toward the surface, she savored the sensation. After the heat of the jungle, the cool water caressed her flesh in sensual, decadent strokes.

Oh, this feels so good.

As soon as she broke the surface, Phoebe pushed her hands over her head, slicking water from her face and hair. She searched for him, peering between the posts of the dock, but he'd disappeared again.

A strangled scream tangled in her throat and she jerked when she felt something brush past her legs. She spun, treading water, straining to see below the water. But she could catch nothing but shifting shadows from this angle. Another whisper of touch slicked along her bottom, and she darted forward, spinning in the water once more.

Just as she began to imagine all kinds of slimy, scaly monsters lurking beneath the rippling waters, Sebastian came up for air directly behind her. Laughing, he wrapped his arms around her waist and drew her back into him. Their legs bumped and tangled as they tread water.

"Best thing I've ever caught in this pond," he rumbled near her ear. He found her neck with his lips, and she shivered. His hands scooped up, finding her breasts, and he rolled her puckered nipples, plucked and thrummed them between thumbs and fingertips as he continued to lick and nip the side of her throat.

Phoebe caught her breath, closed her eyes, and dropped her head back on his shoulder, savoring the sensation of being nibbled like the finest chocolate. Still, she couldn't make it easy for him. Reaching back, trying not to groan in surrender when his erection pushed insistently between her thighs, Phoebe ran her hands up his sides. And when she found his ribs, she curled her fingers and tickled until he jerked back, laughing.

"Oh, you wanna play it like that, huh?"

But she darted away before he could snatch her back. She twisted in the water to face him. With the blade of her hand, she slapped a wave of water at him. And while he was blinking and sputtering and shaking the water from his face, Phoebe cut through the pond like a fish, swimming for the far shore.

She had a good, solid head start on him, and she swam like a pike, streamline and fast, but still, he caught her. A big hand wrapped around her ankle and yanked her to a halt. Before she knew what was happening, the water closed over her head in a rush. She came up, laughing and sputtering and swiping the water from her face.

He circled her like a shark, the lower half of his face submerged, his narrowed-eyed stare tracking her. Those electric blue eyes dared her to try to flee again. Giggling, she turned slow circles to follow him, never letting him behind her for a second. She risked a glance to the shore, then, when she saw him gathering himself in anticipation, she shot in the opposite direction.

This time, he waited until she was nearly to the dock before he snatched her round the waist.

"Okay, okay." She laughed when he made to dunk her again. "You win."

He rotated her in his arms until they bobbed in the water, facing each other. He kept his hands on her waist. Their knees bumped. It didn't take long before he drew her closer and guided her legs around his waist. The playfulness had left him. The way he looked at her now took her breath away.

"Admit it." His hands slid down from her waist and he cupped her bottom, drawing her closer still.

Frowning, distracted by his hard erection riding so close—but not close enough—to where she needed it, she glanced up. "Admit what?"

"You know what," he insisted. And she was afraid she did know, all too well, what he wanted to hear. What she didn't know was if she was ready to say it, ready to admit it out loud. Not yet.

She thought about using their position to sidetrack him. A little wiggle, a tilted pelvis, and he'd forget all about pursuing this subject. As if he'd read her mind, he arched his back, making it difficult to play the oops-did-I-just-slip-onto-your-dick-my-bad card. Left with no option other than to give him what he wanted, she drew her knees in and shoved against his chest, pushing and twisting until she'd wiggled free like a slippery eel.

His expression darkened. He advanced, she retreated. He took another stroke forward. She glided back.

"Phoebe," he warned.

"No," she said, growing angry. How dare he ruin this? Why did he have to get all serious and demanding? Why couldn't he have just enjoyed the moment? She lifted a hand from the water and pointed at him. "Stop it."

Expression grim, he began breast stroking toward her, his head above the water, his determined stare zeroed in on her. She back stroked, watching him, matching him motion for motion until her heels met the slippery, sloped bottom of the pond.

She found her footing with all due haste and stood. The water lapped at her navel, and his eyes flickered black as his gaze dropped to her bare breasts. Swallowing, she waded backwards. The waterline dropped to her hips, mid-thighs, knees. And his smoldering stare followed.

Still she kept going.

And still he kept following.

Her breath came in shallow pants. Her heart raced. Phoebe jerked her focus to the dock, to the pile of her clothing. But before she could take two steps in that direction, every last stitch of her clothing disappeared. She drew up short, gasping in outrage.

"That's not fair," she snapped, whirling around to face him. "Bring them back."

But they stayed gone.

He was climbing the bank, his head canted down, water sluicing down his beautiful body. Phoebe backpedalled, shooting a quick glance over her shoulder for sanctuary. There was none.

"Stop it," she ordered once more, though she knew it would do no good. The look on his face was too determined, too angry. She thought about running, but where would she run to? The house? *His* house? Talk about walking into the lion's den. Besides, he'd only follow. Hell, he'd probably catch her before she made it halfway across the meadow, just as he'd caught her before she'd made it across the pond.

"We have to go back to camp now, Sebastian."

Nothing. He just kept right on coming.

"I have work to do."

No response.

"Damn it, they could be finding the sword. Right now. We don't have time for this."

No verbal reply. But his brows drew together, and

his step faltered for a moment. Then he drew a resolved breath and kept coming. The look on his face said she might as well be whistling in the wind. They weren't going anywhere. Not until he'd gotten this out of his system.

Damn it, had he caught her slip? Was that why he'd paused?

Lord, he had her so flustered she didn't know what she was saying anymore. She had to be more careful.

Okay. All right then. She'd put a stop to this now. Right now. Right here.

She planted her fists on her hips and stood her ground. "I am not your mate, Sebastian. So you need to just stop this nonsense."

He froze in his tracks. His eyes went demon black. And they stayed that way. His nostrils flared, and his head dipped even more. And he began stalking her. *Really* stalking her. Adrenaline spiked through her system making her tremble.

She could see his patience, his restraint, his self control going up in flames, burning like dry kindling in the depths of his black eyes. Phoebe licked her lips and scrambled backward again.

But he was done playing. Through letting her feel like she had any control whatsoever over this situation. She didn't make it very far before he was upon her. He took her to the ground in an instant, crushing her into sweet smelling grass and delicate wildflower buds.

Sebastian straddled her hips. She wiggled and squirmed for all she was worth, but she couldn't dislodge him. Her temper snapped. Phoebe flailed her arms, swinging a fist at his stubborn jaw. But he deflected the blow and captured her wrists. By the time he pinned them over her head, they were both panting.

"What are you doing?" Phoebe screeched at him. "Get off me."

But he remained silent, staring down at her, burning her with those grim, black eyes. As though he were stamping his possession on her very soul. Damn his rotten hide.

His erection lay, hot and hard and heavy, between them. But he made no move to use it. Just taunted her with what she wanted and what he would not give. Not until he'd gotten his way. She made a fist and prayed her claws and fangs would stay hidden away.

"Damn it, *say* something!"

He snapped his teeth at her. His nostrils were still flared in aggression, and his lips formed a tight line. The muscle on his jaw was bunched, hard as a rock. At least his eyes had turned blue again, but they still shot angry sparks at her.

"You *are* my mate. We aren't leaving here until you admit it. Once and for all. We're also going to get a few other things clear while we're at it. First, you will stop hiding things from me."

She sputtered, "I haven't—"

"Bullshit," he barked. Her mouth fell open, and she gaped up at him. "What happened to your hand that you wouldn't show me earlier? And what did you mean when you said they might be finding the sword right now? Stolas already has the sword, or doesn't he?"

Phoebe pressed her lips tight and scowled mutinously up at him.

"Exactly," he growled. As if she'd just made his case for him. But he wasn't done yet. "Never again will you rush headlong into danger without regard for the consequences. Like when you left the tent this morning without me. Or this afternoon when you left the dig site, again without me. Or when you go about scooping up snakes like they're goddamned puppies. Or when you dangled face down off the side of that freakin' crumbling ruin." Phoebe opened her mouth to argue, but he snapped, "Be silent!"

Taken aback, Phoebe sucked in an offended breath. She clamped her lips together, and she seethed.

"And, above all, never again will you deny that you are my mate. Never will you so much as *think* those words. And you will stop testing me this way."

"I wasn't testing you!" she snapped, his order for silence be damned.

"You do. Over and over." Keeping her wrists anchored above her head, he slid down her body, maneuvering until he settled himself between her squirming legs, just narrowly avoiding a well aimed knee. He growled, clamped a hand on her hip to hold her still, and deliberately stroked the length of his erection along her cleft, making her eyes all but cross. "And I thought I told you to be silent."

Now her eyes wanted to cross for a completely different reason. The bossy jerk. She narrowed them instead and stewed, too angry to string two words together.

"I've fought my instincts where you are concerned. Time and time again, I have suppressed them. No more," he said. She tried to insert a sentence, a word…an angry grunt, but he spoke right over her. "I will not allow you to put a damned relic above your own safety. Not anymore. And I will not allow you to withhold your trust. You will not question my orders when it comes to your safety. I *will* keep you safe at *all* cost." He glared down, searching her face. "Am I understood?"

She was too angry to respond. But she was also stunned by the unshakable, furious resolve in his eyes.

"Damn it, Phoebe," he snarled, giving her wrists a little thump against the ground. Not hard enough to hurt her, but enough to grab her attention. "You. Are. My. Mate. I'm not asking you anymore. Now I'm telling you. *Qui et illisium speccaté*. Now and forevermore. You are mine."

"You've said that before," she stated quietly, some of the heat draining from her. Those words…they did funny things to her insides, every time he said them.

"I meant them then. And I mean them even more now." He eased back just a bit, loosened his hold on her wrists. But he didn't let go, and he didn't relent. "I was created to be your protector, Phoebe. Your lover. Your champion. Your mate. I will not fail you. And I will never, ever leave you. You were meant to belong to me. As I belong to you. Never again will you deny my claim. Nor will you ignore your claim on me."

Phoebe forced a swallow. Her unwilling stare fell to the marks on his shoulder. Her mark. Now she was afraid. Not of him. But of herself, and how much she wanted all he'd said to be true. Irrevocably true.

Say something, she told herself. *Anything. Make him see reason. Make him see this will never work between us.*

But the words, and the conviction behind them, eluded her.

"Say it," he demanded, harsh and unbending. "Admit it, out loud. You belong to me."

A sliver of defiance lanced through the panic. He wrapped her hair around his free hand, fisting it, tugging gently despite his forceful tone. "Say the words!"

She narrowed her eyes, just the slightest, refusing to relinquish her defiance, even now when she knew he spoke the truth. "Fine," she snapped. Then she thrust her chin up and glared at him. "*You* belong to *me*."

He blinked. She could see she'd caught him off guard. But the edges of his sculpted mouth twitched, a grin that almost escaped him. Almost, but not quite. He wouldn't relent. Not this time. And she knew it.

"True. But not exactly what I'm wanting to hear, *caro mita*." *Little heart of mine,* he'd called her. He rolled his hips against her, dragging a reluctant groan from her. "Before we leave this place"—he rolled his hips again—"and I don't care how long it takes, you will admit it. You are mine. Now say it!"

Phoebe bit her lip. Everything inside her wanted to give in, wanted desperately to yield. She barely stifled a moan as he shifted his hips once more. Her body ached for his.

And that was when she noticed fresh beads of perspiration dotting his brow. His face hardened, as if he were calling on all his self control to resist slipping inside her and pounding away his frustration. His eyes were merciless, his body rigid.

"Say it," he ordered once more.

Phoebe swallowed a groan, fighting her own body now. Fighting the need to revel in his mastery, fighting the soul deep desire his claim had sparked. To be his. Completely. Forever. His.

"Say it," came the fierce whisper, laden with

desperation and torment and a need so great it scorched them both. She felt the faintest tremor in his hands then, and she searched his face, his eyes.

In that moment, Phoebe knew she couldn't fight him, couldn't fight this—fight what was between them—any longer. He wanted this too badly.

And, so did she.

"I am yours, Sebastian," she said softly, but with great conviction. "Only yours. Your mate."

Where had those words come from? They were out of her mouth before she could call them back. Shocking her. And, by the look on his face, shocking him as well. Unmitigated relief softened all that sheer male possessiveness, keeping her from instantly regretting her capitulation.

"Nothing will keep me from you," he growled and dipped his head, at last capturing her lips. Seizing them. At the same moment, he shifted his hips and thrust deep. Without warning, without hesitation. Pushing all the way inside.

Phoebe gasped in surprise as raw sensation hit her like a tidal wave.

His hands still held her immobile beneath him, but he laid claim to her body with sure, powerful strokes. At some point along the way, he threw his head back and roared his possession. Phoebe couldn't defend against his passion. She got swept up, carried away. Their bodies fell into primal rhythm, straining against each other, urging each other on.

He finally released her hands, only to reach down, hook her legs, and shove them up till her knees were anchored nearly around his ribs. And he began to really move then, increasing the tempo, driving into her, making her head spin. Phoebe was lost to the sensations pouring through her. She could feel the changes taking place in her body, but was helpless, once again, to stop them. His tongue swept along the sharp length of one of her fangs and he groaned into her mouth.

She must have nicked him, because the coppery flavor of his blood blossomed against her tongue. Her gums pulsed in response. Her eyes began to burn.

He tore his mouth from hers and demanded, "Do it." He tipped his head to the side, baring his throat. "Bite me, *caro mita*. Mark me as yours."

With those words upon his lips, and his body dominating hers, she couldn't hold back any longer. She opened her mouth wide and sank her fangs into the side of his throat. It wasn't with the purpose of drawing his blood, though the salty tang of it seeped into her mouth, nonetheless. It was the act in and of itself that ruled her. The possession. The primal need to mark her territory.

And when she felt the unexpected sting of *his* fangs sinking into *her* shoulder, her body erupted. Phoebe clutched him tight and rode wave after wave of pleasure so bright, so brilliant it bordered on painful. She whimpered against his flesh as he began to come. The feel of his solid, hard length, buried deep inside her, jerking and jetting, shot Phoebe soaring skyward yet again, pushed her even higher when he rotated his hips. He gave one final thrust and roared against her skin, long and loud.

Chapter Eighteen

Phoebe floated back to reality. She was only vaguely aware of physical sensation as Sebastian carefully retracted his fangs from her skin and then swiped his tongue along her flesh. Phoebe experience a brief pang of loss, but the first blossoms of embarrassment swiftly began to take root. Mortified, she realized her fangs were still embedded in his neck. The moment she withdrew them, blood began to well, and she panicked.

"Lick them," he said, his voice calm if a bit hoarse.

Phoebe's brows drew together. No, he couldn't mean—

"You have to lick the punctures for them to close otherwise they're just going to keep bleeding."

Oh, dear Jesus.

Closing her eyes, she tentatively did as he'd instructed. She'd already had the taste of him in her mouth, so this was not the shock she'd expected. The act of running her tongue along his skin bothered her far more, however, as it sent sparks of desire showering through her already overloaded system.

Phoebe blinked and then looked closer, peering hard at the sealed puncture wounds on his throat in disbelief. "I have healing spit?"

And apparently no filter after mind-blowing sex either. She hadn't meant to voice that incredulous question aloud.

"No. Well, not all the time," he said, smoothing the hair from her brow. He smiled down at her, the picture of a well sated male. "But right now, during and after sex, your body produces certain chemicals, one of which is designed to heal your partner—*me*—should you decide to use those sexy little fangs of yours."

He thinks they're sexy?

Phoebe didn't quite know what to do with that.

He dropped a kiss to her lips as she tried to map out the logic of chemical reactions. She didn't know what to do with that either. Phoebe nearly cried when she felt him pull out and move away, her emotions were so raw. But he only lay down on the fragrant grass beside her before drawing her into his arms.

He tucked her head into the curve of his shoulder and pressed a soft kiss to her damp hair. "Why were you so resistant to admitting we are mated?"

Let me count the ways...

She licked her lips, and then chewed on the bottom one while he waited in silence. She watched her fingers as she traced small patterns across his chest. And then her eyes widened, and she flattened her palm against his skin. In the encoded alphabet her father had taught her, she'd been tracing the word *mine* on him, over and over, without even realizing it.

"Maybe I have a feeling you equate this mating thing with my obedience. And, let me warn you right now, that's never going to happen," she finally replied. She knew she was deflecting but couldn't help it.

He huffed out a laugh. "Believe me, I'm not stupid enough to demand obedience. I've yet to see a mate who even knows the meaning of the word." He nudged her with his shoulder until she looked up at him. "But you better get this through your beautiful head. This *mating thing* is real. And it has already happened. This is a done deal. So, don't bother to ask me to undo it, because *that* will never happen."

He stared hard at her now, and she finally, reluctantly, nodded. The muscle in his jaw bunched. So, he'd been expecting immediate and unquestioning acquiescence? Too bad. She was doing the best she could here.

They lay there in silence for a long time. Eventually, Phoebe relaxed against him, enjoying the way his body felt alongside hers, all hard muscle and warm male. He traced lazy lines up and down her arm and over her back. Phoebe closed her eyes and sank into the pleasure, going boneless.

"Is there..." Her voice trailed away as embarrassment took over.

"Is there what?"

She drew a bracing breath. She should have kept her mouth closed, but the questions were beginning to pile up. Still, she couldn't quite look him in the eye as she asked, "Does there always have to be biting? I mean, can't we just have normal sex?"

"Normal sex?" He chuckled.

Irritated, she poked him in the ribs. "You know what I mean."

Sebastian twisted suddenly, rolling her beneath him, pinning her, forcing her to look at him. He traced the line of her jaw with the back of his knuckles as he stared at her, perfectly serious now.

"I'm sorry. I shouldn't have laughed. I want you to be comfortable asking me anything. No matter what it is. Understood?" When she nodded, no hesitation at all, his smile nearly blinded her. He dropped a kiss to the tip of her nose, and then assured her, "Yes. We can have normal sex. There doesn't always have to be biting involved. As far as I know, biting usually only happens when emotions are running high. Or when a mating is new, while partners are still…finding their way with each other. While they're still learning to trust each other and are establishing the parameters of the relationship."

This information went a long way toward putting her at ease. To know it didn't always have to be that way between them, the complete loss of control, the overwhelming urges…the marking. That they might have a normal relationship despite what she was—what *they* were—made her feel a little less like a freak.

So lost in thought was she that, at first, she didn't realize her focus had drifted to his mouth. Not until she felt the insistent nudge of his arousal pressing against her womanhood. Startled, she met his gaze. Her breath got tangled up in her throat at the look on his face, at the fire simmering in his brilliant blue eyes. Eyes that flickered black.

"Shall we test the theory?" His grin dared her as nothing else could.

Phoebe licked her lips. Emboldened by his expression, by the rapt way he watched the tip of her tongue moisten her lower lip, she tilted her hips up in invitation. And she smiled, feeling brave and desired, wanton and wonderful.

Sebastian needed no further encouragement. He dipped his head and brushed a whisper soft kiss to the corner of her mouth. And then another. And another.

Slowly working his way across her bottom lip until they were both breathing heavily. Sebastian tangled his fingers in her hair, cupped the back of her head, easing her into the right angle as he deepened the kiss. His big body moved over hers and he braced his weight on his elbows. Sebastian repositioned his hips and slid his rigid length along her aching, wet cleft over and over, until they were both shuddering. Phoebe wrapped herself around him, clinging, holding tight.

Just when she didn't think she could take it a second longer, he rotated his hips, and then slid home, slow and easy. He kept them to a leisurely pace, stroking her skin, her hair, her face. He nipped and nibbled kisses along her jaw, down her throat, along her scar. And when the crest hit them, when the surge of pleasure swept them up and over, he held her in a tender embrace.

Phoebe peered up at him, locking gazes with him until her vision blurred and she cried out in wonder.

When it was all over, he rolled with her, draping her over his chest like a blanket. He held her there as their breathing evened out and the world slowly crept back.

A huge weight had been lifted from her shoulders. Yes, she'd felt the changes in her body. Felt her fangs begin to emerge. But she'd been able to control it that time, and she'd forced her fangs back. Judging by the burning sensation, her eyes had still turned. But changing eye color was a long way from trying to chew his skin off. She was ecstatic, filled with hope for the first time in longer than she could remember.

She pressed a tender kiss to the side of his throat, thankful beyond words. Sebastian smoothed his calloused hand down her spine, and he kissed the top of her head. No words were needed just now. And she basked in the sensation.

Just as she decided a nap seemed in order, she felt him stiffen beneath her. He heaved a deep sigh, his broad chest rising and falling, moving her head right along with it.

"We should go back," he said. "I'm sure Ricardo is wondering where we disappeared to."

Phoebe sighed too. As much as she didn't want to move right now—or possibly ever again—he was right. Ricardo would worry.

"I think I could use a shower first," she said, pushing up off him.

In the blink of an eye, she was as clean as if she'd just stepped from said shower and clothed in her jungle gear. She lifted her eyebrows, looked down at herself, then shot him a questioning glance.

Sebastian smiled ruefully at her as he conjured her glasses and handed them to her. "If I get you anywhere near a shower, it's going to be at least a few more hours before we head back to camp."

Now she frowned. "But—"

"I'll make love to you again," he interrupted bluntly.

Heat flooded her face. She ducked her head, though she couldn't help the small smile tugging at her lips and slid her glasses up the bridge of her nose. Fully clothed now himself, Sebastian stood, caught her hand, and tugged her to her feet. He slipped an arm around her waist and pulled her close.

"Ready, *caro mita*?"

She glanced around them at the meadow and the

pond, then peeked up at him, feeling very shy all of a sudden. "Can we come back sometime?"

His smile stretched ear to ear. "Any time you want. Just say the word."

Phoebe grinned and nodded once more. Sebastian dipped his head and captured her lips. She slipped her arms around his neck and met him, kiss for kiss. Somewhere along the way, hardly even noticeable for the powerful sensations kissing Sebastian invoked, she caught a wisp of that falling sensation she'd come to associate with shimmering. And when she opened her eyes again, they were standing inside their tent back at base camp.

"I want to check in with Ricardo, then I think I'll spend the rest of the evening examining Dad's journal."

"Can I help with anything?"

"Not really," she said, smiling apologetically. "Ricardo doesn't even know how to decipher Dad's code."

She watched him for a moment, and then, she made a decision. Call it impulse. Call it gut feeling. Or maybe it was some primitive instinct driving her. She didn't know what pushed her, but whatever it was, she was as sure of her choice as she'd ever been sure about anything in her life.

"Actually," she said as she twisted her hair out of the way and back up into a bun at the base of her neck. "There is something you can do."

"Sure. What do you need?"

Point of no return, she told herself. "You can help me translate Dad's journal."

He frowned now. "I don't know the code."

"I'll teach you."

He stared at her for a long moment, surprise etching his face. And then, without warning, he swept her into a hug tight enough to make her bones creak. Caught off guard by his exuberance, Phoebe laughed aloud.

"Tell you what," he said, setting her back on her feet. The journal and the arrowhead shaped rock reappeared on the desk beside her. "I know how anxious you are. Why don't you get started? I'll go let Ricardo know we're here, and then I'll be right back."

"What about the line of sight rule?"

"If you can bend, so can I…just a little anyway. I'll be right outside the tent. And I'll only be gone for a minute. If anything happens, if you need me, just yell, okay?"

Compromise. She kind of liked this new dynamic.

Smiling, Phoebe nodded and took her seat at the desk. She readjusted her glasses and reached for the journal as Sebastian left the tent.

But she hadn't gotten more than a line or two translated when she heard the tent flap swish. She glanced up from her work. She should have known.

Phoebe quirked a brow. "Well that didn't take long."

Sebastian said nothing. He just stood near the entrance, staring at her with an odd expression. Without a word, he strode forward until he reached her side.

Suddenly uneasy, Phoebe stood. "What's wrong?"

Oh no! Dread hit her. Hard. Had something happened to Ricardo while they'd been gone? Fear and worry congealed in the pit of her stomach. Slowly, silently, he reached out, captured her hands, and pulled her out from behind the desk so she was facing him fully. And then he slowly removed her glasses. He dropped them onto the desk without taking his eyes from her.

He kept peering at her with the strangest look on his face, his probing stare searching every inch of her countenance. What the hell was going on?

"What's wrong?" She reached up and laid her palm against his chest. He started, glancing down at her hand. And when he looked back up at her, his expression had changed. He looked...shocked? Surprised? Off balance, for sure. "Sebastian, you're really starting to worry me."

"Your mother was Danika." His voice sounded hoarse, strained. *Different*. With an unsteady hand, he reached up and traced his fingertips over her cheekbone and down the side of her face. He captured a loose strand of hair and rubbed it between his fingers for a moment, before lifting it to his nose. He dragged in a deep breath. Why was he smelling her hair? And then he cupped both cheeks and held her still as his gaze devoured her.

"Yes." Phoebe frowned. "It was. How do you know that?"

"How could I have missed it before?" he whispered, shaking his head.

"Missed what?" Phoebe insisted. "What's going on?"

"Get your hands off my mate!"

Phoebe jerked at the angry shout. She whipped her head around to see Sebastian standing just inside the tent flap. For an instant, the world stopped spinning as she glanced back and forth from the Sebastian standing a few inches away from her to the one standing at the tent opening. She couldn't speak. Couldn't compute.

What on earth?

And then the Sebastian standing next to her took half a step back.

And he morphed.

A tall, lean demon stood before her now. Skin a brilliant crimson with black tattoos snaking their way along his arms and across his ribs. Long, jet black hair. Eyes a bottomless coal black. His fangs were clearly visible as his smile stretched wide.

Sïnsobar!

Phoebe hopped back, nearly toppling over the chair behind her in her haste to get away. The Sebastian by the door charged across the tent, focused on the demon smiling at her. With one last searching look, Sïnsobar vanished in a cloud of wavering air.

"Damn it," Sebastian snarled as he rounded on her. "Are you all right?"

He reached for her, but she instinctively drew back. Her eyes were wide. She couldn't catch her breath. What was real? What wasn't? Was this yet another trick? How was she to believe her own eyes anymore?

"Phoebe?" Sebastian said, drawing up short.

"How do I know it's really you?" Phoebe whispered, shaking her head.

He searched her face. And then he said softly, "*Qui et illisium speccaté.*"

Phoebe's breath caught on a sob, and she launched herself into his arms. Sebastian wrapped her up tight, holding her until she stopped shaking.

"How can he do that?" she finally asked, her voice muffled against his shirt.

Sebastian took her by the shoulders and led her to

the couch where he tugged her down beside him. "Sïnsobar is Carpathï. They are a breed of skin-shifters, or maybe a better term would be shape shifters. They can take on any human form, though most can't hold the stolen shape for very long. Sïnsobar is…special. He can hold form for extended periods of time. Days, if necessary, I've been told."

"Why didn't he take me, like he did before?"

"He knew I'd just follow his shimmer trail. It'd be too fresh, and I'd catch up faster than I did before. And he probably figured you'd put up a fight this time, now that he knows what you are."

"What I am? I'm not anybody. I'm just me."

He took her by the shoulders and gave her a little shake.

"Damn it," he barked. "You have to stop it. Stop denying or pretending or whatever the hell it is you're doing. Sïnsobar can get to you. He just proved that. He did it once. He could do it again. It's time for you to own up to what you are, figure it out. And figure out what you can do. You have to be able to protect yourself in case…in case I can't be there to do it for you."

She looked up at him, feeling so small. So inconsequential.

"Damn it, he did a real number on you, didn't he?"

She frowned. "Who? What are you talking about?"

"Your father."

"My father? He didn't do anything to me. What are you talking about?" Now she glared at him. Why was he dragging her father into this, making her dad into the bad guy here?

"It's the only answer I can come up with as to why

you won't take the blinders off when it comes to what you are."

"He kept me safe. He loved me."

"I don't doubt that he did. In his own way. But he should have told you the truth. At the time, hiding what you are might have been the right thing to do. But hiding won't help you now. Now you have to face it. Face it, *caro mita*, or it could get you killed. And I can't live without you. You're my life now. I love you."

That drew her up short. She blinked up at him, at a complete loss for words. Just when she thought she had things figured out, he threw a curveball at her.

"Sebastian...I—"

"No, don't say anything. I know that wasn't fair to toss it out there like that. But it's true. I've waited for you forever—I just didn't realize it until I found you. You're what I was missing. And now that I've found you, I don't intend to lose you. So, you're going to have to set aside whatever hang-ups you have and face reality. Ignoring what you are...that won't make it go away."

"And what am I?" she shouted, angry at him for making her do this.

He ran his hands lightly up and down her arms. Gentle. Soothing. "You are a demoness, love. But your scent is human, which is really confusing. You don't, or haven't yet, manifested any abilities. And you haven't fully morphed, so I can't say as to what breed you are."

"What do you mean, fully morphed?" Her eyes grew round. "You mean I could change fully into...into a monster? Like him? Like Sïnsobar? Or like one of those...those *things* in the cave?"

"Not a monster, sweet." He pressed a kiss to her

forehead. "And not necessarily like him."

"Until that day in the cave when I saw all those others, until I saw you, I thought that's what all demons looked like in their true form. Like him. Like Sïnsobar." She fingered the scar on her throat.

Sebastian frowned, tilting his head as he took her hands in his. "Why would you think that?"

Phoebe let out a shuddering breath. "When I was a small child—the day my mother left—I saw her change. I never told my dad. She looked just like Sïnsobar does. The red skin. The black marks on her arms. The long black hair. The eyes and fangs. She—"

Phoebe broke off abruptly as memories, long suppressed assailed her. She pressed her lips together and closed her eyes, shaking her head.

"Tell me," Sebastian urged softly.

"We were at the park. It was late, getting dark. We were on our way back to the car when this man stepped out of the shadows. He grabbed her, I remember. And his eyes were red. Like bright, flame red. She yelled at me to run, and I did. Only I didn't run far. I hid in the bushes, and I watched. She changed into…" Phoebe's voice trailed away, and she licked her lips. "She looked just like Sïnsobar. She killed that man—that demon— with her bare hands, and with her fangs. And then, just like that, she was back to normal."

Only then did she realize she'd been rocking back and forth. Sebastian pulled her into his arms. "Finish it," he urged.

"We went home."

"What else happened?"

Phoebe didn't want to face the pain again, didn't want to take those memories out and look at them. But she did. Because he was right. She needed to remember, so that she knew what she was up against.

"When we got home, Mom sent me upstairs to play. But I could hear them shouting downstairs. I crept to the top of the steps, and I listened. She kept telling Dad that we all needed to go away. That they'd found her, and that she couldn't go back. I don't know who *they* were, or where it was that she didn't want to go back to. Dad was so angry. He yelled at her, said it was all her fault."

"Did she tell him about the demon in the park?"

"I don't know. I got frightened because I'd never heard them scream at each other like that before. And then Dad told her—" She cut herself off as she finally let herself remember. "Dad told her to go. That I would never be safe as long as…"

"As long as she was around," Sebastian finished for her.

Phoebe nodded, tears streaming down her face.

"She stopped at the bottom of the stairs, just for a moment, and she looked right at me. Her eyes turned black. Demon black. But she didn't say a word. She just turned and left. I never saw her again."

"Before she left you, she must have put some kind of masking spell on you, maybe even bound your powers. I didn't notice it at first, not until I took you to Asher for a cure for the venom. The elixir he gave you must have inadvertently begun removing the spell. Or drastically weakened it. Whenever you experience strong emotions, you give off spikes of energy. And every time you begin to morph, the hole in the spell grows, exposing you. Exposing your abilities. Little by little."

"I don't morph." But even as the words left her mouth, she knew them to be a lie. How many times had her fangs come out around him? And what about her hand at the ruins, how it had turned bright red, tipped with black claws?

"Yes, you do, *caro mita*. Most of the time, you just probably don't realize it. Whenever we kiss? When we make love? Your eyes turn black. Sometimes only for a split second. But they turn. And when you get supremely pissed off? Your ears draw to little points."

Her hands flew to her ears.

"Not now," he said, smiling. "So far, that only seems to happen when I really push your buttons."

Phoebe dropped her head. How could she deny the truth any longer?

"Phoebe," Sebastian said gently. "It's entirely possible that Danika left to protect you. That she thought the only way to keep you safe was to stay as far away from you as possible. She probably bound your powers somehow and bespelled you, and then left, thinking you'd be safe with your father."

Phoebe was silent for a long moment, nestled in the shelter of his arms. Could it be possible? Had she spent the better part of her life hating her mother for all the wrong reasons?

He drew a deep breath, as though to speak, then let it out and remained silent.

"What?" she prompted.

"You realize it's entirely possible, from your description at least, that your mother was Carpathï?"

"Like Sïnsobar?"

He nodded.

"A skin-shifter," she said softly.

"Yeah," he confirmed. "And that would make you one as well."

She swallowed.

"How does that work?" she asked in a small voice.

"I don't know," he admitted, piercing her with a steady stare. "But we will find out. You're not in this alone."

She rolled that around in her head. It was strange, having someone like Sebastian in her life. Someone committed to her. Someone so concerned about her, worried about her wellbeing and her happiness. Her father had loved her. In his own way. But he'd always been focused on the sword first and foremost. And then there'd been the ruins.

Her mother had put her first. But she'd left. To avoid becoming someone's prisoner. To keep her daughter from becoming one.

"So, that could happen to me? Some random demon could come along and…and take me away, lock me up, keep me like a pet? Or a slave?"

"No, love. That will never happen to you."

Phoebe tipped her head back and peered at him, desperate to believe. "How can you be sure of that?"

He pressed his lips to her forehead, lingered there. "Because I've already claimed you. And no demon is stupid enough to challenge me."

She huffed out a breath. Could he be any more arrogant? But his confidence comforted her in a strange, probably completely twisted way, and she settled her head against his chest. Her thoughts whirled.

"So Sïnsobar could impersonate anybody?"

Sebastian nodded. "Most of the time you'd be able to tell. Talk to him about something only that person would know. Sooner or later, he'd get tripped up. But it's still dangerous because in the meantime, he'd be able to get close to you. Close enough to touch you, to shimmer away with you, or kill you, and you'd be none the wiser. Not until it was too late."

Phoebe shot to her feet, filled with panic. "We have to warn the others, Ricardo and Marco. We need to—"

And then she sat, dumbfounded. She turned wide eyes to Sebastian. "How do we know he hasn't...that they aren't..."

Grim, Sebastian laced his fingers through hers and gently squeezed her hand. "We don't."

Chapter Nineteen

"Well, we can't just sit here and do nothing," Phoebe said at last. Sebastian watched, filled with pride, as she pulled herself together. "First things first. You need to send the journal and the stone away again, wherever it is that you sent them before. We can't risk Sïnsobar getting his hands on those."

He hadn't expected that. He was learning all sorts of new things about his little mate. One of which, she may be taken by surprise, but she bounced right back and flourished under pressure. And she was practical. With a thought, Sebastian vanished the items in question. "I'll conjure them back for you whenever you want them."

"I know," she said in that absent sort of way she had when her mind was already on the next subject. Sebastian grinned despite the dire situation. "What next?" she asked softly, as though speaking to herself.

Before he could respond, she was already in motion, thinking on her feet, pacing the confines of the tent as she ticked points off her mental list. "You and I have to stick together. There's no question there. If he can impersonate you well enough that it fooled me once, I don't want to take that chance again."

Now his grin nearly split his face. Well, that would certainly save on arguments later if she thought it was her idea.

"Somehow, we have to figure out if Ricardo is really Ricardo," she went on. "That should be easy enough. But I don't know what to do about Marco. I don't know him well enough to say if it really is him, either way. And we need to find that damned sword before they do."

That caught his attention. "Phoebe, stop."

He caught her hand as she passed by and tugged her around until she finally focused on him.

"You say that like you believe it's here. Close by." When she bit her lip, he lost patience. "We're in this together. We are mated. No more secrets."

He could see it the moment she made up her mind. And he didn't know whether to be relieved or pissed off that she hadn't gotten to this point sooner.

"If my suspicions are correct, then yes, the sword is very close by."

"Explain," he demanded.

"According to Dad's journals, when he had Dr. Brewster examine the sword, he also commissioned him to have a replica forged. I believe, on that first excavation we returned to right after the fire…an excavation that brought us here to Calakmul… That my father hid the real sword in the ruins. And I believe the sword that was stolen was the replica."

Sebastian stared at her, stunned. "But any demon that got close to it, that touched it, would know it was a fake. They wouldn't have been able to sense any resonating energy source—"

"Dad took care of that." She shot him an uneasy look. "He had Dr. Brewster take fragments of the bone, chips of the stone, and slices of the skin and inlaid them into the replica, hoping that if there were paranormal properties present, the DNA samples and the shard of Jasper would give off enough energy to fool any thieves. At least, until the real sword could be moved if necessary."

"Smart," Sebastian said. Hope soared as grudging admiration for Phoebe's father grew. The man had been smart. Cautious and smart. At least, he had been when it came to the sword. Now when it came to his wife and his daughter, on the other hand, that was another story. "It must have worked, because, as far as we know, Stolas believes he has the real sword."

"Good. Now, I haven't been able to translate much yet, but the lines I did get to so far are promising. I'm more certain now than I was before that—"

A huge explosion rocked the campsite. Sebastian dove for Phoebe. Wrapping his arms around her, he took her to the floor and covered her with his body. The blast had been so close that his ears were still ringing. Keeping a protective arm wrapped around her head, and the bulk of his body hovering over hers, he leaned up and looked around.

The corner of the tent was on fire. Smoke was already beginning to billow inside. Through a tear in the fabric, Sebastian could see shadows moving outside. Phoebe pushed up from the floor.

"What happened?"

"We're under attack."

"Ricardo," she whispered. Then, before he could anticipate, she shoved herself up and was sprinting out of the tent.

"Damn it," he hissed as he followed her.

He found her crouched between Ricardo and Marco near a pile of overturned crates. Ricardo had a rifle, and he was firing at anything that moved. Phoebe had procured a pistol, and she, too, was returning fire. Only the demons that were pouring into the camp weren't shooting with the same caliber. Plasma balls flew willy-nilly through the darkness, igniting whatever they landed on, including Ricardo's tent.

Sebastian morphed. He had no choice. There were just too many demons to fight. His primary concern was getting to Phoebe. How she'd managed to cross the camp to get to the others so quickly was a mystery to him, but he had his suspicions. Perhaps she had a specialized power all her own.

Swarms came at him, right and left. When a bullet whizzed by his head, he shot a sharp look to the humans crouched near his mate. Phoebe already had her hand on the barrel of Ricardo's gun, pushing it in another direction. She shook her head vehemently and she shouted at the old man.

Confident his mate had the situation in hand, and that he wouldn't be suffering from lead poisoning in his ass before the end of the fight, he continued slashing and smashing his way through camp.

A shiver of awareness went down his spine when he heard a dark laugh from nearby.

Ashïek.

Damn it. He had to get to Phoebe. *Now.*

As he ripped the head from one fallen foe, he stepped over another on his way to her side. And then his heart lodged in his throat. Ashïek shimmered right behind her.

Before Sebastian could shout warning, before he could move, Ricardo spun about and made to shoulder the rifle. But the demon was just too close, a plasma ball already formed in his palm. Sebastian sprinted toward them, but even as he did so, he knew he'd be too late. Phoebe's focus was on the demon standing over Marco, claws extended on a downward, lethal slash. She had her gun up and was already squeezing the trigger, not that the bullet would stop the demon for long. Ricardo shot one glance over his shoulder, long enough to take note of Sebastian's approach, long enough to realize that Phoebe's back was unprotected.

And then Ricardo threw himself to the side, directly into the path of the plasma ball aimed straight at Phoebe's back. The projectile hit the old guide square in the chest. Sebastian arrived in time to catch him before he hit Phoebe. She whirled around, her wide-eyed stare going from the huge, charred hole in Ricardo's body to Ashïek's smug face.

One second Phoebe was there. Shocked. Horrified. Grief-stricken. And the next, an enraged Carpathï demoness bent on destruction had taken her place.

Sebastian blinked. He'd been expecting this. Well, not *this* exactly. But he'd been expecting to see her morph, sooner or later.

But to actually see it…took his breath away.

And stunned him long enough for a sneaky Charocté to get in a lucky shot. Pain slashed across his ribs, and he bellowed. He had time only for a backhanded blow to his attacker before he had to leap after his mate. She was already charging after Ashïek, murder in her eyes.

Two more Charocté leaped in her way. She cut them down without a second glance, her focus solely on the bastard who'd killed Ricardo. More demons jumped between Sebastian and Phoebe, slowing him, hampering his progress. She couldn't face Ashïek, not alone. She wouldn't survive.

Panic closed his throat. Fear clutched his heart.

Ashïek fired a plasma ball at Phoebe. Sebastian roared, sure he was going to watch his mate die. But she spun and dodged at the last second, and the plasma ball whooshed past her streaming pitch-black hair. Sebastian was certain his heart had stopped dead in his chest in that sliver of time.

He tried to catch up to her, but she was like a streak of lightning, moving so fast he was having trouble tracking her. Suddenly she had a plasma ball in her hand. At first, he thought she'd caught it, but then he realized it was hers, that she'd formed it. But, untutored as she was, her aim was bad, and she set the ground at Ashïek's feet aflame.

But she'd caught Sebastian's foe by surprise—that much Sebastian could see. Ashïek danced back from the flames, his expression thunderous. Sebastian would have laughed aloud had it not been for the fact that, even now, a Ralsha was sneaking up on his mate from the side. Sebastian was currently battling three of his Ashïek's minions. He pulled in his focus and made to shimmer to his mate when a flash of movement caught his eye. Suddenly Marco was standing between Phoebe and the Ralsha. A plasma ball formed in the palm of Marco's hand and then the Ralsha was aglow, screeching as it erupted into a moving ball of flames.

Marco took up an unmistakable, defensive position at Phoebe's back, sticking to her like glue though she was bouncing all over the camp in pursuit of Ashïek. Marco shot down two more demons intent on Phoebe before Sebastian could join them. And all the while,

Phoebe focused on Ashïek with single-minded purpose.

Ashïek lobbed another plasma ball at Phoebe. This time she wasn't fast enough. Though it didn't catch her full on, it scorched the side of her thigh. She screamed in pain. Sebastian lost his focus, and a Charocté jumped on his back, latching on to one of his wings, jerking and yanking. Sebastian roared. He beat his wings, catching a minion nearby, decapitating him. But he couldn't dislodge the Charocté on his back. He roared again, reaching behind him, grappling, struggling as the Charocté wrenched on his left wing until tendons strained and popped.

And suddenly Phoebe was there, darting all around him, slashing at the minions who'd thought to bring the great Vengeance down. She vaulted onto Sebastian's shoulders, put her knee on the back of the minion on Sebastian's back, and ripped the Charocté's head clean off. She was already racing to another attacker before the demon's body had fallen from Sebastian's back.

Sebastian could only spin, arms extended, prepared to battle the next attacker as he tried to track her. But no one even got close to him. Soon, Sebastian stood amid a pile of demon body parts, catching nothing more than fleeting glimpses of his mate as she annihilated his enemies.

He caught a glimpse of Ashïek, standing just at the edge of camp. Lucifer's general watched Sebastian's mate with shrewd consideration. And then he shimmered away.

Finally, when there were no more demons to kill, Phoebe stopped running. She stood before him, her back to him, crouched defensively, waiting for the next wave of demons to come.

"Phoebe," he called softly. He didn't want to startle her.

She glanced over her shoulder. The moment her gaze locked on him, she straightened, frowning. And then she looked around. Now that the haze of bloodlust was fading, reality came crashing down. With an anguished cry, she raced to Ricardo.

Sebastian followed, standing guard as she knelt beside the old guide's body and sobbed. He scanned the clearing. There was no sign of Marco—or rather, of Sïnsobar. At least, that was who Sebastian assumed it had been. Why Sïnsobar had protected her that way, Sebastian couldn't figure out.

Had he been merely protecting a demoness of his breed? Had he connected Phoebe to Danika somehow? If so, what was Sïnsobar's connection to Danika? Why would he risk Ashïek's wrath to protect Vengeance's mate?

He'd have to figure it out. Just not now. Now they needed to move. There was no telling whether or not Ashïek would be back, and whether or not he'd be bringing reinforcements.

Sebastian bent and scooped up a struggling Phoebe, helping her to her feet. She leaned against him, limp in his arms as she continued to sob. Sebastian curled his wings protectively around her, all the while he watched for movement.

Phoebe wasn't quite coherent yet. And when she looked down and got her first real good look at herself, she began screaming.

Sebastian took her by the shoulders and shook her. "Phoebe. Damn it, snap out of it." He hated being an asshole, wanted only to hold her tight and comfort her.

But they couldn't afford for her to fall apart right now.

Her cry strangled off. But now she was whimpering. Which, honestly, wasn't much better. The pitiful sound was ripping his guts out. "Phoebe," he demanded, shaking her again. "Look at me."

Finally, huge black eyes turned his way. They welled and overflowed. Tears continued to track down her cheeks leaving tracks through the splashes of blood on her face. She was covered in the stuff. Soaked with it.

He drew his focus in and conjured them both clean, though he didn't morph back. Not yet. Not until he knew they were safe.

"Baby, look at me. Focus." When she finally complied, he changed his grip to a soothing stroke. "Are you hurt?"

She made to glance down, but he stalled her. "No. Look at me. Do you hurt anywhere?"

She shook her head. She was probably numb, already going into shock. He glanced down, doing a quick visual inspection. Her thigh was raw, blistered and charred. Other than that, he didn't see so much as a scratch on her.

"Your thigh has a burn." When she started to look down again, he quickly diverted her attention back to his face. "Stay with me, okay? Look up here. We're going to get you taken care of, all right?"

She nodded.

"Breathe." He pushed his palm along the side of her face, hooking her hair behind her ear. "Can you do that for me, *caro mita*? Can you just breathe?"

Again, she nodded.

"We're going to shimmer now. Back to the farm,

okay?"

She said nothing, just stood docilely as Sebastian closed his arms tight around her. He couldn't shake the sight of Ashïek's plasma ball whizzing past her head. His hands were still trembling as he shimmered with Phoebe to his kitchen back at the farm.

Sebastian guided her to a chair, and he conjured a First Aid kit. He dropped to his knees beside her and peeled back the ragged edges of her pant leg. And his stomach rolled. Her flesh was burned so badly. Blistered and split. Blackened. He dabbed at the wound, doing his best to pick charred material from the injury without causing her more pain than necessary. His chest ached. He should have protected her. He should have never let her take Ashïek on like that.

Sebastian glanced up at her, she hadn't so much as flinched this whole time. Her stare was vacant. And she hadn't morphed back to human form yet.

Sebastian knew real fear then. What could he do for her? How could he make this right?

"Well, well, well…would you look at that. The great Vengeance, brought to his knees at last."

A river of ice lanced straight through his veins. Still crouching, Sebastian spun, placing himself directly between his mate and his age-old nemesis. Once again, he'd lost track of his surroundings. He was losing his touch.

"Aww," Ashïek taunted from his perch on the countertop. "Did you honestly think you would get to *keep* the girl? Here's a news flash, Vengeance. Deep down, you're still a bad guy. And bad guys don't get to keep the girls." He glanced around the room. "So homey, by the way. You've turned into a regular old

Martha Stewart, haven't you, Vengeance?" He shook his head and tsked. "Such a waste of talent."

Before Sebastian could respond, a massive explosion rocked the house, knocking Sebastian on his ass and tipping Phoebe from her chair.

Chapter Twenty

"Ah, that'll be Dimiezlo. Now there's a demon who knows how to make an entrance."

Another explosion, this one much larger than the last, shook the house on its foundation, nearly deafening Sebastian. Something groaned overhead, as if the very roof threatened to come down on their heads. Smoke began to fill the air.

Sebastian shot to his feet and pushed a nearly catatonic Phoebe behind him. Ashïek lobbed a plasma ball as he vaulted from the counter. Sebastian deflected the missile with one of his own. He fired another off in quick succession, clipping Ashïek in the shoulder. All out battle ensued, but they were too evenly matched, and the only thing taking major damage was Sebastian's house. Wood splintered and caught fire. Appliances exploded. Huge holes were blown in the walls.

Sebastian had to work double-time to keep Phoebe behind him and protected while still keeping Ashïek on the defensive. Another explosion rocked the floor beneath him, and Sebastian lost his footing for a moment, going down on one knee. It was the opening Ashïek had been waiting for. He slammed into Sebastian, sending them both crashing into the living room. Phoebe was knocked through the doorway ahead of them.

Sebastian caught a glimpse of her as she went sailing over the couch a second before Ashïek summoned a sword and slashed it across Sebastian's chest, cutting deep. Blood sprayed in a wide arc. Sebastian stumbled back with a pained grunt. He summoned his own sword and managed to fend off the next blow. But his wounds weakened him, and now Ashïek stood between Sebastian and Phoebe. Steel clanged against steel as Ashïek advanced, ruthlessly driving Sebastian back, smashing his head against the fireplace mantel.

Phoebe let out a blood curdling cry and leaped onto Ashïek's back, taking both Ashïek and Sebastian by surprise. She gouged at Ashïek's face and neck with her small claws, ripping at his hair. She wrapped an arm around his throat and dug her knees into his back.

Ashïek, off balance, staggered back, his arms pinwheeling for a moment. He grappled with Phoebe, but she was fast, and she was fueled by rage. Sebastian, his vision dimmed by the blow to his head and the severe loss of blood, struggled to his feet. He had to get to Phoebe before she got hurt.

With a choked roar, Ashïek reached up and caught a handful of Phoebe's hair and jerked her forward. She went somersaulting over his shoulder and landed on her back at his feet. Ashïek lifted his blade high, preparing to plunge it through Phoebe's chest as she lay there with the breath knocked out of her.

As the blade came down Sebastian dove to cover her. The blade hit one of his wings and deflected, but the poison-dipped point penetrated his back, piercing a lung. Sebastian rolled to the side taking Phoebe with him.

Ashïek charged after them, sword raised for another killing blow. He brought it down, but Sebastian swiftly sealed his wings around them like a cocoon. The blade sent a shower of sparks flying as it connected with Sebastian's metallic armor-like feathers.

A furious war cry came from the doorway. Sebastian caught sight of Sïnsobar as he swooped inside the room. In that moment, Sebastian thought they were done. Or that he was, at least. He'd battle till his last breath to give his mate a fighting chance. But he was a realist. There was no way he'd be able to take them both on, not while defending his mate, not wounded as he was. He should have called the others for help. Now it was too late.

Sïnsobar lowered his head and hit Ashïek like a freight train. The two went careening into the far wall. Picture frames crashed to the floor and shattered. Flames punched through the ceiling. A loud crack came from upstairs, and the house shuddered.

"Get her out of here," Sïnsobar yelled.

It took Sebastian a moment to realize the Carpathï was talking to him. And still it made no sense. Why was Sïnsobar helping them?

With a groan, he rolled over and wrapped his arm around Phoebe's waist. She was just beginning to push up on all fours, though she swayed drunkenly to the side. Blood dripped from her nose.

The last thing Sebastian saw of his home was Ashïek and Sïnsobar grappling and crashing around the living room. He wrapped his arms and his wings around Phoebe and used the last of his strength to shimmer them away.

Sebastian couldn't control the landing. He'd lost

too much blood. His vision was already winking in and out. His grip on Phoebe was tenuous at best, his hands slick with his own blood. When they landed, they landed hard. He went skidding across the marble floor, and Phoebe bounced out of his arms.

He tried to speak, tried to call out for help, but the only thing that came out of his mouth was a spray of blood. He was seeing completely in shades of gray now. He recognized the room, the foyer of Gideon's plantation. He'd managed to get that right, at least. His breath left him in a pained whoosh as he tried to rise. He couldn't even lift his head off the floor. Pounding footsteps came rushing near. Then again, maybe those were the last of his heartbeats.

He gradually became aware of someone crouching over him.

Phoebe. My Phoebe. My fierce mate.

She hovered over him, growling low in her throat. A plasma ball crackling over her open palm, threatening the two dark shadows that entered the room at a run. The brightness of plasma balls in the distance drew his focus.

"What the hell," Xander's deep rasp echoed throughout the room, ringing in his ears.

"Is that what I think it is?" Gideon demanded.

"A fucking demoness," Xander growled.

"Sebastian, man, can you hear me?" Gideon called.

Sebastian tried to respond. More blood bubbled at the corner of his mouth and he began coughing. Christ, he was hacking up a lung here, drowning for sure.

He turned his throbbing head, blinked woozily. His sideways view of the scene made him want to laugh. Xander and Gideon hovered at the edge of the room, regarding Phoebe like some kind of miracle. Or a deadly force of nature.

Hell, she does kind of look like it, doesn't she?

God, he was getting delirious.

"Wait," he managed to croak. More bloody coughing ensued. Finally, when he finished hacking, he stretched out his hand, gaining everyone's attention.

Blackness was creeping steadily around the edges of his vision now, and he knew he didn't have much time left.

"My...mate..." he rasped, "Phoebe...safe..."

It was all he could get out before the darkness claimed him.

****

Phoebe crouched protectively over Sebastian as the two demons extinguished the plasma balls in their hands and slowly straightened at Sebastian's words. Phoebe glanced down. When she realized Sebastian had lost consciousness, she gave a little cry and dropped to her knees beside him. She immediately reached for his face.

"Sebastian! Sebastian, wake up!"

He was still breathing, but just barely. A pool of crimson was beginning to form beneath him, slowly spreading across the marble floor. Oh, dear lord, he was losing so much blood. She pressed her hands to his chest, hard. But the gash was just too long to cover and, feeling helpless, she began to sob.

The tall blond demon dropped down beside her. Instinct had her hissing a warning at him.

"It's okay," he said in a low, calm voice. He held his empty hands up to her. "We're friends. Let us help."

A thick white towel appeared out of nowhere, and

the blond demon pressed it to the wound on Sebastian's chest. The towel went completely red in minutes.

"Move on back now," the blond instructed with a heavy southern accent. "You have to let us see what needs to be done here."

Phoebe fell back on her heels and then scooted back as the other demon joined them. He wore his hair in a buzz cut, but he had a dark five o'clock shadow. He looked like GI Joe...with flame red eyes.

GI Joe and the blond demon exchanged glances.

"It's deep," GI Joe said, his voice rough as sandpaper.

"Gonna have to cauterize it," the blond one said. He glanced over his shoulder. "Call Niklas."

Phoebe looked around, only then realizing there were two women standing in the doorway. One of the women, a tall, leggy, model-type jerked a phone from her pocket and began dialing.

Phoebe looked back to Sebastian. She couldn't take it, couldn't stand seeing him like this. She moved around the blond and knelt at her mate's head. She stroked his cheeks, smoothed his hair from his face. And her tears poured.

"Don't bring him round just yet, sweetheart," the blond demon instructed. "Trust me, he ain't gonna wanna be awake for this."

A new wave of energy shimmered into the room, and Phoebe instantly went back on guard.

"It's okay," the blond one said. "He's one of us."

The newcomer flew to Sebastian's side and dropped to his knees beside GI Joe. "Sweet heaven," he whispered.

"He should have begun healing already, but he's

not. Must have been poison on the blade. We gotta cauterize this wound. Now. You're gonna have to help hold him down."

"No!" Phoebe yelled, moving forward aggressively. He was wounded bad enough as it was. They weren't going to burn him too.

"Darlin', if we don't, he'll bleed out."

She looked up at him uncertainly.

"It'll be okay," the newcomer assured her. His ice blue eyes bore into hers. Then he looked over her shoulder at someone behind her. "Maggie?"

The blond one immediately stiffened. "No way."

"Shhh, Gideon," a short curvaceous woman said as she moved into the room. "Everything's going to be just fine."

A wave of warmth washed over Phoebe. She felt like she was suddenly floating on a cloud, with not a care in the world. Only that couldn't be right, because Sebastian was hurt. Badly hurt. Maybe even dying.

She frowned, blinking furiously. Sebastian. She had to help him.

A gentle hand touched her shoulder. And the warm, fuzzy feeling intensified, wrapping around her, holding though she tried her damnedest to shake it.

"You need to hurry," Maggie instructed. Though her voice was pitched low and easy, it held an unmistakable note of strain. "She's very strong. And she fears for her mate. I don't know how long I can hold her."

Phoebe let two sets of soft, gentle hands ease her back, away from the three men working feverishly over Sebastian. She watched as they tore his shirt off. And she barely flinched when they maneuvered him around,

307

pinning wings and arms to the ground at his sides.

Then the blond straddled Sebastian's waist. Phoebe went up on her knees. She shook her head, resisting the fuzzy cocoon. They'd hurt him. They weren't being careful enough. She made to move closer, but soft hands held her back. A cool, smooth hand came up to press against her forehead.

Phoebe dropped back on her butt. The room all but spun. She felt...drunk.

Whoa. What a buzz.

The short woman—*Maggie, yeah, that was her name*—Maggie knelt directly in front of her, blocking her view. But there was something wrong. Maggie had a thin trickle of blood seeping from her nose. Blood...

Sebastian. Where was he? He was bleeding too. She needed to help him.

"I'm losing her," Maggie said as she dropped to her own butt and wobbled to the side.

Phoebe glanced over and frowned. The blond demon was straddling Sebastian. And his hands were glowing. She blinked. Refocused. No. Those were fire balls...no, plasma balls, she corrected. He was burning Sebastian's chest.

And Sebastian was fighting, teeth gritted, flailing against the floor as the other two held him down.

Phoebe exploded into motion. She hit GI Joe like a tank. They went rolling across the floor and she smashed an elbow into his face. Just like that, she was on her feet, charging back into the fray. A well-placed fist sent the blond one sailing before she turned her wrath on Blue Eyes.

"Son of a...grab her!" someone yelled.

"I can't. She's moving too fast," came the reply.

A muffled grunt met her ears as she slammed into GI Joe once more. Why wouldn't he just stay the hell down? She darted away before he could get a grip on her, and then she wheeled around looking for Blue Eyes. Or Blondie. They were both going down for hurting her mate that way.

"Phoebe," Sebastian whispered.

Phoebe froze. And then she flew back to his side, the others forgotten.

"Don't...they were...helping..."

"But—"

"Trust them...safe now..."

His eyes fluttered closed, and he was out again. She glanced to his chest. The long gash had been sealed closed and all that was left was a long strip of bright pink, blistered flesh."

Blue Eyes approached cautiously. "He's going to be okay."

She flicked a glance to his split lip, caught a glimpse of GI Joe's swollen eye. She refused to feel bad. But then she saw the blond demon hovering over the woman—Maggie—as he held a tissue to her nose and glared holes through Phoebe's hide. Now she felt guilty.

Phoebe glanced down at the hands cradling Sebastian's ash colored face. Crimson hands with little black claws. She sat back on her heels, hard, and she held them up, staring at them, shocked. Disgusted.

"Help me," she whispered, her eyes welled with tears as she looked around the room. "I don't know how to change back," she admitted her shame aloud. And then she dropped her head and sobbed. "I can't...I don't know how."

You could have heard a pin drop.

Gentle hands cupped her shoulders. She looked up into kind brown eyes and a beautiful smile filled with empathy. "We're here to help. Everything's going to be all right now."

Phoebe blinked. "I'm so sorry," she whispered.

The woman's smile grew. "I know. There now."

She enfolded Phoebe in a careful embrace and rubbed slow circles on her back. At length, she pulled back and patted Phoebe's cheek.

"I'm Carly," she said. "And that is my mate, Niklas." She pointed to Blue Eyes. Then she pointed out each one of the others in the room, tagging each with a name. GI Joe was Xander. The scowl on his face made her look away, until the beautiful woman Carly called Kyanna moved into his arms and poked him in the ribs.

"Pleased to meet you," he growled, though he didn't sound happy about it at all.

"The good-looking guy over there is Gideon. He's usually pretty easygoing. He'll stop glaring at you as soon as his wife's nose quits bleeding. And that's Maggie bleeding all over his shirt." When Phoebe started, sucking in a sharp breath, Carly rushed to reassure her, "Oh, honey, I'm just kidding. She's not even bleeding anymore."

Phoebe eased back on her heels.

"Have you never morphed before?" Kyanna asked, moving closer, ignoring Xander's warning growl.

Phoebe shook her head. "No. Not all the way."

That earned her some odd looks from the room at large. Was that not normal? God, she was a freak, even among monsters. Phoebe ducked her head and closed her eyes.

A throat cleared, and then Kyanna said, "That's all right. It happens, ah, I guess." Murmurs of agreement soon went around the room.

No. It didn't. Phoebe could tell, just from the tone. But it was kind of them to lie. She could feel the panic rising again, and the fear. She just wanted to crawl in a hole somewhere. Alone. Not surrounded by Sebastian's well-meaning friends.

"Maggie," Niklas said, his voice pitched soft and low. "Her colors are changing again."

"No!" Gideon barked. "No more. I don't care if she starts shooting rainbows out her pointed little ears. Maggie is officially off duty for the night."

Phoebe frowned as she turned to watch Gideon and Maggie engage in a quiet if heated debate. At length, Gideon moved behind his mate, wrapped his arms around her waist, and rested his hands flat on her stomach.

"No," he repeated firmly.

Xander cleared his throat. "We need to move him."

The men moved into position around Sebastian, and Phoebe tensed.

"They're just going to take him upstairs so he can rest more comfortably," Maggie hurried to assure her. Nodding, Phoebe got to her feet and moved back so Niklas, Xander, and Gideon could heft Sebastian up from the floor. The sight of his battered body made her teary all over again.

As the trio moved past her, Xander took one look at her and barked, "Pull it together, demoness. He can't deal with you falling apart right now."

Phoebe's gaped at him. Her tears forgotten.

Kyanna gasped. "Xander!"

He rolled his eyes and began moving the others along toward the stairs. Maggie came to stand beside Phoebe and slipped an arm around her shoulders. She offered Phoebe a conspiratorial smile, and then turned to glance at the demon who'd just put Phoebe, very rudely, in her place.

"Don't worry. He'll grow on you."

Chapter Twenty-One

Maggie, Kyanna, and Carly took her to Sebastian's room. They helped her bandage his wounds, and then sat with her while she waited for him to wake up, a united front of solidarity in the face of their mates' disgruntlement.

"Try closing your eyes and breathing deeply," Kyanna suggested. "Kind of like meditating. Imagine what your eyes normally look like. The color of your hair. The shade of your skin."

Phoebe did. Just as she'd been trying everything they'd suggested for the past hour. Well, when they weren't grilling her with the kinds of questions she suspected well-meaning sisters might utilize when meeting their brother's girlfriend for the first time.

Nothing happened, and she began to fear she'd be stuck looking like this for the rest of her life, however long that might be.

Nerves had her pushing to her feet and pacing the room.

"Oh!" Carly exclaimed, drawing the other women's attention. "Look at her leg!"

Phoebe glanced down. Her thigh had been throbbing for so long, and with Sebastian's ordeal, she'd nearly tuned it out.

"Maybe that's why she isn't able to change back," Maggie suggested. "Let's get that cleaned out."

The three women advanced on her like a battalion of field nurses. By the time they were done with her, even the smallest of scrapes had been thoroughly cleaned and bandaged.

"There," Carly said as she smoothed down the last piece of medical tape. "All done."

The three women sat back and stared expectantly at her. After a while, and a collective puzzled shrug, they eventually began wandering off, one by one.

"If you get hungry later, the kitchen is downstairs to the left, just off the foyer. Help yourself. If you need anything at all, Gideon and I are down the hall, second door on the right," Maggie said. "And Niklas and Carly will be spending the night as well. They're at the other end of the hall, third room on the left."

"Thank you," Phoebe murmured with a small smile.

Maggie slipped out and closed the door behind her with a soft click. Phoebe climbed onto the big bed beside Sebastian and curled up, careful not to bump him. Not an easy task, given how much space his wings took up. But she managed. She lay there for what felt like hours, just watching him. She was tired, emotionally wrung out, but she couldn't fall asleep.

Heaving a sigh, she eased from the bed and tread quietly to the door. As she reached out to turn the doorknob, she caught a glimpse of her hand. Gasping, she spun around and rushed to the vanity across the room, patting her face, running her tongue along her teeth.

Relief swamped her at the sight that met her eyes. She was back to normal...or well, humanlike. She felt herself begin to tense up again, and quickly squashed that line of thought. She didn't want to be red anymore, and she feared if she didn't settle down, that was exactly what would happen.

Phoebe's stomach growled. She shot one more glance at the bed. Sebastian seemed to be resting comfortably. So she slipped from the room and tiptoed down the hall toward a grand staircase worthy of Scarlett O'Hara.

Phoebe ran her fingertips down the banister, her gaze tracking her surroundings as she'd failed to do before. Maggie's home was really beautiful.

She crossed the foyer, noting that someone had cleaned up all the blood. But her footsteps slowed as she reached the kitchen. The rattle of a plastic bag and clink of plates alerted her to another's presence, and she stopped walking. Phoebe caught her lower lip between her teeth. She didn't feel like being social, not just yet. And what if it was GI Joe—no, his name was Xander. What if it was Xander? Truth be told, he scared her a little.

She slowly turned and began tiptoeing back toward the stairs.

"You already made it this far, darlin'. Might as well come on in."

Phoebe froze. She closed her eyes, groaned inwardly, and then let out a deep breath. Turning around, fingers fumbling with the soft hem of her borrowed T-shirt, she stepped inside the kitchen.

Gideon stood at the counter near the refrigerator. He wore a pair of tattered jeans, zipped but not buttoned, and not a stitch more. His golden hair was mussed, his feet were bare. He had the look of a man who'd just rolled from some lucky woman's bed—that lucky woman being Maggie, of course.

Phoebe clasped her hands behind her and rocked back and forth. "So…"

He turned to fully face her, and leaned back against the counter, crossing his arms. His assessing stare traveled quickly over her before returning to consider her hair.

"Well, I gotta say, I didn't expect brown."

That caught her off guard.

"The green eyes, yeah, but not brown hair."

"Why not?"

He prodded at a bruise the size of her fist along his jaw. "If you don't mind my sayin' so, you got one hell of a temper on you, darlin'. Red suits you better," he said with a wink. But his roguish grin stalled out any offense she might take.

"Sorry about, ah, earlier." Lord, at this rate, she'd be scraping her toe across the ground and ducking her head.

He let her squirm for a moment more, and then he broke out laughing. The sound rolled through the room, rich and warm. "Don't worry about it. Any one of our mates would have done the same, my own included. How's the big guy doing, by the way?"

"Okay, I think. He's sleeping." Phoebe felt the muscles in her neck and shoulders begin to relax. She eased farther inside the room.

"Rest will help him heal better than anything else right now. Hungry?" he asked, returning to his task.

She couldn't see around his broad shoulders, so she went to stand beside him to watch him work. She studied the array of ingredients on the counter, puzzled.

"What are you making?"

"PB and J," he said, licking a daub of purple goo from his thumb. "With jalapeño, pickles, bananas, and cheddar cheese. Want some?"

She shook her head, scrunched her nose up, and stifled a gag. "No. Thanks."

"It's for Maggie." He glanced up. The grin he offered her was an adorable combination of goofy, giddy joy and boastful male.

"Really?"

"She's pregnant. She has cravings."

He sounded so proud of that bit of information, she laughed aloud.

"Congratulations," she told him, amused.

"Thanks!"

She watched as he carefully trimmed the crust and then cut the sandwich into four precise triangles before moving them to a clean plate.

"Can't you conjure?" Again with the lack of filter. She could have kicked herself. But she couldn't seem to help it either.

Gideon glanced up and blinked, his expression surprised. "Yeah. Why?"

Phoebe eased back a little and wrapped her arms around herself. "Uh, well, Sebastian mentioned everyone has different, um, abilities. That not everyone can do certain things. I just thought…" She nodded toward the plate and the sandwich he'd constructed and shrugged.

"Oh, well." He dusted his hands, and then turned to face her, leaning a hip against the counter. "Yes, I can conjure. Unless I'm hurt, or right after I morph. For some reason, morphing takes more out of me than it does some of the others. I make the sandwiches for

Maggie by hand because…well." He paused, as if searching for the right words. "Because I guess it makes me feel like I'm doing something important for her. I want her to know how much I love her, and this is one of the ways I can show her."

Phoebe melted then and there. How could you not like a guy who was so sweet and loved his wife so much? Loved her and went out of his way to do little things to show her.

"There's so much I don't know about this…this…" She couldn't even find the right words.

He shot her a grin. "We're figuring that out."

She reached over, picked up one of the leftover slices of cheese, and nibbled the edge.

"So you've never morphed before, huh?"

She shook her head.

"How is that possible?"

Phoebe glanced at the bottle of soda on the counter. "Are there anymore of those?"

"Sure," Gideon said. He opened the fridge and pulled one out, cracked the lid, and handed it to her. "Whole fridge full. Maggie says they help settle her stomach." He frowned. "You feeling sick, darlin'?"

Phoebe shrugged. "Just a little off. Probably too much excitement if you know what I mean."

Gideon nodded, but he seemed to be watching her a little closer now. "I better get this up to Maggie. But seriously, you need to know we're all here for you. When you're ready to talk, if you have any questions, anything…all you have to do is let us know what you need."

Phoebe held the 7-Up to her chest as she felt herself getting emotional. "Thank you. I mean that."

Gideon scooped up the plate and the soda. He took a few steps, and then doubled back to grab a pint of mint chocolate chip ice cream from the freezer and a spoon from the drawer. With another nod, he walked toward the door.

At the doorway, though, he stopped and looked back.

"Phoebe?"

"Yeah?"

"Welcome to the family."

Phoebe blinked, and by God if tears didn't start welling in her eyes. But before she could respond, he vanished.

She sipped soda and stood there for a moment more, staring at the empty doorway, lost in thought. She took another bite of cheese. And her stomach rebelled.

Forcing herself to swallow the bite in her mouth, she grimaced. Phoebe looked around and found the trash can. After pitching the rest of the cheese, she gulped half the bottle of soda, grabbed another bottle from the fridge for the road, and made her way back upstairs.

When she stepped back inside the room, she drew up short. The bed was empty.

"Sebastian!"

He staggered into view, bracing his hand on the bathroom doorway. His hair was damp, and steam rolled from the room behind him. "Yeah?"

"What are you doing out of bed?" She rushed inside the room, deposited the soda bottles on the bedside table, and hurried to his side.

"I'm fine," he assured her, but his words were slurred, and he was unsteady on his feet.

"No, you're not. Get back in bed." She inserted herself under his arm and he lumbered across the room beside her.

"You changed back," he remarked, glancing down at her.

"Yeah, I'm not really sure how. I just realized suddenly I was back to normal." She shrugged and eased him around until he dropped back on the bed. "You changed back too."

He took a deep breath, stretched, and grimaced, his hand going to the fresh bandage on his chest.

She worried her bottom lip. She shouldn't have left him alone. "Are you okay?"

"Yeah, just a catch. By morning I'll be good as new." He patted the bed. "Come here."

"That's probably not a good idea. You need your rest."

"I can't rest until I have you in my arms. I need to know you're safe."

Melting.

She couldn't even fight it anymore, was tired of trying. She turned the lamp off and climbed up on the bed beside him.

"Where'd you get the clothes?" He fingered the collar of the oversized T-shirt.

"Carly asked Niklas to conjure them for me."

"You like boxers and muscle shirts. I can—"

"No, this is fine for tonight." She snuggled up to his side, mindful of Gideon's comment about conjuring in an injured state.

"You could always take it off," he suggested, the leer in his voice unmistakable.

"I don't think so. You're in no condition to—"

"Wanna try and find out?"

"Sebastian! No!" She poked his hip, gently.

He chuckled and cuddled her closer. Phoebe wrapped herself around him, careful of his bandages. The silence and the darkened room was like a cocoon, the sense of safety lulled her.

Just when she thought he must have drifted off again, he whispered against her hair, "Did you really give Xander a black eye? Or was I hallucinating?"

"Sebastian," she hissed, mortified. But a long moment later, ashamed of herself, she whispered, "Yes."

He started chuckling. And he got louder. And louder. Until he was laughing so hard and so loud the bed shook, and she feared the others would come to check on him.

"Go to sleep." She harrumphed and turned over, giving him her back.

He curled himself around her, snuggled her close and—still chuckling—whispered in her ear, "That's my girl."

****

The next day, just as he'd predicted, Sebastian was as good as new. His chest now bore a long, fresh pink scar, and he was a little sore. But other than that, he was completely healed. Phoebe, apparently, couldn't get over it. She kept asking if he was all right. And she'd insisted on looking at his chest, several times. Not that he minded. Sooner or later, he'd convince her he was one hundred percent, and he'd seduce her back into bed if he had to.

He sat on a log swing in Gideon's backyard watching the river slowly drift by. Phoebe lay beside him, her head on his lap.

They'd spent the better part of the day with the others. The group, as a whole, had been giving Phoebe a crash course in demonology. They'd told her about various other demon species, explaining abilities and trying to determine if she had any gifts of her own. So far, the only thing they'd pinned down for sure was her speed.

"I'm sorry about your farm, Sebastian."

A heavy weight settled upon his chest at the reminder. He'd been doing a pretty good job of not thinking about it. But it had been like an elephant in the room. His place was gone. His haven. Yeah, he was disappointed. Sad. Pissed off, even.

But then he looked at the woman in his arms, and he smiled.

"It doesn't matter."

She frowned up at him. "But it does! How—"

He shushed her by laying a finger to her lips. "It doesn't matter because I still have you. You're safe, and that *is* all that matters." He feathered his fingers through her hair thoughtfully. "We'll rebuild. Either there, or somewhere else. We'll make a home for both of us."

Tears pooled in her eyes, and she blinked, turning her head away.

"Sound good?" he asked, suddenly uncertain.

"Sounds good," she echoed, her voice a little hoarse.

Smiling, Sebastian turned his gaze to the river. But then he glanced back down. If she could shimmer, he could send her away in an emergency. He wouldn't have to worry so much if they were ever separated and pinned down like they had been before.

"Try to shimmer, just one more time," he urged.

She heaved an irritated sigh and sat up. "I can't."

"Have you tried, honestly?"

"Stop nagging," she snapped.

"But you should be able to shimmer. At least, in a limited capacity. All Carpathï can. It should be an inherited trait. You've closed your mind."

She turned away to gaze out over the river and ignored him. He studied her face. She had dark shadows beneath her eyes, her skin looked faintly gray, and her cheeks were hollow.

"Are you feeling all right?"

"I'm fine." But her expression was pinched, belying her words.

"You hardly touched your lunch." Come to think of it, she'd skipped breakfast completely. He narrowed his eyes.

"Too busy talking, I guess."

She had yet to talk about Ricardo. He'd tried to broach the subject, more than once. But she shot him down every time, closing herself off and withdrawing until she would barely acknowledge him. Her grief was eating her alive. And he couldn't get through to her.

He reached over and rubbed slow circles on her back. Bit by bit, he felt her relax beneath his hand. Finally, she leaned back and let him draw her into his arms.

Frustration drove him to try, just one more time. He pressed a kiss to the side of her forehead, and spoke in low, soothing tones. "We agreed no more secrets, right?"

She immediately tensed.

"Tell me what's wrong. Talk to me."

She pushed to her feet and began walking away from the log swing. Sebastian shot up and followed. He grabbed her by the wrist and spun her around. She tried to break free, jerked at her wrist, and then, when that didn't work, she slammed her palm against his shoulder. Still, he wouldn't budge.

"Damn you, let me go."

"Never. Tell me what you're so afraid of."

"You saw what happened," she finally snapped, pushed to her limits. "You saw what I did to—"

She broke off and turned her head away, closing her eyes tight. Sebastian captured her chin and drew her back to face him.

"You saw what I did to those demons that attacked us at camp," she said, quiet now, unable or unwilling to fully meet his gaze. "You saw what I did to your friends. What if I got mad, really mad, at you? What if I hurt you that way? I couldn't live with myself."

"Is that what's bothering you?"

Her head drooped forward, and her shoulders sagged. "I'm a monster," she whispered. "How can you want me? How can you stand to be around me?"

His heart hurt to hear her talk about herself this way. He released her and took a step back. At his actions, she seemed to cave in on herself. But he had to get through to her, once and for all. She couldn't go on like this.

It was breaking her.

Chapter Twenty-Two

Sebastian centered his energy, drew it in, and he morphed. He snapped his wings open, extending them to their full, impressive glory.

"Look at me, Phoebe," he commanded around a mouthful of fangs.

Grudgingly, she peered up at him.

"You trust me, don't you?"

She nodded without hesitation.

"You know I would never hurt you, right?"

Again, she nodded.

"Then you have to trust me on this. I am the same as you. Maybe not Carpathï, but demon all the same, yeah? You won't hurt me. And you are not a monster. You are my mate, as I am yours." He drew her into his arms, and she didn't resist. Pleased, hopeful, he rubbed his cheek against the top of her head as he folded his wings around them. "You are smart, and compassionate and gentle. But you're also strong when you have to be. Resilient and brave. And I am proud to call you my mate."

She curled into him, but he urged her back a little and cupped her face, forcing her to meet his probing stare.

"Never question how much I want you." He searched her eyes. "I love you, Phoebe."

She blinked. Slowly, with heartbreaking

tenderness, she eased her arms around his neck and pulled him down. And then she hugged him tight.

Sebastian morphed to human form and hugged her right back, lifting her clear off the ground. He set her back on her feet, and he captured her lips with his. The taste of her, the soft yielding of her lips against his, the way her body melted against his sent desire rushing through his system.

But then she broke the kiss and tilted her head, pressing her forehead to his. "I love you too," she said softly. And she smiled up at him, her eyes filled with tears.

Sebastian came undone. He let out a whoop of joy and lifted her from the ground again. Only he didn't stop there. He spun her in circles and peppered her face with kisses.

"Stop! Stop." She laughed. "You're making me dizzy."

He set her back on her feet, but then he rumbled in her ear, "Dizzy? *Caro mita*, I'm about to blow your mind."

In a heartbeat, he shimmered them to the room they'd been using while at the plantation. In less time than it took for her to draw her next breath, he had her naked and on the bed beneath him.

"Sebastian," she moaned as he kissed his way down her body.

Man, he loved it when she said his name like that. He decided then and there that he'd make it his personal mission to get her to say his name, just like that, at least once every day for the rest of their lives.

He lingered over each and every sensitive point, wringing more erotic little sounds from her. And when he pushed deep inside her, and she clung to him so sweetly, his heart felt as though it might burst from his chest.

****

Phoebe sat at the kitchen table pouring over her father's journal. She'd been meticulously teaching Sebastian the complicated code her dad had created, and she was impressed with how quickly he was catching on.

Her fingertips traced one puzzling passage as she read and then re-read the characters. Phoebe pinched the bridge of her nose, blinked, readjusted her glasses, and then took a third go at the paragraph.

"What?" Sebastian asked, watching her. "Did you find something?"

"Maybe," she said, her focus locked on the dark slashes and marks in her father's heavy hand.

"Phoebe, are you feeling all right?"

She was too busy translating to pay much attention to the sudden note of concern in Sebastian's voice.

"I'm fine," she murmured, absently waving a hand in the air. "Look at this." She angled the journal toward him as she pointed out the particular text. "In the Kingdom of the Snake, where the priests drew…" She paused, thumbed back a few pages for reference, then flipped back to the passage. "Where the priest drew first blood and the birds find roost, a key will reveal the truth."

She looked at him, brimming with excitement. Excitement, and just a touch of nausea. "Calakmul was the seat of what was otherwise known as the Kingdom of the Snake. It's one of the most structure-rich sites within the Maya region. There are roughly a hundred and seventeen paired stelae meant to represent the rulers and their wives. For more than twelve centuries, Calakmul was a major player in Mayan history. Its domain was marked by the extensive distribution of the glyph of the snake head sign, known as Kaan."

Phoebe fingered the arrowhead shaped rock she'd recovered from the base of one such statue in the jungle. "A key will reveal the truth," she repeated softly.

"You think that rock is a key of some kind?"

She glanced up and grinned despite the pounding in her head. "I think so."

But he frowned. "I know you said you're fine, but you're really pale." He reached up to touch her face before capturing her hand. "And clammy. When did you last eat?"

Phoebe blinked as a swirl of dark spots clouded her vision for a moment. "I—"

Suddenly a ripple of profound unease coursed through her. Beside her, Sebastian shot to his feet, bristling.

"What is that?"

"Angel," he warned, his tone dark.

He urged her to her feet and pulled her to the foyer. Gideon and Maggie were already rushing in from the den; Niklas and Carly hurried down the staircase.

"Angel," Niklas barked.

"Wait," Maggie urged, breathlessly. She closed her eyes for a moment, and then smiled. "It's Samuel."

Gideon shot her a look. "Are you sure?"

Maggie nodded.

Gideon looked to Sebastian and then Niklas. "It's okay. Samuel is an ally."

"He's an angel," Niklas warned as he gently but insistently pushed Carly behind him.

"He's an ally," Gideon insisted. "He's the one that gave us the tip about the name we should look for. How the *balance of the world will be weighed in the hands of Rehsa*. And he blessed Maggie and the baby."

Niklas glanced to Sebastian, who in turn looked to Gideon.

Sebastian nodded. Niklas nodded. Neither one looked very happy. Gideon strode forward and opened the door. Phoebe sucked in a sharp breath. A handsome, ginger haired male stood in the doorway. His bright blue eyes were so remarkable she nearly missed the brilliant, white wings at his back.

Nearly, but not quite.

"Peace be with you," he said in a voice that washed over her like sunshine.

But just being this close to him made her skin feel tight, and her heart beat with the urge to do battle.

"Breathe," Sebastian advised quietly near her ear. He laced his fingers through hers and squeezed. "It's your natural reaction to angelic presence. Just breathe. Try to relax."

"Come in," Gideon offered.

A wide smile split Samuel's face. He walked inside. Well, maybe *floated* was more accurate. Gideon took a quick peek outside, and then closed the door behind him.

"I come with important news," Samuel said, his hands clasped before his pristine, white long-sleeved shirt.

"You found more on the prophesy?"

"Alas, no. Not yet." He opened his mouth to say

more, but then frowned as his gaze snagged on Phoebe. "You are unwell, child."

All eyes turned to her. Sebastian's grip tightened.

"May I?" Samuel looked from Phoebe to Sebastian and back again. Sebastian darted a glance at Gideon.

"It's all right," Gideon said.

Samuel moved closer at Sebastian's nod. The itching sensation in Phoebe's skin was nearly unbearable now. The need to explode into action almost more than she could control.

Samuel lifted one hand and pressed his palm to Phoebe's forehead. He closed his eyes, and a troubled frown darkened his features.

"There is something here that makes her ill. It affects you all—all of you but the Human, the Halfling and the Guardian. But it's very bad for her."

"The ward stones," Sebastian hissed. "Damn it, how could I have forgotten?"

"Of course," Gideon said, eyeing Phoebe. "They'll make her sick. She's not used to them. Not like we are."

"I know my touch unsettles you, child," Samuel told her, "but if I could, just one more time?"

Phoebe gave a reluctant nod.

The angel settled his hand upon the top of her head and closed his eyes one more time. She had the strangest sensation of something...pulling...being drawn from the top of her head. The headache and the nausea, while not completely disappearing, got drastically better.

"Thank you," Phoebe said when he lifted his hand away.

He smiled at her. "You are welcome. But you must not stay here any longer than necessary. You will sicken again. And, if left too long like this, you will die."

He stepped back then and clasped his hands before him once more. At his pronouncement, Sebastian turned stiff as stone. She squeezed his hand, but he shot her a dark look. A warning, if ever she'd seen one. He'd be chewing her out later for not telling him she was sick. That was plain as day. She heaved a sigh.

"Your news?" she asked, turning to the angel.

"Ah, yes. Several in my flock have heard of a place in New Orleans where there has been a concentration of evil. They've heard rumors of a demon of great power being held captive. And of ghastly sounds coming from a warehouse where the evil seems to be at its worst."

Niklas stepped forward. "Have you sent anyone to investigate?"

"Yes." A fleeting look of sorrow passed over the angel's face. "Three of my flock went to the location. They did not return, and they do not answer their summons."

Niklas, Gideon and Sebastian exchanged knowing glances.

Phoebe frowned. "What does that mean?"

"They have returned to the Maker," Samuel stated solemnly.

"Where is this warehouse?" Sebastian asked.

Samuel gave them the coordinates. "I would be happy to stay behind and watch over your mates until your return."

Niklas stiffened, as did Sebastian. If his hand squeezed hers any harder, he'd shatter bone.

But Gideon was the first to speak. And his words shocked Phoebe to her toes.

"Thanks, but our mates are perfectly capable of taking care of themselves. Besides, we have Phoebe to look after them now. They're in good hands."

Samuel bowed his head. "As you wish." He turned to the door but then paused. "Maggie, may I have a word."

"Of course." Clearly puzzled, Maggie approached the angel. Gideon dogged her heels, not letting her out of arms reach.

Despite his benign demeanor, and the fact that he'd taken away most of her illness, Phoebe was glad to see Gideon's caution. She just couldn't shake her sense of distrust of the angel. Maybe Sebastian was right. Maybe it was just a demon's natural response.

Still...

"Your father—"

"No," Maggie cut the angel off, and Phoebe was surprised by the vehemence in the woman's voice.

"My apologies. Michael would like to request a visit with you."

"Has he accepted my husband?"

The strained look on Samuel's face was all the answer she apparently needed.

"You've delivered his message. And I thank you for your blessings and your assistance with our search," Maggie said, the essence of diplomacy. "But you may tell Michael, if you would be so kind, that unless and until he is ready to accept Gideon as my mate, as my husband, and as the father of my child, I have nothing to say to him."

That being said, she stepped back into the shelter of Gideon's waiting arms. Gideon tucked her into his embrace and murmured something against her ear.

Maggie nodded and patted his arms.

"As you wish." Samuel bowed his head to the room, and then he glided out the door, closing it softly behind him.

Niklas turned to the others. "We need to go."

Gideon already had his phone to his ear. A second later, as he lowered the phone and shoved it back in his pocket, Xander and Kyanna appeared in the corner of the room.

"I have to take Phoebe out of here," Sebastian said.

"What? No, you don't," she argued. "You need to go with them. Save Mikhail."

"You heard Samuel. The ward stones are slowly killing you. I have to get you out of here before you get any worse."

"I'm fine."

"Yeah, I've heard that before."

"Well, I mean it now. I really do feel much better. Whatever he did helped. A lot. So you need to go. Find Mikhail. And then you can come back for me. I'll be all right till you get back. I promise." She shot Gideon a grateful glance. "Besides, I have a job now too."

Gideon grinned and nodded, pointedly ignoring Sebastian's peeved scowl.

"Now," Xander prompted impatiently from his post near his woman.

Sebastian stared long and hard at her for another moment. "All right. Okay. Fine." He glanced over his shoulder at Gideon. "Dude, if she gets any worse, I'm gonna kick your ass."

"Me?" Gideon feigned an innocent look. "Why me? What'd I do?"

Sebastian scowled at him. Then he turned and

pulled Phoebe into his arms for a soul-searing kiss. Her head spun, and her heart raced. She didn't think it had anything to do with the ward stones this time.

At a pointed throat clearing, Sebastian broke the kiss. But instead of letting her go, as she'd assumed he would, he cradled her head in his hand and pressed the side of her face to his chest as he held her tight.

"*Qui et illisium speccaté*," he whispered against her hair.

Chapter Twenty-Three

The moment Sebastian shimmered inside the warehouse, the stench of rotting flesh hit him like a brick wall.

"Oh, sweet Christ," Xander growled, pressing the back of his hand to his nose.

Sebastian glanced around, sword drawn and at the ready. The warehouse appeared empty but for that God-awful smell.

"Spread out," Niklas barked.

As a unit the four of them fanned out and began searching the warehouse. Sebastian pulled up a tarp and pushed aside a huge crate to peer behind it. A rodent the size of a Mastiff skittered over the toe of his boot and scurried away. Sebastian dropped the tarp, shook his leg and let the shiver of disgust wiggle over his shoulders and down his spine. Okay, maybe not a Mastiff, but certainly a small poodle. By the saints, nothing made his skin crawl worse than a rat. He'd take an entire nest of Garnochs over one of those little fuckers any day.

A shrill whistle split the silence. He spun on his heel and sprinted up the rickety wooden steps, heading toward the source of the sound.

Sebastian skidded to a stop just inside what must have once been an office. His stomach revolted and he had to turn aside, squeeze his eyes closed, and force the bile back down. Giving himself a hard mental shake, he rushed farther inside the room to join the others.

They'd finally found Mikhail.

God help us all.

The Demon of War hung suspended from a massive, rusted meat hook that had been anchored to the wall. The oxidized point of the hook went all the way through him, and protruded from his sternum. His head hung forward, so they had yet to see his face. But the rest of him had been ravaged. Beaten to a bloody pulp. Sliced. Bruised. Amputated.

Skinned.

Broken.

His chest was barely moving. His elbows were manacled and chained to the wall, as were his knees. Pointless to chain ankles or wrists, Sebastian supposed, when the victim had no hands or feet to keep restraints anchored.

All around the room, body parts littered the floor. Hands, feet, tongues, ears, lungs, livers. Other parts no male wanted to consider. Basically anything that could be cut off or cut out and still regenerate.

Anything.

Covered in blood, both dried and fresh, swarmed by flies, the appendages formed gruesome piles of carnage. And in the middle of that pile laid a woman's cold, dead body. Her throat had been savaged and, judging by the lack of blood around her, she'd been drained dry.

Sebastian's heart broke for Mikhail. To torture the Demon of War like this, continuously cutting off, cutting *out* body parts, bleeding him half a step shy of Oblivion, driving him out of his mind with hunger because of his injuries, and then putting an innocent throat before him like a lifeline? Sebastian could barely wrap his mind around that kind of depravity...and he knew of only one demon capable of that level of brutality.

Well, two. After all, it had been Mikhail's chief duty to torture victims this way while serving Lucifer. Taking them right to the point of death, then yanking them back. But Mikhail had never reveled in it to this extent.

Sebastian knew of only one demon who would take such unmitigated glee in torture of this magnitude.

Ashïek.

After this, Mikhail would be crazed. Feral. They'd probably have to find a way to contain him until they figured out how to handle him and determine if he was even safe to unleash on the world again.

"Get him down," Sebastian barked when he realized the others were standing as he was, staring in shock.

Just as they moved forward to reach for Mikhail, the air near Sebastian wavered. Sebastian leaped into action, barely managing to pull up at the last second before he delivered a killing blow to his own mate.

"Phoebe?" he choked.

And then he leaped forward to catch her as she fell to her knees and vomited. He tugged her hair back from her face, holding it out of the way until she quit heaving. He helped her to her feet and over to the corner with the least amount of...well, Mikhail.

"What the hell's going on?" Xander bellowed as he and Niklas supported Mikhail's weight while Gideon carefully guided his big body up and off the hook.

Sebastian was too busy checking to see if any of

the blood soaking her clothing belonged to her to ask questions. Her skin was Carpathï crimson, her hair jet black. And her eyes, despite the bottomless black color, were wide with shock. He clamped his hands on either side of her face, forcing her to look at him and only him. He didn't think she'd even had a chance to take in her surroundings yet. That was probably a damned good thing. The sight of Mikhail—everywhere—would be sure to send her over the edge.

"Talk to me," he demanded. "How did you get here?"

"Shimmered," she panted. "Thought of you…came to you. Don't know how, just…*felt* my way to you." She pressed a fist to her side and winced, bending slightly the way a runner might after a grueling race.

By now Niklas and the others had lowered the still unconscious Mikhail to the floor. They crowded around Sebastian and Phoebe and were all clamoring for answers.

"Shut up," Sebastian roared. Then, to Phoebe, he urged in a more reasonable tone, "What happened?"

"Attacked…less than a minute after you left. Like they were waiting, watching." She puffed. "Demons…everywhere. My God, so many of them."

He was losing her. He gave her a little shake, bringing her back to here and now.

"We tried to call for help, but you didn't answer."

Niklas and Gideon reached for their phones, checked displays, and swore.

"Jamming device," Xander announced, kicking a small black box in the corner.

"How did they get past the ward stones?" Gideon demanded. "No demon should have been able to touch them."

No one had an answer.

Niklas shouldered his way into the mix. "Is Carly all right?"

"They're all okay." Phoebe nodded, and the relief in the room was palpable.

"We fought off as many as we could. But they just kept coming. I didn't know what to do, and then Kyanna was yelling and cussing at me, ordering me to shimmer."

She groaned and wobbled, bending over at the waist. For a moment, Sebastian thought she was going to get sick again, but she straightened and dragged in a deep breath.

"I didn't know where to go, where to take them that would be safe."

"You shimmered *with them*? You've never shimmered before, and you shimmered *with my helpless pregnant wife*?" This from an incredulous Gideon.

Phoebe shot him a look that would have given Sebastian pause had it been aimed at him.

"Your *helpless pregnant wife* exploded eight demons—maybe nine, I lost count—with some freaky blue balls of energy. And it was shimmer with her or let her die. There were just too many to keep fighting. And when Kyanna got hit, we just couldn't hold them off anymore."

That shut Gideon up.

But now Xander was the one exploding. He shoved the Seer aside and got right up in Phoebe's face.

"Where is my wife?" he snarled.

"She's all right," Phoebe breathed, wincing again.

"Damn it, stop crowding her." Sebastian threw an

elbow. "Let her talk."

But Phoebe swayed once more and dropped to her knees. Sebastian went down with her and wrapped his arm around her waist for support.

"Took them to the ruins. To Calakmul. At the top of the second structure, there's—"

"I know the way," Gideon snapped. And then he was gone. Xander and Niklas were hot on his shimmer trail.

Sebastian wrapped his arms around Phoebe. How was he ever to keep her safe? If she wasn't petting snakes and diving for careless workers, then she was smack in the middle of demon battles. Trouble followed her around like a lost puppy.

"We have to get Mikhail someplace safe," he told Phoebe. "Is the plantation even standing?"

"I think so. But it's a mess."

"Well, it's better than nothing. Can you stand? We need to get Mikhail back, see what we can do to help him."

"I don't think so, Vengeance," Ashïek said from the doorway. "War and I were having so much fun together. Besides, you and I have some unfinished business."

Sebastian snarled as he jumped to his feet. In a split second, he morphed, snapping his wings open behind him, creating an instant shield for Phoebe. "News flash. Stolas has been taking credit for your handiwork."

Ashïek shrugged. "He has a poor imagination, and a lack of vision. Besides, do you really think anyone else would have this kind of"—he waved his arm around at the carnage—"creativity?"

The grin on Ashïek's face enraged Sebastian.

Sebastian summoned plasma balls in the palms of both hands. "You're a dead demon."

Smug, Ashïek tilted his head. "I don't think so. You see, I know something you don't."

"What's that?"

"Your female will be your downfall." With that, Ashïek launched himself at Sebastian.

They hit the far wall, smashed through, and then went tumbling through the air until they crashed on the concrete a story below. As though waiting for a sign, Ashïek's minions began pouring into the warehouse. Some attacked Sebastian from behind while he squared off against Ashïek. Others aimed for the stairs and the office above.

Phoebe!

Sebastian snapped his wings open and took flight. In the first swoop, he knocked a swarm of minions from the stairs. In the second swipe, he brought the stairs themselves down.

The windows in the office shattered, blown from the inside out, and Sebastian caught a glimpse that turned his blood cold. Minions had already gained access to the office. Even now, Phoebe was fending off two of them while the third crept up on her from behind. But the angle was bad, and he couldn't risk a plasma ball. He might hit his mate by accident.

He flew toward the office, but then jerked to a stop when a heavy chain wrapped around his ankle. With a mighty roar, Ashïek gave a yank, and Sebastian careened to the ground.

Panic swelled. He had to get to Phoebe.

But once again, Ashïek was standing between him and his mate. Sebastian saw red. Nothing would stop him. He would get to his mate. Or he'd die trying. He let go of the tight leash he kept on his temper. Let go of his self control, of his restraint. It was like the day in the cave, when he'd rescued her the first time.

No, it wasn't like that.

This was way worse.

He decimated wave after wave of minions in a complete blood bath. And then he turned his wrath—the wrath of Vengeance—on Ashïek himself. Ashïek fought back like the demon he was, vicious and ruthless, but Sebastian was unstoppable. He had something to fight for now. Something Ashïek could never truly understand.

Swiping up the chain that had been used to bring him to the ground, Sebastian wrapped it around his fist, and then used it as a whip. He slammed it against Ashïek over and over. Every time the demon tried to crawl away, Sebastian would grab him by the ankle, drag him back, and pound on him some more.

Only when Ashïek was a pulpy mess, babbling incoherently, did Sebastian kneel on his chest. He clamped both huge hands on either side of Ashïek's head and lifted it from the bloody concrete. He looked into Ashïek's eyes, waiting for the sliver of awareness to surface. And when it did, he snarled, "You lose."

He wrenched Ashïek's head from his body.

Sebastian stood—Ashïek's head in one hand, and a plasma ball in the other—and he roared loud enough to shake the rafters. He dropped the plasma ball on Ashïek's chest, then tossed the decapitated head on top.

His age-old nemesis was dead, defeated by his own hand. Sebastian expected to experience some sort of powerful emotion. Joy. Victorious. Invincible.

All he felt was relief.

With a mighty swoop of his wings, he propelled himself to the second floor. He dug his fingers into splintering wooden planks and ripped half the wall out. And once again, he was amazed.

Phoebe, still fully demonic, crouched protectively over an unconscious Mikhail. She'd just lobbed a plasma ball, and her final opponent went up in a screeching ball of flames.

And standing at her side—fighting by her side—was Sïnsobar.

Again.

His heart thumped hard. Sebastian flew inside the room and tucked his wings back so they wouldn't catch on the ragged opening. This was the third time the Carpathï had protected Phoebe in battle. What the hell was going on? It was high time he got some answers.

He made to grab Sïnsobar by the front of his shirt, but Phoebe lunged between them.

"Wait," she said, holding a hand up to warn him back. "He saved my life."

"Exactly," Sebastian growled. "He's done it more than once. I want to know why."

Phoebe relaxed infinitesimally and moved to his side so they could both face the Carpathï.

Sïnsobar stood before them, tall and proud, his crimson skin—skin so very like Phoebe's—splashed with blood. As he opened his mouth to speak, the air in the corner of the office distorted once more. Gideon and Niklas appeared. They took one look around at the destruction and shook their heads. Then they caught sight of Sïnsobar and both went into a battle crouch.

"Wait," Sebastian ordered.

Both his friends sent him questioning glances, but they straightened and extinguished the plasma balls in their hands. Sebastian turned back to Sïnsobar. Gideon came to stand at his side, while Niklas went directly to Mikhail.

"Get him out of here," Sebastian said.

With a nod, Niklas placed a hand on their fallen brethren and shimmered him away.

"Answer me," Sebastian ordered, turning back to the Carpathï. "Why do you keep rushing to my mate's defense?"

"She is a Carpathï demoness. My kind. One to be protected."

"Bullshit. You yourself handed her over to a cave full of minions to be raped and tortured and feasted on."

"That was before I knew who she was."

Who, not *what*. Little alarm bells went off in Sebastian's head.

The Carpathï turned to face Phoebe now, making it clear his attention and his answer was for her and her alone. "Your mother is Danika, yes?"

Phoebe regarded him with suspicion. "So?"

"Danika is my sister."

"A member of your clan, you mean?" Sebastian clarified. Hoping against hope.

"No." Sïnsobar angled his head to give Sebastian a pointed stare. "My *sister*. Full blooded spawn of the same parents. Direct bloodlines."

Sebastian groaned aloud. Gideon burst out laughing, which earned him an evil glower from the Carpathï.

"So you're what…my uncle?" Phoebe asked, her forehead pinched together.

Sïnsobar regarded her for a moment, and then tilted his head in acknowledgement. "You may address me as such."

Phoebe's lips compressed. "I don't think so."

From across the room, Sïnsobar scowled, clearly displeased that she wasn't more eager to jump on the family train.

Phoebe leaned close to Sebastian and asked, "Why do *you* not look happy about this?"

"Because, darlin'," Gideon interrupted. "Familial ties among the Carpathï are very, very strong. I think it's pretty safe to say that your days of peace and quiet are over."

Phoebe looked around at the decimated building and turned huge eyes on Sebastian. "*This* is peace and quiet?"

Gideon burst out laughing once more before he too shimmered away.

"Temptation is correct. Familial ties among our kind are very strong. Which is why, now that you've mated my niece without my permission you will help me," Sïnsobar said, turning to Sebastian at last.

"Hold the phone one damned minute." Phoebe stiffened and took an aggressive step forward, placing herself squarely, protectively in front of Sebastian. But he was having none of that. He grasped her around the waist and tugged her to his side. He wouldn't dream of trying to shove her behind him. He'd probably end up with a hole in his back. Phoebe shot him an irritated scowl but went on as if she hadn't been shuffled to the side. "Sebastian doesn't owe you a damned thing. Mating him was *my* choice, one I made willingly. I don't care whether you give your blessing or not. You didn't care about what those…those *things* were going to do to me in the cave. Don't think for a second I'm going to believe you care about me now just because we share common bloodlines."

"Our species is ruled through male hierarchy. I am the head of our line. It is my duty to protect you. And as a Carpathï of my line, it is your duty to gain my approval to mate." Sïnsobar glowered at Phoebe. He probably thought he could intimidate her into compliance. Sebastian thought about warning him that the tactic wouldn't work. Instead, he decided to sit back and watch the Carpathï fail in an epic way.

"Yeah? Well, my *human* half doesn't care jack shit about your approval. In fact, my *human* half says you can take your approval, or lack thereof, and stick it where the sun don't shine."

Crash and burn, baby.

Sebastian couldn't have been prouder of his mate. However, he was curious as to why Sïnsobar would make such demands of him. "Help you how?"

"You will help me locate and free my sister Danika."

Phoebe took a step forward, but Sebastian tugged her right back. "She's alive?"

Sïnsobar nodded. "She was captured by a portal, much like the one rumored to have captured War and the mates of the Slayer and Temptation."

"She's alive," Phoebe whispered, lifting a hand to cover her mouth. Sebastian tightened his arm around her, fearful she might collapse.

"For my mate," Sebastian swore solemnly, "I will find and will free Danika. But only for my mate, not for you."

"*We* will," Phoebe piped up.

"We will," Sebastian corrected after a pointed elbow connected with his ribs. "But we will do it without you."

"I can be of assistance."

"I don't trust you as far as I can throw you. Besides, if you could be of that much assistance, you wouldn't need my help."

"*Our* help," Phoebe corrected.

"*You* will stay out of harm's way," Sïnsobar instructed Phoebe. "Which reminds me, Vengeance. As head of her clan, and as her uncle, you and I need to have a chat about the way you've been letting her run wild."

"Letting her?" Sebastian choked and began coughing.

Phoebe helpfully pounded on his back.

"If you require instruction on the proper way of things, I will be happy to show you," Sïnsobar said.

Now it was Sebastian's turn to laugh. He glanced down and met Phoebe's mutinous glower. "Good luck with that," he told Sïnsobar.

Sin looked between the two of them and shook his head. Once again, he addressed Phoebe. "I will always be near should you need me."

He bowed his head, touched his forehead briefly with one hand, and then swept that hand toward her before he shimmered away.

Just as Sebastian turned to pull Phoebe into his arms, she glanced down. And a look of horror twisted her features. "Is...is that a *lung*?"

Sebastian clapped his hand over her eyes. "Hold on to me," he instructed.

"Wait!"

Sebastian frowned at her.

"We have to go to the ruins." She shook off his hand and beamed up at him, her face alight with excitement. "To Calakmul."

"The others will already have their mates back."

"I know," she said, shaking her head. "This isn't about them. Or not directly."

"Then why—"

"When I was trying to shimmer, trying to figure out where to go, I felt this tug. I knew I had to take them there, to Calakmul. Don't you see? I'm drawn there. My power is strongest there. There's a reason for it."

Sebastian tilted his head and waited.

"I think the sword is there. And I'm pretty sure I know exactly where."

Sebastian's smile grew. "Take me there."

"It's at the top of the—"

"No," he insisted, shaking his head as he wrapped his arms more securely around her. "I want *you* to shimmer us there."

Her eyes widened, and panic filled her expression. "Oh, but—"

"You can do this, Phoebe. I have faith in you."

She blinked up at him like he'd lost his ever-loving mind. But then, by slow degrees, determination took over.

"I can," she finally said, and pressed her lips together. She put her arms around him, and Sebastian watched as her face—her precious, beautiful face—screwed up in a severe frown of concentration.

Sebastian was well-versed in the ways of

shimmering. But it was always unsettling when you weren't the one in control. Still, he gave himself over to her, trusting in her to get them there safely.

The world fell away and returned with a jolt. Their feet hit the crumbling stone, hard. As soon as they solidified, Phoebe lurched sideways. If he hadn't had a tight hold of her, she would have slipped right off the side of the ruins. He jerked her back, taking several cautionary steps away from the edge.

She was puffing and her eyes were wide, but she was recovering quickly. She pressed a palm to her temple and blinked.

"Sorry about the landing," she said, grimacing.

He laughed. "You did great, sweetheart!"

"No, I almost—"

"Almost doesn't count," he murmured, laying a finger against her lips. "First time I shimmered, I ended up halfway inside a tree. Trust me on this. You're a natural." He dropped a kiss to her lips. "Okay, so where is this sword?"

"Oh! Right," she said, slipping from his arms. Phoebe hurried inside the temple and Sebastian followed.

The chamber was surprisingly large, with a massive stone altar in the middle of the room. Or what was left of a stone altar. The enormous slab had been shoved askew and tilted onto its side, the corner was broken, and a network of cracks snaked across the surface. The altar itself had been decimated. The very floor of the room had huge holes smashed into it, as if beefy fists had slammed into the aged stone. All around, scorch marks marred the carved surfaces where great chunks of ancient, irreplaceable works of art had been demolished.

"My God! What happened here?"

Sebastian watched as Phoebe paced the confines of the room. She slowly reached up with trembling hands and lightly brushed her fingers over a blackened hole high up on the wall.

Sebastian surveyed the burns. "Demon battle is my guess." He moved farther into the room, then drew up short. He couldn't believe his eyes.

There in the rubble of the altar rested a fist-sized, mangled ball of blackened gold and jewel bits. Crouching, he picked the hunk of precious metal up and examined it. Could it be? Had this been the Amulet of the Gods? The very talisman Gideon had been searching for to break his curse?

So it was real after all.

"What's that?" Phoebe came to peer over his shoulder.

Standing, Sebastian bounced the ball in his hand once, twice, then tossed it back into the rubble. "Nothing of importance anymore," he said with a big grin.

Phoebe shot him a questioning smile, before turning away. He watched as she returned to the doorway, and then began counting off paces. Six steps in, she turned left, paced ahead four steps, stopped at the wall.

"Please conjure the key."

Sebastian called forth the bejeweled rock she'd found in the statue and handed it to her.

Phoebe held the key in one hand and used the fingers of her free hand to trace a seam in the wall in front of her.

"Why six and four?"

"Hmm? Oh, it's my birthday. June 4th. Ah, here you are," she finished on a whisper.

Phoebe brushed debris from the crevice, and then, after considering the hole she'd uncovered, she twisted the rock in her hand, considered, and turned it over again.

And then she inserted the rock key. Pushed and jiggled until a loud pop echoed throughout the chamber.

Phoebe glanced at him, her eyes wide and excited. That excitement was contagious, and Sebastian found himself grinning too. Phoebe turned back to the key, but Sebastian grabbed her wrist, stalling her.

"What?" she asked, a puzzled frown darkening her brow.

He stepped closer, put a hand on her hip, and angled his head, bringing his face close to hers. "No matter what we find here, we're in this together, yeah?"

She smiled. "Yeah."

"I love you." He pressed a fleeting kiss to her lips. And then he moved behind her, taking a protective stance.

She started to twist the key, then paused, turned to grab a fistful of his shirt and dragged his face down to hers. "I love you too."

She gave him a much longer, much more leisurely kiss. Just when he decided to hell with the sword and was seriously considering dragging her down to the floor to have his wicked way with her, she released him and pushed out of his arms. With a giddy laugh, leaving him standing there on wobbly knees, she spun around and gave the key a triumphant twist.

Stone grated on stone, and a long panel of ancient

glyphs slowly began to slide out of the way. Sebastian yanked her back, afraid the stone might roll forward and crush her, but it only fell harmlessly to the side. And as they shifted to peer into the hidden compartment, a shaft of sunlight broke through the clouds.

Phoebe gasped, and Sebastian whistled.

A dusty sword was propped against the back wall. Forty-five inches in length. Three inches across the fort. The indentation running down the length of the straight double-edged blade was etched with glyphs. The cross guard was inlaid with silver. The bone grip was covered in red, leathery-looking skin with some kind of distorted black markings. And a single, rough cut, blood red stone was set in the pommel.

Phoebe turned her face to smile up at him, so radiant Sebastian's heart ached at the beauty of it.

Chapter Twenty-Four

The sun had set long ago, but the full moon bathed the waters in shades of silver and shadow. Sebastian took Phoebe by the hand and led her to the water's edge.

"What are you doing?" She tugged, but he wouldn't let go.

"We're going skinny dipping to celebrate." He vanished their clothing with a thought. And then he morphed back to human form, knowing she'd be more comfortable that way.

That was something else they were going to have to work on. Getting her comfortable in her skin, literally. Phoebe squawked and tried to cover herself, but he was having none of that.

Sebastian turned and started walking backward. He caught both her hands and held them slightly out to the sides, so he had a good view as he pulled her along in his wake. The sight of her naked went straight to his head...and his groin.

"You know, you're pretty sexy in red," he said, his voice gone husky with desire.

"Sebastian!"

"Phoebe!" He mocked her and chuckled as the water slowly crept up their legs.

He tugged her off balance, and she tumbled into his arms. Pinning her to his chest, Sebastian moved deeper in the water. She dropped her forehead to his shoulder and whispered, "I don't know how to change back. When I changed last time, it just sort of…happened. I don't know what to do."

"Do you want to?"

"Yes."

"All right. But know that I still want you, no matter what you look like."

"I can feel that," she whispered. He was sure she could, as his erection was currently rock hard and trapped between them.

"Okay, draw a deep breath—"

"I've already tried this," she interrupted.

"Phoebe."

"Well, I have. Besides, how do you know what I'm supposed to do all of a sudden?"

"I made a phone call. A very expensive one. Now, be quiet and listen."

She peered up at him suspiciously. "Who did you call?"

"*Phoebe!*"

"Okay, okay."

"Draw a deep breath. Try picturing in your mind what it feels like when you summoned plasma balls. The gathering of energy, the way it coalesces, the way it surges and ebbs."

She nodded.

"Now see if you can send that energy elsewhere. Not to the palm of your hand, but to your nails, to your eyes, your hair, your skin. Your very cells."

Suddenly Sebastian was standing in the water, with his arms full of…an exact replica of himself. Surprised, he dropped her and lurched back a step. She'd just skin shifted. Right before his eyes.

Holy shit!

Phoebe gasped and sputtered as she splashed up out of the water. Sebastian was relieved to see that she was his Phoebe once more, and not a clone of him.

"What the hell?"

"I'm sorry! I'm sorry!" Sebastian grabbed her around the waist and pulled her back into his arms.

"What was that for?" She turned hurt eyes his way as she wiped wet hair from her eyes.

How to tell her without her freaking out? "Um, you slipped," he finally settled on saying.

Tomorrow. He'd tell her tomorrow. For now, just for tonight, he wanted this moment.

She gave him a wary look, but she let him draw her close. "You're not upset about Sïnsobar being family, are you? Or that we have to find my mother now?"

"No." He smoothed a stray rope of wet hair from her cheek and watched, fascinated, as a bead of water rolled down the side of her face and pooled at the base of her throat.

"We're going to have to keep that sword hidden away," she reminded him.

"Yep." He bent to lap at the little hollow by her collarbone. He swept her back up into his arms and set his lips to her skin.

"Mikhail was in pretty bad shape." She gasped aloud and shivered when he found a particularly sensitive spot. "Shouldn't we check on him?"

"The others will let us know if they need help."

Her breathing turned shallow as he slowly slid his hands down her sides, over the gentle flare of her hips, and he reached for her knees.

"We're pretty much homeless, you know," she breathed.

Sebastian drew her knees higher on either side of him, guiding her ankles around to lock them at the small of his back.

"I figured we might try camping for a while," he said with a small smile against her skin.

God, he loved the way her head fell back like that when he kissed her neck. And there was that sexy little moan. His dick pulsed in response, and his balls drew up tight. He slid his hands along the bottoms of her thighs. And then, gripping her tight little ass in both hands, he angled her just right and slid home.

She moaned his name, just how he liked it, and then she tipped her forehead to his. "*Qui et illisium speccaté*," she whispered.

Sebastian wrapped his arms around her and held tight. He had the whole world, right here in his arms. And he was never letting go.

Now and forevermore.

Epilogue

Maggie tore down the stairs. She couldn't catch her breath. Her mind raced.

"Oh, no. No, no, no," she whispered furiously as she threw the door to the newly remodeled study open and burst inside.

Gideon was around the desk and grabbing hold of her before she made it halfway across the room. "What's wrong? What happened?"

Maggie clutched the front of his shirt. Her wild-eyed gaze swept the room, touching briefly on the three couples gathered round the fireplace.

"I just checked on Mikhail—"

"Damn it, Maggie! I told you not to—"

"Gideon, listen to me!" She fisted her hands in his shirt and tugged. "He's gone. Mikhail's gone!"

Look for these titles by Brenda Huber
Now Available:

MINE
CRAVINGS
SHADOWS
QUEEN'S CHESS

Texas Series:
TEXAS BRIDE
TEXAS BLAZE

Chronicles of the Fallen:
THE SLAYER
THE SEER
TEMPTATION
VENGEANCE

Coming Soon:
WAR

Don't Miss the other titles in Brenda Huber's Chronicles of the Fallen Series!

TEMPTATION

A demon with nothing left to lose. A Halfling who will prove him wrong.

Chronicles of the Fallen, Book 3

With the destruction of the Amulet of the Gods, Gideon's last hope of Divine forgiveness is lost. Cursed to never know the touch of another, he spirals closer to losing control. But, for the sake of his brethren, he takes on one last mission.

His simple task, to guard a very special Halfling, quickly becomes a complicated mess. The feisty woman sets fire to his blackened soul. Curse or no curse, he will stay by her side—even though he is more of a threat to her than the demon prince plotting to take over the world.

Despite the dubious "blessing" of her birthright, Maggie is happy with a career she loves, a place of her own and a circle of good friends. But Gideon—The Demon of Temptation—seduces her out of her comfort zone and plunges her into a world she's never known.

Entangled in the blurred lines between good and evil, desire and destruction, Maggie's only chance for survival is to trust her very life to the one man who doesn't even trust himself.

Warning: Contains an unpredictable demon surviving on the edge, and a desperate Halfling determined to live life on her own terms. And so continues the journey of six fallen demons and the women who capture their hearts.

THE SLAYER

The darker side of his nature just can't let her go.

Chronicles of the Fallen, Book 1

Born of heaven, forged in hellfire and damnation, Xander roams the earth as an unlikely protector of the innocent. Grudgingly embroiled in a demon uprising, Xander must help his brothers-in-arms recover four Sacred Relics rumored to be Lucifer's downfall.

The stakes are simple. If he fails, a new regime will assume control of the underworld and the boundaries between hell and earth will crumble. If he succeeds, long-awaited salvation could be his. But when a beautiful innocent is caught in the crossfire, the price of redemption could be too steep.

Kyanna Hughes is a hereditary Guardian, sworn to protect a sacred Relic at all costs. From the cradle, she was taught to hate all things demon, but her unwanted attraction to Xander turns everything she's been taught upside down.

The danger she faces involves more than her heart. For Kyanna is not only a Guardian, but a keeper of secrets so dangerous, that to keep them out of demon hands even the angels in heaven would see her dead...

Warning: Contains a demon with a notoriously single-minded determination to save the world, and a sworn enemy for whom he will risk eternal damnation. And so begins the journey of six fallen demons and the women who capture their hearts...

THE SEER

Not even the fires of Hell will keep this demon from his mate.

Chronicles of the Fallen, Book 2

All whisper his name in fear, for *The Seer* was the right hand of Lucifer, the Collector of Souls. Condemned by Heaven, a fugitive from Hell, Niklas's only hope for salvation lies in protecting the innocent from demons bent on ravaging mankind

After uncovering a plot to overthrow Lucifer, Niklas and his compatriots scramble to retrieve crucial Sacred Relics before the plot's mastermind gets to them. For if Lucifer falls, so too shall fall the barriers between Earth and Hell.

Carly Danner's life is turned upside down when she stumbles upon a demon summoning, plunging her into a dangerous realm of temptation and forbidden love. Left with no choice, she must trust the most unlikely of protectors, a darkly sensual demon with a fearsome reputation.

As the tangled web of desire and betrayal draws her deeper, Carly walks a blurred line between good and evil. And Niklas must decide if redemption is worth losing the woman who stole his heart.

Warning: Contains a demon willing to put the world at risk for the love of one woman, and an innocent human who would sell her soul to save the demon she can't live without. And so continues the journey of six fallen demons and the women who capture their hearts.

Thank you for purchasing
this publication of The Wild Rose Press, Inc.

For questions or more information
contact us at
info@thewildrosepress.com.

The Wild Rose Press, Inc.
www.thewildrosepress.com